186

THE MAH-JONGG SPIES

ALSO BY JOHN TRENHAILE

A Man Called Kyril

A View from the Square

Nocturne for the General

John Trenhaile

The Mah-Jongg Spies

E. P. DUTTON   ☐   NEW YORK

Published in the United States by
E. P. Dutton, a division of New American Library,
2 Park Avenue, New York, N.Y. 10016.

Library of Congress Cataloging-in-Publication Data
Trenhaile, John.
The Mah-Jongg spies.
I. Title.
PR6070.R367M34   1986   823'.914   85-29282
ISBN: 0-525-24391-7

OBE

Designed by Nancy Etheredge

10 9 8 7 6 5 4 3 2 1

First Edition

F/Tre

ACKNOWLEDGMENTS

My thanks are due to Anthony McGrath, Director of Baring Brothers & Co. Ltd., for telling me about desalination plants and how they are financed, while at the same time guiding me through the complexities of the financial transactions that figure in this book. I must emphasize, however, that such improbabilities and downright errors as remain are my responsibility alone.

I record with pleasure and gratitude the innumerable favors and gifts of hospitality showered upon me in Singapore by Mr. Khoo Teck Quee, his wife, children, family and friends; and by many others who in their different ways made my stay in the Far East such a happy and memorable one. If I have borrowed beyond the bounds of politeness, *duibuqi*.

Hongkongside, I am grateful to Sir Denys Roberts KBE, JP, Chief Justice of Hong Kong; Mr. Kenneth Mok MBE, FBIM, solicitor and judge; and Deputy Commissioner Chan Wa Shek ISO, JP, for their invaluable suggestions and comments on the manuscript at an early stage. In those few remaining areas where I have allowed literary license to override factual accuracy, I throw myself upon the mercy of the court and can urge no mitigation.

But when all is said and done, all debts acknowledged if not repaid, there still remain two persons above the rest who must share responsibility for whatever in this book is good. With a generosity that is wholly characteristic they gave me first their time, then their unrivaled knowledge and experience of the places I have attempted to describe and finally a novel complete in all respects. This book belongs to them—they watched it grow, they helped to make it, it is theirs; and to them I now respectfully dedicate it, with love and honor and a gentle reminder to one of them that we live in a world where every prospect pleases and only man is vile. . . .

For
Lee Yuk Tong
and
Khoo Hock Tin
"Elder Brother and Younger"

"Under heaven, all are one."
—CHINESE PROVERB

"All the rest is context."
—JOHN FRASER,
*The Chinese: Portrait of
a People*

A NOTE
TO THE READER

China is a land of one language but many dialects. The officially blessed version of spoken Chinese is called Mandarin. With a few exceptions I have used the Chinese *Pinyin* system of romanizing Mandarin, even though some names, such as Beijing, will be more familiar to Westerners in the Wade-Giles style (Peking). I did, however, lack the nerve to inflict the reader with Xiang Kang, the Mandarin version of Hong Kong.

Chinese family names come first, followed by given names. Qiu Qianwei is pronounced "Chew Chi-en Way." Zhao Yi Qiang sounds something like "Jow" (as in jowl) "Yee Chee-ang." Qingqing is pronounced "Chingching" and Kaihui, "K'eye-Hway."

In the People's Republic of China the *fen* is the smallest unit of currency; there are ten of them to the *jiao* (or, colloquially, "*mao*"), and ten *jiao* equal one *yuan*, or dollar. The *yuan* is worth approximately UK £0.25, or US $0.35.

☐ xiii ☐

Prologue
A GAME PROPOSED
1984

As soon as the black Zil came to a halt, half a dozen guards materialized from the shadows, their Kalashnikov A-47s raised shoulder-high, to form a human corridor between the car and the house. Robert Zhao stepped out, saw the uplifted weapons and hesitated. There's nothing to be afraid of, he told himself: you're a guest . . . He dithered an instant longer, then pushed through the double entrance doors without looking to right or left, heedless of the mansion's imposing façade and desperate only to escape the wounding January cold, which in a few seconds had numbed his extremities. Major General Krubykov, who was accustomed to the climate and had a Russian sense of occasion, followed at a more leisurely pace.

"I am sorry about the weather," he said affably. "Coming from Hong Kong you must feel it, I suppose."

Zhao did not reply at once. He stood in the center of the vast hall with hands in pockets and shoulders hunched, the very picture of misery. Although he had walked from the car straight into the house his overcoat was caped with snow and his feet felt damp. The dacha was scarcely warmer than the night outside. His Chinese blood, used to tropical climes, felt thin as water. Zhao sank his hands deeper into his pockets with a shiver. "A bit," he muttered.

"Come," said Krubykov, slapping his guest on the back. "I'll take you up, give you some vodka. That'll warm you!"

Zhao shuddered at the barbarian's touch. He was about to turn under the pressure from Krubykov's hand when his attention was arrested by a portrait that seemed to fill the whole of the far wall. He recognized the subject instantly; confirmation, if any were necessary, was at once provided by the inscribed plate at the bottom of the frame: IOSIF VISSARIONOVICH STALIN.

Krubykov, seeing the direction Zhao's eyes had taken, quickly increased the pressure on his back. "Come," he repeated, a little less pleasantly. "It's warmer where we're going."

He escorted the Chinese up the stairs and along a passage. The house smelled damp and neglected, as if nothing had been done to it since the turn of the century. The predominant colors of the moth-eaten furnishings were red and gold, the lampshades bore frayed tassels and the heavy velvet curtains showed faint traces of mildew. It was a depressing place. When Krubykov stopped before the last door on the left and knocked, Zhao stole a sideways glance at him. This man seemed reasonably civilized, for a Russian: he wore a well-pressed suit of decent cut, his short, silver-gray hair was neatly waved and his hands were properly manicured. Krubykov presented himself to Zhao, and to most other foreign visitors, as an experienced man of the world; but all of a sudden he was a little less sure of himself and his guest wondered why.

The door opened and Zhao stepped into the plainest room he had ever seen. Its ceiling, walls and furnishings were pure white. Most Russians found the atmosphere cold and bleak; but to a Chinese like Robert Zhao white signified death, and on him the effect was chilling.

A fire roared halfway up the chimney, its golden glow softening the pallor of the bleached stone hearth. Zhao instinctively made his way toward it without waiting to be asked. As he stood with his back to the flames, feeling the tips of his fingers begin to tingle, he groaned with relief.

"Good evening, Mr. Zhao."

He looked up, startled, his quick eyes darting everywhere at once. The voice of the man who had just spoken was thick with catarrh and sounded rusty, but the English accent was almost as impeccable as Zhao's own. For a moment he scanned the room in vain, his perception lost among all that whiteness. Then he focused on the desk beneath the window.

The man sitting there was almost completely bald. His round face was old and wrinkled but it had the excellent pink color that normally goes with a healthy lifestyle. The body, by way of contrast, was abnormally thin, so that the man's white suit hung off his shoulders in loose folds. Large, thick spectacles magnified his baby-blue eyes into cold marbles which stared at Zhao without favor or malice, almost without interest, as if the Chinese were a dog or a child who had wandered by mistake into the presence of adults.

Zhao struggled to disengage his stare from the round orbs that disfigured the face of the man at the desk and said, "Good evening. You are . . . ?"

"Kazin. My name is Kazin."

The speaker did not rise to greet his visitor; he merely lifted a hand from a thick stack of papers that lay on the surface of the desk in front of him and waved toward a white leather sofa. "Please. You would like a drink, perhaps?"

Zhao hesitated for a moment before he shrugged off his wet coat and lounged across to the sofa, tossing the garment to Krubykov with the same arrogant gesture he would have used to his houseboy at home. The major general caught it with a grimace of distaste, but kept silent. Zhao unfolded his tall, elegant figure onto the cushions and stretched lazily, seeking to convey boredom. His thin, handsome face was fixed in an expression of wholly artificial politeness which complemented his earlier disposal of the coat. "I would like some brandy," he said, and could not forbear from adding, "if you have any."

"We have it. Krubykov?" The officer nodded and went across to a drinks cabinet, where he poured Zhao a generous tot of cognac. Kazin watched the Chinese sip it, noted how his expression softened into one of unwilling appreciation, and smiled. "You must find Moscow very cold, I am afraid." Kazin's harsh voice was not attuned to small talk: the sound of it accorded ill with his outwardly friendly smile. "They tell me that in Hong Kong today it was fifty-nine degrees Fahrenheit. Almost spring, wouldn't you agree?"

Zhao flicked a speck of dust from the trousers of his neatly pressed Savile Row suit and nodded carelessly. "Oh, indeed. You are in the Moscow Narodny Bank, Mr. Kazin? A director, perhaps?"

Kazin looked across to Krubykov and the two men exchanged smirks. "You could say so." He took a drag on his cigarette, examining the smoke through narrowed eyes as if the idea entertained him. "The bank is, how shall I put it, the bank is frequently accustomed to act in accordance with my instructions. A director, yes, you could say so. A shadow director."

Zhao fidgeted impatiently. "I was expecting to meet a member of the board; also, a minister. A finance minister."

"Well, yes, that too. In a way. My actual title is chairman of *Komitet Gosudarstvennoy Bezopasnosti*."

Zhao coughed. He did not understand Russian. "You are with the Ministry of Finance?" he ventured.

There was a long silence. When Kazin did at last speak, Zhao jumped. "I am with the KGB, Mr. Zhao."

There was another, even longer pause. Zhao's features remained as impassive as ever, but all three men were aware of a new stillness in the room, a greater depth of silence that made what had gone before seem positively rowdy by contrast.

The Chinese cleared his throat. "This is . . . unexpected." His voice lacked much of its former assurance. Kazin rested his chin in his hands and subjected Zhao's face to critical examination, the results of which seemed to disappoint him.

"I understand that," he said slowly. "You were invited to Moscow, in secrecy, to discuss financial matters of mutual interest. Naturally, a man of your stature, one so *important*, was expecting to meet bankers, ministers. But this way we can avoid a lot of unnecessary formality."

Kazin broke off, and slowly lowered his hands to the desktop. Zhao had begun to find his lengthy pauses unnerving.

"We can?"

"We can. Officials, politicians, tchah!" Kazin waved a hand contemptuously. "I think you will prefer to deal principal to principal. We want to talk about the same things. About money. About power. About *that!*"

He flung out an arm and Zhao, following his line, saw pinned to the wall nearest the door a large map of Southeast Asia on which someone had drawn a thick red circle around Hong Kong. At the top of the map, in the same red crayon, was written a date: *19 September 1988*.

"Do you know the significance of that date, Mr. Zhao? Oh, please smoke if you wish."

Zhao had already drawn out his gold cigarette case and now he lit up, taking each movement slowly so as to give himself time to think. His initial sense of shock at finding himself to be the unwitting guest of the KGB had worn off. He knew that whatever happened at this meeting would be of enormous interest to Chinese Central Intelligence, which had been known to pay well on occasion, and he resolved to miss nothing.

"No," he said at last. "The date means nothing to me."

Kazin seemed to lose interest. He turned to Krubykov and said wearily: "Tell him."

"It is the day on which Thomas Edward Young attains the age of sixty-five years," the major general said. "You know Mr. Young, of course?"

Zhao shrugged. "Of course. If we are talking about the same person, he is the chairman and chief executive of the Pacific & Cantonese Banking Corporation in Hong Kong."

"Of the Corporation, yes. Who are your bankers, are they not?"

"Among others. A man like me has many bankers, Mr. Krubykov. I really don't see how my affairs—"

"And to whom you owe money. A great deal of money. Let us see now . . . " Krubykov walked across to the desk and pulled the thick pile of paper toward him. It was a folded computer printout. "Ah yes, as of this morning, twenty-seven million, eight hundred thousand, and forty-three Hong Kong dollars, odd cents. When I say 'you,' of course I mean you personally, your various companies and their subsidiaries."

Zhao stubbed out his half-smoked cigarette. "I would like to close this meeting now, Mr. Krubykov. I do not think we have anything to talk about."

"I think we do." It was Kazin who spoke. He lolled back in his chair and started to rock to and fro, never taking his eyes from the Oriental's face. "I must tell you, Mr. Zhao," he said after a while, "that no one leaves this house without my permission."

Zhao licked his lips. "I am a guest in this country. I have certain rights. I repeat: There is nothing to discuss."

The silences were becoming ever more ominous. When Krubykov smiled, Zhao knew real relief.

"I would advise you to stay," Krubykov said quietly. "Rights, as you call them, or no rights. You see, we have been buying your paper. There is rather a lot of it about at the moment. Not as much as the Corporation owns, but enough to liquidate you quite thoroughly, I think. I shall be happy to give you the figures, they are here in the desk drawer. So please. We can do this amicably. Or we can do it under pressure. To do it amicably will be so much easier on us both. Particularly in the light of the offer we wish to make to you."

"Offer?" Zhao spoke very quickly, too quickly.

"Yes, offer. How would you like to take Mr. Young's place? To become chairman and chief executive of Asia's second-largest bank?"

Zhao's gasp seemed to fill the white room for a long time after the last puff of breath had crossed his lips. Before he could respond, however, Krubykov was speaking again. "You do agree, I take it, that the Corporation is a desirable prize?" When Zhao did not answer immediately, he went on. "It is very old, very respectable, very soundly based. Its loan book is immaculate, its procedures unimpeachable. What you would call a 'blue-chip' house, yes?"

Zhao nodded slowly, like a man still regaining his wind.

"And one with a curious function to perform. There are times—please help us, Mr. Zhao—there are times when the Corporation and the Bank—I mean of course the Hong Kong & Shanghai Bank, and also Standard Chartered, combine at the request of the government to perform tasks normally carried out only by an issuing house, a national bank. Is that not so?"

"Yes. Sometimes." Zhao spoke unwillingly, like a man who senses that he is being led down a treacherous path. "But I do not understand—"

"The Corporation is a power in the land, your land. One of the greatest financial institutions Asia has ever seen." Krubykov patted the printout in a gesture that was almost affectionate. "We intend to own it," he said.

"You intend . . . *what?*"

"To own it. We intend to acquire a majority of its Founders Shares. Well, we intend to *control* it, I should say. In this country the distinction between control and ownership tends to blur somewhat."

Zhao's eyes had suddenly become very alert. Krubykov saw that he had the full attention of the Chinese and smiled pleasantly. "Let us try to establish some common ground. First. You will perhaps know that the Far East is very important to the Soviet Union, strategically as well as economically."

"Of course."

"So that when the Chinese mainland takes over Hong Kong in 1997, our position there will become . . . uncomfortable."

Zhao's lips curled. "Say rather—untenable. It is already uncomfortable, more than uncomfortable. You have no base there, none whatsoever."

"Well, I won't quibble. On any analysis, before 1997 comes we need to establish such a base."

"You can't."

"And why?"

"Because you tried in Hong Kong once before, in 1977, and you failed. That entrepreneur, Eddie Wong. He gave the Moscow Narodny Bank security over companies owning prime Hong Kong sites. The British government wrested them from you and swore that it would never happen again."

"Nor do we intend that it should. The Wong fiasco will not be repeated, set your mind at rest about that. We are not interested in Hong Kong land, not at this stage, and in any case we accept that no Soviet financial institution would ever again be permitted to take a mortgage over any part of Hong Kong's soil. So, then. How much do you know about the way in which the Pacific & Cantonese Banking Corporation is run? About its constitution?"

"I know what everyone else knows."

"Then let us concentrate on that."

"I cannot see why—"

"I am interested, Mr. Zhao. Your views are important to us. Please."

Zhao shrugged. "If you insist. The constitution was set by act of Parliament in the nineteenth century. There are articles of association, of course. None of the fundamental provisions can be altered except by legislation."

"Very good. Please go on."

"There is a board of directors and the usual collection of shareholding members, let me see . . . A shares, prefs, B deferred . . ."

"And Founders."

"Yes, and fifty Founders Shares."

"Which are very special. Special for a number of reasons. What are they?"

"I really haven't the least idea."

"But of course you have! Why are Founders Shares different? What makes them distinctive, desirable?"

"Well, I suppose . . . because they are concentrated exclusively in the hands of one family, the Youngs of Hong Kong. Is that what you mean?"

"Yes, partly. But do continue, please."

Zhao pouted and dredged about in his memory. "Also . . . well, also because those shares are worth, at today's prices, something in the region of three or four million pounds sterling *each*."

"Not a very precise figure."

"No. It depends how you value the preferential rights that Founders Shares carry on a dissolution. Together they nullify all of the Corporation's other shareholders. The owners of the Founders Shares can between them at any time either dissolve the bank or prevent it from being dissolved. I suppose you would say that is special?"

"Yes. And thirdly, because under the Corporation's constitution these precious shares cannot be pledged, charged or mortgaged in any way except by means of an instrument executed in the presence of a duly appointed magistrate of Hong Kong. Am I right?"

"Yes. So I believe."

"And that precaution was built into the articles of association for the very good reason that the shares, most unusually, are bearer shares—in other words, possessing the certificates is as good as owning the shares. A lender who took possession of the share certificates would be regarded for all practical purposes as their owner."

"That is so. Obviously, no one would surrender his Founders Shares certificates to a lender in those circumstances."

"But conversely, of course, someone who did not possess the certificates would have very few rights over the shares. When he came to enforce his security, he would find himself in some difficulty."

"Quite so. And of course, that's the whole point of backing up a loan with adequate security: you have to be sure that if the borrower doesn't pay you'll at least be in a position to sell the collateral. Hence the need for particularly stringent formalities when lending on the security of such shares—in the case of the Corporation, an instrument attested by a magistrate."

Krubykov nodded, as if pleased. "Three very good reasons why those shares are to be regarded as special, and I do not understand you to disagree. Who owns the Founders Shares, Mr. Zhao?"

"As I've told you, the Youngs."

"Yes—but which of the Youngs?"

"I do not know. No one knows. Except their lawyers, I suppose."

Krubykov looked across at Kazin, who now was standing by the fireplace, and the two Russians laughed. "We know," said Kazin.

Zhao shifted forward onto the edge of his sofa, no longer making even a pretense at inscrutability. It was a remarkable change of attitude on his part, but in Hong Kong knowledge of that magnitude represented money and power. "You do?"

"Yes, we do," said Krubykov. "Twenty of the Founders Shares belong to Simon Young, the head of one of Hong Kong's principal trading groups, Ducannon Young. Another ten at present belong to his father, Thomas. The remaining twenty are vested in trustees of the estate of Thomas's late brother, David. Those two individuals, Thomas and Simon, thus theoretically have power between them to dispose of the Corporation tomorrow—"

"Ah yes, because under the articles, on a resolution to dissolve only the votes attached to Founders Shares—"

"Are eligible to be counted. Indeed. So whoever controls the Founders Shares controls the Corporation. And of course, whoever possesses the share certificates, controls the Founders Shares."

"How do you know this?" Zhao's voice vibrated with suspicion. Now he was backtracking fast: he felt he had allowed himself to be carried away, that in the eyes of these contemptible foreigners he must have lost much face.

"We are, among other things, intelligence gatherers, Mr. Zhao. We garner and we sift. People do us favors, sometimes for money, sometimes under threat"—Krubykov smiled at the word "threat" and hesitated an instant, as if to savor it—"sometimes from pure ideological commitment. All kinds of people. Bankers. Lawyers. Clerks in attorneys' offices whose job it is to keep the filing cabinet tidy. You may take it that our information is accurate."

Zhao shook his head, reluctant but wanting to be convinced.

"Even if you're right, you'll never get your hands on them. Never. It is utterly inconceivable that those shares would be disposed of outside the Young family, and the share certificates are guarded night and day, in the Corporation's vaults."

Krubykov raised his hands. "Oh, please do not trouble yourself about that side of the matter; we are quite capable of handling it ourselves. No, what we need to discuss with you is what might happen in the event of our one day owning the shares. We would need to appoint a new chief executive; that chief executive, as you rightly said, cannot be Russian; and so we return to where we began—would you be interested?"

Zhao leaned back thoughtfully while his brain riffled through a dozen possibilities, analyzed and rejected many plans, focused, came to rest. "As a career it might be considered . . . entertaining."

"And of course, it would enable you to pay off your largest creditor—the Corporation itself. To say nothing of the KGB, who have bought, as I say, a substantial proportion of your other commercial debts."

There was a long pause. "The price?" Zhao said at last.

"The price is very simple. You would have to act in accordance with certain instructions which we would give you."

There was another heavy silence. "What instructions, exactly?"

Once again, Kazin and Krubykov exchanged glances. "It will be our intention to call in all the Corporation's outstanding loans," said Krubykov. "And then to close the lending book to Hong Kong traders. Forever."

Zhao's expressionless face suddenly crumpled. "*What?*"

"I think you heard correctly," said Krubykov.

"You would call in . . . *all* debts?"

"And foreclose where immediate payment was not made, yes. And then perhaps shut down the Corporation for good; we would have to see. Your own position, I need hardly add, would be protected in such an event."

"But . . . but scarcely a *hong* would be left standing!"

"Exactly! That is our aim: nothing short of the entire financial destruction of the British Crown Colony known as Hong Kong. It would not stop with the *hongs*; they are merely trading companies, of greater or lesser power and resource. Our assault will undermine the banking community as well. Are your sympathies with the banks, Mr. Zhao? Really?"

Zhao pouted. "Never mind the banks. What about the ordinary people? The small service companies, the restaurants? They couldn't begin to cope with such a disaster."

"No, none of the middle or smaller companies could hope to survive. Some of the majors might ride it out, we do not know; although Ducannon Young itself would be bound to fall. But the strategy is perfectly clear: we would refuse to give time, we would refuse to lend further. Our projections show what the effect of closing Asia's second-largest bank in those circumstances would be. As a financial center, Hong Kong would fold overnight. The Corporation would be left owning something in the region of twenty percent of all land subject to the three treaties that presently govern diplomatic relations between Britain and China concerning Hong Kong. And then"—Krubykov bared his teeth in a grin— "Beijing may have Hong Kong, and welcome to it!"

"I think you are a madman, Mr. Krubykov. The British and the People's Republic of China would never let that happen. They would stop you."

"How?"

"By putting together a financial lifeboat. By bailing out the debtors."

"Not, I think, the British. Their responsibilities are nearly at an end, and propping up Far Eastern financial traders, commercial pirates, bandits, is hardly likely to win elections in England."

"Beijing, then."

"Where are they to get that kind of money? And why should they spend it on capitalist roaders, isn't that what they call them?"

"Then they won't even try. They'll invade, send troops and force you to cancel all you have done."

"No, they will not."

"Why not?"

"Because they know what we also know, that the moment the first Chinese soldier sets foot on Hong Kong soil, the world's largest banks will forthwith send what I believe are melodramatically styled the Titanic telexes."

"The what?"

Krubykov chuckled. "A silly phrase, isn't it? Let me explain: For many years now there has been an understanding between the fifty largest banks in the world that in the event of invasion of Hong Kong by the Chinese mainland, telexes will be sent draining the territory dry. In less than a minute, the time it takes to cable money, all the foreign-dominated funds at present in Hong

Kong will simply disappear. Go. Vanish. So in either case, Moscow wins. The People's Liberation Army of the People's Republic of China will march in to take possession of an empty shell. And let us be frank with you, Mr. Zhao—we really do not care which way it happens."

Zhao could not begin to come to terms with what he had just learned. "You are wrong," he said mechanically. "Hopelessly wrong."

"Why?"

"It's—" Zhao raised a hand to his forehead and began to massage his temple. "It's like a scheme devised by a . . . a lunatic," he said at last.

Krubykov laughed, not at all put out. "But a lunatic with a successful record. You as a Hong Kong businessman, you of all people, should appreciate the force of *that!*"

Kazin suddenly turned away from the fireplace and strode toward Zhao, who shrank back, afraid. His yellow skin had taken on a gray hue, leaving only an unhealthy tinge of pale mauve around his lips. But Kazin bypassed him and went up to the map on the wall, drawing a stubby red crayon from his pocket.

"Let me fill in another piece of the jigsaw," he said. "For a brief moment in the nineteen thirties, Thomas Young's father, Richard Young, controlled all fifty Founders Shares. He gave twenty of them to Simon outright. Then he set up a trust and put the rest of the shares into it. The trust's known as the Richard Young Settlement and it contains some extremely detailed and intricate provisions. But because he knew the terms of that settlement would cause family friction if they leaked out, he kept its existence a secret from everyone except Tom, who was then his favorite. Mark that and remember it—Simon Young, Tom's son, knows nothing of this settlement."

"Go on. What did this settlement do?"

"According to the trust, twenty of the Founders Shares belonged to David Young and his successors, while ten were assigned to Thomas—*but only during his life or until he ceases to be chairman of the Corporation.* And on September 19, 1988"—Kazin tapped the date with his crayon—"he will be sixty-five, when, under the terms of the Corporation's articles, he must resign his chairmanship. You see what that means?"

"It means . . . that as soon as he resigns he will lose his ten Founders Shares."

"Yes."

"That could be changed," Zhao blurted out. "The article of association which obliges him to resign could be altered."

"Only by an act of Parliament, which the British would not be foolish enough to promulgate."

"You cannot be sure of that."

Kazin shrugged. "It's quite immaterial. As I say, Thomas Young owns the shares only until he resigns or dies. Parliament in Westminster can set the date of his resignation. I"—he tapped his breast mockingly—"*I*, Oleg Kazin, can, if necessary, set the date of his death."

Zhao looked away. Kazin knew that this Chinese businessman was no stranger to the use of violent means to attain a commercial end. After a moment's pause in which to let the message sink in, he resumed: "At which point, death or resignation, I care not which, six of his ten Founders Shares will pass to his son, Simon, thereby giving him a one-vote controlling interest. And through him that controlling interest will come—to us!"

Zhao, mesmerized, stared at Kazin. The chairman, seeing the effect his words had produced, was well pleased. "The year 1988 is crucial," he said abruptly. "Everything must be done, all must be in place, by then, no later. *The timing is absolutely essential!* I have started the clock, Mr. Zhao. The seconds are already ticking away. In your present—how shall I say it—*delicate* financial position, it is even later than you think. Well?"

When Zhao said nothing, Kazin turned back to face the map and with two vicious strokes deleted Hong Kong from the face of the earth. He used such force that the crayon tore the map, leaving a crinkled streamer which reminded Zhao of wallpaper stripped from a mansion that once had been grand but now was nothing; and as the image solidified it was as if the same two strokes repeated themselves in his intestines like the crisscross slashes of a Japanese suicide.

Kazin turned once more. "So tell me," he said affably. "What do you think?"

One question had increasingly come to trouble Zhao during the interview; and now, after a very long pause, he gathered himself together enough to ask it.

"Why do you need to enlist me in this . . . this folly?"

"Why you?" the chairman repeated. He advanced slowly toward Zhao's sofa, while Krubykov approached from the fireplace to guard his other flank. Zhao looked up at the ruthless faces above him and realized with a horrid flash of insight that there was no time left, no hope at all; and at the same moment he divined the answer to his own question.

"Mr. Zhao," Kazin said quietly. "In order to carry our plans through, we need someone who is intimately connected with the Young family. As you are. But that's not all. It is inevitable that Chinese Central Intelligence will find out about our plans. We need to know when they do. We need to know how they intend to counter them. We need hard, specific information at every stage. We need, in other words, a spy in the enemy's camp: someone in whom Chinese Central Intelligence repose implicit trust."

He sat down on the sofa next to Zhao and placed a friendly hand on the Oriental's knee. "A friend of the Youngs, a friend of China—not an easy combination to find. How fortunate we are, then, to have found you, Mr. Zhao."

I

BUILDING THE WALL
1985-1986

1

Simon Young arrived at Beijing's Metropolitan Airport to discover that the afternoon flight to Tokyo had been delayed for one hour. He checked in and decided to go for a stroll down the blue-tiled concourse, good-humoredly doing his best to ignore the attention he attracted. When he first traveled to China, any foreigner would automatically draw a crowd. Now, visitors from abroad were becoming so common that the average inhabitant of Beijing scarcely bothered to turn his head at the sight of Caucasian skin. But Simon Young differed from most other Westerners in one respect. He stood six feet four inches, and the Chinese were fascinated by his height.

He came to a halt in front of Yuan Yunsheng's celebrated mural, *Water Festival: Song of Life*, and stood before it, lost in contemplation of the vibrant scene. After a while a little crowd began to gather, keeping the kind of respectful distance that the *waibin*'s extraordinary stature warranted. Simon eventually woke up to the fact that he had an audience. He continued to gaze at the mural for a few moments longer before suddenly wheeling around with a smile on his face. The circle of curious Chinese dissipated within seconds, leaving him alone in what had suddenly become a deserted stretch of the terminal's floor.

Deserted, that is, except for one man, who stood his ground.

Simon began to saunter toward the stairwell. But in order to take the shortest route, he would have had to march straight through the only person who had stayed to gape. Simon altered course and his observer swiveled as if to follow. The Englishman slowed his pace and for the first time really looked at this solitary voyeur.

The man was in his early thirties, Simon judged, although it was difficult to tell, because he had one of those ageless, smooth moonfaces that convey the simplicity of both the very old and the very young. His hair was thinning; but at least it looked clean, which his clothes did not. He resembled a typical peasant, but— Simon's eyes narrowed—a peculiar example of the class. He wore a soiled blue uniform jacket and denim trousers rolled up to the knee; but in his right hand he carried a large, expensive-looking case, a gold ring glittered on his little finger and his feet were shod in a pair of glossy leather shoes.

To someone less well versed than Simon Young in the multifarious arts of Hong Kong imitation, the ritzy bag might have passed for Louis Vuitton; but the orange strap was a giveaway. Fake hide straps always turned that color when exposed to the wet; Simon had known it to happen many times. Still, the bag was vastly superior to anything he'd ever seen in the hands of a Chinese peasant.

The man had a bizarre smile. When he saw Simon staring at him he parted his lips to reveal the tips of his teeth placed neatly together, just touching. There was something disturbing about his demeanor. It was unnatural. It made him stand out, in a society where to be indistinguishable from the mob was considered a cardinal virtue.

Simon Young tightened his grip on the handle of his briefcase and gave the Chinese a wide berth. There was still nearly an hour to go before they called the Tokyo flight and suddenly he wished it was time to board. He could feel the odd man's eyes burning into his back.

Simon went to sit down on one of the black vinyl chairs at Gate 46, opposite the Bank of China's money-changing bureau. It was the airport's slack period; not many passengers walked the concourse, so he had plenty of space to himself. He pulled a copy of the *Far Eastern Economic Review* out of his briefcase and began to read an article on desalination plants. After a while his mind began to wander. Simon already knew all there was to know about desalination: for more years than he could count he had lived with the dream of building such a plant for the benefit of Hong Kong. But then the People's Republic of China had guaranteed a supply of fresh water to the colony and the dream had waned, just as his interest in the magazine article was waning now. He tossed the magazine onto the seat beside him and raised his arms above his head in a long stretch.

It had been a good trip, he reflected; better than expected. The Chinese had bought Ducannon Young software to service their new accounting system for state subsidies, a prototype of which was being developed in Zhuhai Special Economic Zone, so the prime object of his visit was achieved. Then a chance remark over dinner had opened up the possibility of supplying prefabricated light industrial buildings to Jilin Province; but that would mean expanding DY Construction's production line by eight percent, which in turn meant a lightning trip to Japan to talk to Nomura's finance boys. It was tiresome, but necessary.

He looked up to check the clock and noticed that the odd man who had stared at him earlier was standing about ten meters away, talking to two others. Simon frowned. Something was wrong. He didn't know what it was, but the setup bothered him. With his right hand he casually felt inside the pocket of his coat, ensuring that his wallet and passport were still in place.

The other two men who had joined the first were equally strange in appearance. It was almost as if they had deliberately set out to make themselves as conspicuous as possible. The eldest, who looked to be in his fifties, was very thin, with a narrow, pinched face; he wore a large red wooly hat that must have been extremely uncomfortable in Beijing's afternoon humidity. His eyes kept flickering over the first man's shoulder to where Simon was sitting. And with a little start of alarm, Simon saw that he too was carrying a large, smart bag—pigskin, this time, with gold combination locks.

The third man presented an even greater puzzle. He was young, a teenager or no more than twenty at most, but his hair was grizzled and his lips were distorted in a leer. Simon lowered his gaze and there, as some instinct had told him to expect, was a third, elegant cabin bag. This, the largest, was made of crocodile skin.

They were the weirdest group of men Simon Young had ever seen in the course of innumerable visits to China. He stuffed the magazine into his briefcase and stood up, wanting to put some distance between himself and these three men. As he rose the trio simultaneously turned to look at him, and their faces dissolved into smiles. There was something profoundly unnerving about those smiles; all three men showed the tips of their teeth just touching, their lips drawn back to reveal the gums. They reminded Simon of children struggling to force themselves into a camera shot. He marched straight ahead at a brisk pace, glad to get away.

According to the reconstruction made by the Public Security Bureau, what followed took exactly fifteen seconds.

He heard a shrill cry of fear behind him, that was the first thing, and he faltered in midstride. He swung around to see that the three men had fanned out and were advancing swiftly toward the Bank of China's bureau. Then the thug on the extreme left, the oldest, held his bag up to his chest, wrenched open the locks and extracted a machine pistol.

Someone shouted: "Get down!"

The airport became bedlam. Screams echoed, people cannoned into one another, Simon saw a woman snatch up a child, run, trip and fall flat on her face, crushing the child beneath her. Somewhere high above his head a siren sounded.

"Get *down!*"

Memories of half-digested newspaper reports came flooding into Simon's mind—Beirut, Athens, hijack . . .

A uniformed member of the Public Security Bureau was shaking his arm. "Get down," the policeman repeated, in English. Suddenly he kicked out his foot, hooked it around Simon's ankle and brought him down to the deck. The Englishman's chin landed on the tiles with an agonizing crack. He tasted blood as it started to ooze into his mouth from the wound where his teeth had bitten through the inner cheek. The noise around him had reached an intolerable level. Women and children were screaming and weeping, men shouted, whistles blew, but, like the victim of a nuclear attack expecting the shock wave after the flash, still he waited for what he knew must come—the sound of automatic fire and the smell of cordite.

There was a momentary hush; even the siren ceased. In the next second, Beijing's Metropolitan Airport became a slaughter-house.

The man who had first attracted Simon's attention was leading the other two by several paces. As Simon watched, he raised his gun and fired some twenty rounds. Simon, deafened, held his hands to his ears, groaning with the shock. Volley after volley echoed through the cavernous terminal building like a pneumatic drill worked in a confined space. Nausea flooded Simon's stomach.

When the firing ceased, he could not prevent himself from looking up. Now the man on the far right raised his weapon. In the split second left before he fired, Simon caught a glimpse of a teller sitting behind the Bank of China desk. From the expression on his face, Simon judged that he had not had enough time to feel either hurt or afraid, just surprised. Astonished. Perhaps outraged. Then the next shower of bullets struck the plate glass immediately in front of him.

One green-tinted sheet trembled for an instant; then a crack appeared at the top and rapidly ran the length of the entire pane before the glass shattered into pieces and fell to the floor, leaving a jagged hole. The teller's mouth jerked open and he raised his forearm to his eyes while tumbling to one side. Then a bullet must have caught him, for a gory crack suddenly appeared in the side of his head and something sprayed against the green wall behind him, forming a grotesque splodge that soon developed one long and two shorter tails, as if someone had flung a can of crimson paint.

The firing ceased; the concourse became as quiet as a church. The three men reached the remains of the Bank of China's till, used the butts of their weapons to shatter what was left of the glass, and clambered in. Their leader rummaged briefly behind the counter before tossing three large cashboxes to his associates. When they had finished looting, they came back onto the floor of the concourse and made off toward the exit.

Suddenly one of the assailants noticed the Englishman looking straight at him. He grabbed the leader by the arm and pointed. Then, while Simon watched helplessly, all three halted and turned in his direction. The one wearing the wooly hat muttered something as he jerked back the bolt of his gun. Simon saw the muzzle lift and, even while he watched, his mind perversely insisted on recording the minutiae of how one's own death came. The black hole in the end of the muzzle looked very small, too small to allow the passage of something as deadly as a bullet. It was surrounded by three concentric rings etched deeply into the gunmetal. But, surprisingly, it made no noise. Nothing came out.

Simon raised his eyes a fraction, to see only blank expressions on the terrorists' faces. The men continued to stare down at Simon Young and he gazed back at them. No one spoke. It was the fourteenth second.

Hu Chuangmei squeezed her palms tightly together and muttered a few words. The bones on the backs of her freckled hands, fine as knitting needles, stood out alarmingly. Then she cast; and the ancient coins fell jangling onto the table in front of her. Hu squinted down at them, bringing her head to within an inch of the table's surface.

"Water trapped by earth," she cried. "The Army!" The old woman raised her head and, addressing herself to the ceiling, began to chant:

"The Army. The Army must have perseverance
And a strong leader.
Good fortune and no blame."

She lowered her eyes to Sun Shanwang, who was sitting opposite her, and snapped: "Read!" The deputy controller of Chinese Central Intelligence opened the *I Ching.* It was an empty ritual, for Hu Chuangmei knew every line of the work by heart, but in this room things must be done correctly. Sun found the place and slowly began to read.

"In the earth is water,
Symbolizing the Army.
The superior man increases his following
Through benevolence toward the masses."

Hu Chuangmei nodded approvingly and said, "Six in the fifth place." Sun Shanwang ran his finger down the page until he found the lines.

"Six in the fifth place: wildlife enters the fields.
There is benefit in catching it and no blame.
The eldest son should lead the Army.

The younger carries corpses.
Continuing is ominous."

He closed the book; and for a long time there was silence.

The large room dated from a more gracious, imperial age. Its wall panels, scarcely faded by the passing of time, portrayed a peaceful garden scene, with some human figures reduced in size to indicate their relative unimportance in contrast to their natural surroundings. The long black wood table stood by the tall windows, overlooking an ornamental lake. Hu Chuangmei and Sun Shanwang sat at one end, facing each other. At the head of the table, his back against pillows, was China's director of Central Intelligence, a very old man, who stared sightlessly down the room to the distant doors. Now he turned with a smile to face the fourth occupant of the room sitting next to him.

"We cannot continue to do nothing," he said, in a voice that scarcely disturbed the room's stillness. "We must act. Vigorous leadership is needed."

The man thus addressed extended his forearm and delicately adjusted the amount of shirt that showed at the cuff of his well-tailored jacket. "I agree," he said.

"Vigorous and experienced leadership, Baba." Hu Chuang-mei's voice was respectful but firm. "At thirty-six, this man is too young."

"He is young, younger even than our friend the Chrysanthemum here. This is good. You must not let your experiences in the ten terrible years affect you, Hu *tongzhi*. They should not blight your life. We must learn to trust our youth again."

"Hah!" Sun Shanwang shook his head. "To be young is good. I can remember. To be vigorous like our colleague here, Zhao *tongzhi*, is also commendable, although he is not as young as this man you talk of. But—to come from an unsatisfactory background, not so good."

"It was his fortune." The old man's voice sounded very patient. "He escaped. He was educated in the West, like Robert Zhao here. He was educated in the finest universities of the West. Princeton for economics—he is a man of economics. Mathematics. Harvard Business School and a master's degree in Business Studies. He is a man of business. We need this. Is it not so, Chrysanthemum?"

Robert Zhao suppressed the irritation that his Mah-jongg title always provoked in him and nodded. "It is so."

"Yes, but . . . " Sun Shanwang rose from his chair and began to pace about the room, anxiously rubbing his hands together. "But his ancestry, his bloodline." He shot a keen look at Hu Chuangmei, who failed to meet it.

"Indeed, indeed. His great-grandfather and his grandfather were aristocrats. They both were noble lords."

"Exactly."

"Yet I do not wish to enlist his ancestors." Baba and Hu Chuangmei, who were husband and wife, exchanged secret smiles. "I wish to enlist him. Just as I chose to enlist the Chrysanthemum, who sits here by my side, his background notwithstanding. Besides, Sun *tongzhi*, you forget—this man also had a father. A good man. One who was with Mao Zedong in the caves at Yenan. One who took care to educate his son to the best standards. Such good fathers produce good sons."

"Not always." Sun shook his head. "Good fathers sometimes produce bad elements. Why was this one's father so keen for him to leave the Middle Kingdom, hah? Trouble came; this man left."

"Yes, he left. He was brilliant, even as a child. He went to the West to apply that brilliance, to acquire the skills we so badly lack." Baba's voice was patient and persistent. "The father began the work of redeeming the ancestral line: so now this man, with the help of Zhao *tongzhi*, will take on where the father left off."

"Baba is right." Zhao spoke up on his own initiative for the first time. "I must be able to deal with whoever is chosen for the job. He must understand the practicalities as they arise from day to day. I cannot be expected to work with an ideologue. We need sense, not slogans. Baba, may I meet the man?"

"Not yet. I will tell you when he is ready."

"I hope you will think he is ready soon, then."

"Why?"

"I need to assess his skills. He must not only be well versed in the economic side of it; he must have practical ability also. We shall not be operating in a vacuum." Zhao paused, as if reluctant to continue. "If, or rather, when the Russians discover our plan, they will hardly leave us in peace to develop it. The man you choose must be capable of dealing with these things."

"You will not have long to wait, Chrysanthemum." Sun Shanwang tapped the face of his watch as he spoke. "It would not be convenient to be at Beijing Metropolitan Airport at this moment. The project is further advanced than you know."

Baba nodded in agreement. "This afternoon, we have begun our work of preparation, Zhao *tongzhi*. The candidate I have chosen will be ready soon enough. Please accept my views on that."

"Of course." Zhao directed a sharp, malicious glance down the table. "I have confidence in your every decision, Baba."

"Yet you should take heed." It was Hu Chuangmei who spoke, her cracked, aged voice resonating harshly in contrast to that of her husband. "The lines are ominous. They talk of corpses. 'The *younger* carries corpses' . . . yes. You should take heed. 'The *eldest* son should lead the Army.' That is what the lines say. This one, he has not suffered like the rest."

"Suffering . . . " Baba continued to stare unseeingly down the long room. After an interminable silence his wrinkled face cracked into a tired smile. "I need this man. And because I need him . . . he will suffer. Perhaps."

The traffic policewoman on duty at the corner of Beijing's Sanlihe and Zizhuyuan roads jerked her left arm down and raised her whistle to her mouth. At once a dozen bicycle wheels eased forward across the line. She made them wait a moment longer, sucked in her cheeks, lowered her right hand and prepared to blow.

In her elevated kiosk she was better placed than the perspiring cyclists at her feet to hear the car's horn. She quickly turned her head to the left in the direction of the West City; for a moment all she could see was the broad, blue avenue flanked with high lamp standards, each bearing its single loudspeaker, then her eyes focused and her jaw dropped. A Red Flag limousine was racing toward her down the center of the highway.

"*Ting!*" Stop!

But the cyclists were already streaming out into Zizhuyuan Road, oblivious to her cry. Only when she blew her whistle as hard as she could did the rear guard, scenting trouble, resignedly lower their feet to the ground once more. The horn sounded again, very close now, and then the car was on them.

The driver did not even slow down. As the car crossed the intersection it was traveling at a steady sixty miles an hour. It winged the leading cyclist, hurling him into the road. His machine bounced aross the bonnet of the long, sleek sedan before being flung on top of its owner, who groaned and lay still.

A hush descended on the crowded scene. For a moment everyone stared into the distance at the back of the fast-receding Red

Flag, but only the policewoman in her raised nest could see the tiny black head framed by the rear windscreen: a small and somehow insignificant figure to be riding in the back of such a powerful car. Then her gaze shifted to the vanquished cyclist as he rose unsteadily to his feet with the help of two friends, who hooked their hands under his armpits and assisted him to the curb.

The policewoman took another breath and blew a long trill. It was her job to keep order in the road. Death and endless trouble might brush too close, but all that mattered was the fact of their passing. Life went on. What point was there, then, in making a drama out of it . . . ?

Qiu Qianwei, the occupant of the Red Flag, was scarcely aware of the incident at the intersection. It was his first ride in China's prestigious official car, so all his concentration was focused on making the most of the experience while it lasted.

He reached into the breast pocket of his white cotton shirt and took out a pack of Double Happiness cigarettes. The hand that held the match was shaking slightly, sole indication that Qiu Qianwei had mixed feelings about this ride in a Red Flag.

It belonged, insofar as something in the People's Republic of China could belong to anyone, to the Seventh Department of the Central Control of Intelligence, also traditionally known as the Mah-jongg Brigade. Many high-ranking cadres had endeavored over the years to eradicate Mah-jongg terminology and usage from the Seventh Department's affairs; all of them had failed. Thus it was that the job of official Mah-jongg driver, a highly prized sinecure for which many backdoor favors changed hands, was still assigned to "West Wind." The present incumbent viewed his passenger, "Winter," with suspicion and curiosity. This was hardly surprising, since Qiu's duties in Economic Intelligence rarely necessitated his absence from HQ at 15 Bow Street Alley, and on the few occasions when he was required up at Brigade he took the number 302 bus. West Wind couldn't understand why so much fuss was being made of Qiu Qianwei, but in accordance with sound departmental practice he kept his views to himself. You never could tell. Qiu might look puny and unimportant, but sometimes even a blind cat happened upon a dead rat.

Qiu was worried. A summons to Brigade almost certainly meant trouble; a summons backed up with a Red Flag signaled endless permutations of potential disaster. Leader Deng rode around in such a car. Qiu knew only too well that he had little in common with Deng. All he asked of life was that he be left alone to work with his electronic calculator, his figures and his charts. Once in the real world, he was out of his element.

He drew hard on his cigarette, suppressing the cough that the cheap tobacco gouged from his throat, and wished he'd bought the Winstons when they had been offered. But at nine mao the pack, they represented an almost indefensible extravagance and besides, it would have meant trading with Old Tian, whose account with Qiu was presently weighted rather too much in Tian's favor.

The car slid past the high gray walls of the Friendship Guest House and continued on its way toward the wooded green hills. Qiu frowned, his mind stuck fast in the groove of economic duplicity. On the seat beside him lay a flat package done up in white paper. It contained seasoned smoked pork. The cadre picked it up and weighed it in his hands. There ought to be more. For three mao he usually got seven good, thick slices. Here there were only six, yet he had paid the same. What did that mean? Mrs. Lin at the commissariat was sending him a message, that was obvious, but . . . what exactly was the message? Working out the answer would require thought, and time. But it would also have to wait, because now the driver was slowing for the turn-off to Haidian and there were only a few minutes of the journey left.

Before the car could turn into brigade headquarters, however, it had to give way to a black Shanghai sedan which was emerging through the massive wooden doors onto the road. Qiu caught a quick glimpse of a tall Chinese sitting in the Shanghai's backseat; an overseas Chinese, evidently, for the arm raised to the window was clad in stylish cloth of a Western cut. Qiu puffed out his cheeks. It was all very well for those *Huaqiao*, they needn't trouble themselves about the price of pork . . .

As the car eased to a halt in the courtyard the solid doors rolled shut behind it. Qiu stepped out into the moist evening heat, pushing the black-framed spectacles onto the bridge of his nose and screwing up his face into a squint against the sunlight. In September it was invariably cooler up here in the lush woods by the Summer Palace, but not much. He knew that once he left the shade of the surrounding gray stone walls he was going to melt. He found it difficult to breathe, his heart had begun to beat in a series of irregular thumps. There was trouble in the air, real trouble. He could smell it.

"*Xiaodi.*" Little Brother.

Qiu swiftly dropped his cigarette onto the concrete and ground it out. Then he blinked and turned toward the imperious voice that had spoken from the gatehouse. Sun Shanwang stood there, hands on hips, his tall, wiry body straight as a ramrod. Qiu knew that Sun was sixty-five years old, but the deputy controller always seemed untouched by time.

"Hah, Little Brother, welcome, welcome . . . "

The words "welcome, welcome" belied their speaker's tone. Sun Shanwang's narrow face wore its familiar pinched, pained expression of disapproval, and Qiu hastened to placate his superior. "Good evening, Comrade Sun. Thank you for sending me the car."

"Too urgent for the bus, Little Brother. You are for the Old One."

Try as he might, Qiu could not staunch the rush of air through his lips; he knew at once that Sun had heard. The senior cadre's mouth compressed in an unspoken reprimand, but already he was hobbling away toward the main building. Now the evening seemed even warmer than ever, and thoughts of the price of cigarettes were far from Qiu's mind. But as he started off in Sun's wake he remembered, with a stab of horror, the smoked pork. He had left it on the backseat of the car. Qiu wheeled around in time to see the Red Flag waft out of the courtyard, bearing his six-slices-that-should-be-seven with it.

That was what happened in the world outside. Trouble, nothing but trouble. First the pork, now goodness knows what. He had never seen the Old One. But he had heard . . .

"Come this way, Qiu."

They entered the main building through an archway made of red pillars topped with gold. The columns supported two blue dragons, guardians of the tiered, green-tiled roof. It was an impressive edifice, but as the two men traversed the cool, gilded corridors of the old house, penetrating ever more deeply into its recesses, away from the bright midsummer light, Qiu noticed nothing except the patches on the heels of Sun's black corduroy shoes scuttling along the polished wooden floor in front of him.

"Hah, in here . . . " Sun was standing before a wide door, on the panels of which was portrayed a haunting watery moonscape. "Please follow me, Little Brother."

Qiu dug his fingernails into his palms and adjusted his lips into their customary, neutral smile. "I am grateful for your kindness, Comrade Sun."

He took a step forward, still conscious only of Sun's back. Then the deputy controller stepped to one side and there it all was. The scene. The room. Exactly as the stories were told.

It was very large and the ceiling was high. The parquet flooring, highly polished, formed an intricate circular design. At the far end, a *li* away or so it appeared to Qiu, enormous windows gave onto a blue evening sky brushed by gently waving birchtops. He knew that on the other side of those windows there was a lake, not unlike the one depicted on the walls, but without its beautiful long boats and modest ladies . . . and the huge table, yes, that was there too, and so was the Mah-jongg set.

Sun Shanwang marched down to the end of the table, where he took up position at Baba's shoulder. "Qiu Qianwei," he said tersely.

"Hah, hah . . . Qiu *tongzhi* . . . "

The Old One had called him "comrade." Qiu raised his eyes a fraction and stared down the long table at the room's only other occupant. His nerves had begun to affect his sight: he saw as if through the wrong end of a telescope. A vast distance away sat a wizened old man, propped up by bulky cushions and supported at the back by a padded triangular rest. His face was the color of the paper on which they printed the *People's Daily*, but even from so far away Qiu could see that this old man had a smile, and it was kind.

"Come, come . . . " His voice was a very soft whisper. Qiu stepped forward, trying to keep his face molded into an expression of dispassionate respect. So frail, so very frail. The Old One seemed scarcely to breathe. On seeing Qiu approach, his wrinkled face very slowly wound itself into an even broader smile and he raised his hand an inch from the embroidered quilt that, on this hottest of days, lay across his knees.

Qiu swallowed. All the blood in his body seemed to lift itself into his head and sweep away again, leaving him weak—for he realized that he was supposed to take that papery hand in his own. And he could not do it.

The Old One smiled, ever so gently, and nodded. "Yes," he whispered. "Take, take . . . "

Qiu hesitated. Then, very slowly, as if afraid of breaking the old man's bones, he bent down and for a second cupped the proffered hand in his palm. He stared at the two hands, one of which had embraced Mao Zedong, and for an instant he seemed to float off the floor . . . then the moment passed, and he breathed again. "Sit, sit."

Sun Shanwang rammed a chair hard against the backs of Qiu's knees, thereby injecting a breath of realism into the situation, and Qiu sat down abruptly. He was still very close to the Old One, however, and he had no intention of diverting his gaze; for he knew that he was in the presence of Revolutionary history and that even today there were Red Guards who would cheerfully give up their lives if only they could sit in this chair first. His hand had touched the Old One's, which in turn had touched the Flame . . .

"It is kind of you to sacrifice your time for me, comrade." The voice was thin and insubstantial, like its owner; the words came out in short, slow sentences. "I am an old man now. You can see for yourself. You have many things to do. Many demands on your time." The look of anguished negation on Qiu's face seemed to be the answer the old man sought, for he smiled his patient smile and said, "Those of us who are left . . . can no longer play a role. See how we in Central Intelligence are reduced to spending our days . . . " He lifted his hand as if the effort cost him pain, and gestured feebly toward the table. Qiu tore his eyes from the ancient face before him and looked down. The Mah-jongg pieces were scattered about the surface in disarray, one game over, another yet to begin.

Sun slid into a chair opposite Qiu and scowled at him. "What do you say to Father, hah? No words to speak?"

"My time is quite worthless, Baba. Especially when compared to your own. Please allow me to render every assistance."

"Thank you, Little Brother. I need your help."

"*My* help?" Qiu was incredulous.

"Yes. I hear many good reports of you. Your attitude is correct. Your viewpoint is straightforward. It is in accordance with the Party's own. Also, I hear much of your intelligence. Genius, even that. Genius."

The silence was very long.

"Will you help me, Little Brother?"

Qiu's reply came out, too quickly, in a quiet hiss. *"Dangran."* Yes.

The old man lethargically nodded his head. "Thank you. Thank you." From under his triangular, hooded eyebrows he observed how the red fire of Revolutionary ardor burned in the young man sitting beside him, and was pleased. He reached out toward the table, but his strength seemed to desert him, for he lay back against the cushions, chest heaving. He allowed his head to loll to one side, letting Sun read the message in his eyes, and nodded. Sun at once leaned forward and carelessly picked up one of the tiles lying face down in front of him.

"Here you are, Little Brother. This is for you." He tossed it toward Qiu, as if indifferent, but the expression on his closed face was manifestly hard. He doesn't approve, thought Qiu, and the knowledge brought its own unpleasant brand of excitement.

He looked down, careful to keep his face expressionless. The tile was made of ivory and it weighed heavy in his hand. The plain back was painted sky blue. The front . . . he flipped it over and as if from outside himself watched his fingers uncurl, their muscles disabled by shock.

Cream background, a rough, thick red rectangle bisected by a slashing downward stroke, red the color of blood. *Hong long.*

Baba said: "I ask you to consent to be my Red Dragon, Little Brother."

Red Dragon. At thirty-six, Qiu heard himself appointed brigade commander of Central Intelligence with the new rank of colonel in the PLA (the People's Liberation Army); the salary of a deputy alternate Politburo member; and the right to expect goodness knows what else besides in years to come. Oh yes, and a bullet as the price of failure . . . Qiu squeezed the tile, deriving irrational comfort from the feel of its hard edges grinding into his flesh.

"What is the significance of the year 1997, Little Brother?" It was Sun Shanwang, the deputy controller of intelligence, who spoke. "You may ignore its being a year of the Ox . . . "

Qiu's fingers folded over the tile, clenched it for an instant, and uncurled again.

"Nineteen ninety-seven, Little Brother . . . ?"

Qiu's head snapped up. "Nineteen ninety-seven . . . is the year when we shall recover what the imperialist lackeys took from us. Hong Kong will revert to the Middle Kingdom." But his thumb continued to stroke the ivory; moist flesh against the smoothness of time, a reminder of everything that endured . . .

"That is right." Now the old man spoke, raising his voice a tone so as to penetrate the mists engendered in the young cadre's brain by possession of the tile. "But Sun Zi reminds us. One thing to capture . . . another to hold." His eyes traveled sideways, and Qiu followed his glance. A few feet away from the table stood a revolving bookcase on a stand. The spines of two tomes were visible: *Ping Fa*, the *Principles of War*, by the ancient philosopher general Sun Zi, and the *I Ching*. On seeing the latter Qiu's body rippled with a sudden chill. He had not seen that. Seen-it-but-not-seen-it.

"I want you to build me a wall."

Qiu presented his smiling face to the controller of China's Central Intelligence Service and spread his hands. "A wall, Baba . . . ?"

"Yes. A wall around Hong Kong. I do not mean one of bricks and mortar—but nevertheless, a wall such as the capitalists and the Soviets will never breach again. Not as long as the Middle Kingdom lasts. But—the matter is urgent, very urgent. We must start the building now. You can do this for me, Little Brother? With your skills and your knowledge? You can build for me this wall to protect our inheritance? As you could build a wall in the game . . . " He gestured toward the tiles. "The task is long. The difficulties are great."

"My poor abilities will not serve, Baba. I lack practical experience of such matters. I can only make things worse than they were before, with my clumsy ways."

"I think you are too modest, Little Brother."

"I am afraid when I think of how I shall disappoint you."

"Yet I have hope."

"Then obedience requires me to submit. This, naturally, I do with a fervent and earnest heart. I shall rely on the thought of Chairman Mao. As interpreted by his disciple, Leader Deng," he added hastily.

"I know it. Although you have many things to master before you can build my wall. As yet, you are but a man of theories. I know this. You will receive help and encouragement from Comrade Sun. He will be your mentor. Trust him. You are younger brother, he is elder. From now on, your family and his are one."

"Thank you, thank you."

"Also, you will have other teachers. One in particular, the Chrysanthemum. You have much to learn about Hong Kong, Little Brother. The Chrysanthemum is skilled in the ways of commerce, of business. He will help you. In time."

"The Chrysanthemum?"

"He is a businessman of Hong Kong, who understands banks. There is a Russian bank to be destroyed. It is not only a bank. It is the headquarters of the Russians' spy network throughout the Far East. The greatest danger we have ever faced. I want you to ruin it. The Chrysanthemum will help you. There is another businessman, Simon Young—he too will help you. You must make this bank lend Simon Young a huge amount of money, and then see that it is not repaid."

Sun, aware that Qiu was reeling, hurriedly said: "We have much to discuss, Red Dragon. But Baba is tired. We will talk in the morning. For now, it is best if you go to your new quarters."

"May I ask—"

The words froze upon his lips. Directly opposite him a panel in the beautifully decorated wall slid open to reveal a bent black shadow, its face invisible in the fading light of dusk. Then it hobbled forward into the room and to his astonishment Qiu saw that it was a shadow with substance, an old woman leaning on a stick, her free hand tucked behind her back.

"Baba is tired, did you not hear?" Her voice was cracked and hoarse, the voice of a peasant, but something told Qiu that this was no serf. Although her back was twisted almost double it was obvious that she did not lack energy or spirit, and her black pajamas were of the finest quality. Her feet . . . for a second Qiu's permanent expression dropped to be replaced by a look of naked curiosity before he could resume the mask. Her feet had been broken and bound. That could mean she was highly born.

"*You!*" The old woman raised her stick, leveled it across the table, and prodded Qiu in the chest. "Baba needs rest. He needs tea. He needs food. *Out!*"

Baba's face displayed patient resignation, as if he had witnessed this scene before and knew he could do nothing to change its course. Sun Shanwang, however, for the first time that day showed a hint of satisfaction. Qiu realized that his audience with history was over. He edged his way backward, unable to take his eyes from the Old One's face until right at the end when, as if by magic, the door swung open behind him and allowed him to pass through, out of their presence, the three people inside the room staring back at him with the serene impassivity of waxwork figures, framed in empty time.

Qiu found his wife sitting on a stool, surrounded by packing cases, with the shards of a broken cup in her hands and tears flowing down the plump cheeks of her plain face.

"Qingqing! What's the matter?"

She jumped at the sound of his voice and wiped her nose on the back of her hand.

"Nothing, nothing. Happy to see you."

His face softened a fraction and he allowed her one smile from his limited stock. Qiu's smile was peculiar: for a second the very edges of his lips would flicker out of true into an exaggerated curve while his eyebrows rose halfway up his forehead. If you blinked you missed it. The facial gesture conveyed politeness, but involved no emotion.

"You don't like our new quarters—is that it?"

"I like very much. Thank you, *Airen*."

They stared at each other, still numb with the shock. Earlier that day he had left her in the apartment on the borders of Fengtai and Tongxian, and that was one life; now here they both were, ensconced in a house of the Central Intelligence Mah-jongg compound, and another life seemed to have begun. In the course of a few hours, without reference to him, the authorities had transported his wife and their communal possessions from surroundings of spartan sufficiency to a home of enviable comfort. The couple were used to having every aspect of their lives ordered by the state but, even so, nothing had prepared them for such a momentous change.

"Where is baby Tingchen?"

"In our room, in his cot. He was asleep when I last looked."

"Is mother here as well?"

"Yes, upstairs. In her room."

"Upstairs . . . ?" It was a house, Qiu reminded himself sharply; of course, there was more than one story. "She has her own room?"

"Yes." Qingqing risked a wan smile. "Mama's sulking."

Qiu's own mechanical smile flickered across his face. "Hah!"

"She doesn't like the orderly."

"The *what*?"

As if in answer he heard the clang of saucepans tumbling down next door and at once he strode toward the kitchen, only to stop on the threshold with one foot still upraised.

"You are who?"

The fat woman standing by the sink appeared to take no notice. She was wiping her hands on her greasy gray *sam-fu*; only when they were quite dry did she turn toward the doorway, frown and say, "Colonel, this kitchen is not good."

Qiu swallowed.

"Not enough places to store things. You will see about this, please. Tomorrow. No need to do tonight," she added, as if by way of gracious afterthought.

Qiu backed away from the doorway, keeping his eyes fixed on the woman. Qingqing had unpacked a stool for him. He groped his way toward it and sat down. He opened his mouth but, before he could speak, another strange voice intruded on his muddled brain.

"Hah . . . Colonel, please excuse."

Qiu swung around to be confronted with a middle-aged man in the uniform of the People's Liberation Army, nervously twisting his cap in his hands.

"You are who?"

"Your driver, Colonel. You want the car tonight, hah?"

Qiu did not move his head but his eyes strayed to Qingqing's face. No help there.

"The car is where?" he said at last.

"Outside, Colonel."

"I see." Qiu did not get up at once. He continued to stare at his wife, who carefully kept her face under control. It was impossible for the PLA driver to know what they were thinking, if indeed they thought anything at all. At last Qiu rose from his stool and strolled across to the window, but casually, as if this were an unplanned stop on his way to do something else. Qingqing watched his back, anxious for a cue. She noticed how as he approached the window his shoulders suddenly sagged and then quivered slightly. At last her curiosity got the better of her and she jumped up to be by his side.

They stared out for a long time, saying nothing; then simultaneously they turned away. After Qiu had counted up to ten he swung around, but the green Mercedes was still there.

The driver continued to twist his cap and keep his eyes firmly fixed on the floor.

"Hah . . . car tomorrow at eight, okay?"

"*Hao.*" Right.

After the man left Qiu and Qingqing continued to stare at each other without speaking, afraid that words might break the magic spell that had them in thrall. At last he bent down to pick up the remains of the broken cup. "Better make a start, eh?" he said.

There was much to be done; the household went to bed late that night. Qingqing thought her husband was exhausted, so it surprised her when he pounced, draining off all his nervous energy into her placid body with a few quick thrusts. But there was something she very much wanted to say; and when he had finished and lay still she felt that, no matter how great the risk, this was the time to say it. After a long, calculating pause she summoned up her courage, stretched out one hand to touch him and, once she had satisfied herself that he really was asleep, whispered, "Whatever they want . . . whatever it is . . . please . . . *succeed.*"

2

The Chinese woman was turning away from the grill with a slip of paper on which the teller had written her balance when she became aware of a commotion at the other end of the banking hall. Her eyes strayed instinctively to the huge oak-cased clock above the revolving doors. Twelve noon: the noise must signify that her father-in-law was on his way to the Hong Kong club, with all the ritual paraphernalia that his progresses in and out of the Corporation usually involved.

She knew it would have been stupid and childish to go and hide behind a pillar, so instead she stood quite still in the middle of the marble floor, hoping that he would not notice her. But he did. He always did.

"Jinny!" Tom Young's commanding voice easily carried the length of the hall. Simultaneously the phalanx of gray executives who surrounded their chairman wheeled to the left, bearing down on the hapless Chinese woman. Jinny Young's face froze; she looked as if she were anticipating a physical assault.

"How nice to see you." Her father-in-law took one of her hands between his own and gave it a squeeze, while the gray phalanx looked on impassively.

"Thank you, Tom. You seem very fit."

It was true. The chairman of the Pacific & Cantonese Banking Corporation was tall, lean and lightly tanned; he always looked like a man who had just returned from a cruise.

"My doctor says there's something about the making of money which agrees with my constitution." He spoke abruptly, without any attempt at the courtly humor that the words might have conveyed in another man's mouth. "What brings you here?"

"Oh, just seeing if I have any money left." She could not resist adding, "I am a customer of yours, you know."

"Do you?"

Jinny's mouth had developed a tic. "Do I what?"

"Have any money left?"

"A few cents, maybe." She smiled up at him timidly, willing the banker's façade to crack, but his expression remained as fierce as ever.

"Good." Still clasping her hand he led her aside, out of the gray phalanx's earshot. "I've been trying to speak to Simon all week. Is he avoiding me?"

"No, I'm sure not." She smiled idiotically, resenting the way he made her want to ingratiate. "He has been abroad for the past few days. Beijing, Tokyo, Taipei—"

Tom Young frowned, as if this answer was just about as wrong as it could be. "Well, tell him to phone as soon as he gets back, will you?"

"Certainly, Tom. Can I say it's about anything in particular?"

"You can tell him to get his damn treasurer off my back, if you like." His lips almost got as far as a rueful smile, as if he were dimly conscious that this was not quite the way to address one's son's wife in public, even if she were Chinese. "I've told him before, I'm not lending on his scatterbrain projects and that's flat!"

Tom Young had been at commercial war with his son for almost as long as Jinny could remember. Their quarrel had its origins in one of Simon's earliest property speculations, Ko Shan, but by now the skirmishes raged so far and wide that Jinny couldn't begin to guess what was raising her father-in-law's blood pressure to such a degree.

"And now, my dear, if you'll excuse me . . ."

Before Jinny could draw breath Tom Young had once more enclosed himself in his protective gray human tank and rumbled off toward the doors. For a moment she stood looking after him with a neutral expression on her face, while her rapidly beating heart subsided to its normal rate. You have to bear this, she told herself dispassionately. It is part of your fate. The price of happiness.

She hurried away from the Corporation's headquarters, glad to be liberated from the oppressive gloom of its Victorian splendors, and hailed a cab to take her to the King Fook Gold and Jewelry Company in Des Voeux Road. Inwardly she was seething but no one looking at her would have known it; her appearance did not differ markedly from that of any other rich Chinese *tai-tai* on her way to the shops.

At last Jinny's rage wore off and her mind began to busy itself with sums. She had more than enough money to pay for her husband's present but things were not as simple as that. She had to consider how best to approach the negotiation in such a way as to save money while at the same time preserving her inner feelings of sacrifice and love. The smile on her lips widened a fraction. Economy could take a backseat today. She knew exactly what she wanted and she intended to have it.

The object of her desires was a set of studs with matching cufflinks, each piece a diamond mounted in black onyx. Jinny had been sparring with her favorite shop assistant for several weeks now. He led her into his private sanctum at the back while they mouthed pleasantries as usual, but both of them knew that this was dealing day.

"Those studs," Jinny said casually. "The stones are very small."

"But excellent quality, Mrs. Young."

"Oh, maybe. I can't think of anyone who'd actually wear them, that's the problem. Such a speculative buy."

"Would you care to see them again, madam?"

"Why not?"

He laid the tray on the desk between them and proffered a glass, but Jinny had already taken her own out of her handbag. "Small," she said after a while. "Like I say. And scratched, a couple of them."

The man smiled. "I couldn't possibly offer you imperfect goods, Mrs. Young," he said, reaching out to remove the tray.

"Leave them."

He smiled again, and withdrew his hand.

"How much?"

He named a figure and she laughed. "For madam," he said hastily, "there is always a special price. Shall we say . . . one-third discount?"

"They're really not worth that kind of money," Jinny said as she scooped her glass back into the bag. "Thank you all the same."

"Would you care to place a value on them?"

She named a figure approximately two-fifths of his original price. The shop assistant spread his hands in a warding-off gesture, like one who knows that his next remark will offend. "Please give me some face, Mrs. Young."

They haggled. Suddenly Jinny became impatient. It was late, Simon's plane would be landing soon. The man, sensing her change of mood, seized the psychological advantage by reducing his latest figure a tiny fraction and they closed at once.

She had paid over the odds, but today for some reason she did not care. Simon would soon be home. Nothing else mattered. They had been married for nearly twenty years and whenever he went away she still missed him like a moonstruck girl.

Jinny took a cab to the house and as Ah Kum answered the door to let her in said, "Calls?"

"Dr. Lim of the Red Cross phoned." Ah Kum scratched her ear, trying to remember what she was supposed to say. "He wanted . . . to tell you that"—her eyes widened in relief—"that he has lost his minutes of the last meeting of the Vietnam Orphans Committee and could you please let him have a photostat of yours."

"All right. Anything else?"

"Yes."

Jinny waited impatiently. "Well?"

"Ah . . . Your calligraphy class has been put back to Wednesday afternoon, three-thirty."

"What a nuisance. I shan't be able to go; phone Mrs. Khoo and tell her I've got a Save the Children Fund dinner that day. . . . Oh, don't you bother, I'll do it myself. Now. Master will be home soon."

"All ready, all ready."

"Ready, are you? We'll see."

She went to Simon's study and laid the leather jewelry box on the exact center of his blotter, where he could not fail to notice it first thing. Then she turned to Ah Kum and said, "I will inspect now."

Ah Kum followed her mistress through the house from top to bottom, marveling at such thoroughness. Every surface capable of bearing dust was fingered, every coverlet straightened, each vase moved a fraction. It isn't natural, reasoned Ah Kum to herself; after twenty years she ought to be playing Mah-jongg or bedding a lover, not searching high and low for dirt. Then she caught a glimpse of the light in Jinny's eyes and her own expression softened. Love—that's what came of marrying a foreign devil, with his romantic, impractical ways, handsome bastard though he was. Rich devil, too. Still . . .

The tour of inspection ended in the living room with Jinny making a minute adjustment to the silver-framed photograph of the children that stood on an occasional table by the door. Above the table hung a mirror. The two women, mistress and servant, looked into it together and perceived different images. Jinny, suddenly depressed, stared at herself and saw a once-lovely face now verging on middle age, its makeup less than perfect; hair that was brittle and suffering from split ends; a neck that no longer was smooth. But when Ah Kum regarded the reflection of her mistress she saw a fine-boned, beautiful woman in the prime of life: well-permed, expensively dressed, with rounded features rendered a touch erotic by the presence of a single black mole on the hairline above the right, perfectly almond-shaped eye.

Jinny raised a hand to her forehead and adjusted a lock of hair. Her hands were her most exquisite feature: the fingers long and tapering, the skin unmarred by age. Ah Kum watched them enviously.

Two pairs of eyes met in the mirror and simultaneously the women sighed, then smiled.

The doorbell rang. Jinny stiffened. For a second, every line of her body seemed to quiver with energy; then, just as suddenly, she was still.

"Master?" said Ah Kum doubtfully. "He is early."

"Don't stand there gawping, Ah Kum. Answer the door!"

Jinny followed the servant into the hallway, pausing by the mirror to smooth her hair one last time. She heard the door open and turned to greet her husband with a smile.

But it was not Simon who stood on the step.

*   *   *

Every man has his own special way of coming home and Simon Young was no exception. Most of his peers in Hong Kong regarded him as an eccentric Englishman—eccentric even by the standards of that distinctly individual colony. While the *tai-pans* of the other great trading *hongs* were wafted in their Rolls-Royces from Kai Tak Airport through the tunnel to "Hongkongside" and the air-conditioned mansions in Shek-O, the managing director of Ducannon Young preferred to take a taxi to the Star Ferry and finish his homeward journey with a trip across the harbor. Sometimes, if he had no luggage, he even forsook the taxi and went by the 200 bus.

Today, however, he had a suitcase with him and he hailed a cab. The drive to the ferry began with a long gray bobsled run between high tenement walls, with their protruding poles of washing, which he always found depressing, so he used the opportunity to scan the newspapers. *Ta Kong Pao* had nothing to say, but then the Communist press in Hong Kong was notoriously boring as well as predictable. The *South China Morning Post* had an article on the coming fusion of the four stock exchanges, which Simon read with mounting irritation. How ludicrous it seemed to promulgate reforms of that kind just twelve years short of handover. The People's Republic of China would decide what happened to the Hong Kong exchanges, not Britain.

At the ferry he headed for the second-class entrance, thereby saving himself twenty cents, and humped his case down the ramp. It was evening, the ferry was full, but he found himself a place at the front where he could stand among the homeward-bound workers and look out over the harbor. It was good to feel a breeze on his face again and smell the rich tropical scents: intangible but real benefits which no car journey could ever confer. In late September the heat and humidity steadied at a tolerable level; and this evening the skies were clear, affording him a view of the Peak. Simon breathed deeply. Twelve more years to go. A gross of months . . .

As the ferry eased its way toward the island his eyes narrowed. Work on the Hong Kong & Shanghai Bank's new headquarters went on day and night now; he had been away for less than a week, but even so, progress was noticeable and the building was all but complete. People couldn't understand the rush. "You're mad," Simon's father had bluntly told the Bank's president. "You're

□ 44 □

going to finish just in time to hand it all over to the mainland Chinese . . ."

Simon slung his jacket over his shoulder and strode up the ramp with a long, loping stride while Chinese and Europeans alike scuttled out of his path. Anyone in Hong Kong who stood six feet four inches tended to carry his own space around him like a force field. Besides, he was well known, his reputation went before him and no one cared to get in his way.

Luk Seng Kay was waiting at the barrier as arranged, his familiar worried frown even deeper than usual.

"*Nei ho ma?*"

"*Hoh-le, hoh-le, dor jeh.*" Luk felt somehow slighted when his employer addressed him in Cantonese. The managing director of Ducannon Young was entitled to have English spoken at all times, or so his servant thought. "Boss, we got a big problem at home."

Old Luk and his wife Ah Kum had looked after Simon's family for many years. The husband was in his late fifties and one of nature's pessimists, but Simon knew him well enough to realize that he had come home to a genuine crisis. "What's up, *Lao* Luk?"

Luk carried his bags over to the waiting Porsche and loaded them swiftly into the trunk. "Visit," he said as he stiffly folded himself into the passenger seat, knowing that Simon would want to drive. "We got visitor, from that place." He jerked his thumb over his shoulder. Simon was startled. He wasn't expecting anyone from the People's Republic of China.

"Who?"

"*Gongganju.*"

"Police? Public Security Bureau?"

"Right, right."

Simon accelerated across the Chater Road lights and headed toward Wanchai, grateful for once that Luk had borrowed Jinny's Porsche. The streets were packed with people, locals and tourists. Normally he would have enjoyed the busy spectacle, not minding the traffic jams, but such unwelcome news made him eager to be home.

"Who's looking after this chap?"

"Lady."

"Mrs. Young's alone?" Simon's voice was harsh with reproach. "I leave Ah Kum with her, tell her to keep good eye out."

Twenty-odd years ago Mr. and Mrs. Luk had swum across Deep Bay on their way out of China, braving the sharks and the

Royal Hong Kong Police to "touch home base" and win their freedom. Since then they had proved their worth many times over. The news that Ah Kum was in the house with Jinny reassured Simon a little.

They were nearly at the Aberdeen Tunnel. He saw a narrow chance and took it, shooting the car like a red bullet aimed between two lorries and a bus while Luk smacked his lips in appreciation. "Who brought him to the house?"

" 'Sistant Commissioner Police Reade."

Officially, Reade was attached to the Commercial Bureau of Special Branch. Simon knew that in addition he was DI6's local resident. He went down a gear and slammed through a gap that suddenly opened up on the far lane. Yes, he wanted very much to be home.

The Youngs lived in a rambling three-story house built high up out of the side of a cliff a few minutes' drive from Repulse Bay. Simon sent Luk to garage the car and went in through the kitchen. As he expected, Ah Kum was standing against the inner door, one ear pressed to the panels.

"They're still in there," she hissed. "Together!"

From the look of bafflement on her face Simon deduced that she had not been able to hear very much of the conversation.

"Is Assistant Commissioner Reade with them?"

"He left."

Simon was startled. "When?"

"About twenty minutes gone."

"I see." Simon frowned. "Any tea?"

"Inside, Boss."

Simon took his briefcase through to the lounge with him. He hesitated for a second in the doorway, long enough to register that he was entering a totally silent room. Jinny rose to meet him, a bright smile on her face, and he noticed with pleasure how the tight-fitting electric blue *cheongsam*, modest and suggestive at the same time, clung to her trim figure. He preferred her to wear Chinese clothing, although she, in common with so many well-off Oriental women, affected to like Western styles.

He very much wanted to give his wife a hug. In London he could have done it; but not here, not in front of a Chinese visitor. So instead he bent down to kiss Jinny on the cheek. "Hello."

"Hi." Her smile was uncertain, and with a sudden quickening of the heart he saw her lower lip tremble. "Simon, I'd like you to meet a guest. This is Mr. Qiu of the Public Security Bureau of the People's Republic of China. Peter Reade brought him, but he had to leave."

Simon looked over her shoulder to see a short, small-framed Chinese with a bespectacled, boyish face sitting by the window in a wickerwork chair. Now this guest rose quickly and walked toward Simon, his hands nervously rubbing the small of his back as if not sure what to do next.

"*Qiu tongzhi. Ni yao bu yao shuo putonghua?*"

"Thank you, Mr. Young, but I am anxious to polish my English, if you have no objection. Of course you know that English is now our official second language?"

"I had read that, yes."

"And please . . . I shall not be at all offended to be called 'mister,' as I am sure you will prefer. Do I call you *tai-pan?*"

Simon laughed. "Lord, no. We haven't had any of that nonsense for years."

"That's what I thought, but it's always better to check, isn't it?"

Simon held out his hand. "Mr. Qiu, I must compliment you on your English. It is truly excellent."

After a moment's hesitation Qiu took his outstretched hand and briefly squeezed it. "Oh, you embarrass me, Mr. Young. I am only too aware of the mistakes I make all the time. Please overlook my errors and correct me whenever you can."

"I know there will be nothing to correct."

"You are too kind."

"Do sit down. Have you had tea?"

Jinny touched his arm. "Ah Kum made it a few moments ago. Sit down, relax. How was the trip?"

Simon gratefully lowered himself into the nearest armchair and expelled a deep breath. While they exchanged a few meaningless remarks about his journey he continued to watch Qiu carefully. The little man's face gave nothing away. He studiously avoided looking toward husband and wife as they talked, but didn't seem to know what to do instead. Eventually he went back to his chair and, after a short internal debate, sat down.

"Are you all right?" Simon mouthed; and although Jinny nodded, he was concerned. His wife had been permitted to emigrate from China more than twenty years before, but the Middle Kingdom never quite lost sight of its children. Jinny preferred to avoid all dealings with representatives of the mainland except when her husband's work necessitated it. Simon took a sip of tea and realized that it was superior Lung Ching, the famous "Dragon's Well." Jinny apparently thought their guest worthy of some extravagance.

"How was your journey, Mr. Qiu?" he asked.

The question seemed to flummox Qiu. He half lifted himself out of his chair, sank back again and gripped the arms tightly. "Fine, fine, thank you."

"Mr. Reade brought you, I understand."

"Yes."

"A very nice man."

"Oh yes."

"We have been friends for some years now."

"Hah?"

Softly, softly, thought Simon to himself. The point will emerge in time. Today, tomorrow, next year.

"Beautiful house you have, Mr. and Mrs. Young."

"We have been very fortunate in many ways. This house is reasonable when compared to some." Simon's eyes flickered around the lounge, retaking possession. Its white walls were tinged with just the faintest suggestion of green. Over by the window embrasure, three bamboo chairs lacquered the color of fresh mint surrounded a square glass-topped table that supported a Lalique bowl containing fragrant potpourri. Qiu's wicker chair occupied a corner nearest the artificial fireplace, in which stood one of Jinny's Oriental flower arrangements. Simon's books filled white, glass-fronted cases on either side of the mantelpiece. A deep-piled carpet, the color of coriander, stretched from wall to wall. The understated message was one of cool, Eastern tranquillity. Simon was very fond of this room, the product of his wife's good taste.

"I am glad to be able to offer you its hospitality," he said. Simon made it a rule never to denigrate his house, however much Chinese convention might require it. "You are seeing it at its best, after I have been absent from it for some days."

He saw the momentary flicker of irritation behind Qiu's eyes and awarded himself a mark.

"Please forgive me, but I am afraid I do not understand."

"The best government is when the emperor is far away."

Qiu's face remained impassive, denying Simon confirmation of whether he recognized the classical maxim, so alien to centralized Communist thought.

"Darling, perhaps Mr. Qiu would like some more tea."

"Oh yes . . ." Jinny Young got up a shade too quickly and walked across to Qiu's chair with the pot. The nape of Simon's neck had started to prickle: Why didn't Jinny do as she always did and call Ah Kum to do the serving?

"Mr. Reade said you might be prepared to assist me, Mr. Young. I don't like to trouble you, but perhaps you can help."

"If I can, Mr. Qiu. I am sure you know that I have modest dealings with China now."

"Extensive would perhaps be a better word, Mr. Young."

"You are very kind."

"If I may say so, on the contrary. You have been kind to China."

"We have tried to live together in harmony, let us say."

"And in the course of your business dealings you have come often to China. Three days ago, in fact, you were in Beijing."

Simon paused before answering. "Yes . . . ah, Mr. Qiu, I believe I can guess why you are here. The airport . . ."

"You are right, Mr. Young."

"A very shocking thing, Mr. Qiu." Simon saw that Jinny was becoming impatient. He reached for his briefcase and extracted the newspapers, turning up an inside page of *Ta Kong Pao* before handing it to her. "Who were they?"

"Terrorists, Mr. Young. Armed bandits, robbing the airport's bank. Such violence has been unheard of in China for many years."

Simon thought of the Cultural Revolution, of old friends who had disappeared forever, and clenched his teeth. "Indeed."

Jinny read the article and looked up, her face incredulous. "An armed attack?" she whispered.

Simon nodded. "A teller was killed, I believe."

"But you were there, Mr. Young . . ."

Jinny's face registered shock. "You were—"

"It's all right, darling." Simon raised his hand. "I was there, as Mr. Qiu says, but I was never in any danger. They passed me by."

Qiu leaned forward eagerly. By now he was sitting on the very edge of his chair—another millimeter and his bottom would be suspended in space. "Yet you saw them, did you not?"

"Yes. I answered questions at the time, Mr. Qiu. The Public Security Bureau will have my answers on file."

Qiu's face changed; at first Simon wasn't sure what had happened. For a split second the corners of his mouth curved upward but his lips did not part . . . was that meant for a smile? His little face looked solemn enough now: a frown creased his forehead and the downturned lips were thrust outward. Qiu pushed his spectacles further up the bridge of his nose.

"The answers you gave were very good, Mr. Young. Very clear. It is the best description we have. You noticed them because they were carrying expensive cases, yet they were dressed like peasants. There were three of them, I think?"

"Yes."

"You have given a description of the clothes they were wearing, height, build, even facial features. May I compliment you, please? It is very unusual for a foreign visitor to be able to distinguish Chinese faces one from the other in that way."

"I have lived here a long time, Mr. Qiu. All my life, in fact."

After pouring the tea, Jinny, for some reason known only to herself, had gone to sit on a pouf to one side of Qiu, folding her arms around her legs and resting her head sideways on her knees. For several minutes Simon had been conscious of a growing unease brought on by this unnatural tableau. Suddenly he realized what was troubling him. In one of the guestrooms there hung a classical Chinese painting of the Emperor Qin Shihuangdi presiding over the execution of some subversive scholars. To one side, a little in front of him, knelt a concubine, her head lowered and her hands clasped in supplication. She was interceding for the victims, pleading for mercy. Qiu and Jinny did not physically resemble the emperor and his concubine, but their respective positions and levels were the same.

"Mr. Young"—Simon came back to the conversation with a jolt—"Mr. Young, it would assist me, my department, if you could visit Beijing in the near future. We think those men have been caught. They are being held in the capital. We need a positive identification."

"But surely there were many other eyewitnesses—"

"None of them can give such a good description as yours."

As always in dealings with the People's Republic, wheels moved endlessly within wheels. Simon found himself hunting for the commercial angle, the political slant. Ostensible high-profile cooperation, of course, that went without saying; having a foreigner, a Hong Kong foreigner, issue a public denunciation against terrorists . . . or were they bank robbers? He knew he would have to talk to Reade.

"I am anxious as always to give what help I can, Mr. Qiu. But my schedule is a tight one. I was not planning to return to China in the near future. Let's see . . . this is the last week in September. The end of October is really—"

"Can we not persuade you to come earlier? All your expenses would be met. First class, of course."

"It is not a question of expense, Mr. Qiu."

"Then what *is* the question?"

It was so unexpectedly tart that for an instant Simon could not believe he had heard correctly. Qiu switched on his mockery of a smile and as promptly turned it off again.

"May I have a day or two to consider how best to proceed?"

"If you insist. One day would be better than two."

"I understand. How can I contact you?"

"Through Mr. Reade, please."

Simon raised his hands an inch from the arms of his chair and lowered them again preparatory to getting up. Qiu saw the delicate signal and at once reverted to his previous vein.

"I am so sorry to have taken up so much of your time, Mr. Young. Please forgive me, especially when you have just returned from a journey. After you left China you went to Tokyo, I think? And then to the other place?"

Simon was tired, his tact had worn paper-thin. "To Taiwan, yes."

Again the flashing, dead smile. "To Taiwan. And now, please do excuse me."

"How are you getting back into town, Mr. Qiu?" Simon knew he had no choice but to make the offer: "Can I arrange some transport for you?"

"Thank you, but I can easily walk to the bus stop. I like to take the bus. I can see so much that way. I ride on the top." He had reached the door, where old Luk was already waiting to see him off the premises. "Just as you do. Good-bye, Mr. Young . . . Mrs. Young."

He nodded and passed through into the passage. As the living room door closed, Jinny got up from the pouf and ran to embrace her husband. " 'Just as you do,' " she mimicked crossly. *"Fang-pi!"*

"Language."

"Well Simon, honestly. I mean to say—"

"If they can't find out that the head of Dunny's has some

peculiar habits they're not the people I take them for. And going by bus is a fairly public thing to do." He went across to the phone on its table by the picture window overlooking the bay and dialed a number. "*Wei* . . . Assistant Commissioner Reade, please. . . . Hello? Peter? Peter, what the hell is going on . . . ?"

As soon as Jinny heard him say Reade's name she quickly rose and left the room. Five minutes later Simon found her taking a bath, with only her face exposed in the midst of a rich lather of bubbles.

"What *is* so special about my Roger & Gallet bath gel?" he said plaintively.

"It smells nice, that's what."

Simon sat on the side of the oval bath and felt around in the lather until he encountered one of her feet.

"Ow!"

"Thank you, darling," he said quietly.

"For what?"

"For the studs and links. They're exquisite."

Jinny's lip trembled. "You are welcome. You are worth it, because you appreciate nice things."

Simon released her foot and softly slid his fingers up her leg. Her skin felt soft and silken-smooth to him; whereas the firm, slightly abrasive texture of his fingertips sent a shudder rippling up Jinny's thigh. Her eyes were half-closed, her cheeks flooded with blood, she began to bite her lower lip . . .

But when his hand drifted still higher, she jerked her legs together, trapping him. "Simon!"

"What?"

"Never mind 'what?' So innocent!"

"Of course." His forefinger waggled, ever so gently. "We're married. Why don't I come in there with you?"

She smiled at him, but her eyes said no—time and place were wrong. Simon gently withdrew his hand. "Reade sounded a bit miffed, I thought."

"Oh?" Jinny soaked a washcloth in hot water and folded it over her eyes, using it to mask her recovery.

"Yes." Simon smiled, seeking to bleed his words of all offense. "He implied that when he brought Qiu here you rather pointedly suggested he should leave."

Jinny blew a channel through the bubbles immediately in front of her mouth and allowed her body to float to the top of the water.

"Jinny, is that true?"

"Of course not. It's just that . . . well, this Qiu . . ."

"Yes?"

Jinny removed the washcloth. "He's from Sichuan, that's all. From Chengdu."

Simon said nothing for a while. He played idly with the water, shushing it between his wife's legs, a distant smile on his lips. "So. Qiu came from your own province, the place where you were born. And you knew he wouldn't talk about home in front of Peter, is that it?"

"You don't approve."

"I think it was . . . incautious."

"If you say so. Thank you for your criticism. I shall try to benefit from it. And now, shall we discuss the Four Moderniza-tions?"

"It was incautious. Silly." When Jinny's face remained closed he went on: "Did you learn anything?"

She shook her head.

"Did you seriously *expect* to learn anything?"

"Maybe."

"No message, no threats?"

"Nothing. He pretended not to know. He knew, of course."

"Certainly he knew. You're an overseas Chinese now, with a brother and sister still living in Sichuan. You were allowed out, they weren't. The *Gongganju* exist to know things like that and exploit them."

Jinny looked away.

"Did you hear me, Jinny?"

"I heard."

When Simon stood up and reached for a towel, Jinny said, "Will you make me a drink, please? I'll be out in a moment."

"What would you like?"

"Daiquiri."

Simon's eyebrows rose. Jinny saw. "You make me feel like an alcoholic," she grumbled.

"It makes a change from your usual grape juice, that's all. Right. One daiquiri coming up." He moved to the door. "Give me a shout when you're ready."

"Simon."

He paused, one hand on the side of the open door, and looked back.

"I didn't mean to offend Peter Reade."

"You didn't. He thought it was all rather a joke."

"Are you going?"

"To get your drink . . ."

"I didn't mean that. I meant, are you going to Beijing?"

"I doubt it."

"Peter thinks you should go."

Simon raised his head. "How did you know that?"

"It was the way he introduced Qiu to me. Something in his manner. Respect."

"For Qiu?"

"Yes. And for . . . the request itself, I think. It's true, isn't it?"

Yes, thought Simon, remembering his recent phone call— Peter wants me to go, all right. "I'll get your drink now."

"You should go. To Beijing. You should."

"Why?"

When she did not reply immediately he turned back and for a heart-stopping moment saw that his wife had disappeared. But then she floated up through the bubbles, spouting water like a dolphin, and he consciously felt himself relax; indeed, it astonished him to note how tense he had been.

"You should go," she said simply.

3

It was a fine autumn morning: breakfast time in the Qiu household. The family—Qiu himself, his mother, Qingqing and their baby son Tingchen—were seated at a round table, in the center of which stood a steaming bowl of pork porridge. This had been cooked up by their new orderly, known simply as *Ayi*, or Auntie. Qiu and baby Tingchen were making a hearty meal of it. Qingqing ate cautiously, every so often directing a questioning look at her mother-in-law. Old Mrs. Qiu sat with a scowl on her face, eating nothing at all.

Mrs. Qiu and *Ayi* did not get on.

For every one of Qiu's thirty-six years his mother had cooked his meals. Even after his marriage she had continued to rule the kitchen with a bamboo rod, much to the relief of Qingqing, who had neither flair nor love for the culinary art. But now it seemed that *Ayi* had other ideas, and since she, unlike Mrs. Qiu, came with the house as part of its fixtures and fittings, her will looked like it would prevail. *Ayi* did the cooking in this house; Mrs. Qiu did not. Since the Qiu family had moved in more than three months ago there had been arguments without number, some of them heated. Qiu merely ignored these dissensions, while Qingqing's feeble attempts at reconciliation met with total lack of success. She went to each matriarch in turn, pleading with her to "think of it from the other person's point of view," or "try to arrange a compromise," but somehow the community techniques that she had learned in her job as secretary of a district Party committee seemed ill-suited to the difficulties that beset her own home.

This distressed Qingqing, but it was not the sort of problem she could take to her husband. In China it had always been the woman's lot to suffer under a mother-in-law's heel. Now Qingqing felt as if she had two mothers-in-law.

"Please eat, Mama," she ventured timidly.

"No appetite," grumbled the old woman. "How to eat this . . . pap! Cooked in a house not my own by a . . . a . . ."

"Good meat, Mama." Qiu was enthusiastic about the new kitchen arrangements. He hadn't eaten so well for a long time. When his father died some years ago his mother's cooking suffered a downturn from which it never fully recovered.

"Meat, pah! More gristle than sinew and more sinew than flesh."

"Could only afford once a week, until now," Qiu observed matter-of-factly, and diverted all his attention to his son. Tingchen sat bolt upright in a new high chair, a spoon in each hand. Facially he resembled his father: pronounced cheekbones, narrow frowning eyes and lips that seemed to be perpetually set in a grim curve of disapproval. Although he was more than three years old he still used a high chair and he could not feed himself; but his parents did not see him as backward. Indeed, by Chinese standards he was advanced for his age.

Qiu smiled at his son, holding his peculiar facial grimace a second or two longer than usual, and picked up a morsel of pork with his chopsticks. "Can?"

"Can."

Slowly, like a courtier kowtowing to the emperor, Tingchen bent his body forward until it was almost parallel with the table, thus giving his anxious father a chance to inspect his short, spiky hair for lice, and swallowed the meat before sitting upright again, the frown on his face, if anything, deeper than before.

"*Hao bu hao chi?*" Taste good?

"*Hen hao.*"

Qiu was delighted. Baby Tingchen's vocabulary expanded daily. "Good boy," he clucked. "More can?"

"No more."

Qiu reached for his son's bowl and scraped it clean, holding it to his own mouth and scooping the gray rice gruel into it with rapid sweeps of his chopsticks. When he had finished he burped, nodded politely to his mother and stood up. "Anything to do?"

"Can you see to Tingchen's business, please?" said Qingqing.

Qiu lifted his son out of the high chair, draped him across his shoulder and with his free hand felt around inside the slit cut in the back of the baby's trousers. Nothing. Before very long they could risk buying grown-up pants for him. "Come, baby," he said cheerfully. "Toilet!"

He bounced Tingchen out of the room, humming a tune. The little boy belched softly in conscious imitation of his father, waving a hand to his mother and grandmother who continued to sit glum-faced at the round table.

"He is a very enthusiastic and earnest father," said Qingqing. "I am most fortunate. Thank you, Mama."

But this fine October morning even flattery failed to ease "Old Buddha" 's joints; she tut-tutted noisily and levered herself out of the chair with her cane.

"Will you be upstairs, Mama? If you're not too tired later on, perhaps you might help me with the marketing? I welcome your ideas . . . but only if you want, and if you feel well."

Old Buddha made no reply. Qingqing addressed her last words to empty space.

Qiu put his head around the door. "Baby Tingchen's with *Ayi*, they're playing in the garden. I'm afraid I'll be late tonight. Meeting."

"Will you want an evening meal?"

"Maybe."

Qingqing would have liked to press him for a more definite answer but knew it was hopeless. She sensed that her husband was still unsure of himself in his new job and the last thing he wanted was to be nagged by her. "Fine, fine."

Qiu nodded and walked out of the house. Even though they

had moved in a month ago, it was still a big moment for him when he passed through the front doorway and strode down the path toward the car. As he reached it he could not resist turning back for a look at his domain. It was a two-story brick-built house with a gray tiled roof, constructed along with nineteen other identical dwellings in the early part of the decade. The metal windowframes were painted a pleasing blue to match the guttering underneath the roof where the architect had given its edges a slight upward turn, and there were two chimneys, one for the central heating flue and one for the open stove. The house was big as well as handsome. Whenever Qiu looked at it he felt his heart swell.

But his face clouded. Houses had to be paid for. There was a job to be done. Qiu sighed. Why, oh why, had they picked him?

He stepped into the back of the green Mercedes and said, "Computer block. Overseas Territories Wing."

The journey took less than five minutes. A white-coated girl met Qiu at reception and accompanied him down a passage covered with shiny linoleum until at last they reached a hermetically sealed sliding glass door. The girl tapped on it with a five-fen coin to attract the attention of a man standing with his back to them; when he turned around, Qiu recognized Sun Shanwang.

Sun touched a button and the door slid back with a hiss. Qiu stepped across the threshold.

"We'll go to that office," said Sun. "In there . . . we can borrow it for as long as we want."

They walked across to a glass-walled office with a large window overlooking the dusty central garden. Sun offered Qiu a chair. As Red Dragon sat down he cast a discreet glance toward his superior, trying to assess his mood. But you never could tell with Sun Shanwang. His spare, almost skeletal body moved stiffly, the result of too many freezing nights spent on damp floors during the Cultural Revolution, and his wizened face had long ago learned the wisdom of keeping secret that which should not be known. He had a habit of pursing his lips into a tight circle, suggestive of disapproval.

"Smoke?"

Qiu hesitated. He knew he was at the start of a long, perhaps a lifetime's, relationship with this man, and as always he thought in terms of an account. Everything had to balance, or be made capable of balancing, at any time. So if he accepted this cigarette he placed himself under an obligation to Sun that had nothing to do with work: he incurred a social debt that must one day be discharged. Sun was offering American cigarettes, Marlboros. He, Qiu, had only inferior Double Happiness on him. If Sun chose to call the debt in the course of this meeting, Qiu would be unable to meet his obligation. Sun would not complain of that, since the effect was to increase the obligation, the equivalent of charging interest. But Qiu would be placed at a disadvantage. To use a Western phrase much disliked by all Chinese, he would lose face. Since Sun was a superior, it was essential for him to cultivate a good working relationship with him. Yet Sun did not like Qiu, Qiu did not like Sun, Qiu needed Sun but only fractionally more than Sun needed him . . . The permutations, the complications, were endless.

Qiu shrugged. He wanted a smoke. "Thank you."

Sun's lips did not purse, which Qiu took for a good sign. The older man lit up and sat back in his swivel chair, rocking gently to and fro. Qiu thought that with his graying hair and rectangular spectacles he looked suspiciously Japanese. At last Sun smiled.

"Are you liking your new quarters, Red Dragon?"

"Thank you, yes."

"Your wife is content?"

"Very content, thank you."

"I'm pleased. You're very young, Qiu Qianwei. Thirty-six is young to be a colonel in the People's Liberation Army, true-not-true?"

"True."

"Young to be Red Dragon. Do you agree?"

"I agree, Elder Brother."

Sun took a drag on his cigarette and breathed out slowly, savoring the smoke a second time as it drifted past his nostrils. "China is changing, is that not so?"

"Yes."

"Men like yourself . . . educated, with exposure to Western business methods and a knowledge of capitalism in practice . . . such men are rare." A faint smile wrinkled his lips. "You went abroad at the right time, Comrade Qiu."

"Yes."

"Your father was prescient. He knew what was coming, I think."

Qiu looked down at the desk, embarrassed. People said that Sun had lost a child in a street riot. "I was lucky enough to win a scholarship," he said quickly, and instantly regretted his forwardness.

"Lucky . . ." Sun seemed to think the word inappropriate.

"Can you help me over one thing, please? Can you tell me why young people lack all imagination? During the Cultural Revolution, why was I always cleaning toilets, eh? I know how to clean a toilet. I did it for three years. I can think of a hundred ways of degrading me, none of them involve cleaning toilets. Please explain, Little Brother. They were your generation. I would welcome your views on this."

Qiu tried not to think of the times to which Sun was obliquely referring. "Attack the headquarters!"—those were Mao *Zhuxi's* words; but he, Qiu, had left, en route for college, Harvard Business School and an altogether different society. "I'm sorry, Elder Brother, but I cannot."

Sun sighed. "Please let me have your views on this, one day."

"I will, I will."

"Now I have those figures for you." The older man reached into a briefcase beside his desk and tossed Qiu a printout. "That is what you requested, I think."

Qiu seized it avidly and began to study the numbers, every so often sliding his spectacles upward with a jerk of his middle finger. "Excellent," he breathed at last. "Perfect. The model . . . perfect."

"This is acceptable for your purposes?"

"Oh yes."

"You realize how confidential such things are?"

"I understand fully, Elder Brother."

Sun made no attempt to keep the incredulity off his face. "You really do believe that this is how the bank will behave in practice?"

"Oh yes. Take a capital figure and a stated rate of interest pegged to US prime rates, develop the assignment against a projection of world trade and money supply in the known light of Soviet Communal Bank's cash flow over the past six years and likely budget in the next eighteen months, annualize the return—"

"Enough!"

Sun Shanwang's fist hit the desktop, making Qiu jump. "I am sorry, Elder Brother," he said quickly; and for a moment there was silence while Sun breathed heavily. When at last the older man had regained his self-control, he said, "Please be good enough to explain."

"I am sorry," Qiu repeated. But how was he to explain such things to one who had no experience of them? "There is a model," he began hesitantly. "It is possible to predict how a bank will behave in the future by examining what it has done in the past. If you want to assess the likelihood of its granting a particular loan, first take the capital sum, apply to it what you know about interest rates and see how attractive it looks in the light of the bank's balance sheet and management accounts. You put yourself in the position of the bank's own directors, with all the information known to them."

Sun regarded his subordinate curiously. Qiu was not experienced in the ways of the intelligence world and Sun had little respect for his practical abilities, regarding him as too academic, too theoretical. But when Qiu was in his element, dealing with statistics, economics, figures—all the things, in short, which he had left China to learn—he became transformed. His face was excited, light gleamed in his eyes.

Sun repressed his doubts and asked: "Ducannon Young the same? Even though it is not a bank?"

"Yes. Not all of the Ducannon Young companies are obliged to disclose their full-form annual accounts in Hong Kong, but because the group is traded in London under stock exchange rule five thirty-five we can easily gain access to the relevant figures. Our contacts within the company can supply any missing factors. From this data it is perfectly possible to project a model of Ducannon Young's loan repayment performance capability and supply side for the coming year. And . . . it works."

"It works, you say, in theory and in practice. But what of the commercial morality?" Sun frowned. "Do you really believe that a Hong Kong businessman with a reputation at stake will agree to take part in such a scheme? Think of it—he will be lending his name to a plan to borrow an immense amount of money from a Russian bank to build a desalination plant, and then bring about a deliberate default with the specific aim of ruining the lender and causing it to close its doors."

Qiu had to fight to keep the condescension out of his voice. "Please understand, Elder Brother, that in Hong Kong the traders have ideas of business ethics that differ from ours. Things which would cause a scandal in Beijing or Shanghai are perpetrated there daily, by people fighting just to stand still, to stay where they are. In Hong Kong, if a man borrows money and finds an excuse not to repay it, he is regarded as a hero. No, morality will not enter into this thing."

"Now that you have met the man, is that still your view?"

"I was informed that, out of all the bad elements, he would be most likely to serve. Now that I have talked with him, I agree."

"And . . . you are certain? About the financial model?"

"On these figures, yes."

Sun nodded slowly. "You are in command, Red Dragon. This is your assignment, not mine. But I am perplexed by one aspect."

"Please tell me, Elder Brother, and I will help you if I can."

"Why should Soviet Communal Bank lend so much money unless it has the security of a mortgage over the site of the desalination plant?"

"Ah. It is a question of what is possible, Elder Brother. Some years ago, the Moscow Narodny Bank nearly gained control of some Hong Kong land in just that way."

"How, 'gain control'? A mortgage is a security, isn't it? The man who lends the money has the right to sell the property which secures the debt; he does not become its owner."

"This is true. But if the debtor does not pay, the lender has the right to sell the property."

"To himself?"

"No, no—that is not permitted. But he can always sell it to a friend."

"Ah, is that how it works?"

"Yes. In Hong Kong, mortgages of land to the Soviets are therefore forbidden. They must content themselves with lesser security, or forgo the transaction altogether."

"So maybe they will choose to forgo?"

"I do not think so. That is the whole point of this financial model. The figures are bold, but they do represent a way for SCB to worm its way into the Hong Kong capital market. And no doubt the bank will also be looking for a chance to bring about a default, thereby opening up the possibility of a sale of the security. So yes, the calculations will stand up, Elder Brother." Qiu did not have to pretend. Once he had the figures before him he knew how to interpret them. It worked. *It worked!*

"Let us hope so." Sun looked at his watch. "Young arrives at Beijing Metropolitan Airport on the fifteen forty-five Cathay Pacific flight. Relying on your emphatic assurances, I will authorize procedures for the next phase. You may meet the flight as planned."

"Hah, thank you, Elder Brother."

"This has been a productive and helpful meeting for me. Thank you for your assistance."

The two men rose and shook hands, their tight smiles betraying nothing of what they felt. Qiu left the computer complex, blinking against the fierce light, and waved his hand. Within seconds the green Mercedes had come to a halt beside him, sending clouds of dust spiraling up into the dry autumn air.

The driver opened the door for him and he climbed in with a sigh. Figures. He was at home with figures: they made good servants. But soon he had to emerge into the real world of difficult and irrational people—who made bad masters.

"*Chongwenmen*," he snapped. "Today, not after next Spring Festival."

The two men dined quietly in one of the side rooms kept specially for foreigners at the sprawling, seven-story-high Beijing Roast Duck Restaurant in the southwest area of the city. It was a hot night, so they sat by an open window with a joss stick on the table between them to discourage the midges.

Simon perversely derived almost as much pleasure from his surroundings as from the food. The restaurant was crowded, the service on the rough-and-ready side. An attempt had been made to spruce up the dining rooms since his last visit: some red lanterns were strewn from the ceiling and there were now tablecloths, but the soy sauce still came in a plastic bottle and the chopsticks were made of Bakelite. Qiu had a row with one of the managers concerning a cracked bowl, which the waiter had refused to replace. In China, change came gently and over a period. Simon complimented his host on the food, as convention required.

"But you have eaten hardly anything! And I can well understand why—the cooking here is shameful."

"If I may say so, it is a delight. And I have eaten until my stomach groans with the effort of retaining so much heavenly food."

"Sure? Please let me order more . . ."

"Really, I couldn't."

"Another Tsingtao?"

Simon drained his glass. "No more beer for me, thanks. But don't let me stop you."

Qiu pulled out his cigarettes and offered the pack to Simon.

"No thank you. I do not smoke."

Qiu, who knew that, affected surprise. "I thought all wealthy capitalists enjoyed big cigars!"

"I have better things on which to spend my modest income. Healthier things." Simon had brought a round paper fan with him.

Now he picked it up by the stem and began to wave it gently to and fro. "Cooler things."

"Cold dew will soon be here. October eighth."

"Ah yes. Thank goodness. And then, let me see . . . 'hoar frost descends,' is that right?"

"I think you know China very well, Mr. Young."

"My knowledge of this beautiful country is in fact quite limited. Some of your fellow countrymen have been kind enough to give me a small education, that's all. I learned the lunar calendar when I was a boy."

"Forgive me for prying, but is it right that you were educated partly in Hong Kong?"

"I studied at the university. There was only one then, of course."

Neither man mentioned Young's first-class economics degree: it would have been tactless.

"The new one is very impressive, I am told."

"I believe so. Mr. Qiu . . . may I please ask you something?"

"Of course."

"What is the schedule for tomorrow? I would like to make plans."

Qiu stubbed out his cigarette. "I see no reason why you should not be on the first plane back to Hong Kong tomorrow."

"Ah, but the first plane is at seven forty-five."

"Yes, I know. If you will now come with me, we can conduct all our business tonight."

"Tonight?"

"Yes."

Qiu called for the bill. When it came he held it up to the light and peered through his thick spectacles at every item, raising several irritable questions with the waiter before reluctantly counting out the money in scruffy notes held together with bits of tape. "Come," he said to Simon, the business side over. "I will fetch the car. This need not take long."

But when they descended to street level Qiu promptly disappeared and Simon looked around in vain for his Capital Car Company Shanghai sedan. Like most city streets in Beijing, this one was underlit. Crowds jostled him, the innumerable pedestrians either not recognizing that he was a foreigner or—more probably, bearing in mind his height—not caring. Simon strained his eyes to right and left, sometimes dodging back onto the sidewalk to avoid a group of bicyclists without lights. There was no car. He began to feel uneasy. Most of the nearby shops were darkened but, diagonally across the road from him, flashing red neon strips molded into the shape of a dragon suggested a nightclub. Nightclubs were a relatively new phenomenon in the capital and so far the authorities were adopting an ominous wait-and-see policy toward them. Simon had heard unsavory rumors about such places. Large numbers of men and a handful of women were lounging around the doorway of this one, and with every second that passed more of them noticed the tall Englishman. Just as two or three of the loiterers started to cross the street, Simon felt a tap on his arm and, on looking down, was relieved to see Qiu Qianwei.

"Sorry, sorry. This way please, Mr. Young."

To Simon's astonishment, Qiu led him to a smart green Mercedes and held open the nearside rear door. When the Englishman hesitated for a second Qiu flapped his hand and showed signs of impatience. As soon as Simon got in next to Qiu someone slammed the door. Then the chauffeur came around to the driver's seat; and Simon saw that the man was wearing the olive green uniform and red lapels of the People's Liberation Army.

"Just what is going on, Mr. Qiu?"

"Please be patient. This won't take long."

"I had a hired car—"

"Already taken care of; please don't worry about it. We can transact all our business very quickly."

"We're visiting Qin Cheng Prison Number One for an identification parade—at this hour? With a PLA driver?"

But Qiu did not reply. Simon glanced out of the window. They were going roughly northeast, traveling very fast. As they crossed Xuanwomen Street he thought he caught a glimpse of a traffic policeman holding up the flow to let the Mercedes pass through on red and his heart began to pound unpleasantly. This trip was turning sour. Peter Reade had virtually insisted that he come, but nothing in the brief had prepared him for being hijacked.

He leaned forward to address the chauffeur. "Please take me straight to my hotel," he said firmly; but the driver ignored him and Qiu remained silent. Simon reluctantly sat back, aware that he could do nothing more.

At Qian Men the driver swung right, his tires squealing, giving Simon only a swift glimpse of Tiananmen's curved roofs picked out in rows of brilliant lightbulbs, and the vast square thinly illuminated by garish, blue-white globes. He realized that they were heading for the dreary two-mile-long stretch of road along either side of which ran Beijing's least successful housing project—ten-story glass-and-concrete apartment blocks that looked beautiful from the outside but lacked adequate water pressure, gas mains, elevators or effective central heating. Simon knew from the Hong Kong grapevine that a German study had recommended tearing them down and starting again: a solution unacceptable to any Chinese government.

The car slowed, turned in off the street, and came to a stop in front of one of these apartment blocks. The driver switched off the engine.

"Please come with me," said Qiu. "There is nothing to be worried about—this is my home. Please!"

Simon unwillingly followed him inside, feeling he had no choice. Qiu lived on the first floor in modest, albeit extremely cramped, comfort. The place was furnished in quasiclassical style, with good quality watercolor reproductions on the walls and brightly woven rugs on the bare concrete floor.

Simon saw an old man sitting by the window, with his eyes closed and one arm resting on a nearby table.

"Please meet my uncle," said Qiu. "He is blind and deaf; in any case, he speaks no English. Please do not feel inhibited by him. He is the only surviving representative of the family's older generation. My parents are both dead."

"I am sorry to hear that."

"Some years ago now. Fortunately, my uncle needs very little, and the neighbors are caring people."

"You must be relieved."

"Would you like some tea? I shall in any case make some for myself."

"Yes, then. Thank you."

"Sit down, Mr. Young."

Simon did so. He was fascinated. As Qiu passed through into the kitchen he laid a hand gently on his uncle's shoulder and the old man responded by reaching up quickly to squeeze it, but that was all. Qiu did not even look down. The uncle continued in exactly the same position, his visionless eyes fixed on a point over Simon's left shoulder. He was all skin and bone, wearing only a gray vest over baggy pants. Simon wondered uneasily whether he could sense his presence.

As if reading his mind, Qiu put his head around the kitchen

partition and said: "He does not know you are here yet. I will introduce you." Simon wondered how; but then Qiu came back with the tea things, which he placed on the old man's table, and beckoned the Englishman to approach. He took hold of Simon's forearm and wrapped his uncle's frail hands around it. At once the old man raised his head, as if listening. Qiu spoke a few words in a dialect unknown to Simon and after a pause the uncle nodded vigorously.

"He can't really hear me but he knows I'm talking, and that reassures him. He feels my hand and yours at the same time, that tells him you're a guest. Please sit down."

Qiu poured tea from the gaily enameled pot into three bowls and replaced their lids. "I am sorry to ask you to spend time in such poor surroundings, Mr. Young."

"On the contrary: I find your apartment both comfortable and tasteful."

Qiu shrugged. "In Beijing, Mr. Young, privacy is hard to come by. By day, it is impossible for me to see you without other foreigners in Beijing getting to hear of it. By night it is difficult, but by bringing you here there is at least a chance of keeping our business private."

"I understand that. But what is private about an armed attack on an airport bank?"

"You can forget about the attack. Have some more tea?"

Simon slowly extended his arm and allowed Qiu to fill his cup to the brim.

"We are no longer interested in it."

"Good lord! But someone was killed . . . the teller."

Qiu shuddered inwardly, remembering how the attack had been mounted by men of the Mah-jongg Executive Unit, by his own colleagues. At first he'd refused to believe that story, until Sun Shanwang himself repeated it, with a reminder of how glorious it was to die for the Middle Kingdom, and then Qiu had no choice but to believe. "Yes, it was terrible, terrible. But at least it does have one advantage."

"*Advantage?*"

"Yes. We very badly wished to talk to you in Beijing at a time when you showed no desire to come here. The attack at least gives us an excuse to bring you to China."

"Excuse? I'm sorry, but I'm not following all this. You could perfectly well have talked to me when I was here last month."

"Unfortunately, certain decisions had not at that time been

taken. It was not convenient. But, as I say, the attack on the airport bank has provided us with an excellent pretext for recalling you to the mainland. Nobody can question it: as far as the outside world is concerned, there was an attack, you identified the attackers, it is obvious that at some time—perhaps more than once—you would have to return to China at the request of the police." Seeing that Simon was about to protest, he raised his hand. "And may I respectfully suggest that when you return you inquire of Mr. Reade on this business. He will supply the . . . missing links. He will also be able to tell you something about us."

It occurred to Simon that the room was soundproof. No noise arose from the street below. The old uncle felt along the table for his cup, adroitly removed the lid, and took a sip. He replaced the lid without a sound. The room was completely silent.

"Who is 'us' in this context?" Simon asked.

"Central Intelligence, Seventh Department. The Mah-jongg Brigade."

"The what?"

"Mah-jongg Brigade." Qiu grimaced. "Long ago, intelligence gathering in China was thought to resemble a game of Mah-jongg. There were only a very few intelligence officers in imperial times and they adopted the names assigned to Mah-jongg tiles. Old habits unfortunately die hard."

Simon stared at him. "You mean, it still goes on?"

"Yes."

"So which tile are you?"

"It really doesn't matter."

Simon frowned and rubbed his forehead. "You are telling me . . . that Reade knows all about this."

"On the contrary, he knows as little as we thought we could get away with. It is *you*, Mr. Young, who are going to be told all about everything. Please excuse me if I smoke."

He lit up, rolling a cloud of smoke toward Simon. "I don't believe this will take long. What does the name Eddie Wong mean to you?"

Simon unfolded his long legs and rubbed the tops of his thighs to help the circulation. "He was a Hong Kong businessman," he said, choosing his words carefully. "He borrowed from Moscow Narodny in Singapore, to finance a residential-cum-leisure complex on Lantau Island."

"The deal went wrong."

"Shall we say that the bank thought it necessary to call in the debt, and that thereafter there were complications."

Qiu smiled. "I admire your sense of tact. It is almost Chinese in its refinement. The truth is that Wong defaulted, couldn't pay and the bank foreclosed on the shares in the Panamanian and Liechtenstein companies which held the Crown leases underlying the development. I do not have to spell out to you, of all people, the possible consequences."

"No. Moscow came within an ace of obtaining a direct financial stake in a Crown colony, one due to be handed back to Beijing a few years later. If the bank had managed to foreclose and get ownership of the actual soil, it would have been catastrophic for you."

"Yes. If it had not been for some superb investigative reporting by *Target* magazine it might actually have worked. Now the rules have been changed, and no Soviet bank will ever again be allowed to take security over Hong Kong land."

"True. But even in the Wong case, there was a happy ending. Beijing and London put together a lifeboat, bought the bank out. It was Cha Chi Ming . . . isn't he your senior money man in Hong Kong?"

Qiu nodded. "He bought the shares back, yes. But at a price. Moscow Narodny ended up accepting thirty million dollars Hong Kong in exchange for a debt that was never worth more than twenty-seven million. Mr. Wong's reputation was slightly dented; but, after all, this happened in a place where such things are, one might say, the warp and woof of business. The account was closed, Wong lived to fight another day. More important, so did the bank."

"Yes. What is this to do with me, Mr. Qiu? I didn't deal with Mr. Wong, and I happen to know that the Corporation never financed him."

"No indeed: the Pacific & Cantonese Banking Corporation has always been admired here for its acumen; never more so than during your father's chairmanship. Whereas of course Ducannon Young, its trading offshoot, has better things to do with its money than deal with the Wongs of this world."

"We prefer not to think of ourselves as an offshoot, Mr. Qiu. Dunny's has always been an autonomous entity."

"Naturally." Qiu smiled again; Simon thought he had never seen such an insincere expression on a human face. "I will tell you what this has to do with you, Mr. Young. Ever since the Wong fiasco, we have been constructing a plan here in Beijing: a plan to ensure that when our rightful property is finally restored to us, it comes back intact. Moscow Narodny has now been supplanted by the Soviet Communal Bank, and Soviet Communal is nothing but a nest of spies. Its financial operations are insignificant when laid alongside its remarkable and extensive capacity for the gathering and analysis of intelligence. We mean to erect a wall around Hong Kong which the Russians will never be able to breach. We intend, in short, to eradicate the Soviet Communal Bank's Far Eastern operation."

"You intend to do *what*?"

"To eradicate—"

"But that's ridiculous!" Simon allowed his contempt to show. "The Russians will never let you get away with that."

"The Governor of Hong Kong is greatly in favor, Mr. Young. So are the head of Special Branch, the financial secretary and DI6. For you see, once you get rid of the bank, you get rid of the KGB as well. The Russians have no other means of entry to Hong Kong. Or didn't you realize that?"

"No. I most certainly didn't."

"I would go so far as to say that the destruction of SCB is the single most important intelligence project intended to be accomplished over the next five years. I am aware of nothing else that has been accorded such high priority."

Simon said nothing for a while. Qiu was calmly proposing the destruction of one of Asia's most recently successful financial institutions, in the apparent expectation that the managing director of a major Hong Kong trading house would acquiesce. "Go on," he said quietly.

"You will know the old maxim: 'Owe your bank a thousand, and it has you at its mercy; owe it a million, and you have it at yours.' We propose to put the maxim into practice."

"How?"

"By persuading the Soviet Communal Bank's Singapore branch to lend one hundred million pounds sterling to finance the construction of a desalination plant at Tsim Bei Tsui, on the north-western coast of the New Territories."

"What? I can't believe you're serious."

"Why not?"

"Because I think you're pulling my leg. Everyone in the Far East knows about my plans for building a desalination plant in Hong Kong. It was a dream that took years out of my life. Then just as I was on the point of finding the money, Hong Kong solved its water shortage problem by negotiating a deal with the People's Republic to take water from the East River. We don't need a desalination plant anymore."

"You do if China decides to turn off the taps."

"Well yes, but you won't."

"Won't we?"

"What are you saying, Mr. Qiu?"

"You're not very interested in politics, I think?"

"Not very, no."

"Let me educate you a little, then. Suppose the PRC were to attempt to renegotiate the deal recently struck with the British government—say five years from now."

"We have to assume they won't."

"Suppose they did. Suppose circumstances changed. My government would propose a renegotiation. Westminster could decline to vary the terms already agreed. What pressure might Beijing then seek to apply?"

"Ah . . . that's what you meant when you talked of turning off the taps."

"Yes. Depriving Hong Kong of its newly acquired source of water would be a good way of bringing Westminster to heel."

"And that's why you think the Governor would be in favor of a desalination plant, because—"

"Because it would preempt one possible source of pressure in the run-up to changeover, yes."

"But the PRC would never agree to the project. And without Chinese mainland say-so, Hong Kong wouldn't dare proceed with anything that large."

"Oh, the PRC would be in full agreement, Mr. Young."

"I don't see why. If the whole point of the project is to give Westminster leverage against Beijing—"

"The whole point of the project is to ruin the Russian bank, Mr. Young, don't forget that. And there is a commercial angle, too. The Shenzhen Special Economic Zone is proving a drain on this country's resources, including its water. Beijing would not be averse to seeing Hong Kong independently supplied by means of a desalination plant."

Somewhere behind Simon's back, the old man groped for his cup once more and drank. This time there was the merest clink as he replaced the lid. Nothing else disturbed the silence.

"Yes, it used to be a pet project of yours, Mr. Young. You

had, *have* a great desire to do something for the benefit of Hong Kong before you leave it, and a deep respect, love even, for the Chinese people. What better monument to Ducannon Young could there be? But now let us examine the practical difficulties."

Simon grunted. "You admit there are difficulties, then?"

"Yes. The Corporation's coffers are closed, your father will not lend; and while the Corporation will not lend, all usual sources of finance are denied to you, because what fool will lend to a son whose father does not trust him? Forgive my blunt speech, but that is the major difficulty which you face in realizing your ambition to see this project through."

"You are blunt indeed." Simon made no attempt to disguise the bitterness in his voice. "My family quarrels are no concern of yours. Forgive *my* blunt speech."

"Of course. The only mitigation is that these things are fairly common knowledge, would you not agree?"

"I still don't understand why you're telling me this. Even if I were prepared to have dealings with Soviet Communal Bank, and I'm not saying I would be, they'd never lend that kind of money except in syndicate."

"They'd lend alone against the security of the Corporation's Founders Shares, Mr. Young."

Simon raised his head, very slowly, feeling himself to be in the presence of either a madman or a rogue. "No."

"I think so. You own twenty out of fifty issued Founders Shares in the Pacific & Cantonese Banking Corporation—a major bank whose status in the Far East is unique. Those shares were created by your great-great-grandfather and have passed to you by direct inheritance. Apart from a value of something over three million pounds sterling each, under the articles of association those shares entitle the owner to a seat on the board for himself or his nominee. They also carry decisive voting rights on any proposal to dissolve the Corporation, so that the registered owner of a majority of such shares could force through a resolution to put the bank into liquidation. Oh yes, Mr. Young, the Soviet bank will lend. You have what I believe the bankers call . . . *collateral.*"

Simon shrugged. "Even if what you say is true, I still don't believe that any bank would lend such a sum except in syndicate."

"Not so. If Soviet Communal thought it saw a chance of getting its hands on those shares through a foreclosure, it would lend and lend all on its own, shouldering the entire risk. No one else would be allowed to share the prize. And of course, a foreclosure is exactly what the Soviets would intend, right from the start, with the additional advantage that since the Founders Shares are bearer shares, they could be made to vanish into safe hands overnight."

Simon started to raise his hands to his forehead, then seemed to think better of it and stopped short. His face wore the look of a man who is trying to explain something to a nice but incredibly dim child. It was a good impression, but Qiu saw the interest glittering in the Englishman's eyes and was not deceived.

"Mr. Qiu. *Mister* Qiu. Let us suppose for one moment that there is some reason behind what you say. Let us suppose the Russians would lend, that the money was there, that the shares could be made available. What in the name of goodness leads you to think that I'd be mad enough to get involved in such a . . . a *lunatic* scheme? That I would risk my Founders Shares in a venture of that kind? What's in it for me?"

He saw the answer a split second before Qiu gave it and his hands involuntarily clenched.

"Because the mortgage of the shares which you signed would be valueless, Mr. Young. We would see to that. You need have no fear."

"Valueless." Of course. *Of course!*

"Quite. When the bank came to realize its so-called security, it would find that it had no rights at all, none whatsoever. It would be one hundred million pounds short and it could not hope to survive such a loss."

"So I'd be left with a spanking new desalination plant, a contract to supply water to Hong Kong on commercial terms, but no obligation to repay the money I'd borrowed. And where would that leave my commercial reputation?"

"Sorry?"

"I live and work in Hong Kong. My companies all are based there. I have to do business daily with people who know my affairs inside out. Once it became known that I had lent my name to such a scheme, who would want, who would *dare* to deal with me?"

Qiu blinked. "In Hong Kong? You think it would matter if word got out that you had borrowed money and then found a way out of repaying it? You would be seen as a hero!"

Good grief, it's true, thought Simon; but all he said was: "It would matter to *me!* And to others as well. So I ask you again: Where would it leave my commercial reputation?"

"Intact, when the story was told. Besides . . . even if your fellow businessmen cared about all that, which I dispute, after 1997 you'd find you had all the commercial reputation anyone needed. With a European board of directors and Chinese staff. With us."

Simon opened his mouth wide, but for a long time no words came out. At last he said, "You're telling me that . . . that after 1997 you'd be prepared to see Dunny's go on . . . as before?"

"Yes."

"With European management and locally recruited Chinese staff . . . alone of all the *hongs*?"

"Certainly."

"No strings, no restrictions?"

"None."

Simon shook his head from side to side, very slowly, like a man in shock. "That's a bribe, Mr. Qiu. That's the biggest all-time damn bribe I've ever been offered, or ever likely to be."

"Tempted?"

"Yes, by God! Who wouldn't be? You're asking me to take an incredible risk, but the prize . . . oh yes, I'm tempted all right."

"Then that's not a bribe, Mr. Young. It is a deal. Now let me try something else." His voice was smooth as Cathay silk. "I regret having to introduce a new note into the discussions, but time is almost desperately short and I need an answer soon. I want you to discuss this with your wife."

"Why?" Simon was enraged; the word came out like a pistol shot.

"She has a vested interest in this project. To say nothing of the Luks, your valued servants, but we can afford to leave them out of the calculations, I think. Whether the People's Liberation Army pardons their little misdemeanor is not within my control, although I must tell you that killing a guard in order to escape from China would normally be punishable by execution. Your wife is different. You will find that she is in favor of this proposal."

"Why the devil should she be?"

"Because she has a brother and a younger sister in Chaiyang, in Sichuan. I saw them, not long ago. They are, at present, in reasonably good health, although their circumstances leave something to be desired. Whether those circumstances improve or deteriorate depends on you, I should think."

"Threats? You're threatening a Hong Kong businessman? Oh,

come on, Mr. Qiu. Please arrange for me to return to my hotel now."

"Soon."

"*Now.*" Simon stood up. "I have had enough. You are prepared, actually prepared to threaten me indirectly, threaten my wife's brother and sister . . ."

"They are my brother and sister too, Mr. Young. Did Jinny not tell you of our relationship?"

For a moment Simon stood staring down at Qiu; then, without warning, he collapsed back into his chair. And the Chinese, looking at his guest's face, suddenly understood why other races called the English "white."

After Qiu had handed Simon into the care of his army driver he did not return to the apartment at once, but instead stood in the hallway, methodically cleaning his spectacles with a square of tissue. He felt very tired. The interview had left him feeling drained and dispirited. He was not used to this kind of thing. Had it gone well? Was it a disaster?

No, it was not a disaster. Qiu's instincts were becoming quite finely attuned to his new job; he knew that the meeting had gone satisfactorily.

He went back upstairs, walked along the passage and banged on the door of the flat adjacent to the one in which he had entertained Simon. It opened a crack large enough to allow the occupant to inspect him.

"You got it all?"

"All, Colonel. Voice reproduction was perfect. We'll have the film for you first thing tomorrow. We're just packing up the equipment."

"Good."

Qiu walked back to the apartment where he and Simon had talked. "Uncle" was still sitting by the table near the window, his sightless eyes fixed on exactly the same point as before.

"He's gone. We are leaving now."

For a moment the old man did not react. Then he raised his arms above his head, yawned loudly, and stretched.

"Very good, Red Dragon." He scratched himself under the right armpit and yawned again. "It went well."

Qiu exhaled a long, low sigh of relief. "Thank you, Elder Brother."

"*Nali, nali,*" said Sun Shanwang.

4

Ducannon Young ran its worldwide operations from a headquarters building that, in common with those of all the other first-rank trading *hongs*, enjoyed a panoramic view of the harbor. Unlike its rivals, however, the company long ago chose a location standing back a little from the waterfront and facing on to Queensway. Dunny's had never moved since its foundation in the late 1870s, although several structures had successively stood on the same site. The present one, next to the new Supreme Court building, was twenty stories high and largely faced with aquamarine-tinted glass—David Young's choice at a time when he still controlled the company. His nephew, Simon, would have liked to tear it down and start again, but it was not the time for such extravagant gestures. The construction industry functioned against a background of mounting pessimism about the colony's future. Major rebuilding projects would have to await the year 1997 and whatever convulsions of fortune the changeover might involve.

The top floor housed only the boardroom and an apartment for the managing director's personal use; Simon stayed there occasionally when there was a crisis on or if a typhoon was imminent, but he disliked sleeping away from home. Most of his daytime working hours were spent in the boardroom, which doubled as his private office, although more and more frequently the international nature of Dunny's corporate business obliged Simon to travel a good deal. At lunchtime he was due to fly to Singapore, but first he had to chair a meeting. The prospect gave him little pleasure.

He was at work in his favorite position, standing at a high clerk's desk by the plate-glass window whence he could keep an eye on the harbor. Simon rarely failed to draw inspiration from the scene below, and this morning he was in need of it. He had spent several hours sifting through the final draft of a confidential five-year plan for Ducannon Young Electronics Ltd, weeding it of unjustifiable optimism, making lengthy notes in the margin and generally trying to improve upon the subsidiary board's collective handiwork. It was a dreary task and he flicked the document into his out tray with a sigh of relief. He had just begun to study an early-draft architect's drawing of a new Public Utility Board building in Kuching, for which DY Construction Ltd planned to tender a bid, when the intercom buzzed.

"Yes?"

"Your wife is here, Mr. Young."

"Ask her to come in."

A moment later the door opened and Simon turned away from his desk. Jinny was at the door but behind her, in the gap, he could see his secretary hovering. "Oh Mary . . ."

"Yes, Mr. Young?"

"Phone me through the morning gold fix as soon as you get it, please. Even if the meeting's still in progress."

"Certainly, sir." Mary Street's exact age was unknown but she must have been in her mid-fifties now; she had joined the company as a teenage girl. Dunny's pursued a deliberate policy of recruiting Chinese staff but, following an unbroken tradition that dated back to the last century, the directors had English secretaries. Although these women were called "secretaries," in truth, however, they customarily performed personal assistant and other functions that ranged from answering the phone to acting as surrogate mothers. That was why Mary waited in the background after she had shown Jinny Young into the boardroom; she always knew when something was up. As managing director's number-one secretary, her responsibilities obliged her to contain the damage. No wife was equipped for that job. Especially when, as now, the wife was suspected of causing the damage . . .

"That's all for the moment, Mary. Keep ACP Reade in the outer office until I buzz, but tell George Forster to come straight up. Don't let Reade see him."

Mary nodded and silently closed the door.

"Am I early?" Jinny asked. "Don't let me disturb you."

He shook his head. "It's all right. Did you get Diana's birthday present?"

Jinny was nettled by his failure to acknowledge her efforts to look good for him on this visit to the office. She was wearing a black dress with a slightly flared skirt and white collarette, adorned by a simple silver brooch. The outfit made her look demure, responsible—the managing director's wife, in fact. But the managing director did not notice.

"Yes, I got the present. What do you think?" Jinny began to rummage inside a gold and black plastic carrier, eventually pulling out a dress.

"Very nice. Yes, I like that. D'you think the school will let her wear it, though?"

Jinny shrugged. "It will be good for her to have it anyway. I've left things a bit late. Does it matter if I courier it?"

"You can use tonight's bag—tell Mary on the way out. Card?"

During this brittle exchange Jinny delved into the carrier and pulled out an envelope. The two of them went through the annual ceremony of signing their daughter's birthday card.

"There's a letter for Mat, too. Can you sign that? Then both our children are taken care of for a while."

"Thanks. I've been meaning to write to him, but—"

"I know. Please don't worry. It is a mother's duty to write to her son. But I like you to sign it as well, because then he feels you're involved."

"Of course. Here, let me do it now."

Jinny handed him the letter. "I bought some paper," she said. "I can wrap Diana's present while we're waiting." She went to sit at one end of the long boardroom table, spreading out the wrapping paper in front of her with the kind of care normally reserved for pure silk. Simon watched her reflection in the plate-glass window, wondering why so many Chinese chose to expend their emotional energy on beautiful but inanimate things.

Jinny, for her part, suppressed the tight feeling in the pit of her stomach and made yet another attempt to bring the domestic ship back on course. "You're very silent this morning," she murmured, without raising her head. And every other morning, she was thinking.

"Nothing to say." Simon's words produced a thin film of moisture on the window, a fine mist that endured no longer than the words themselves.

"So how long does this continue?" Jinny tried hard to keep her tone light, but there was no mistaking the tension underneath.

"Does what continue?"

Jinny folded, taped, folded again, not wanting to rush her answer. "Silence," she said at last.

"We've discussed things. I understand your point of view."

The answer annoyed her. "Why do you English always pretend to understand? You're not buying groundnuts off me, Simon. You make it sound as though—"

"You have a brother who turns out to be a cadre in Central Intelligence and a mysterious uncle who lives in Beijing. You didn't know about the uncle. It must have been a shock. What more is there to say?"

After twenty years of living with Simon she realized that the reference to her uncle was supposed to be sarcastic; but it had taken her a long time to learn about sarcasm. "Do you have to talk to the window like that?" she asked.

He turned away, the irritation showing on his face. "Sorry. I'm angry—with myself, not with you."

"And why is that?"

"Because I should be reacting differently. I should have a greater awareness of the difficulties facing you. Of course, you could not tell me the truth. You had every reason not to tell me." He smiled at her, a real smile with genuine warmth in it. "I'm not doing this very well, am I?" Then his face clouded again. "It's just that—"

"What you resent is my failure to tell you before you last went to China, isn't that it?"

He shrugged. "It might have helped."

"You think it's so easy."

"I *don't.*"

The submissive role traditionally assigned to a Chinese wife no longer suited Jinny. "But you *do!*" she said bitterly. "He warned me. You think I didn't *want* to tell you? Qiu warned me not to."

"I see. Is Qiu his real name, by the way?"

"No." Jinny averted her eyes. "Of course not. Do you think I've been lying to you about my birthname? He is Wang, like me."

"Oh, Jinny . . ."

"How do you think I've felt, all these years? 'Living a lie,' isn't that the phrase you use? They told me at the beginning, 'If we let you go, if we let you marry this man, you must say nothing about your past, *nothing.*' And I obeyed. Was I stupid?"

"No, I don't mean to suggest—"

"Of course I obeyed! I have a brother, I have a sister, they stayed behind. Was I supposed to sacrifice them?"

They stared at each other, further apart than ever. "Why don't you understand?" Jinny wailed bitterly. "All your life you've lived here, you should know by now that the Far East isn't England. England, with its fundamental freedoms, and rights, and laws the same for everyone."

"Yes. I do understand that."

"Don't you know how much I love you?" she murmured—and instantly regretted it.

"Don't you know *me?*" he replied, feeling equally helpless.

Before either of them could respond to the pleading in the other, they heard a soft knock at the double doors to the corridor. Simon, suddenly glad of the interruption, called, "Come in."

The doors opened to admit George Forster, Ducannon Young's treasurer and finance director: a short, stocky man with a bald strip dividing the remnants of his bushy hair into two neat halves.

"Hello, George. Come in and sit down."

"Thanks. Jinny . . ."

"George." She had finished wrapping up the parcel. Her need to talk was palpable and Forster looked inquiringly at Simon, seeking a cue. Before he could give it the intercom buzzed again.

"Yes . . . ah, thank you. Let's have it." Simon looked up. "Morning gold." Forster came to stand behind him, where he could look over the managing director's shoulder as he wrote. Simon jotted down the price at which gold had been fixed and raised his eyebrows, but Forster merely shook his head.

"Nothing," he said, as Simon recapped his fountain pen. "It's up, but Tokyo twitches, that's all. We're not at the start of another run. Forget it."

"I still think we could do better with our three-month money."

Forster shrugged. "I'll get us more into the Eurodollar market, if you want. It's looking reasonably good at the moment."

"That's not going to solve things, though, is it? What did the Corporation give us last night?"

"Three and seven-sixteenths under base."

"The bastard." Simon spoke without rancor, accepting a problem that wouldn't go away.

"We could always move. Say the word."

"No." The two men smiled, but without humor. "Father can keep Dunny's overnight funds. God knows, it's just about all he does get from us these days."

Jinny watched them through half-closed eyes, faintly contemptuous of their boyish seriousness. Simon at work reminded her of Simon playing with their son's train set, or teaching him the rudiments of cricket. Boys' games, that's all. So solemn. So childlike.

Simon picked up a bound report and tossed it onto the table next to Forster. "What are we going to do about this desalination business, George? Reade'll be here in a moment, I have to tell him something."

"That's easy. Tell him we can't afford it. It's an excuse no one can argue with and anyway, it's the truth."

"Although we could borrow."

"Not from the Corporation. As long as your father runs the Corporation and has his Founders Shares—"

"He's not going to lend the money we need to build a desalination plant."

"Or any other capital project of long-term benefit to China."

"So, to cut a long story short, you agree with me that we're stymied unless we're prepared to go in with Qiu and approach Soviet Communal Bank."

"Which you don't want to do."

"Correction—which I can't ever be *seen* to want to do. Don't confuse the issues, George. I'm as keen as hell on this scheme. It's a public-spirited project where for once the figures happen to come out right. What matters at the moment is keeping it under wraps."

"Oh, Simon . . ." Forster hitched one leg onto the table and folded his arms. "Come off it. For one thing, this is Hong Kong, not Zurich." He gestured toward the far end of the room, where a red phone stood on a small table beside Simon's desk. "Your father could call you now on the private scrambler, ask you to his box at Saturday's races and Dunny's would jump five points in heavy afternoon trading. What secrets do any of us have these days?"

"You said, 'for one thing.' What other factors are there? Be devil's advocate. Tell me all the reasons why I can't borrow from the Soviets, because at the moment I'm damned if I can see a good one."

"Well . . . the Chinese involvement, first of all. Then, track record. SCB hasn't got one. It seems to have taken over a lot of the Moscow Narodny operation but we're all still waiting to see what happens. Dunny's shouldn't be seen getting into bed with any newcomers. Especially Soviet newcomers."

Before Simon could reply the intercom buzzed again. "Assistant Commissioner Reade is here to see you, sir."

"Send him in."

Reade entered the office with quick, silent steps—one businessman, pressed for time, calling on another. He was short, no more than five feet eight, and he walked with the slightly artificial, erect gait of a man who is ashamed of his beer gut and wants to hide it. His thin, sandy hair was brushed straight forward onto the brow, where it petered out in untidy wisps. Reade looked rather older than he would have liked. Reade was vain.

As the commissioner approached, his shoes making no sound on the thick carpet, it occurred to Simon that here at least was a man whose secrets remained intact. Reade, in his white shirt, maroon tie and dark gray suit, was indistinguishable from the many thousands of anonymous businessmen with "interests" in Hong Kong who thronged the island's streets and hotels; which was fitting, for as well as being DI6 resident, Reade helped run the Special Branch's commercial unit and as such wielded his own very special kind of influence over those he most resembled.

"Peter . . . good of you to come."

"Good of you to see me, Simon. George . . . Hello, Mrs. Young."

Jinny nodded, a reserved smile on her face. She was afraid of Reade: afraid of the power he wielded, the forces he represented.

"I've asked Jinny to be here for reasons which I don't think you'll find hard to understand," said Simon.

Reade smiled, his thin mustache crinkling, and shook his head.

"Do you mind?" Simon asked.

"I don't *think* so. Not at this stage." The smile that Reade turned upon Jinny was wholly cosmetic. "We have to live with things as they are, isn't that so?"

Jinny lowered her eyes. She remembered the old days, when Hong Kong was different, when Hong Kong was special. She was the wife of one of the most important and influential businessmen in the colony, but still she could not quite rid herself of the irrational fear that Reade might return to his office to make a couple of phone calls, and she would be on tonight's plane bound for nowhere, without appeal or recourse.

Simon indicated that everyone should sit down. He took the chair at the far end of the long boardroom table opposite Jinny, with George Forster on his immediate right and Reade on his left. "Well now, Peter. I've leveled with the government. You know as much as I know. What do you want me to do?"

"More to the point, Simon, what do you want to do? Mind if I smoke?"

"Please. And you already know the answer to your first question. I used to nag the Governor about my desalination plant, on and off, for years. I don't have to remind you of how it shaped up: we had a water problem; we boasted the third-largest container port in the world, the third-largest gold dealing center, one hundred and twenty-nine banks; and there were still times when we couldn't even guarantee that there'd be carafes of water on the boardroom table."

Reade lit up a Turkish cigarette, quickly filling the room with its delicate aroma. "His Excellency doesn't mind being nagged, Simon, especially by people like you. It's part of any governor's job."

"But in those far-off days, accepting my proposals wasn't. Anyway, it didn't matter, because after a while the problem went away. China gave us all the water we needed. Now, suddenly everyone's interested in desalination again and I'm still the only one who's drawn up plans and done the figures. So yes, I want to build the ruddy thing."

Reade laughed and then drew deeply on his cigarette. "Go ahead, then."

Until that moment Jinny had been leaning her arms on the table and staring sideways out of the window, with one leg crossed over the other and a bored look on her face. Now she straightened up and for the first time looked at Reade. George Forster, who had been fidgeting, became perfectly still.

"Could we have that again, Peter?" Simon's voice was controlled but Reade had been in the game for too long to be fooled by a man's voice. He knew the timbre of excitement.

"Certainly. Qiu got the political angle just right. London's uneasy as it is about struggling through the next dozen years without the Chinese attempting to force a renegotiation of the terms. London wants to take out some insurance, and that means, among other things, ensuring a replacement water supply. Forget about the money for the moment. If you can solve the problem of finance, you can have a contract, a tripartite contract on proper commercial terms, to supply Hong Kong with water."

"Tripartite?"

"You, the British government, Beijing."

Simon raised his hands and clapped his temples. "The PRC. Even though on paper it's against their political interests?"

"Yes. They don't think of it like that, of course. They want to bring down the Russian bank. So they're coming in, with some money, but not much. It'll have to come out of the Shenzhen Special Economic Zone's allocation, which as you know is not limitless. Once the plant's up and running, Hong Kong would pay for the water at market rate with a subsidy from Shenzhen which increases on a sliding scale as 1997 comes closer; after that, it's all down to Beijing. Comments?"

Simon said nothing for a while. "George?"

Forster shifted uneasily in his chair. "You said, 'Forget about the money.' But that's the very thing we can't do. Where's this money to come from, Peter? We're talking about a minimum of a hundred million pounds. You know we can't handle that all by ourselves, no one could."

"What about the Corporation?"

Simon snorted. "Come on, Peter. You know what father's like. He'd rather die than put Corporation money into this—especially when it's my idea in the first place!"

"But have you asked him?"

"Many times. The answer's no."

"And as long as father won't lend to son, no one else is going to."

"Right."

Reade stubbed out his cigarette and presented Simon with a

neutral, smiling face. "Then I'd say your options were remarkably limited." His eyes strayed to Jinny. "It's Qiu's funny money idea or nothing."

"That presupposes I trust Qiu."

"Don't you trust him?"

Simon again looked across at Jinny and smiled thinly. "Not much."

"Interesting. We do."

"I see."

"The official British line is that Qiu speaks for his government. And although you say you don't trust him, nevertheless at his suggestion you've already made a written invitation for a loan, haven't you, Simon?—all nicely backed up with facts and figures." Reade paused, wanting his bombshell to have maximum effect.

"You can't be serious!" George Forster had been listening to the conversation with mounting incredulity; Reade's latest contribution was too much for him. "Are you saying the Governor would allow Soviet Communal Bank a toehold here?"

"That would depend on the security offered, wouldn't it?" Reade replied. "I agree that Dunny's wouldn't be allowed to get away with mortgaging the site to the Russians. That's out, totally. I also stress that the government would look to you to preserve confidentiality, whatever terms you managed to negotiate and with whomsoever you negotiated them. We can't afford a crisis of confidence at this stage and any suggestion that the Russians were involved in the project would cause precisely that."

Throughout this speech Reade's eyes were fixed on Jinny's. Now he seemed suddenly to make up his mind. "Listen to me, Simon. There are any number of Anglo-Chinese joint ventures on the drawing board at the moment; you know it, I know it. Some of them are backed for reasons that have nothing whatever to do with economics or welfare. They're vehicles. Don't ask me 'vehicles for what?' because I shan't tell you; it's none of your concern. All that matters is that His Excellency is giving you the official green light. Your job is to get on with it and build the plant. The rest is up to me and"—this time Reade did not just look at Jinny, he openly smiled at her—"people like me. Opposite numbers. Perhaps even allies, of a sort."

He leaned back slowly, replacing his tortoiseshell cigarette case in the breast pocket of his suit like a man who has had his say and is packing up to go. George Forster drummed his fingers on the table with a frown. Simon rose and began to move restlessly about the long room, one hand in pocket, jingling loose change. He was trying to identify what was in it for Reade, to decide just how far he trusted the official British version. Only his wife sat in remote silence, looking at Reade through the opaque eyes of a prophet.

"No," she said aloud, and Simon stopped pacing.

"What?"

"Nothing."

Simon turned back to Reade. "So Qiu had it right, after all," he said softly. "You're gunning for the KGB and using me to do it."

Reade spread his hands. "Perhaps. It's not all codebooks and Mata Hari's, you know. I'm being more frank than I ought to be, Simon. Don't expect me ever to repeat what I've just said, because you'll be disappointed."

"Oh, I get the picture all right. You're happy to push me into the arms of Soviet Communal because it suits your book, but if it comes unstuck—"

"You won't see Her Majesty's Government for dust. Correct." Reade stood up. "We're only thinking aloud at this stage. Confidentiality—please remember that. Any deal you did with an outside source would be subject to the Official Secrets Act. Anyway, let us know if you believe there's any mileage in it." He raised his right hand very deliberately to consult his watch. "And don't miss your flight. Or Mr. Qiu—I gather he's in Hong Kong?"

Simon's eyes contracted for a moment, then he smiled. "Dear Peter—always subtle. I hope you've tipped them off to save us a couple of window seats."

Reade returned the smile. "No. But there may be times in Singapore when you feel a little crowded. Don't worry about it. Prime Minister Lee Kuan Yew's a great friend of ours, we have to let him know the bare bones, and more people care about your welfare than you might think. By the way, do you feel like telling me why you're going to Singapore, Simon?"

Simon hesitated. He quite liked Reade and had never yet had cause to distrust him. But the enormity of what he was getting into gave him pause. So much was at stake; Simon wished he could believe that, even now, he understood just how much. "I have a meeting with intermediaries," he said guardedly. "An introduction to Soviet Communal Bank is being arranged."

"Ah. Will I see you at the Hong Kong & Shanghai bash on Saturday?"

"Yes. I'll be back by then. Oh, but of course you knew that, do forgive me." He walked to the intercom and flicked the switch with unnecessary violence. "Mr. Reade is leaving now. Please see him out."

As the door closed behind the assistant commissioner, Simon wheeled round to meet Forster's eyes. "How the devil did he know we'd already made a written submission to Soviet Communal?"

"There isn't much Peter doesn't know. But that staggered even me. Are you going to play this game?"

Simon grinned. "I'm not sure, George. I think so, yes. One thing's certain—I'm not going in with Peter and Qiu, not the way they intend, anyway."

"I don't get you."

"If we take Soviet Communal's money, we're going to keep all our options open. We hold the reins, dictate the terms, decide what's repaid and when."

"But of course, we'll repay."

"Will we now? Why, for heaven's sake? This is 1985, George. You're becoming a shade quixotic, aren't you?"

"Think of our commercial reputation."

"I have thought of it. What reputation do any of us have these days? If I see a chance of not repaying that money and still hanging on to my shares, I'll take it. Anybody who's survived here for more than ten minutes would do the same."

"Maybe, but Dunny's has always traded honestly. We pay our debts."

"Not always. There've been times. We always *try* to pay our debts."

"Aren't you forgetting something else—something that ought to mean even more to you than to me?"

"What?"

"Are you seriously going to risk losing those Founders Shares for anyone, even Her Majesty's Government? They're bearer shares, remember. Once they're out of your sight, you may not find it so easy to get them back again. For that reason alone, if we do business with SCB it ought to be real business, honestly transacted."

Simon smiled at him and looked at his watch. "I've got a plane to catch; Qiu'll be waiting for me. Jinny, darling, are you coming down?"

"One other thing before you go," said Forster quickly, forestalling Jinny's answer.

"Make it fast."

"If you decide not to repay, you're in danger of losing your Founders Shares. But if you *do* repay, you'll be running foul of both Qiu and Peter Reade. Steer clear of this, Simon."

"Thanks. I'll think over what you've said. But I'm late."

"You're really going?" Forster said uneasily.

"Oh yes, I'm going. Until this morning I still wasn't quite sure. But I'm certainly going now."

Qiu was waiting for the car, as arranged, at the side entrance to the Bank of China's main building, in Bank Street. He stepped toward the Rolls but Simon forestalled him by getting out first.

"Good afternoon, Brother-in-law Qiu. Have you eaten?"

"Yes, thank you, Mr. Young."

"That's rather formal. Please feel free to call me Simon, if you wish."

Qiu's shrewd eyes narrowed and Simon could see that he was tempted. "Of course." Meaning no thanks.

"Would you like to put your case in the car? My chauffeur will meet us at Kai Tak."

Qiu's eyes flickered toward the Rolls-Royce and now the look in his eyes was greedy. "We're not going by car?"

"No." No, it is time to reeducate you somewhat, young brother-in-law.

Qiu handed his suitcase to the driver with obvious reluctance and as the car pulled away from the curb his eyes followed it, even when Simon was speaking to him.

"We have plenty of time today, Qiu Qianwei. We'll take the 200 bus, see Hong Kong as it deserves to be seen."

The two men sat right at the front. It was midmorning, the bus was only half full, so there were few to remark this odd couple—the Englishman in his safari suit and Qiu wearing what Simon thought of as a "Taiwan Flash" outfit, an embroidered short-sleeve shirt with tie over tight gray slacks held up by a snakeskin belt. As the bus emerged Kowloonside and began its long crawl up Tsim Sha Tsui East the Chinese turned to Simon. "Why take the bus?" he asked.

"Think of all the money we're saving."

Qiu smiled and for once Simon was able to detect a spark of

genuine enthusiasm in his expression. "I am not saving anything. What about you? The Rolls-Royce is there anyway, isn't it so? It still has to be kept full of petrol and oil, and someone must wash it. The driver must be paid whether you ride in it or not."

"All this is true."

"Then why?"

"I can tell you, but I'm not sure you'll understand."

"How will we ever find out unless you explain?"

"True. Well, then . . ." Simon hesitated, fumbling for words. Now that it came to the crunch he found the reeducation of Qiu Qianwei harder than he'd expected. "I am a citizen of Hong Kong. This is my place. I walk its streets, ride its buses and its subways. I listen to what the people are saying. I like the people in a way I don't like anyone else. I pay taxes to help keep it all going. I *belong* here. Hong Kong has fed and clothed me over the years. I owe it a lot. And I don't know anywhere else in the same way as I know this place."

Qiu blinked his long, slow blink. He was puzzled. Young was quite unlike most of the Westerners he had ever known, while at the same time retaining some of their worst characteristics: greed, hypocrisy and a wholly unjustifiable sense of superiority, to name but three. *Quan yang zhi xing*—foreigners have the nature of dogs and sheep. Yet this man did have some civilized values; what he had just said about Hong Kong proved it.

"That is why you want so much to build a desalination plant?"

"Yes, partly. Although of course, there are selfish reasons as well. Even before I met you, I realized that it would be to my commercial advantage after changeover if I was seen to be helping the colony, working for its welfare. And now it seems that if I go along with your plans, I can actually make a profit as well."

"That is frank. But I am more interested in what you said about liking this place and its people. You are not Chinese. You are English. Do you really prefer Hong Kong to, say, London?"

"I hardly know London at all. I try to avoid going to England. It's, well . . . I don't want to decry my own people, my own land—"

"There, you see, you think of it as your own land."

"Please hear me out. I was going on to say that London has become a strange place to me—dirty, noisy, full of arrogant, rude people. All right, you can say the same about some parts of Hong Kong—but at least Hong Kong's still got some go. It's got optimism, spirit. London hasn't. It wasn't always like that. But you can't ever put the clock back, can you?"

Qiu shook his head. Young's words made him feel almost sad. In his own lifetime China had changed more than in the previous thousand years. So much was lost. So little was gained.

For a while they rode in silence, each thinking over the other's words. During the past few days there had been times when Simon had come very close to hating Qiu for what he had done in Beijing, but certain features of his character were curiously attractive. He was a funny little chap. If only the Chinese weren't all so obsessed with their own inherent superiority . . .

"Mind if I ask you something?" he said at last.

Qiu appeared to awake from a reverie. "Ask what?"

"See there." The bus was stuck in a traffic jam and showed no sign of moving. Simon pointed out of the window. Qiu looked and saw in the street a teeming sea of black heads with only the occasional flash of blond marking out an obvious foreigner.

"I don't see anything," he said suspiciously.

"All those people. Crammed into so little space. How do your security services keep an eye on them?"

"An eye?"

"Surveillance."

Qiu sniffed and looked straight ahead. "I don't know what you're talking about."

"Everybody realizes that the People's Republic of China is able to monitor what goes on in Hong Kong with remarkable efficiency. Even our own Special Branch can't compete. How do you do it?"

Simon kept his amusement well concealed while he watched the struggle that displayed itself on his traveling companion's face. For about half a minute Qiu's gaze slid toward Simon and as quickly slid away again, that irksome twitch of a smile coming and going, while he tried to resist the temptation to display his higher knowledge.

"Don't you know?" Qiu said at last.

"I wouldn't ask if I knew."

"But you must know."

"Why?"

Qiu shrugged and gestured toward the window. His hands were long and slim; the upward-turning fingers tapered to fine almond-shaped nails. It occurred to Simon that they were the sort of hands that might have belonged to a scholarly mandarin from an earlier age.

"You see the street, there," Qiu said at last. "What sort of street is it, would you say?"

Simon looked. It was a typical Hong Kong scene: food stores, bric-a-brac emporia, restaurants, camera shops, postcard vendors, the occasional bookstall half hidden away down an alley. He could smell frying meat, petrol fumes, acrid dust and decaying food-stuffs. Drivers sounded their horns, people jostled one another off the pavement, cyclists struggled to keep upright. Storekeepers stood in their doorways, looking this way and that for customers. The bus inched its way forward through a smoggy haze of pollution, while above the passengers' heads were strung innumerable red, gold, green, blue and mauve signs bearing Chinese characters of every size, several of them advertising the ubiquitous "villas," or rooms rented by the hour and no questions asked.

"A usual back street," Simon said.

"Yes. It is usual. Suppose you wanted to . . . keep an eye, I think you said, on this street. What would you do?"

"I have not the slightest idea."

"Take her, then. Look . . . in the doorway next to the Golden Ming restaurant."

Simon followed the line of his finger and saw an old woman standing with her hands behind her back, the right one clasping her left forearm and a serene smile on her face. She wore a purple tunic over baggy black slacks and sandals on her otherwise bare feet. She blended into her background like a tree in a forest.

" 'All Mount Sumeru in a mustard seed,' " commented Qiu.

"Ah, you mean she's a world in miniature—she's represen-tative, typical?"

"Entirely so. And somewhere in China she has a cousin. Or a son. Or a brother. Somewhere, it doesn't matter where. We . . . can always find that person, however far away he may be or however hard he may try to escape or"—again that sideways flicker of the eyes, again the microsecond smile—"however high that person may climb."

"And once you find that person, you have a key."

"Which will unlock the door to that old woman's heart. And from there it is but a single step to unlocking every door along this street, for the old woman knows what goes on behind them all, as old women do everywhere. Now I think you understand, Brother-in-law?"

"A little." He thought of Jinny, of the deception she had maintained for nearly twenty years. "A little."

The jam was slowly beginning to dissipate with the help of a traffic policeman. Simon cast a glance in the direction of the old woman, saw that she had been joined by a companion and grinned. "I think she would be a very good choice of spy, Brother-in-law Qiu."

Red Dragon looked again. His beady gaze lighted on a Chinese youth who had appeared in the doorway behind the old woman and taken her by the arm. They were laughing together, but that was not what had caught Simon's attention. The boy, who looked to be in his late teens, wore tight white trousers, a black shirt open at the collar and a gold medallion on a chain around his neck. His hair was permed into a high wave at the front, liberally highlighted with rusty red. As the two men watched from the bus, another person appeared in the same doorway, a white man nervously clutching a camera. The boy quickly turned, patted the Westerner on the cheek and blew him a kiss. The client smiled wanly and scuttled off as quickly as he could. The boy made a disparaging moue, said something to the old woman, who laughed; then he took off in the opposite direction, combing his hair.

Simon saw that his companion's eyes were smoldering as they followed the gilded youth down the street.

"Do you know what we do to homosexuals in China, Mr. Young?"

"No."

Qiu's eyes reverted to the Englishman's face, but slowly, as if he were reluctant to abandon sight of his prey. "We shoot them," he said quietly.

"Is that right? I had always heard that there were no homosexuals in China."

"That's because—"

"You shoot them, yes of course. Ah! We're on our way again." As the bus moved off, Simon could not resist a parting shot. "I still think the old woman would have been a brilliant choice. A mine of information, I'd say. Wouldn't you?"

"*Hah!*"

5

Singapore had always fascinated Simon. It reminded him of a place in a child's fairytale picturebook. On page one was a pagoda, exotically embellished with dragons and bells; you turned over to find a tropical grove, half concealing an old-fashioned house; another page, more greenery, this time enveloping a bank or a shopping complex. But always the greenery; for, to him, Singapore was a garden city.

By the time the cab reached Scotts Road the rain had stopped, the clouds had rolled away and the setting sun sat low in a pale mauve sky.

"Ah, Cheam."

Qiu blinked, his senses quickened as always by the Englishman's enigmatic provocations.

"What is Cheam, please?"

"It's a suburb of London where I was at prep school—you'd call it junior high school. The houses were just the same"—Simon waved at the passing scenery—"large and solid and respectable, like the people who live in them. The same design, too. We could easily be in Cheam. It's one of the fascinations Singapore has for me. 'Everything under heaven.' Qiu Qianwei, please tell me something about the man we're going to meet."

"Ah, Mr. Ng. He is mainly retired now. In Hong Kong, as you know, we have our semiofficial front men."

"Like Mr. Robert Zhao, for example. He is a friend of mine, but he works for you."

"Exactly so. In Singapore things have to be conducted very differently. But there are certain businessmen who are not without sympathy for China and do what they conveniently can to further her interests. When you meet Mr. Ng you must not assume that he is our puppet. He is able to do us certain favors, on his terms rather than ours. Do you follow me so far?"

"Yes."

"One thing he is able to do is make an introduction to the Soviet Communal Bank chiefs. So, when you prepared your written submission, asking for a loan, it was he who delivered it, in person. He is strictly a free-lance go-between."

"I see."

"You must please be very careful what you disclose to Mr. Ng. He has extensive interests throughout the Far East. If he unfortunately came to have information which might enable him either to prevent harm to his family businesses or to advance their fortunes, he would unhesitatingly use that information without considering the effect of his actions on China."

The cab turned right just short of the Equatorial Hotel, then right again, pulling up outside a square, two-story, cream-colored mansion with a gray-tiled roof. There was little to distinguish it from the properties on either side. An elderly Chinese was sweeping up puddles of water from the drive, using a long-handled broom of stiff palm leaves. Simon paid off the driver and turned to find that Qiu was already deep in conversation with the gardener.

"Mr. Ng, may I introduce Mr. Young of Hong Kong."

So this was not the gardener, after all. Now it was Simon's turn to blink. "Good evening, Mr. Ng."

The old man leaned on his broom and smiled shyly. "Hah . . . hah, Sir Young."

"Would you prefer to converse in Mandarin or Cantonese, Mr. Ng?"

Ng's eyes lit up. "Cantonese, if agreeable." He extended one hand, punching it straight out in front of him like a karate expert taking stance. The skin was soft and slightly waxy, as if permanently mildewed by the damp climate.

"It is a great honor to receive the head of Ducannon Young in my house," he said. "Welcome, welcome."

"The honor is mine." Simon's reply sounded grave, but his heart was at peace. Ng represented to him the very best kind of Chinese: elderly, serene and dignified, one who dealt with triumph and disaster just the same.

"Please enter."

Ng walked slowly in front of them, leading the way at a shuffling, unhurried pace. His shoulders were rounded and his figure was frail, but Simon noticed how he held his head up, taking an interest in what lay before him; and the Englishman sensed that this old body housed a young spirit. They passed under the lean-to porch that most large Singaporean houses have to protect visitors from the rain as they get out of their cars, and proceeded into the kitchen. An old gray-haired woman was standing at the sink, washing rice for the evening meal; she acknowledged her master with a toss of the head but the rhythmic swishing of her hands never faltered. Then they were in the living room: a strange habitation for one of the wealthiest men in Singapore. The parquet floor, scrupulously clean, was bare of anything except an old rug and a few items of furniture that had seen better days; the plastic-covered sofa had a small tear in it, the prints on the walls were mass-produced, while the desk, piled high with prospectuses and bills, looked as if it had come from a secondhand furniture emporium in Chinatown. A large TV set and video recorder provided the only contemporary touches in an otherwise modest room.

As Simon sat down the servant came through from the kitchen bearing a cup of tea which she set before him on a cane coaster. The cup did not quite match its saucer. Simon smiled, remembering how his father had once described to him the difference between the billionaires of Singapore and their counterparts in Hong Kong. "In Hong Kong you can tell a man by the registration plate of his Rolls-Royce: did he buy it this month or last? But if you want to find a rich man in Singapore, go to the hawker stalls late one evening and look for an old man in pajamas and carpet-slippers drinking soup." When Simon asked why, his father merely shrugged and said: "The old man in slippers doesn't present much of a target to his government, does he? It's obvious."

Simon's smile faded at the memory. For Tom Young, everything was obvious and always had been. How unlike the man sitting opposite him now! Ng's gentle face was circled with lines and his upper lip projected forward into a point, causing a faint resemblance to a benevolent tortoise.

Simon was sipping his tea when another Chinese entered the room, aimlessly swinging a tennis racket from side to side. This man seemed to be about forty and was dressed in white shorts and a T-shirt. He smiled briefly at Simon, then bent low to whisper in Mr. Ng's ear.

The old man's face clouded. "Mr. Young, it seems that your presence here has been noticed already."

Simon replaced his cup on its saucer, keeping his face expressionless. "Oh yes?"

"You were followed from the airport. One of the cars we recognized and expected. The government here"—Ng's smile was more than polite, it displayed mild relish—"but the other we cannot yet identify. My third son is making inquiries." Simon saw that the tennis player had silently disappeared. "I suspect that SCB is taking more than a passing interest in your visit."

"Oh dear. I have brought trouble to your house."

"Not at all." Ng's manner was becoming increasingly lively. "I lead a very quiet life here, since my retirement. I can stand some excitement." His smile faded. "I do not want in any way to curtail your plans. Still less to offer advice to one of Hong Kong's most distinguished entrepreneurs. But if you were to consider spending a quiet evening here in my house, instead of going out . . ."

Simon hesitated. The prospect of inactivity always bored him. His instincts told him to go down into the city, make a few phone calls, listen, learn . . . but no, his host's advice was good: when engaged in such a sensitive project, it was important to keep a low profile. "You have read my mind," he said. "Thank you."

"Not at all, I am glad to see you here. Perhaps we could have a talk? I see so few people these days, visitors are a rare pleasure. Perhaps we can leave the . . . the *excitements* to Mr. Qiu here?"

Qiu had been standing by the window, looking out across the garden. Hearing these words, he turned around.

"Mr. Qiu, my sister will be coming here shortly," Ng said.

"She has been researching the position. I understand she would like to take you on a short tour of observation. There are some strangers in Singapore on whom she would welcome your views. I too."

Qiu raised his eyebrows. "From the land of snows?"

"From Russia, yes, but that's not all. Mr. Robert Zhao is also here, on a visit from Hong Kong. Do you see any connection with your presence, Mr. Young?"

"No," said Simon. "Should I?"

Ng shrugged. "His association with the People's Republic is well known. What do you think, Mr. Qiu—is there a link?"

"I do not know. Mr. Zhao has many interests and he is free to travel where it pleases him. Certainly he is not here at *my* request."

"I see."

"A coincidence," muttered Qiu. "You said strangers, Mr. Ng. Who else is here?"

"Two other men arrived from Moscow yesterday. We have managed to identify one of them as a low-grade *liu-mang*, a hoodlum who used to be here in the Moscow Narodny heyday: presumably they have called him in to provide background information. The other man, I feel, is a more serious proposition. But I do not yet know who he is. My sister hopes that your resources will enable us to find out more. Meanwhile"—the old man turned back to Simon—"I would welcome your comments on the Pacific markets, Mr. Young. Do you have a view on Australian mining shares?"

"An enthusiastic view with regard to some of them."

"Ah! Then we have that in common. And software companies, perhaps?"

Ng was still smiling but Simon's concentration suddenly became absolute. "Perhaps."

"You will know, Mr. Qiu, that our honorable guest has something of a reputation in Asia where software is concerned?"

Qiu shrugged, apparently indifferent.

"Yes. There was an initial difficulty, I believe?"

"Difficulty, Mr. Ng?" Simon's voice was low but it contained something Qiu had never heard before. A note of menace. Of danger. He pricked up his ears.

"It is an interesting story, Mr. Qiu, maybe you haven't heard it." Ng seemed determined to address himself to his fellow Chinese but Simon was not deceived. He attuned all his senses and waited.

"Ducannon Young's subsidiary, let me see, DY Electronics, was it not?"—he turned questioningly to Simon, who nodded—"had managed to negotiate a solus agreement with IBM. A great coup. Not everyone in Hong Kong was pleased. One man in particular was nettled to the point where he was prepared to engage in a little dishonorable piracy. A Mr. Ao?"

The tilt of Ng's head betokened a request for confirmation, but his eyes negatived the message and Simon said nothing.

"This Mr. Ao came to an unfortunate end, one week after the fruits of his piracy first flooded the market. A Royal Hong Kong Police cutter was cruising the harbor early in the morning when the lookout noticed something afloat in the water. On closer inspection it turned out to be a plastic bag containing helium, for buoyancy presumably, and a man's head: also, his genitals and a knife carved with the insignia of the Hung Society Second Lodge. The bag was connected by rope to what was left of the man himself; he had been in the water for some days by that time. An interesting message. Tell me, Mr. Young, have you had any trouble with industrial pirates since then?"

"None."

The elderly Chinese's eyes twinkled with appreciation. "I thought it unlikely. I'm sure you must have heard that story many times, Mr. Qiu. Please forgive me for boring you."

Qiu treated Simon Young to a look in which skepticism competed for supremacy with respect. "No," he said at last. "I don't know that story."

Simon slowly turned his head until he was facing Qiu and said, very deliberately, "That really doesn't surprise me. It is not a matter in the public domain. These things have a habit of becoming embarrassing, don't they, Mr. Ng?" But his eyes remained fixed on Qiu's for a long time and it was Qiu's gaze that fell first.

"I think I hear my sister's car," said Ng. "Please meet her. You will like her, Mr. Young. She is an admirer of yours."

Simon made a great effort at mental adjustment. Ng's relentless exposition of the Ao saga had shaken him; now he was expected to deal gently with another, presumably equally old Chinese. There was a loud clattering and banging in the kitchen, followed by the sound of raucous Cantonese argument. Simon sighed.

"Hel-*lo*, Simon Young. Glad to meet you. I'm Maudie."

As Simon rose to his feet with a smile he realized that his preconceptions were utterly false; Maudie was in her late forties, he guessed, but someone who took that much obvious care of herself might have been anything from thirty to fifty and still leave a man guessing. She was the tallest Chinese woman he had ever seen, wearing a white, open-necked blouse over Gloria Vanderbilt jeans that looked as though they had been painted onto her hourglass figure, the artist stopping at the precise point where her calf-length, soft leather boots began. She stood in front of him, hands on hips, with long curly black tresses falling forward across her shoulders and her fleshy lips parted in a good-humored grin.

"No-lah, please don't get up. I'll come down to you." When Simon resumed his seat she draped herself along the arm of his chair, one booted leg crossed casually over the other, and swept a lock of hair out of her eyes. "So you got in this afternoon, isn't it? How's Hong Kong? I suppose it's still filth-*ee* rich, yah?"

"We manage somehow."

"Pooh, manage! Hear this man! Last time I was in HK I bought a mink coat, and some little Lebanese wanted to charge me a thousand Hong Kong for keeping it in cold store for one month, and I told him where to get off. Ai, but I mean to go and live there some day. I have my own beautician's business, you know. I can charge what I like up there where the *r-r-rich* people are. Not like here. Hi, Bro."

Mr. Ng nodded complaisantly.

"And you are Qiu, isn't it? Yoo-hoo, Qiu."

Red Dragon had to push his spectacles up the bridge of his nose once or twice before they could be induced to stay in place. His eyeballs seemed to have swollen to several times their normal size. At last he gave up the attempt to articulate his thoughts and merely nodded.

"We're going out, Mr. Qiu. The Mercedes is in dock, so we'll take the BMW. We go now, come on-lah!" Simon felt a cool hand brush his neck and then Maudie was up. "Glad to have met you so soon, Simon Young. We shall have lunch at '1819' tomorrow when business is over, yah?" She tossed her head, once again flicking the hair out of her eyes. "Oh how I detest business, money, money, money all the time. So *bor*-ing." She swung around to face him. "Take Maudie to lunch and it's not boring, isn't it? See you."

She whistled loudly at Qiu, who after a moment of outraged hesitation trotted off in her wake like a grouchy dog. When the Englishman finally managed to tear his eyes away from Maudie's pert departing posterior he found, to his embarrassment, that Ng's eyes were full upon him. For a long moment the two men sat in silence; then Ng tapped the arms of his chair.

"Younger sister, you understand," he said.

Maudie's style of driving was not exactly erratic: it was entirely consistent, but consistently bad. She drove with one hand on the wheel, using the other alternately to brush the hair from her forehead and wave to acquaintances, real or imagined, in nearby cars.

"You're very quiet, lah?"

Qiu cautiously opened one eye and registered that they had stopped for the pedestrian crossing outside the Mandarin Hotel. "Nothing to say."

"So you are the big finance whiz kid, yes?"

"Maybe."

"You've got an economics degree, hah?"

"Yes."

Maudie slammed into gear and launched them down Orchard Road. "Where from?"

"Princeton. And master's in Business Studies from Harvard," he could not resist adding, to remind himself that he was, after all, somebody.

"Wow-*ee*! My ex was Yale man himself."

"What?"

"Ex. Ex-husband. He's a very big finance hot-shit accountant here in Singapore. Yale and Harvard don't get on, isn't it? I like Harvard the best. Generous. Not like Yale; Yale men are all mean bastards. You generous, yah?"

"Not very."

"Yah!"

"Where are we going, please?"

"People's Theatre, Chinatown."

Qiu's other eye opened. "Why are we going there?"

"Soviet Communal Bank's in town, that's why. And the big man's going to see a Chinese Opera this evening."

"How do you know?"

"Because Bro has someone in SCB, he's got someone everywhere. Why, aren't you pleased to be going out with me? A lot of men here in Singapore would give their buck teeth to go out with Maudie."

She turned right out of South Bridge Road, tires screeching in protest, and slowed to a crawl for the crowded streets of Chinatown. The horn produced no appreciable effect on the pedestrians in her way, who would stop in midstride to stare at the BMW in bewilderment, trying to work out what they were supposed to do. "Oh my *God*," said Maudie in despair. "Why don't that Harry Lee just pull the whole lot down, yah? 'Kay, Qiu, here we are. You get out and I'll park. It'll probably take me a while. Wait over by the entrance."

Qiu stood on the pavement and looked about him. The terrace fronting the People's Theatre was crowded with people of all ages and races, so evidently it was a popular show. A huge red banner picked out in gold Chinese characters proclaimed the arrival of the Guangzhou Opera Group with their celebrated performance of *Madame White Snake*. Qiu wandered across to sneer at a poster pinned up beside one of the theater's three double doors. Everyone knew that Cantonese opera was inferior to its genuine Beijing counterpart, but what point was there in expecting these capitalist barbarians to realize that? The crowd was enthusiastic and—Qiu looked about him with growing astonishment—young. He had expected all these bespectacled *tai-tais* in their loose-fitting *sam-fus*, but the sight of so many boys and girls wearing smart Western-style clothes amazed him.

Maudie suddenly rematerialized by his side. "Okay, Mr. Qiu. I got here. Lucky for you! Last time I ate at the Tanglin Club it took me one hour to get from the door to my table. Was my date mad!" Maudie shrugged extravagantly. "Why should I care? If you've got friends, you want to hang on to them. Anyway, my date was one of those mean bastards." Maudie pushed forward to the head of the nearest crocodile of people patiently filing their way inside the theater. "Yale," she explained, tossing the word over her shoulder at Qiu with the careless flick of a keeper feeding the seals.

Immediately inside the door of the already darkened auditorium stood an Indian whose job it was to check the tickets. Maudie showed him a pass; the Indian nodded. Then Qiu noticed another man, Chinese, standing behind the first. As their eyes met, the second man raised the thumb of his left hand to his ear and scratched. Qiu immediately rubbed his right shoulder with his left hand, using only the third and fourth fingers. Both gestures were concluded in less than a second.

"Follow me, please." The second man led Maudie and Qiu across the front row of seats and placed them just to the right of center stage. Although the performance was getting under way the chatter in the auditorium had scarcely diminished. Maudie settled down happily in her seat and began to explain the plot.

"There's this white snake lady in heaven, see, and she has a maid of course, and comes down to earth where she falls in love and has a baby, natch, because no birth control in those days, isn't it, yah? But the priest says she must go back to heaven and leave hubby and baby and they catch her after a big battle and put her in the pagoda, 'cause she's a snake, see, and her son gets a degree and everything and one day they let her out for long enough to visit her son but then she has to go back. Got it?"

Qiu sniffed disdainfully. He had to admit that he quite enjoyed opera. At school he had once sung a minor role in *The Red Lantern* for an end-of-term production. He wasn't familiar with any pre-Cultural Revolution works, but the plot would not, he realized, prove to be a problem, because at both sides of the stage stood long narrow screens on which the management projected a running libretto. The clash of gong and cymbals died away, yielding to the more melodious strains of the *erhu*, and he began to relax. But suddenly he felt a hand pluck his sleeve and he looked down, startled, to see that the man who had guided them to their places was now sitting beside him.

"The row behind," the Chinese said softly. "To your right. Three in from the aisle."

Qiu waited for Madame White Snake's aria to end, using the applause to cover his words. "Photos, yes?"

"Photographs done. On the wire already."

"When?"

"Tomorrow morning, early."

"Go now."

Qiu waited almost an hour for the first interval before excusing himself to Maudie and leaving his seat in search of the lavatory. On his way up toward the back of the auditorium he had about five seconds in which to observe the little group seated in the row behind. Two of them he knew well, for they were local directors of the Soviet Communal Bank and he had studied their files. The third face eluded him. It was the stern, impassive face of one in his late fifties or early sixties and it bothered Qiu that although this man was somehow familiar, he could not put a name to him. And the more he thought about that face, the less he liked it.

*　　*　　*

Next day it rained.

Clouds hung low over the city in huge soft smothering pillows while below them the bedraggled inhabitants of Singapore scurried to their places of work. The water flung itself straight down in vertical slats, filling the drainage canals to the brim, flooding pavements, converting roads to dangerous slipways more suitable for sampans than cars. A depressing day, Simon Young reflected, as the chauffeur turned into Killiney Road, past the post office, heading for River Valley Road and the next phase in the construction of Qiu's protective wall around Hong Kong. A day for meeting the Russians. He opened his copy of the *Straits Times* and scanned the headlines before turning to the finance pages. The rain teemed down outside, soaking its way into the jungle vegetation, the palms, the acacias, the bamboos, until the stench of rot rose with the steam into the back of the nostrils.

They were still early and road conditions were hazardous, so the driver took it slowly along Kim Seng Road. As soon as the Mercedes had crossed the Singapore River it turned right. Mr. Ng gestured out of the window. "There."

The Englishman leaned forward, his interest thoroughly aroused. Through the tepid shower-bath of rain he could see a gateway: two square stone columns topped with ornate dragons, from which hung a green iron gate, one hinge gone. The columns were half obscured by densely planted trees and shrubs that overhung the entrance, cutting off his view of the house beyond. Then the chauffeur had pulled in and slowly the drive began to unwind under its carpet of sodden leaves.

When at last the car stopped under what appeared to be a canopy Simon got out. To his left was the garden, beyond that, the road. The driveway fringed a semicircular lawn, in the center of which stood an octagonal stone fountain. A little to one side of it, close by a tall, densely leaved jacaranda tree, was a gazebo, its iron railings and columns fast degenerating to rust.

"Used to be a hotel," said Mr. Ng. "When my grandfather bought it."

Simon turned his back on the dripping garden and looked up. The house was on two floors, painted white, with pale green windows and shutters. He realized that he was standing under not a canopy, as he had first thought, but one whole room built out from the façade. A veranda ran the length of the house, its tiled floor sloping gently toward the steps for drainage. On either side were arches of grand proportions, with sorry-looking roll-up blinds to keep the sun and rain off the veranda and potted plants neatly arranged along the length of their waist-high balustrades. Everything spoke of neglect. The concrete driveway was cracked, like the low wall that bordered the overgrown lawn, and although some attempt had been made to hack back the foliage Simon knew that the garden, once so formal and attractive, would soon degenerate into urban jungle.

"You like, eh?"

"It's a magnificent house, Mr. Ng. I've never seen anything to touch it."

"Very little like it is left in Singapore now. A pity. I shall miss it. Maudie and I grew up here, you see."

"You say you're going to miss it," Simon said slowly. "Are you selling?"

"Oh yes. My offices used to be here; I still keep a room or two in that wing, over there."

Simon looked. To the right of the façade he could just make out an extension, its front door shuttered with an iron gate and bars across the ground floor windows.

"I really don't need an office anymore," Ng said. "So yes, we are going to sell."

"I should imagine any developer would give his right arm to get hold of this place."

"I suppose so. The buyer will doubtless tear it down and build a pink, circular block of air-conditioned flats some fifty stories high." Ng shrugged. "Shall we go in?"

Simon followed his host up the steps, past the cane chairs that flanked the main door and so to a rusty iron shutter which Ng had to unlock with three keys. "Mind the step, please," he said as he stood aside for Simon to enter.

The Englishman put down his briefcase and looked about him with curiosity. He had been in many Chinese homes but none of them as authentically old as this. Straight ahead of him was a family altar covered with a red, blue and gold cloth, on which stood a plate containing four dusty oranges, a vase of flowers long since dead and two brass joss-stick holders. On the wall behind the altar stood a black and white photograph of an old lady. "My mother," Ng said. "She died three years ago."

"I am sorry."

"Thank you. But it was a good release at the end. When she

died, an era died also. Now we can sell at a time of my choosing."

It intrigued Simon to see how he alternated between *I* and *we*—the father-emperor and the family-suzerain. "Is the time ripe?" he asked, knowing that Ng would not resent the question.

"Nearly. We have been offered a good price, but I have asked for more, of course. We shall get it. Eventually."

Simon smiled wryly. With no capital gains tax to pay or exchange control regulations to worry about, who would do better out of it, he wondered—"I" or "we"? Ultimately always "we," the family . . .

"Come. I am afraid this place has been shut up for many months now, but we have done what we can to make you comfortable."

Ng led the way behind the altar. Simon was vaguely aware of other large chambers to right and left, in one of which he caught sight of an old Chinese bed, its solid wooden hardness exuding discomfort; then he entered a remarkable room, a veritable museum, and had no time to concentrate on anything else.

The walls were the same shade of pale green as the shutters. Exposed beams running the whole length of the room offset the ceiling's soiled whiteness. The floor was tiled in an intricate dark brown pattern interlarded with Chinese characters and scenes from the classics. All the doors and windows (there were many) stood tall and narrow, with iron grills across the outside of the windows and roll-up blinds along their interiors. Two propeller-fans turned slowly above Simon's head as he tried to absorb the room's antique clutter. He found it hard. There was so much to see.

Mr. Ng switched on the lights, six sets of two bulbs each protected by dusty glass bluebell shades. They did little to illuminate the room. Immediately opposite Simon was its focal point: an elaborate, two-tiered table altar, flanked by long, vertical rectangular frames containing calligraphic scrolls of immense intricacy and grace.

"We have tidied up a bit," said Ng.

"I hope you did not go to too much trouble."

"No trouble. To be frank with you, I do not want people to find out about this negotiation of ours. I'm sure you think the same way: it has been impressed on me many times that, for you, secrecy is essential. That is why we do not meet at SCB's downtown offices or at my home. You are a conspicuous figure in Asia. A meeting here will attract very little attention—I hope."

"Thank you. I really could not afford to have news of this business become known."

"Good. I see you are looking at my grandfather's portrait."

"Forgive me, yes." The picture hung directly above the altar. "It is very fine."

"Not bad, not bad. Can you read Chinese as well as you speak it?"

"Not so well."

"The writing around the frame extols his virtues, which were many, of course. After all, he was my grandfather. But some of those virtues are not so popular these days." Ng sighed. "He was an imperial official; please don't ask me what he did, because I haven't the least idea. But he came out of China with three wives and twenty-two concubines and settled here in Singapore, where he made a fortune. He was a farsighted man. Not many court officials had the wisdom to leave while the going was good. Can you imagine, twenty-two concubines? Personally I find one wife quite enough. Mr. Lee, our PM, wouldn't like it at all. So many babies . . ."

"They wouldn't like it in Beijing much, either."

"I have enough concerns without troubling myself about the People's Republic. Don't allow our good friend Qiu to mislead you, please. Business is business. A negotiation is a negotiation. I have no sentiment in me."

Simon began to examine the rest of the room. Much of it was occupied by heavy, black Chinese furniture inlaid with mother-of-pearl; there was also a low, japanned table on which rested a pile of yellowing newspapers. At the far end stood six hard chairs surrounding an ordinary dining room table on which someone had placed two carafes of water and some glasses. At first sight it seemed a strange setting for what was about to take place, but Simon did not find it altogether inappropriate. For he was preparing to marry East to West, old to new—and where better to arrange the match than in a room such as this, in the dynamic city-state of Singapore?

"The other parties are arriving, Mr. Young." Simon heard the squeak of brakes at the front of the house and his heart began to beat a little faster. "Mr. Qiu is already upstairs. He has made arrangements for monitoring this conversation. Please remember that."

"I will."

Footsteps echoed on the veranda. While Simon went to collect his briefcase, Ng disappeared and moments later came back escorting three men.

"Mr. Young, I would like you to meet Mr. Tang . . ."

Before Ng could complete the introduction Tang stepped forward to take Simon's hand and say, "Branch manager, Soviet Communal Bank, Singapore. Very pleased."

"Mr. Goh, deputy manager and chairman of the branch loans committee . . ."

"How do you do, Mr. Young."

"And Mr. Borisenko, from Moscow, vice president in charge of Southeast Asia."

"I'm very pleased to meet you, Mr. Borisenko. I do hope you did not come all this way purely on my account."

Borisenko's lips extended in a momentary smile but he did not otherwise respond. He was a tall, well-built man with watery gray eyes and a seemingly perpetual thoughtful frown on his face. He had large hands which seemed coarse for a banker; but his expression was cold enough. A money man, thought Simon. A reader of balance sheets, with perhaps a prospectus or two for bedtime, last thing at night.

No, the picture wasn't quite complete. A flawed money man. The other two wore ties and short-sleeved white shirts over dark gray trousers, typical Singaporean businesswear. Borisenko's shirt was cream-colored.

"Please, be seated." Ng spoke in Cantonese and Mr. Tang at once translated his words into English. The three bankers ranged themselves on one side of the dining room table. Simon sat down opposite them and Ng took the chair at the end, quietly but obviously underscoring his role as umpire. The light from the windows fell across the table onto Simon, leaving the three men on the other side of the table swathed in shadow. Rain continued to pour down in a heavy, monotonous torrent, its columns reflected in the somber light filtering through the slats into the humid room.

Ng spoke. "Sirs, the language of this meeting will be English. I not speak well. I have introduce. I can go-stay. Please tell."

"I think we would like you to remain, Mr. Ng." Tang, who seemed to head the bank's delegation, spoke slowly so that Ng could follow him. "At least, for these preliminary discussions." He laid stress on the word *preliminary*.

"I stay. Please ignore. Need help more, ask."

"We will." Tang spoke with respect. It was clear to Simon that the SCB, on this occasion at least, felt heavily indebted to Ng. The knowledge brought him obscure comfort.

"Mr. Young . . . we have read the submission which your company sent to us. It is, if I may say so, an impressive document."

"Thank you, Mr. Tang."

The Chinese leaned forward to rest his elbows on the table and cradled his chin in his hands. Simon judged him to be in his mid-fifties. He wore heavy, black-rimmed spectacles with thick lenses that magnified his eyes into bulging, oval-shaped marbles beneath a fringe of crinkled gray hair. In the not-too-distant past, Mr. Tang had had a perm. He spoke English with a slight American twang, which no doubt went down well in the Singapore of the 1980s. By way of contrast Mr. Goh, the younger man, was going bald: his hair thinned out on the top of his skull into two distinct ridges. Simon's eyes strayed towards Borisenko. The Russian had pushed back his chair and now sat with his hands folded in his lap, purposely distancing himself from the meeting.

Tang spoke again. "Normally at this stage we would want to ask you questions on the technical side."

"I have come prepared for that."

"I am sure you have. But your submission is so detailed, so precise, that there is very little we need to ask. No, we would like, if we may, to have a more general discussion."

"Go ahead."

"Mr. Young, over the past three years or so there has been a major decline in the demand for desalination equipment. How sure can you be that the materials you need for this project will be available at all, let alone at the right price?"

"Reasonably sure. I of course accept what you say. For example, the Pegler-Hattersley industrial division has noted the slackening demand for some time now."

"Would you consider approaching Pegler-Hattersley?"

"It is possible. The initial approach, however, is likely to be to Daelim Industrial."

"In Korea?"

"Yes. You will be aware that they were part of the Saudi venture which had to be temporarily shelved."

"The joint venture with Mitsui Engineering and Shipbuilding and Sumitomo?"

"Correct. This was to have been in Assir, where conditions are not unlike those we shall be encountering in Hong Kong. The experience which they built up will be of immense use to us."

"What was the budget on that one?"

"Three hundred and forty-four million US dollars."

"But that was two years ago."

"Or more, yes."

"Where does that leave your figures, Mr. Young?"

"Right where they started. You'll find the inflation calculations in Appendix C." Simon reached for his briefcase. "Actually, those figures are more than a month out of date now. Let me run it through the machine for you."

He opened the briefcase to reveal a portable DY Starframe II computer. His fingers played briefly over the keys and a spreadsheet appeared on the screen attached to the inside lid. Goh leaned forward, an expression of greedy curiosity in his eyes. "Nice gadget," he commented; and Simon smiled.

"We do try. Ah yes—there's an uplift of decimal point seven eight one, giving us . . . there you are, Mr. Tang." He swung the briefcase around so that the screen was visible to the three bankers.

Tang made a note and asked, "What about basic equipment? I must tell you that our own inclinations lie toward Japan."

"Ah. Hitachi Zosen."

"Precisely. They have mastered the multistage flash technology for burning seawater, and we would prefer not to have to deal with Westinghouse as originators."

"I understand that. Their Oman experience suggests a good daily production—twenty-two thousand, eight hundred tons, as I recall."

"Exactly right. You know your brief, Mr. Young."

"I should. I have lived with this project for many years now. There would not be the slightest objection to Hitachi Zosen."

Tang nodded and half-turned toward Goh, who pursed his lips. "Hah, Mr. Young . . . maybe we should consider specifics now, ah?"

Simon shifted in his chair so as to give Goh his undivided attention.

"You want to borrow one hundred million UK, ah?"

"Yes."

"What are you putting in?"

"Project management, expertise and five million cash initially."

"Hundred million is a lot of money, Mr. Young."

Simon smiled and said nothing. Goh continued. "See if I understand the mechanics. You're going to form a new company, right?"

"Yes. The new company will be agent for the venture."

"New company borrows all the money, right?"

"Yes."

"What collateral does this new company have?"

"None. The collateral comes from elsewhere."

"The site?"

"No chance, Mr. Goh. Not after Eddie Wong and your colleagues at Moscow Narodny."

Goh grunted and shook his head in a gesture of resignation. "O-kay. We accept that: no chance of the site. So what do you have instead, Mr. Young?"

Simon smiled but did not reply at once. He had considered how to play his solitary trump card and knew that there was only one way. "I've got twenty Founders Shares in the Pacific & Cantonese Banking Corporation, Mr. Goh."

Apart from the steady splashing of the rain, no noise penetrated the airless room. To Simon it seemed as though he were attending some kind of court-martial. It reminded him of the Surrender Room on Singapore's Sentosa Island, where there was a wax tableau of the formal Japanese capitulation at the end of the Second World War. The three men opposite him neither moved nor spoke. They might have died.

Simon found himself once again looking at Borisenko. The Russian continued to stare at his hands, oblivious to his surroundings, but Simon knew that the other two were waiting for a sign. It did not come.

Mr. Goh said, "Mind if I ask you a few personal questions?"

"No."

"What's your connection with the People's Republic of China? How come they're prepared to deal in on this with you?"

"My devotion to Anglo-Chinese trading relations is sufficiently well known."

"That's all?"

"There are certain understandings as to what might happen to Ducannon Young after 1997."

"We assumed that. What are they?"

"I'm not at liberty to say without the specific authorization of my trading partners in Beijing."

Goh shook his head. "Wrong answer for these people. You're looking for Russian money on a Chinese contract? You know we won't agree to that."

"Is that so?"

Goh took a look at Simon's contemptuous face and was silent for a few moments. Then he asked, "Why not go to your father? What's wrong with the Corporation's money all of a sudden?"

"Because my father does not regard the PRC as a viable trading partner either now or in the future. You know this, Mr. Goh. Everyone in Asia knows it by now."

"And so if DY wants Corporation dollars it has to confine itself to projects of which your father approves?"

"Yes."

"What's he going to say if we lend you a hundred mill?"

"Jesus Christ Almighty!"

Borisenko laughed. The two Chinese turned to look at him, again awaiting their cue, but still the Russian declined to give it. The hands folded in his lap appeared to exert a hypnotic fascination over him.

"We would want certain understandings of our own." It was Tang who spoke; Simon swiveled in his chair so that he was facing him again. "Go on," he said.

"We'd want all your long-term deposits, for a minimum of three years."

"One year."

"Two, with an option to bid for a third."

"Agreed, but only if the option interest rate is not less than one-eighth of one percentage point above your then-standard investment rate for comparable amounts."

"Let's say there is sufficient interest in your proposition to make further negotiation worthwhile."

"Anything else?"

"First refusal over all other DY medium- and long-term capital projects for the next five years on terms not less favorable overall than those offered for the desalination plant, the terms to be fixed by independent London arbitration in case we differ."

"No problem."

"We would want a memorandum of deposit charging your existing Founders Shares plus all other such shares to which you might become entitled in the future, coupled with an irrevocable power of attorney authorizing sale in case of default, and share transfer forms executed in blank."

"Why future shares? Aren't my existing ones good enough?"

"Standard bank procedure, Mr. Young."

"I see."

When Simon hesitated Goh asked, "What are those shares worth? In your opinion."

"Sixty million pounds sterling on assets valuation, more on disposal as going concern, more yet if you take account of the built-in directorship and voting rights on a dissolution. It really depends who's buying and what that buyer wants. In the unlikely event of a default, you'd have a seat on the board of a bank which, if the rumors are correct, could leave Hong Kong in the next few years and reestablish itself here, in Singapore, still under my father's chairmanship, where it would be in direct competition with not only the SCB but Moscow Narodny as well." Simon turned to smile seraphically at Borisenko. "I should think the Corporation would destroy you in about ten days. Maybe eleven; my father's a cautious man."

Silence.

"You want a fixed term loan, Mr. Young. Twenty years, with interest capped at a reduced rate and rolled up until the plant comes on stream."

"Yes."

"In the event of a change of circumstances, hard times, could you reschedule?"

"I see no reason why not, once the project was established and proving itself. Especially since our partnership with Beijing should be well under way by then. Many of the investors who are quitting Hong Kong now will come flooding back, especially keen to deal with the PRC's most favored firm."

"You are sure you can deliver that?" It was Goh who spoke.

"Very sure."

"Then why are these partners of yours so reluctant to put up the money now, ah?"

"Mr. Goh, I've already told you that I'm not allowed to go into the details of my special relationship with China. But is it so hard to guess the answer to your question? The timing's wrong. In ten years' time, when Hong Kong has adjusted to the new political arrangements, things will be different."

"And why should we gamble on that?"

"Gamble? With twenty of the Corporation's Founders Shares tucked away in your vaults? I'm the one who's gambling, Mr. Goh, not you."

Borisenko raised one hand from his lap and coughed into it. Tang at once lowered his arms to the table. "Thank you, Mr. Young. This has all been very profitable. Incidentally, we are most grateful to you for coming down to Singapore to meet us."

"It would hardly have been wise for us to meet in Hong Kong. I hope I need hardly say, gentlemen, that these talks must remain a secret."

"We agree: secrecy is absolutely essential on both sides. If our depositors and shareholders came to know that we were contemplating a loan of this size they would become very nervous."

"It's the same on my side, with the added dimension of East-West politics to worry about. Russian-backed loans are hardly popular where I come from."

"I understand. Now, we would like some time in which to consider the matter further. We can, however, promise you an answer within the next three days."

"That is very speedy. Thank you."

"If we decide to proceed, there will still have to be detailed negotiations between the lawyers. We nominate Allen and Gledhill here in Singapore and Johnson Stokes and Masters in Hong Kong. Does that cause conflict-of-interest problems with you?"

"No. The need for secrecy extends to the lawyers; they must be obliged to keep numbered copies of the documents and to destroy all drafts and working papers."

"That would be our intention also. Good. And now we must not detain you longer." Tang stood up and when the others had done likewise he turned to the head of the table. "We would like to thank you for arranging this meeting, Mr. Ng."

"Hah, pleasure."

"Good-bye." Tang addressed himself to Simon for the last time. "Please remember: the time factor is now urgent."

"Understood."

Simon watched while Ng escorted the three men to their waiting car. After it had driven away the old man returned, thoughtfully shaking his head.

"Were you able to follow much of that, Mr. Ng?"

"Some, Mr. Young. Enough, I think, to make me know I did not want to follow any more. Ah, Mr. Qiu . . ."

Simon swung round. Qiu had silently come to stand at his elbow. His face was sour.

"Well?" said Simon.

"Yes, it went well, I think," said Qiu. "But there has been a development. I must return to Beijing."

It was as if someone had laid a cold, damp cloth around Simon's shoulders. "What?"

"The Russian."

"Borisenko? What's wrong with him? Tough, a real banker."

"Did it not surprise you that he kept quiet throughout the meeting?"

"Not really. Local autonomy is important to the Chinese, I'm used to that. Foreign bosses sit in, they don't interfere, why, what has—?"

"His name is not Borisenko. We sent his photograph to China by Fax last night. This morning we had confirmation from Beijing. I knew I had seen him somewhere before but I could not identify him. Now I remember."

"Who is he?"

Qiu drew in a long breath. There were black circles around his eyes; he seemed very tired, as if he had not slept. "He is a major general in the KGB."

Simon Young sank down into the nearest chair. The cold shawl weighed down on the nape of his neck like a tangible thing. "Surely you expected that?" he said, trying to make light of it. "I mean . . . they had to be involved. Didn't they?"

"Not so early. Not at this stage. And not at such a high level. You are going to get your money, Mr. Young—that much is obvious. Indeed, it seems that you are to be railroaded into a quick deal. But I need to go back to China now and talk to others who are better acquainted than I with this . . . Borisenko. As I say, that is not his real name."

Simon stared up at him, suddenly aware that something about the Qiu in front of him was new. The Chinese looked intensely worried.

"His real name is Krubykov. For many years now he has been personal assistant to the KGB chairman, Oleg Kazin. Please take care of yourself, Brother-in-law. Your health has suddenly become very precious to me."

6

Tang Fai Keong had been born and raised in Singapore; he thought he knew it well. But when the chauffeur swung the car off the East Coast Road the Chinese soon became disoriented to the point where he realized, with a little shiver of unease, that he was quite lost.

Warm rain hammered on the car's roof, at times even loud enough to drown out the Muzak coming from the radio. There was no conversation. Tang's companion was a taciturn man. Throughout the journey he stared stolidly out of the window, chewing gum with manic desperation, as if dependent on it for his next breath. Tang kept his own body hunched up in the corner of the backseat, as far away as possible from the Russian bodyguard and the smell of stale garlic that he exhaled. The Chinese banker disliked all Soviets. They were uncouth. Tang Fai Keong was not an adventurous man. His evenings were usually spent at home, in the company of his wife and daughter. He had been anticipating this assignation for some days past, although the prospect gave him no pleasure. Now, as he left the familiar part of town behind him, all his forebodings seemed to be justified.

Tang asked nothing more than to be left alone to do his job in peace. In particular, he could live without deputations from the Moscow head office. The routine annual audit was taxing enough; but Borisenko's visit was of an entirely different order. The Russian alarmed Tang.

Then, to add to his difficulties, there was the strange telephone call from Beijing that he had taken earlier: the memory of it seemed destined to come between Tang and his sleep. An offer such as every overseas Chinese secretly dreams of: to return to the mainland, work for the People's Republic in prosperity and honor . . . but at a price. Was it a coincidence, he wondered, that this should happen on the very day of his rendezvous with Borisenko? Or did it mean something else, something altogether more sinister?

The driver turned the car off the road through rusty metal gates and pulled up beneath an awning that sheltered the front entrance to a large, square, three-story house. Tang got out and glanced back the way they had just come. He could not see much: a well-kept garden with a large expanse of lawn separating him from the gates, let into a high brick wall, a gravel driveway, densely planted trees on the other side of the road . . .

The Russian bodyguard followed Tang out of the car and plucked his arm. Tang jumped. "Come on," the Russian growled. "We're late." The unlit façade of the house gave little away, but Tang sensed himself to be in the presence of money, big money. Very few people could afford to keep up this kind of establishment in Singapore, where space was the costliest commodity on the market. He tried to work out who might own it but the exercise was a hopeless one: rich Chinese kept their wealth in vaults as silent as they were deep.

Tang's bemusement did not last long. As soon as he crossed the threshold his eyes took in the decor and his face, normally a perfect mask of confidentiality and reserve, broke into a guarded smile.

The house was a brothel.

His smile faded. It was not correct of Borisenko to receive a branch manager in this place. But before the thought could take hold a tall Eurasian woman came forward, her hands held together in a deferential gesture of welcome. The dim light afforded by the red paper lanterns made it hard for Tang to judge her age: she might have been anything from thirty upward and she skillfully used the surrounding shadows to shield her face from too close an inspection. Her voice came out as a low musical murmur in which politeness blended perfectly with allure.

"Welcome to the Teahouse of Jade Contentment. Will you please come with me? Mr. Borisenko is already here."

She led the way up two flights of stairs. As they reached the top of the first and the woman turned the corner, Tang started. An unknown man was approaching him with the purposeful tread of one who does not mean to give way. But when the banker stopped, the stranger froze also. After a second of suspense, Tang smiled again. A mirror.

The woman of indeterminate age escorted him to the far end of a corridor containing many doors. Occasionally he was aware of music or soft voices, but for the most part the house remained silent. His feet made no sound on the deep carpet. As the woman laid her hand on the last of the doors Tang felt his heart give a jump and he licked his lips. He had not visited such an establishment as this for many years. Vague memories fought for attention in his brain, combining to raise an anticipation that was mostly but not altogether pleasurable.

The woman pushed on the door, which opened silently, and stood aside, indicating with a smile that he was to enter. Tang walked forward and gasped.

He was standing inside a box of mirrors.

The door swung to behind him and he wheeled around to face his own reflection. Mirrors everywhere—square panels of silvered glass on the walls, the ceiling . . . he looked down . . . even the floor.

For a moment he felt nauseated. Everywhere he looked he saw only himself, reflected into infinity. The sole light in the eerie room was provided by dim yellow globes sunk into the mirrors at irregular intervals, so that the shadows that they cast softened what would otherwise have been a harsh symmetry of space. Tang swallowed hard, forcing his eyes to focus, to distinguish between reality and its multifarious images. Over by the far wall there was a bed; beside it, a table on which stood a flask containing amber liquid, and two glasses; beyond that, a strange chair, not unlike the one in a dentist's office.

This chair was occupied. Tang concentrated on the distant shadows. "Mr. Borisenko?" he ventured hesitantly.

The person sitting in the chair did not answer at once. Then the shadows stirred briefly and an overhead lamp came on to swathe the chair and its occupant in a column of ivory-colored light.

"Good evening, Tang."

For a moment the banker remained paralyzed, while the man in the chair lit a cigarette and studied him with amusement. Tang saw the smoke wreathe this way and that in the ivory beam; then another voice spoke softly and his head jerked downward.

A beautiful girl was uncurling herself from the floor by Borisenko's feet. She was tall and slim and her silver *cheongsam* clung to her like a natural skin. When she was fully upright she looked down at the man in the chair and murmured again, "Do you wish me to go?"

Borisenko reached out a hand and, after a moment of reflection, laid it on her right buttock. The girl kept her face turned away from Tang but something about her stature betrayed fear. She was unnaturally still—too still to be relaxed or in control of herself. This was so out of tune with Tang's youthful memories that he began to feel apprehensive. The girls were in charge. They were invariably courteous, they might pretend to be childlike, but they controlled the situation. Always.

Except this girl, who did not.

Borisenko ran one lazy finger down the cleft of her buttocks and removed his hand. "Yes," he said quietly. "Go now."

The girl swiftly turned away and moved across to the door. She had to pass very close to Tang. He saw that she was young, still in her teens, and that her face was tense. She had difficulty in opening the mirrored door. Tang knew that she was teetering on the lip of some terrible void, but he could only guess at the cause.

"Come over here, Tang." The banker obeyed. He approached the far corner of the room until he was standing beside the peculiar chair. Borisenko's posture chilled him: the inert, silent Russian resembled a corpse. When one of Tang's legs developed a tremor, he hoped the other man would not notice and take it for a sign of weakness.

Borisenko beckoned him closer. "I want to show you something interesting," he said. He flicked a couple of switches on his right armrest and the room instantly went dark. At the same moment, however, two large mirrors in the wall behind the chair slid up, out of sight, to reveal a square of muted light. Borisenko swiveled his chair through 180 degrees, so that he was facing the wall. "Watch," he said.

Tang blinked and realized that the square opening concealed behind the mirrors gave onto the room next door, which was about ten feet square. Things were so arranged that whoever sat in Borisenko's chair could see through the opening onto a king-size bed, draped in a black silk sheet, its headboard placed against one wall. The bed was at a slightly lower level than the voyeur's chair, but since the opening in the wall was deep as well as long, it was possible to see everything without straining. Apart from the bed, the room was empty. The draperies and carpet were white, as were the bed's two cushions. There was no coverlet. Soft light came from strips hidden behind a cornice.

"A two-way mirror," said Borisenko with satisfaction. "The people next door can't see us, but we can see them."

Tang stared at the floor. He had no desire to see anything. But when Borisenko fidgeted restlessly in the chair beside him, he could not resist jerking his head up to see what had attracted the Russian's attention.

A tall, wiry Malay had entered the room next door. He was wearing only a thin red sarong around his waist. He had evidently just come from the shower, for he was vigorously rubbing his jet-black hair with a towel. He tossed the towel away and gave his hair a final rub with his hands before unrolling his sarong and stepping out of it. As the Malay threw himself down on the bed his eyes flickered upward in the direction of the opening for an instant, and Tang thought he saw a flash of rueful humor in the young man's eyes.

The boy had the good, muscular body of a healthy twenty-year-old. He lay on his back and bent his legs up, resting the heels close to his raised buttocks. As he began to scratch the dark, matted hair around his balls, Tang turned to Borisenko and said quietly, "Will you excuse me, please. I will wait downstairs and you can call me when you are ready."

"Stay." Borisenko closed his fist around Tang's left forearm with enough pressure to stop the blood. "Watch."

Tang felt humiliated. It was intolerable that someone of his seniority should be treated in this way, and by a barbarian at that. But—he was forced to admit it—there was something dreadfully fascinating about the room on the other side of the mirrors. Now there were two people next door; the Malay had been joined by a Chinese girl, who also was naked. Tang looked at her and gasped aloud. She was incredibly young, no more than fifteen at most, and her smooth yellow skin contrasted brilliantly with the dark, betel-hued limbs of the boy. She was shorter than he and she had none of his wiriness. Her buttocks were firm, the breasts not yet fully developed: when she lay on her side they hung down loosely, but if she turned onto her back they compressed into half-melons on which small brown nipples scarcely showed at all.

The couple lay quietly together, on their sides, face to face. They were talking, smiling, every so often reaching out to touch each other lightly, as one might caress a friend.

At last the boy slowly lay back, reaching round to arrange one of the white pillows behind his neck so that he was half propped up on the bed. The girl continued to lie on her side for a while, right hand gently brushing up and down the dark body beside her, up as far as the nipples, down as far as the crotch. Tang stared at the bed, unable to believe that this was happening. He could see everything, down to the last detail. The boy's penis was thick and circumcised; a drop of moisture glistened at the tip. Now the girl enclosed it with her hand and began to massage up and down with short, delicate strokes.

Tang glanced at their faces. They were laughing. Evidently she was asking the boy if he liked it, for he smiled and nodded, closing his eyes. The girl grew bolder. As Tang watched, the deep red glans bulged, shrank, bulged again; and another drop of moisture expelled itself, this time onto the girl's hand. She laughed again and raised her hand to her lips, kissing the moisture away.

She raised herself to a kneeling position beside the Malay, brushed the hair out of her eyes, and squeezed gently. The effect was to make the penis stand and strain upward, as if seeking to escape such delicious imprisonment. With a quick movement the girl changed hands, so that her left one was enclosed around the long shaft, and she used the second and third fingers of her right to stroke the underside of the boy's balls. By now the penis was erect, some ten inches long and as thick as a bamboo pole.

The boy half opened his eyes and pushed down on the girl's head. She took the cock inside her mouth, very slowly, teasingly, a few millimeters at a time, until at last, after about a minute, the whole of the stem had disappeared. Tang gasped again. It was impossible. But the girl had done it.

Because the bed was sideways to the opening, he could see every detail of the tableau. The girl sank her mouth right down to the roots, before lifting her head up to the tip, releasing the glans as if for air, then retrapping it again. The Malay's stomach rippled up and down as he grew closer to orgasm. Now his buttocks were thrusting off the sheet in a controlled rhythm, forcing the girl to moderate her technique or choke. But still she continued to apply the same steady suction, up and down, up and down, while in the room next door the sweat soaked into Tang's shirt, making of it a cold, clammy rag.

"Aaah." Borisenko exhaled softly. Tang, startled, looked down at the Russian to see that he was stroking his chin with the tips of his fingers, round and round, incessantly. The Chinese turned his head back to the opening. He did not want to. But he had no choice.

He saw at once the cause of Borisenko's exclamation. The girl he had encountered when first he came in, the nervous one, had joined the pair on the bed. She was even more beautiful than he had realized at first, especially without her clothes. She was older than the other girl, more practiced in her techniques, more professional; perhaps even a trifle bored. She removed the pillows, so that now the Malay boy was lying flat on his back, and crouched over his face, gently lowering her vagina until the boy could raise his head and lick it. Tang's own mouth fell open. He could see dewy moisture all around the man's lips, could see how the bright red tongue flickered in and out, collecting juice, drinking it . . .

The newcomer began a circular pelvic motion, thrusting her flat stomach in and out, while her hands went down to squeeze the boy's nipples. She spoke to the teenage girl who, without a break in what she was doing, nodded and climbed over the boy's right leg to kneel in front of him. The Malay was coming very close now: it showed in the frantic way his butt lifted off the bed, thrusting his cock upward into the girl's mouth. She placed the forefinger of her free hand alongside the long pink shaft so as to wet it with a downward suck, then used it to massage the opening to his anus. The second girl leaned forward, bringing her mouth to about six inches above the Malay's heaving stomach, and slid her hands down his thighs. His head jerked once around to the right, once to the left and then his mouth opened in a cry.

The younger girl leaned back, removing her lips from the

shaft. As it flicked once, twice, she formed the thumb and forefinger of her right hand into a tight ring which she ran quickly down its length. When she reached the bottom she squeezed, shoved the other, slippery forefinger up the boy's arse and stopped moving.

A wet, white missile of sperm shot out of the pulsating cock. The second girl put out her tongue, adroitly darted her head to one side—and caught the pellet of flying jissom on the wing.

A little groan escaped Tang's lips; but even while he was straining to convince himself of the reality of what he had just witnessed, Borisenko pressed a switch and the mirrors slid down to cover the opening.

There was a long silence.

"In Russia," Borisenko said thoughtfully, "there is nothing like that." He pressed another switch and the room was flooded with light. "Nothing at all."

Tang removed his spectacles and began to polish them with his handkerchief. He was outraged. He felt soiled. And he was shaking from head to foot.

"Sit there." Borisenko stabbed downward with his cigarette. Tang eased himself round the chair and perched on the side of the bed, discovering, too late, that it was a waterbed. Borisenko watched with interest, a glimmer of amusement showing at the back of his eyes, while Tang levered himself upright and tried to smile. He knew what his boss was thinking—that from now on, he, Tang, was guilty of complicity. He could never deny having been present, here in this ghastly room, while next door three people had done unmentionable things. . . .

"Good of you to come, Tang."

"Not at all, not at all." Tang made an almighty effort and succeeded in quelling the tremors that still ran spasmodically up and down his body. Borisenko was master; what choice was there?

The Russian picked up one of the glasses and fastidiously took a sip. He did not offer Tang a drink. When he had replaced the glass on the side table he drew hard on his cigarette and allowed his head to loll backward so that he too could watch the smoke as it became trapped in the soft yellow beam of light above his head. "This Ducannon Young loan," he said at last. "What do you think?"

Tang was relieved to find himself back in the familiar world of business. He screwed up his mouth and pretended to consider the question. "It is very big. Really, it is too big for us to handle alone."

"And why do you say that?"

"In the case of a default, I do not believe the bank could survive. One hundred million sterling . . ." Tang shook his head and unconsciously echoed the judgment of his subordinate, Mr. Goh. "Lot of money. *Lot* of money."

Borisenko smoked in silence for a while. Then he said, "Will Young default, do you think?"

"Very unlikely. He has never defaulted in any payment yet."

"So then—the danger you have mentioned is a small one, eh?"

"Yes, but—"

"But what?"

"With a sum of that magnitude, there should not have to be a risk at all."

In the long pause that followed Tang struggled to attain a less precarious seat on the bed, but it was difficult. At last Borisenko pressed a button on the arm of the chair and it raised him to an upright position in smooth and total silence. Tang was unnerved to see the man rise thus without moving a muscle. His eyes strayed to the wall and he glimpsed a dozen, a hundred Borisenkos all sitting up simultaneously like so many creatures of an invisible Frankenstein.

"You must pull yourself together," Borisenko said. "You are going to lend this money, Tang. All of it."

Tang looked an unhappy man. "All of it," he repeated mechanically.

"Yes. Listen to me."

The banker timidly raised his eyes to Borisenko's face. In the dim light it resembled a dreadful white mask from a No play. "I am listening," he said quickly.

"The collateral offered consists of Founders Shares in the Corporation."

"Yes."

"We want those shares."

Tang stared at him, dumbfounded. "I am sorry, but I—"

Borisenko snapped his fingers impatiently. "As security. We want those shares as security, Tang. We intend to have them. In the event of Young not repaying this loan, Soviet Communal needs to be in a position to foreclose on something concrete. You understand me?"

Tang had completely lost his bearings. "I do not see the purpose of this conversation," he faltered.

"The precise purpose need not concern you." Borisenko settled himself back in the chair and permitted himself a grim smile. "It is enough for you to comprehend that our . . . commercial interests require us to look at and consider all eventualities. We need to maintain and consolidate a position in Hong Kong, once 1997 has come and gone. We shall not be any more popular there, after the mainland Chinese have taken over, than we are now. But if things went wrong with this Ducannon Young loan, those shares would entitle a purchaser to nominate a director to the board of the Pacific & Cantonese Banking Corporation. Imagine it! Nothing like that is ever going to come our way again."

The banker said nothing. Borisenko strove to gauge his reaction but found it difficult—Tang gave nothing away—and for a moment the Russian wondered uneasily whether he had perhaps said too much.

Tang was remembering the morning's phone call from Beijing. At the time he had found it hard to understand the subtle nuances of the message, but now all was becoming clear. The caller, senior vice president of the Bank of China, had not contented himself with offering Tang lucrative employment. In a roundabout way he had also hinted that Beijing was aware of the Ducannon Young loan proposal and that the Soviets would somehow find a way of ensuring that Young defaulted. At the time Tang had found it easy to dismiss such speculation as groundless. Now he realized that in Beijing they were better informed about his superiors' intentions than he was.

He had been a banker all his life and he knew that this was not how you did business. Then, yet again, he remembered his position. "I can lend the money," he said. "If you insist."

"I do insist."

"Please may I ask for an instruction in writing to that effect?"

"Of course. You may have whatever you want, within reason."

"Does that include a full indemnity from Moscow head office in case Young does default?"

Borisenko's face clouded. "It does not."

"May I ask—why not?"

"As you say, Tang, we are talking about a lot of money. This is your bank, your region. We look to you to see that the security offered is sound and that the bank's right to that security is legally foolproof. Is that asking too much?"

"No."

"There are limits, Tang. Within those limits, you may rely on Moscow to help you. But we expect you to do your own job up to the hilt of your own competence. Do you understand?"

"Yes."

"Good. Just as long as you realize that this is regarded in Moscow as the single most important thing to have come our way for years. Got that?"

"Yes, yes."

"And failure is failure, got that also?"

Tang nodded his head.

"Let's hope so. Because I am making you personally responsible for this loan, Tang. From now on, no one is to have any dealings with Young except you. And in particular"—he leaned forward, wagging his forefinger in the banker's face to emphasize his points—"you are to vet the paperwork."

"I?"

"You. The senior official of the bank here in Singapore."

"That is not customary."

"Too bad. If Young sees a way of not repaying this money, he will not repay it. In that he is no different from anyone else. So we must be sure that we have proper security. Everything must be watertight."

"Of course."

"There is no 'of course' about it. Nothing is to be taken for granted, *nothing!*"

"I will see to it."

"For your sake, I hope that is true."

Tang was shaking again, but this time with rage. No one had ever insulted him to such a degree. The indignity involved was colossal. But Borisenko was . . . Borisenko. So the Chinese swallowed, and inclined his head in a stiff gesture of assent.

"And remember this also . . . Young is friendly, far too friendly, with the mainland Chinese."

"Forgive me, but how can that matter to us?"

Borisenko's eyes lost their focus and he leaned back in his chair. "Never underestimate them," he said slowly. "Their people are everywhere. They are in Soviet Communal. Oh yes"—seeing Tang about to protest, he held up his hand—"they are even here, in Singapore, in this bank, *your* bank. They too would like those shares. We must see that they do not get them."

His eyes bored into Tang's. For a moment the banker knew

real fear, as once again he remembered the phone call he had taken that morning and seemed to hear the mellifluous, seductive Mandarin voice . . . then he steadied himself and returned Borisenko's unpleasant gaze without flinching.

"You may rely on me," he said.

"Good." Borisenko stood up and Tang, not without difficulty, managed to do likewise. "In future, you report only to me." Borisenko held out his hand and the banker, after a second of hesitation, accepted it. When Borisenko's fingers closed around his, Tang blenched. They were cold and clammy, as if with slimy dew, and the strength in the hand was cruel. Borisenko showed no sign of letting go. Tang had to stand there, trapped. "We know you are a resourceful man, Tang Fai Keong," Borisenko said at last. "See that your resourcefulness is not wasted in this case."

The Russian abruptly dropped Tang's hand and gestured toward the door. "Tell the madam to bring more whiskey."

Tang gritted his teeth. He was not accustomed to being treated like a brothel servant. But he swallowed that, too. He had no choice but to swallow everything.

The car was waiting for him outside the front door. As he got in and slammed the door behind him he seemed once more to hear that ingratiating voice echo down the line from Beijing; and with sudden disquiet he felt something he had never known before: a conflict of loyalties. "Oh yes," he murmured to himself as the car pulled away, "I shall oversee everything, Mr. Borisenko. I shall attend to it. . . *personally*."

In the upstairs room of the teahouse, "Borisenko" filled two glasses with whiskey and extended one of them to his second visitor of the evening.

"Thanks, Krubykov," said Robert Zhao.

The Russian smiled and clapped Zhao on the back. No trace remained of the domineering regional vice president who had browbeaten Tang a few moments earlier. "You heard everything?" he inquired solicitously.

"Yes. These places are always so well equipped, aren't they? Tape recorders, videos . . . I heard."

"What do you think?"

"I think that if Tang is as important to you as I believe he is, you just made the biggest mistake of your life. No Chinese puts up with being addressed in that way."

The Russian, hearing the tetchiness in his guest's voice, shrugged off the reproof with a charming smile. "People need to be reminded who is boss. I am accustomed to doing that."

"There are other, subtler ways of going about it. I mean what I said earlier: you may have just blown the entire operation."

"Do not trouble yourself about Tang's loyalty. We are quite sure of him."

"Why?"

"He was doing a middle-of-the-road job as number two in a middle-of-the-road bank, here in Singapore. We picked him up, made him a big man. He won't forget."

"He just might, if you continue to treat him with such insolence. For God's sake, why don't you listen to what I'm telling you? You say you need my help, my experience of the Chinese, yet as soon as I point out a danger you ignore me totally."

Krubykov said nothing for a moment. He was tempted to remind Zhao that the KGB needed him for one reason and one reason alone: to spy on the inner workings of the Mah-jongg Brigade. But such bluntness would imply a degree of trust in Zhao that Krubykov was far from feeling, so he confined himself to saying, "When it comes down to basics, everyone is alike. Tang knows we made him and we can as easily break him again. He has no idea of the KGB's involvement in Soviet Communal Bank. Please do stop worrying."

"And yet, if I were working for the opposition in Beijing, Tang is the one man I would set out to ensnare. *The one man!*"

"Of course you would," Krubykov murmured soothingly. "He is a key operative. We always knew that our branch manager here would be extremely vulnerable; that is why we chose Tang."

"Yet you go out of your way to alienate him," Zhao said, shaking his head in disbelief. "You Russians—always the same. Arrogant. Roughshod. If you were the only ones affected, I wouldn't care. But you seem to forget that I, too, have an interest in the outcome of this scheme."

"I don't forget it, not at all. What can I do to pacify you, Mr. Zhao? We have to maintain order in our employees, a sense of discipline. Tang understands that."

"He's too conscientious. If he spots anything wrong, he'll cause trouble."

"There will be nothing to spot."

"You can't possibly be sure."

"But I can. Please listen to me, my dear Mr. Zhao. The mainland Chinese are determined to wreck Soviet Communal Bank—and with good reason. The bank is our only substantial base here in the Far East. We have nothing else of any use. Get rid of the bank and you get rid of Moscow's influence in Southeast Asia. Therefore, they have put together a plan to cause the bank to become overstretched by involving the man Young and his Founders Shares."

"I know all that."

"Well, then. Consider the implications. In order to set up the deal, get it off the ground, Young must provide us with genuine banking security documents. Forgeries simply won't do. The documents he delivers to Tang must be perfectly legal and proper."

"Then the bank has good security, it cannot be ruined and the mainland Chinese will have failed." Zhao sounded exasperated. "It's blindingly obvious to me that the Chinese are going to palm you off with worthless security documents. How else can their scheme be made to work? Why won't you *see* that?"

"Because you are quite wrong. The Chinese intend to do exactly what I would do in their place—substitute false documents at a later stage, so that when the matter is tested in court, as it inevitably will be, the security appears to be worthless *then*. What happens until *then* is of no consequence to anyone, least of all Tang."

"You seem very sure of yourself, Krubykov. I hope your confidence is justified. It's not such an easy matter to substitute security documents as you seem to think."

"Yet my confidence is not misplaced. You heard me give Tang the message; he understands what is required of him. He will check and double-check the papers and will find nothing wrong. A few days later, before the Chinese can effect the substitution, we shall ask him to forward the documents to Moscow for verification, or audit, or something like that—only instead of returning them, we shall keep them. The mainland Chinese will have no opportunity to swap papers around in Moscow, I can assure you of that."

"I hope so," Zhao repeated ominously; and Krubykov spread his hands with a laugh.

"What more can I do to convince you?"

"Get rid of Thomas Young. That at least might do something to restore my confidence in this wretched business. Deal with him now!"

Krubykov, aware of the need to placate Zhao, nevertheless felt his temper beginning to slip. "And why?"

"Once he is out of the way, the son gets a controlling interest in the Founders Shares. When that happens, this whole thing starts to sound worthwhile. Until then, all you're playing for is a minority interest."

"I know that."

"Well then, why the devil don't you act on what you know?" Zhao's voice was starting to sound shrill.

"Because there is no need. The document which Young gives the bank will be framed in such a way as to cover his father's shares as and when they come into his hands."

"I don't like it. Why deal in possibilities when you can be certain?"

Krubykov banged his glass down on the table. "You're starting to provoke me," he said quietly.

Zhao flushed and drained his own drink. "I've told you before," he said viciously, "that's not the way to talk to a Chinese."

"I'll talk to you how I please." Krubykov stood up and wagged his forefinger under Zhao's nose. "Thomas Edward Young stays whole, until we say otherwise. If anything were to happen to him, Zhao, anything at all, we would know where to put the blame. And then, yes, I do promise you—then we would act indeed!"

"So now you don't trust me?"

The question hardly needed an answer. Krubykov said nothing. Zhao stared at him for a long moment before replacing his glass on the table and making for the door. On the threshold, however, he turned. "You can threaten me if you like," he said quietly. "But I make no promises. We need to rid ourselves of Thomas Young."

"So *you* say."

"I do say it. His continued existence is an unnecessary complication of our plans, because as long as he holds on to his allocation of Founders Shares he can block us."

"But as soon as he retires he will lose that allocation and then—"

"Whatever you say, I know that he will never retire, never as long as there is breath in his body. Somehow, he will always find a way of staying on as chairman of the Corporation." Zhao, frustrated beyond endurance, slammed his clenched fist against the nearest mirror. "If you truly want his Founders Shares, you must kill him, Krubykov. And you must do it *soon*."

7

Qiu allowed himself plenty of time for his appointment. He took a red and white 101 bus to Beijing's Beihai Park, riding at the back of the connected double cars so as to avoid the scrutiny of other passengers. He wanted to think.

It was all very pleasant; that was the problem. For what conceivable reason could Sun Shanwang have invited him to lunch at the Fangshan Restaurant? The place was for tourists, famous for its authentic reconstructions of Qing imperial court dishes, and like such establishments everywhere its prices bore little relation to the quality of the food on offer. Even so, Qiu felt his mouth begin to water at the prospect before him. Goldfish duck webs, the house specialty—why not? Tender duck with mandarin fish, egg white, bacon, peas, wine and vegetable garnish all arranged in the shape of a goldfish. And red kidney bean buns to follow . . .

Qiu gave himself a mental slap. Lunches such as this had to be paid for, and not with money either. The invitation signified something important.

He descended at the northern gate of the former Winter Palace, paid his five fen and began to stroll through the park. He had plenty of time. In late autumn the air was fresh but the park was still full. Padded jackets were beginning to make their appearance, especially on children. Qiu approached the *Jiulongbi* and watched morosely as a crocodile of infants were led up to the famous screen. The teacher at the head of the row held a long string looped around each child's wrist: the little girls on the left had their right hands in the loop, alternating with the boys, who were attached by the left. They were brightly clad in reds, yellows and blues, and some of them wore intricate patchwork-quilted tunics which must have cost their mothers or grandmothers many hours of unpaid labor. Qiu sniffed. It ought to be possible for the Party to find a way of harnessing all that free time.

He placed himself with his back to the Hall of Celestial Kings and considered the screen, separated from the concrete path by two low rails and a privet hedge. He was fond of the *Jiulongbi*, had been ever since he first saw it as a child. Against a background of dazzlingly deep cobalt-blue tiles, nine five-clawed dragons danced and writhed their sinuous course, the blue, gold and silver of their scaly coils so realistic that they almost threatened to leap from the wall onto the admiring bystanders below them. Qiu liked the dragons' faces; it was clear that they were all good Party members. Enthusiasm glowed in their protruding eyes: "We're going to come off here and eat you up!" they seemed to say. "One day . . ."

Qiu sighed and moved on. Nine dragons. In Cantonese, *kowloon* . . . which meant, in turn, part of Hong Kong. Suddenly he felt discouraged and cold. Winter would soon be here, along with the ice and perhaps even some snow. He walked faster, puffing a little so that his breath showed against the crisp autumn air, until at last he came to the ferry on the northern shore. He paid another five fen and boarded the barge that would take him across to Qionghuadao, the Jade Flower Isle.

It was a beautiful day, the kind that comes to Beijing only in autumn and not by any means always then. A faint dewy haze hung over the sky-blue lake, shrouding the Jade Flower Isle in a layer of mysterious mist like ultrafine gauze. Qiu stood at the prow and watched Qionghuadao slowly loom up to fill his horizon. There were only a few rowboats in use now; the season was late, the lake cold, but a handful of hardy Beijingese still philosophically plied its tranquil surface. For the most part they were young and in pairs: one boy, one girl. It was a way of obtaining privacy, which in itself was worth a few hardships.

Qiu sighed. His own life was now free of physical deprivation, but that by itself did not bring happiness. He could never quite rid himself of the fear that something might go wrong, and the new life vanish like a dream at daybreak. Over the past few months he had learned a lot, acquired many practical skills, but still he did not feel comfortable in his new role. Qiu longed for a centrally heated library: yes, a library and a chair and table, a file of statistics, a paper to write for some learned journal . . .

He shook himself in an unsuccessful attempt to throw off his depression and resumed his glum study of Qionghuadao.

The White Tower dominated the wooded isle, its huge handbell shape standing out soft white against a sky that for once was free of pollution. Qiu had made this trip many times as a child. One of his earliest memories was of the Tibetan-style White Tower, beneath which his mother and father used to sit on summer Sunday afternoons, idly watching the pleasure boats on the lake far below. Throughout his life, Sunday had represented the only scant moments of relaxation his family ever knew. Normally Qiu would have been working at this hour; he felt a twinge of guilt as he thought of his former colleagues bent over their desks in Bow Street Alley.

His frown deepened. What *did* Sun intend for this meeting?

Qiu disembarked and made his way to the snack bar. He was still early and the boat trip had quickened his appetite. He ordered a *Xiao Wo Wo Tou*, one of the tasty muffins that the Empress Dowager had usurped from the common people to make into an imperial delicacy, and sat down on a nearby bench. He held the bun gingerly by its pink tissue napkin, eating only the very last morsel with his fingers. His mood began to lighten somewhat. It was pleasant sitting there in the sun.

"Ah, Little Brother, there you are."

Qiu had been dozing. His eyes flickered open and he came to his senses with a start. How much time had passed? He tried to stand up, shake hands with Sun and look at his watch all at the same time.

"Hah, welcome, Elder Brother. I hope I have not kept you waiting."

"Not at all, it is I who have delayed you."

"Not at all, not at all."

"Shall we eat?"

Qiu's appetite was in no way diminished by the muffin. He was ravenous. "Only if you are quite ready, Sun *tongzhi*."

"Ready, ready."

Qiu trotted along behind Sun until they came to the Fangshan Restaurant in its superb position overlooking the lake, with the densely wooded hill behind robed in the golds of autumn. It was a mellow noon. The haze still clung to the lake but the sun had bleached the surface of the water a brilliant white and Qiu took out his Hong Kong sunglasses.

"Very smart, Little Brother."

Qiu's lips twitched in their habitual quirky smile. "They make me look like a capitalist, I'm afraid."

"Well, why not?"

Qiu resolved to consult a doctor about his hearing. "Sorry?"

"All the fashion these days. Private enterprise everywhere you look. Good way of solving unemployment, hah?"

Qiu looked cautiously to right and left. They were in the dining room known as The Tower of Azure Light, which at this hour was only half full, but still it was an outrageous thing for Sun to say.

"Ha, ha, very amusing, Sun *tongzhi*."

"Amusing?" Sun looked up from the menu, his eyes blinking behind their spectacles in incomprehension.

"Unemployment. There's no unemployment in the Middle Kingdom, of course."

For a moment Sun continued to gaze speechlessly at his companion; then he laid down the menu and folded his hands on the tablecloth in front of him. "Rubbish," he said.

Qiu's eyes popped.

"I know," Sun went on. "The polite term is *dai ye*, is it not? 'Waiting-for-work.' I call it unemployment. From now on, so must you. I sometimes think, Little Brother, that you forget your new status as Red Dragon. By the way, have you received your copies of *Cable News* yet?"

Qiu squawked and immediately fell silent. *Cable News* represented the very highest level of Party intelligence: it was circulated daily to members of the Central Committee and the commanders of the military regions. The journal contained material equivalent to that which the President of the United States received at his morning briefings. In a country where most people were told nothing about themselves, let alone the outside world, *Cable News* was a source of immense power. It could also be extremely dangerous, for knowledge brought its own very special brand of contamination.

"I was not expecting to receive that," Qiu said falteringly. If the truth were told, he did not care to receive it. All he wanted was to be allowed to get on quietly with his job. "I thought maybe some *nei-can* material . . ."

"What good is *nei-can* to you?" Sun was openly contemptuous. "That internal reference bumpf is all very well for grade-twelve cadres. As I keep having to remind you, Red Dragon, for you things have changed. Have some cold almond paste soup to finish with—it's excellent here."

Qiu, in spite of his nervousness, felt his hunger grow. What luxury! "Thank you, thank you."

"*Bu yao keqi.*"

It was extraordinary, but the waiter came over as soon as Sun raised his hand. Qiu stared. The man was polite as well as prompt. Not only did he write down the order, he actually smiled when he did it. In a city where it could take an hour to order in a top restaurant, such behavior was almost unheard of. It dawned on Qiu that his companion had been here before, and more than once too. But then, he reminded himself dutifully, Sun Shanwang had suffered in his time; it was only right that now he should make up for the past.

"We'll drink some *maotai* to begin with. Wine with the meal but I'll order it later. That's all."

The waiter nodded his head. Another millimeter and it would have been a bow. Qiu stared after him until he had disappeared through the swing doors into the kitchen.

"I hope you like 'Live Carp,' Little Brother?"

"I've never had it, Elder Brother."

"Hah? They fish out a live carp and two chefs work on it together—scaling, frying, garnishing, all that takes them only a few seconds. When they serve, the fish is still flapping. You know, I once saw the mouth keep going even when the fish had been eaten down to the bones? Really. You have to keep the nerve center intact, that is the secret. You will see. Talking of nerve centers"—Sun took a pack of cigarettes from the breast pocket of his shirt and offered one to Qiu—"I want to talk to you about Hong Kong."

"Good. I would welcome some advice."

"Okay, okay. But first, let's drink." The waiter had brought the *maotai*. Sun held up his glass. *"Gang-bei!"*

Qiu drank a little of the fiery liquid, wondering if he would be able to do any work that afternoon. He wasn't used to it; the spirit burned the back of his throat, making his eyes water.

"I like this place," said Sun, who was evidently in an excellent mood. "Imperial cooking, the best. Did you know that last century the emperor used to have one hundred and thirty-six dishes served up to him for lunch every day? What he didn't eat, they threw away."

There was a short silence while the two men contemplated how revolutions are made.

"Now," Sun said. "We have to talk. Everyone's very pleased with you. Apart from your formidable way with figures and high finance, you are learning the business, the *real* business of intelligence very quickly. This is why I'm taking you out to lunch—to show a little appreciation. Also, here we can exchange ideas more freely, in a relaxed atmosphere."

It sounded good, but Qiu thought that in Western society Sun Shanwang would probably have made sure that he ended up with a job that carried not only a good salary but also, and more importantly, unlimited expenses. This was a new phenomenon in his experience and he resolved to be careful.

"You say you want some advice, hah?"

"Yes, please. Can you tell me—have you ever heard of a Hong Kongese called Ao? He was murdered—"

"So Ng told you the story, eh?"

Qiu blinked. "You knew?"

"Yes. It's on the foreigner's file. We're still investigating it. I'll tell you something, Little Brother: Simon Young has some Chinese connections which even we can't fathom. Good *guan-xi*. You need to plan for that."

Guan-xi. Connections, pull. Qiu had never heard the term applied to a foreigner before. "Unusual."

"Correction: unique. He has his own wall around him. One reason why we chose him, of course. That man is going to be useful to us one day. If he survives. Ah, smoked chicken . . ."

Qiu waited until they had been served before he spoke again. It was odd: although the restaurant was crowded by now, no one had come to sit at any of the nearby tables. Nevertheless, his natural caution prevailed. "You think he won't survive?"

Sun eyed him sharply, shrugged and said nothing. He used

his chopsticks to pass Qiu a morsel of chicken, deftly sorting the largest strip of pink meat from the pile on the plate between them.

Qiu munched thoughtfully for a while, then said, "I think he's very tough."

"Maybe."

"Elder Brother, do you think he had this Ao murdered?"

"I don't know. In a way, I hope so. A ruthless operator is what we need. Please eat!"

"Thank you. What are we going to do about Krubykov?"

Sun raised his eyebrows. "Why, what should we do? It is a sign that the Russians are taking the thing seriously."

"Yes, but . . ."

"Never mind 'but.' Krubykov will stay in Moscow where he belongs. Let me deal with him, he's no concern of yours. Much more important: what progress is Young making toward a final decision? I have to tell you, Qianwei, that time is running on." He frowned. "The schedule was always tight. Now, things are not straightforward. We need to hurry."

Qiu laid his chopsticks aside. "His mind is nearly made up. Reade has helped, of course, and his wife will do more. It's a personal thing with him; sometimes I think the commercial aspect isn't his priority. He wants to build that desalination plant. I cannot understand why, but he does."

"Good. Is there anything more we can do to help you?"

"If, as you say, the timing has become even more important, then perhaps he needs a small nudge. Nothing dramatic, nothing to set him thinking. A tiny grain of rice to tip the scales inside his brain. Would you perhaps agree, Elder Brother, that now is the moment to invite the Chrysanthemum to play the part assigned to him?"

"I was thinking the same myself." Sun frowned and looked away, embarrassed. "But there are difficulties," he muttered.

"Ah."

"Listen, Qiu Qianwei. The Chrysanthemum was always a problem. What do you expect? He sits there in Hong Kong, juggling money all day . . . these people are tainted. We use them, but still they are tainted."

"Yet I'd always assumed that the final leverage would come from him. I had counted on it, in fact. The Chrysanthemum's role was central to my thinking."

"I will consider it, Qianwei. Let me speak honestly. Zhao has long been a trusted if somewhat wayward servant. But we've been monitoring some rather strange business activities on his part. I'm sure there's nothing in it, but we're making a few inquiries anyhow."

"In what way strange?"

"First, he has begun to take risks in the market. His debts are mounting—did you know that?"

"No."

"It's a fact. If he continues at this rate, before long he'll be in serious financial difficulty. It will not be the first time, of course; but that's not all. Not only is he running down his assets, he is also redistributing them."

"How?"

"He's shifting a lot of money out of Hong Kong."

"Please excuse me, Elder Brother, but so are many of the other traders."

"To the other place, to Japan, to New York and London."

"Exactly so."

"And to Hungary?"

"*Hungary!*"

"Where now they have numbered bank accounts. And East Berlin. And Havana. Tell me please, Little Brother, I would value your view. What is there in Havana for our Mr. Chrysanthemum? Apart from good cigars."

Qiu was silent after that. Although he munched his way stolidly through the six dishes that Sun had ordered, his mind was elsewhere. He had been counting on the Chrysanthemum. But it was very wrong of the man to transfer his funds to Soviet satellites like Cuba without first asking permission. The news perturbed him greatly. Nothing about the Hong Kong operation was simple, it never had been. But it worried him when so many unforeseen difficulties made their appearance this early in the game. Qiu had always been a defensive Mah-jongg player.

He was quick to offer Sun one of his precious Winstons as soon as the meal was over. The older man accepted with elaborate gratitude and pushed his chair back from the table. "This man Young," he said at last. "Do you like him?"

"Yes." It came out too quickly and Qiu knew it at once. He lowered his eyes. "That is . . . he has some qualities I can respect."

"I understand that."

"But he's proving very stubborn. That's one of the things I wished to ask you about. I don't know how best to proceed."

"What's the problem?"

"He is querying the documentation. I've explained the strategy to him over and over again: We will supply the bank with genuine security documents and then arrange to have them switched later. But Young will not agree to execute genuine documents; he insists on signing the false set for submission to Soviet Communal."

"Presumably he doesn't trust us to effect the switch?"

"That is so."

"It's understandable, then." Sun shrugged. "I don't see much difficulty about this. Allow him to sign false documents and submit them. Meanwhile, prepare genuine ones. You can always effect the substitution later."

"When you say 'genuine ones' you mean convincing forgeries, in other words."

"Certainly, yes: documents that on their face look perfectly regular. Of the best quality, too, with special attention paid to Young's signature. As to the papers which Young himself signs, all you need do is make sure that they contain some small but fatal defect—for example, see to it that he does not execute them before a Hong Kong magistrate. Under the Corporation's articles, that will be enough to avoid the security."

"If I could only be sure that he would allow me to submit the documents to Soviet Communal on his behalf. Then I could make the switch at once."

"Young will do no such thing. He's no fool. No, you'll have to find a way of substituting the 'real' documents for the false ones at a later date."

"But what if the bank detects the flaws in the documents which Young has signed?"

"A minimal risk, in my opinion—as long as you are skillful. But even if they do, you can simply then arrange to have Young sign a genuine set, apologize and start again."

"Revert to the original plan, in other words?"

"Exactly, exactly. By that time Young will have become so enmeshed in the plans for his plant that he won't be able to resist signing whatever we place in front of him."

Qiu sighed. "It is all becoming very complicated."

"Did you ever think this line of work was easy?"

"No."

"Look." Sun pulled his chair closer to the table and folded his hands on the cloth. "There is too much at stake here for me to take any risks. Are you *sure* you understand?"

Qiu nodded.

"Tell me, then. Pretend I don't know anything about this stratagem. Expound it."

"Well. At first, the plan devised by Chinese Central Intelligence was very simple. The sole object of the exercise was to ruin Soviet Communal Bank, nothing else."

"Correct. And how was that to be achieved?"

"By making use of Simon Young: persuading him to borrow from Soviet Communal more money than that bank could really afford to lend. Then, arranging a technical default on the repayments; and finally, ensuring that when the bank came to sell its collateral, the Founders Shares, it could not do so because the mortgage of those shares was a fake."

"That is exceedingly lucid."

"Thank you. But it is only part of the story."

"Yes. Explain that."

Qiu hesitated while he marshaled his thoughts. At last he said, "Simon Young thinks that we are putting the plan I have described into effect. But we are not. The plan has changed and he does not know that."

"Proceed."

"Baba has realized that there is a greater opportunity here. Not only can Central Intelligence ruin the Soviet Communal Bank; it can also acquire Simon Young's Founders Shares, at no cost."

"Very good. How?"

Qiu licked his lips. This was the difficult bit. "The mortgage of the Founders Shares has to be genuine . . . no, sorry, has to *look* genuine, genuine enough to fool a court of law. So that when Soviet Communal Bank sues for its money and tries to sell the Founders Shares, it can, in effect, succeed."

"Yes. And how does that assist Chinese Central Intelligence?"

"It assists them . . . because the bank will sell those Founders Shares to our nominee, the Chrysanthemum."

"Who in turn will give them to us."

"Yes. Having first delivered a draft for one hundred million pounds sterling to Soviet Communal."

"A draft which will eventually find its way back to us. Yes."

Qiu agitatedly drummed his fingers on the table. "But that is the part I still do not understand! *How* will the draft come back? I mean . . . why should it?"

Sun smiled. "We are examining ways of answering that question. Do not let it trouble you. We shall get the Founders Shares; the Russians will not get their money. You'll see." He gently clapped his hands together. "Very good, Qiu Qianwei. Yes, I can see you have understood. And please do not think I underestimate the difficulties facing you. You are dealing with a Westerner. They are different, they are very different. Earlier you asked me, in effect, if I thought he would survive. Now let me ask you a question, one which will perhaps surprise you. How would *you* survive, if you were suddenly taken out of circulation and transported to rural Sichuan, with a hundred million other people competing for the rice in your bowl?"

Very slowly Qiu's mouth fell open and his eyes widened until at last he was staring at Sun across the table like a man who has taken complete leave of his senses. Sun saw his expression and laughed. "Difficult, even for you, hah? For him . . . well."

"Please forgive me, Elder Brother, but . . . what are you talking about?"

Sun smoked for a while without answering. Then he leaned forward to rest his elbows on the table and addressed Qiu in a kindly tone. "This wall," he said. "This wall around Hong Kong. There is more to it, Qiu Qianwei. There is yet another side to it of which you are unaware." He paused, assessing his subordinate through half-closed eyes. "What plans do you have for this afternoon?"

For a moment Qiu could not speak. At last, however, he managed to stutter, "I'm going back to the complex. There's much to do."

Sun laughed. "Nonsense! Come, row a boat with me."

His words threw Red Dragon into a torment of despair. All he wanted to do was crawl away from the table and go to sleep in some quiet spot where Sun would never find him, a comforting nest where Hong Kong and all its many problems could be dismissed as no more than a distressing nightmare. Now Sun wanted him to row a boat. If he accepted, would his superior take that as a sign of laziness on his part? If he refused, would Elder Brother be offended? Was this a trap? To take the rest of the afternoon off could surely be indicative of an incorrect attitude on his part. But openly to thwart an invitation issued by the deputy controller of Central Intelligence . . .

Why did Sun Shanwang want him to ignore the Russian, Krubykov? How could he say it was no business of Qiu's? What was all this terrifying nonsense about Young and Sichuan?

For a few playful moments Sun watched the indecision roll this way and that across his colleague's miserable face; then he leaned forward. "Come," he repeated. "I shall talk to you about Mr. Young, and our Mr. Chrysanthemum. There's much you should learn." He stood up. "You can row," he said graciously. "If that will make you feel any better."

8

There was to be no trifling with the man at the stern. He stood as if bolted to the deck, left hand on hip, the right raised high where the helmsman on the bridge could see it. He was tall and slim and hard as a true sailor is hard, the exposed ridges of his body smoothed and honed to hawsers of muscle uncushioned by fat. His feet were bare. He had rolled his white cotton trousers up as far as the knee; above them he wore only a blue cotton shirt, its material thinned by age and constant use. The face matched the body. It was long and narrow and it tapered to a point at the upturned chin, whence two deep lines ran up the side of his lean cheeks to meet at the temple. Although he was in his early sixties his tightly curled hair was only just beginning to turn from black to gray; and his teeth, all intact and all his own, owed nothing to any dentist. The man's quick, precise movements were those of a born sailor. People sometimes looked at him from a distance and labeled him an artisan, a manual worker of immense resilience and physical skill. Only when they saw his eyes close up did they know themselves to be in the presence of someone very different. His name was Thomas Edward Young. He was chairman and chief executive of the Pacific & Cantonese Banking Corporation.

"Stop engines."

He scarcely raised his voice but the command carried without effort to the bridge, where Luk Seng Kay immediately stabbed down on the two cut-out buttons. As the cruiser coasted gently alongside the jetty Tom Young crouched low to pick up the stern-line and sprang ashore in a single movement, judging the distance, as he judged most things, to perfection. From the prow Simon watched his father lope easily along the planks, the balls of his feet scarcely seeming to touch the wood, and felt the wonted stab of envy. "The old man," that was what he usually called Tom Young, but it was difficult to imagine anyone less old in fiber and being. Simon knew he would not age in that way: smoking long Hoyo de Monterrey cigars, drinking whiskey as though it were tea, working a ninety-hour week.

"Are you going to stay there all night?" Tom's words sounded resentful, as if he disliked being hauled away from his desk to spend Saturday afternoon fishing for sharks in Deep Water Bay. It was so much bluff. Tom liked hunting sharks, just as he liked to grapple with all his fellow predators. But with typical perversity he was venting false displeasure at having thrown away precious hours that could never be regained.

"I'm sorry you were bored." Simon climbed down the ladder and went to join his father at the end of the jetty, leaving Luk to close up the boat. Tom Young shrugged. It was not in his nature to utter meaningless words of comfort. Even when he used to send Simon off to school in England from Kai Tak Airport he would look at his watch without any pretense at concealment. Sometimes his son went through the gate and looked back to find that his father had already disappeared, leaving his mother to wave good-bye to him with a forlorn smile on her face. She was always there; father never was. Only when she died did father begin to pervade Simon's life.

"You'll stay for a drink?" said Simon.

Tom looked at his watch. The automatic gesture was imprinted in Simon's circuits; he could not see it and fail to react. Something always tightened in his stomach, immediately below the breast-bone, but he had never bothered to evaluate the feeling.

"Just one. I want to be back at the bank by six."

"You can shower and change here if you like."

"Change? Why? I haven't any meetings." Tom Young screwed up his lips into an approximation of a smile, as if conscious that the occasion called for a somewhat less abrupt approach. "Does it matter how you're dressed, as long as the business gets done?"

Yes, Simon thought, it matters; but he said nothing. Although he always tried hard to run along with Tom, in matters of business as in so much else their philosophies were very different. Early in his career the two men had quarreled over money, adding commercial ill will to past family history that neither could forget, so that a current of mutual antagonism flickered constantly between them. Simon continued to climb the narrow wooden stairway that led to the house, stifling the petty words that rose to his lips, his vision filled by the sight of Tom's thin, flat buttocks immediately above and ahead of him. Suddenly the older man stopped dead and Simon cannoned into him.

"Christ God Almighty!" muttered Tom. "Look who's here. I'm off. I think I'll have that drink some other time."

He ran up the last few steps. As Simon's head emerged above the level of the terrace he caught sight of a thirties-vintage silver Bentley drawn up in the driveway and he felt his heart momentarily tighten.

Jinny, seeing the two men approach the patio, uncurled herself from a chaise longue and came halfway to meet them. She held a tall, frosted glass in her hand and she was still smiling—but a smile left over from someone else, not manufactured specially for the new arrivals. Tom Young nodded, reached out to touch her arm and walked straight past. Simon kissed her on the cheek but his attention was focused on the poolside bar, where another man lounged elegantly, his back and elbows resting against the padded rail, one straight leg folded over the other.

"My very dear Simon . . . how absolutely super to see you. Do hope you don't mind me dropping in unannounced like this?"

Zhao Yi Qiang was more English than all the English put together. He seemed very tall for a Chinese, almost as tall as Simon, but with the stocky figure that comes from years of high living. His parents had employed a Norland nanny and given him his own tutor (from Eton, naturally) at the age of three. In consequence, Zhao spoke perfect English with an impeccable upper-class accent. Simon sometimes found it disturbing to hear the man talk. The clipped tones seemed a touch unnatural, coming from someone who looked so unmistakably Oriental. But he liked Zhao. Everyone in Hong Kong liked him. The Beijing financiers with whom Dunny's dealt seemed very fond of him too.

And Jinny—did she like him? Simon wondered. The perennial question went unanswered, as always. It irritated him to be so close to Jinny and yet still not know.

"Robert, don't be silly," he said. Zhao had given himself an English forename and expected his friends to use it. "Of course I don't mind. You've got yourself a drink, I see. Get Lennie to freshen it up."

Zhao levered himself upright with a deliberate movement and swung around to face the bar where Lennie Kok Wai, the Luks' son, was already teetering on the balls of his feet, anxious to serve him. The Chinese treated the eager teenager to one of his brilliant, charming smiles and said, "I'll have a freshener, Lennie. Same as before. Ace. Absolutely ace."

Tom Young, who had evidently changed his mind about a drink, now went behind the bar, brushing Lennie Luk aside in order to mix himself a Glenlivet and water the way he liked it. Zhao smiled at him rather less affably. "Young . . ."

"Zhao."

Simon appreciated the way Zhao had greeted him first, before acknowledging his father. Very few people did that. "Golfing today, Robert?"

"Scuba-duba, old bean. I was tootling back from the point so I thought I'd look you up." He lifted his glass. "Honk, honk."

Simon borrowed Jinny's glass and smiled. "Cheers. Give me a gin and tonic, will you please, Lennie?"

"Coming up, Mr. Young."

"So." Zhao lolled across to the table and slumped into a chaise longue. "Jinny tells me that Mat's been selected for the first eleven next term. I imagine that makes you a proud superdaddy?"

"Yes." Simon felt himself blush. He was in truth immensely proud of both his children, but he disliked showing it in front of his Chinese friends. Zhao presented particular difficulty because he always teetered on the border of self-caricature and no one quite knew how to take him. So Simon was relieved when Zhao went on: "What's the tallest *tai-pan* up to these days, mm?"

Tom Young banged the bottle down on the bar and sluiced water into his glass with unnecessary violence. He had always hated Simon's nickname, even in the old days when *tai-pan* as a form of appellation still enjoyed a certain vogue.

"Muck and truck, as usual."

"Haw, haw!" Zhao threw back his head with a stage laugh. "Muck and truck, very good." He half turned in his chair and addressed himself to Jinny. "Did you know, my dear, that that's what we poor but honest traders used to call our mixed cargoes in the old days?" As he said "old days" he held his hands up to the level of his neck and made a mouth with each thumb and forefinger, opening and closing them to emphasize the words. "Also known as 'the good old days' when we Chinese needed a pass to come up the Peak and would have thought ourselves lucky to be the tallest *tai-pan*'s compradores."

Simon tried to see what impression Zhao's words made on his wife. Did she like him? *Did she?*

Jinny looked up and, finding the two men's eyes fixed upon her, blushed. "Honestly, Robert, what was good about them?" she said. "*These* days, you could probably buy us up ten times over out of the petty cash."

Lennie Luk brought fresh drinks. Simon, hearing his wife's words, took a long, thoughtful pull from his glass and said nothing. Robert Zhao's name cropped up a lot these days, in the bars and clubs of Hong Kong. If even one-half of the rumors were true, Zhao might not be as rich as all that—and then suddenly Simon guessed a possible reason for his father's hostility, a creditor unexpectedly meeting his debtor . . .

"I'm off."

By the time Simon looked up, his father had already reached the edge of the terrace. Tom Young threw the words over his shoulder and continued to walk toward his car without breaking stride. "Take care," Simon said mechanically, knowing his father would not respond but needing to say it anyway.

Zhao drew in his lips to make a comical pucker. "Going down to the club for an all-night Mah-jongg beano," he murmured. "Or perhaps the Corporation, to make sure the banknotes are still under the floorboards where he left them. Is it true that he counts them every day?"

"No, no, that's quite untrue. Only on Sundays and bank holidays, when there isn't anyone about." Simon's voice was raw. He didn't care that his father held all Chinese in contempt, especially the ones who owed him money. But he cared quite passionately about the way in which Tom Young chose to show it.

"Haw! Haw! Haw! How absolutely priceless!" Zhao fell silent; his eyes narrowed, as if he were calculating a risk. Evidently it was worth taking, for he leaned forward and cocked his head conspiratorially. "A bit cool, I thought."

"I'm sorry you felt that."

"Yes." Zhao licked his lips and pounced. "Anyone'd think he still remembered Ko Shan."

Simon colored and Zhao, seeing it, at once drew back. "Sorry, old chap. Not funny. Not funny at all."

Simon grunted. "I don't see why not. Everyone else in Hong Kong thinks it's funny."

"Sorry."

"Don't be. I was right about the project, though. He should have lent me the money, I'd have made a packet."

"Yes. But—no, forgive me, I've said far too much already."

"Go on. I know what you were going to say, anyway. Tom saw the property crash coming and wouldn't lend me the money for my first big condominium deal. He was right about the market, of course he was. It's not his fault that the Ko Shan condo bucked the trend and made a fortune for Hong Kong Land."

There was no trace of bitterness in Simon's voice but his expression was taut. Zhao saw it, glanced at Jinny's impassive face and decided that the subject had yielded enough mileage for one day. "So tell me"—he extended a languid arm toward the side of the terrace—"how's your old wall coming along, eh?"

Just below the level of the terrace stood a low ornamental wall. It looked unfinished, but in fact it was very old. Every so often Simon knocked down a section and rebuilt it himself. He had reconstructed this wall several times now, but he still considered it to be "old." Here was a uniquely Chinese way of looking at things: once a particular structure existed on a given site it didn't matter how often it fell or was torn down, because as long as you put it up again it was regarded as the same edifice as always.

"Coming along nicely, thank you, Robert." Simon spoke easily, relieved by the change of subject.

"Still bringing in the jolly old luck, eh?"

"Oh yes."

"But surely you don't believe in that nonsense, do you? I mean, *seriously*, man."

"Building is lucky. You should always be building something. Every Chinese knows that."

"Well, here's one who doesn't." Zhao turned back to Jinny. "What everybody *does* know, of course, is that I built my wretched house on the dragon's eyeball and that's why I never have an ounce of luck any more. Or was it his tail? I'm damned if I can ever remember."

Jinny returned the smile, then lowered her eyes and said nothing. Zhao fascinated her. She did not know how he expected her to respond. Often she wished that he would do what so many of her husband's business friends did, and ignore her. But Robert Zhao never ignored her. From the day they first met, he had striven to impress himself on Jinny.

Simon hastened to fill the hiatus. "Knowing you, Robert, I expect you put the lavatory over the poor thing's balls."

"*Haw!* Yes, well, I expect I did. I like that. Nice one. Must remember that." Zhao's gaze slid like mercury over Jinny's face, searching for signs of distaste at the off-color joke and finding none. "Thing is, Jinny, your husband's such exceptionally good value."

"I think so." Jinny loyally reached out to take Simon's hand, but it was almost as if she were embarrassed by her own gesture.

"Can I steal him, my dear? Just for half an hour or so? Then I must be on my way."

"Of course, Robert. I'll go."

"No." Simon stood up. "You stay here, relax. Robert and I'll go inside."

Zhao picked up his pigskin briefcase and the two men entered the house, leaving Jinny alone on the terrace. She continued to stare into the middle distance until suddenly she was conscious of being watched. She looked up to find Lennie's eyes upon her. The boy quickly turned away, but not before she had had a chance to read his expression and know that he felt sorry for her.

Simon took Zhao into his study, overlooking the pool. He closed the door behind them and went across to the window to adjust the venetian blind. He could see Jinny still sitting on the terrace where they had left her a moment ago. "Sit down," Simon said abruptly.

"Thanks. God, but I love this room. How do you do it?"

"Do what?"

"Manage to combine solid English club comfort with Oriental . . . what's the word I want? Delicacy? Finesse? I never could pull it off myself, although Lord knows I've tried."

"Leather armchairs and an oak desk plus a few Japanese prints and some knick-knacks."

"Knick-knacks, the man says. A thousand Hong Kong says you've got the best collection of *limianhua* outside Beijing."

"No takers. Jinny's much better than I am now. She always knows just where to look for the best bargains."

Zhao had lowered himself into one of Simon's luxurious armchairs. He stretched out to pick up a tiny jade bottle from the occasional table beside him and squinted into its interior. "Look at that craftsmanship! How the hell does the artist get his brush inside to do the painting?"

"He gets up very early in the morning. What's this all about, Robert?"

Zhao replaced the bottle with a sigh, but his eyes lingered on it for several seconds longer. "Today," he said at last, "I went diving with a dickey-bird. The kind that goes *cheep-cheep*." Suddenly his voice became clipped and Simon saw, without surprise, that the harmless caricature had transformed himself into a totally dedicated professional.

"So?"

"He cheeped on about a lot of interesting things. Projects of one kind or another. Construction. Plants."

Simon began to pay attention. He made a mental note to find out who had been with Zhao that afternoon.

"The word *desalination* kept cropping up. Now since I know bugger all about desalination I thought I'd come round and see if my good friend Simon Young can explain it to me."

"It's easy enough, Robert. Lots of people can give you facts and figures. If you're interested in the technical side I'd be happy to arrange some introductions."

"It's not so much introductions that I'm after. It's a partner."

"A partner?" Simon froze.

"Yes. Look here, Simon. We all know you're Hong Kong's desalination king. Out of the blue, I've had a chance to come in on a consortium which wants to go ahead and get the thing built."

"I've heard nothing about this." Simon tried to keep control of himself, but the misery and outrage in his voice were all too apparent.

"Now please don't get uppity."

"Excuse me, but I really do find it very hard to believe that—"

"Oh, but I've got all the plans here." Zhao flicked open the lid of his briefcase, allowing Simon a glimpse of several impressively bound folders. "Believe it or not, Simon, it happens to be true." Zhao was very much in charge of this conversation. "My new associates are coming to the project fresh, and I'm sorry to have to tell you that they're not enamored of your existing plans. They've produced something altogether new. It appears that at least two members of the executive council are prepared to throw their weight behind it."

"Who?"

Zhao allowed a few seconds of silence to enhance Simon's brittle tone before he continued. "Come along. You know I can't tell you that. The important thing is that there's a new market force on the scene and they've asked me to put out feelers."

"To me?"

"Of course. It really is unthinkable that the project should proceed without DY in it somewhere."

"And where exactly is somewhere?"

"They were wondering if DY Construction would be interested in a subcontract for the foundations? A minor contribution, perhaps, but an extremely useful one."

Simon barked a short, sharp laugh. "That's insane."

"There's no property in desalination," Zhao said reasonably. "You don't have exclusive rights there. Or am I wrong? You're very thick with Government House—perhaps you do have rights that nobody knows about. Care to comment?"

Simon said nothing.

"There are . . . would be other advantages. Of your not going it alone."

"What?" The Englishman's voice was bitter. He resented Zhao, resented the deft way in which he had managed to penetrate the defenses.

"The work force would be . . . well now, what is the word I want? International, perhaps?"

"Slave labor."

"Oh come, come. The Vietnamese and Cambodians aren't slaves.

They're very highly skilled. Some of them. And the figures *would* make a wonderful impression on H.E."

"I doubt it. His Excellency doesn't care for slave labor."

"You're very superior all of a sudden, aren't you? DY Construction isn't averse to raking in a few slaves when the going gets tough and deadlines loom."

Simon clenched his fists and said nothing. Zhao surveyed him thoughtfully for a moment, then said: "The trouble with you is that you're all fucked up. If you'll excuse the expression. You live in Hong Kong but you don't quite seem to like playing by its rules."

"What rules?"

"Now don't get sarcastic. You've got a split personality—and you know it! You want to be seen as a benefactor but at the same time you need profits as much as the next man."

Simon kept his temper with difficulty. "Shall we stick with the practicalities?" he said. "You want to build a desalination plant. This project's going to be cheap, isn't it?"

Zhao was about to enunciate an enthusiastic yes when he saw the look in Simon's eyes and hesitated.

"Cheap on paper," Simon continued, "so cheap in fact that the executive council will waive the usual penalty clauses, only to find out later, when it's much too late, that the delivery date was always a myth." He smiled. "How am I doing so far?"

Zhao said nothing.

"Which means going into overtime—double, triple time at weekends, at night, of which the labor force will see precisely"— he held up his thumb and forefinger in a circle—"and then mistakes will be made, from excessive speed. The workmanship will become slipshod. So that there will be expensive repair contracts for years to come. Perhaps even after 1997."

"And so?" Zhao was smiling again. "Assume for one moment that there is substance in what you say, which incidentally I dispute. Who'll be around to do those expensive repairs? Ducannon Young? There may not be much else with which the legendary DY empire can occupy its time, not after the Chinese takeover, which you know and I know will be *total*."

"Oh, I agree. I like your scheme very much. Wish I'd thought of it myself, in fact. Let's see the specification, then."

"Come again?"

"The plans you've got in that briefcase, I'll need to see them before I can give you an answer, won't I?"

There was a long pause, during which Robert Zhao never took his eyes off Simon's face. At last he lazily reached across to draw the bound folders from his briefcase and toss them over to the other man with a smile. "I believe the poker expression is . . . 'see you'?"

Simon snatched them up and began to devour them, running his eyes down each page in less than a second. The figures came jumbling together in his mind, but after a while the overall picture was clear enough. Zhao hadn't been bluffing. He had a scheme—a well-reasoned, soundly based, impressively researched, and above all extremely cheap scheme. A scheme that, if it ever came to a tender, would undercut Dunny's proposals by a considerable margin.

Simon looked up from the last folder and stared at Zhao for a long time without speaking. He was immensely angry, but all his rage and frustration remained pent up inside him, making it impossible for the Chinese to delve beneath the neutral expression on his face. Zhao wondered uneasily what Simon was thinking.

He was thinking that all the really important decisions in life made themselves.

"I'll consider your proposition," Simon said at last. "On a scale of one to ten, where do we stand on urgency?"

"Oh . . . say five?"

"Five. Admirable."

Zhao looked at his watch and suddenly seemed less sure of himself. Simon saw it at once. "Am I keeping you?" he asked innocently.

"My dear chap, not at all." Experience had taught Zhao that Krubykov liked him to make his reports on time, but this was too important to be hurried. "I was horrified at how long I've kept you from your wife, that's all."

Simon stood up; Zhao did likewise. "I'll be in touch," said Simon.

He escorted Zhao to the door. The Chinese turned: "No, don't come down. I'll just say good-bye to Jinny."

Simon went back to the window and stood with hands in pockets, looking down at the terrace. He saw Zhao emerge from the house and go across to the recliner, bend down, reach out, almost touch Jinny's arm . . . not quite. Ah, not quite!

Did she like him?

Did she like him as much as he had always liked her?

Simon wheeled around abruptly, pulled his chair up to the desk and reached for the telephone.

"Hello . . . Simon Young speaking. I'm sorry to trouble you on a Saturday evening, Mr. Ng, but I wonder if it would be possible for you to convey a message to a certain mutual friend of ours . . . Mr. Qiu."

9

When Mr. Tang telephoned to arrange a further meeting, Simon decided that this time he would take Jinny down to Singapore with him. They stayed at the Goodwood Park, where they had spent the first night of their honeymoon before embarking on a Pacific tour. Simon telexed ahead to arrange a surprise: they were put in the same room, the first they'd ever shared. Naturally there were flowers—no one attended to detail like the Goodwood Group—but they also found a completely unexpected bottle of Krug champagne with a note attached to its neck by a pink bow. Jinny picked it up and smiled. "Oh darling, you are thoughtful."

"Not I. Not guilty on this occasion, m'lud. Must be the management."

Jinny held the note up to her nose and sniffed. "Chanel-scented management? At the *Goodwood*?" Their eyes met. "I know who this is from."

"Who?" Simon was genuinely puzzled.

"Of course you know."

"I don't."

"You *do*! Think. Who knew we were coming?"

"Qiu. Dicky Morrison of branch HQ."

"And?"

"Ng." Suddenly his eyes lit up. "Oh no. Not—?"

"His sister, the one you told me about. Maudie! Your *lover*!"

"Ouch! Did I make it sound as bad as that?"

"Every bit."

"And I never even took her to the '1819.' "

"Ah, that's your story. Besides, she wouldn't care—she's got staying power, that one." Jinny threw her arms around his chest. "You have another woman lusting after you, beloved. Your lean, muscular, hungry"—she began to stroke him, sliding one graceful hand between his shirt-buttons until she made contact with his nipple—"body."

"Aah . . . too much."

Jinny began to massage the nipple between thumb and forefinger, drawing excitement from the look that had come into his eyes.

"What's got into you?" he mumbled. "I'm not used to this."

"There's nothing so stimulating to us quiet ladies as another woman giving our husbands champagne. Competition." Jinny gave his nipple a pinch and with her free hand undid first one shirt-button then another.

"Must have a shower," said Simon.

"Why?" Her own eyes were wide with feigned innocence. "You'll only have to wash again"—she ran her hands down toward his waist, nimbly unzipping the fly—"all over"—she began to ease the trousers over his hips—"later . . ."

Simon and Jinny dined in the hotel's outdoor restaurant, content to spend a quiet evening with each other before the new day came to remind them that they were now very different from the starstruck honeymooners of twenty years before.

As Simon stirred his coffee he asked his wife, "Have you thought any more about my proposal?"

"Will I marry you—that one?"

He laughed. "You didn't need much time to make up your mind."

"No. So quick. You were so pushy, even then."

"Was I really?"

"Yes. You had no respect for my situation in those days. A clerk in China's International Travel Agency had to be careful in her dealings with foreigners. You were always embarrassing me, you and you pushy ways."

"Did I cause trouble?"

"You know you did, so you needn't look so innocent. 'Why does that foreigner always come in?' the boss used to ask me. 'Surely no one travels in China that much. And why doesn't he send his secretary for the tickets, instead of collecting them himself?' " One of her beautiful hands stole across the table to squeeze his own, as reassurance that she was only teasing.

"Yet when we wanted to get married, they said yes quickly enough."

"Glad to get rid of me, I expect."

"Perhaps."

She looked into her husband's eyes and frowned. "Are you thinking that they wanted me to spy for them, that they were glad to see us fall in love? You're wrong. They were suspicious. For a time there was even talk of sending me back to Sichuan."

"I've never thought that you were meant to spy on me."

She shrugged. "Perhaps that's what they really wanted all along. We'll see."

Simon smiled uncertainly and for a while continued to stir his coffee in silence. "Actually, that's not the proposal I had in mind," he said at last. "I was thinking of your family: bringing out Mingchao and Kaihui."

"I see. Yes, I've considered that proposal."

"And?"

Jinny shook her head and looked down at the table. "I don't know. I sense it's dangerous. I can't see any further than that."

"In what way, dangerous?"

She looked up at him, impatient at what she regarded as a willful refusal to see. "Making terms with . . . with Qiu, that's always dangerous."

"He's your brother."

"That's how I know."

"What harm can it do to ask?" When she shrugged but did not reply he went on, "He's not an ogre. It's been a long time since you last saw him, remember. I know he can be prickly, but he's reasonable."

"Oh, you always see everyone as reasonable. And they're not." She crossed her arms and began to rub her shoulders. "Not always."

"Why not let me cope with that? All I need is a word from you. Just something to tell me you approve. Of course, if you don't approve . . ."

"I neither approve nor disapprove. Naturally I'd like to see my family reunited, in Hong Kong. I miss them. I've always missed them, every day of my life. And I worry about them, too—why do you think I send them money every year? But I haven't seen youngest brother and younger sister for so long. Not since . . ."

"Since?"

"You know. When they let me go. Then."

"Does it make a difference?"

"Yes. They're Chinese." Jinny's voice was flat. "The Beijing government watches, all the time. I think perhaps it's better just to leave things as they are. Don't wake a sleeping dragon. I think this because I too am Chinese. Sometimes you forget that."

"You make it very easy to overlook, sometimes."

"Is that a compliment, or a reproach?"

"It's a comment. I don't see what being Chinese has to do with this. All I have to know is whether you want me to try and negotiate the release of Mingchao, Kaihui and any other members of your family who survived the Cultural Revolution."

"That's just it." Her voice was subdued. "The word you used just then. 'Survived.' They suffered. I know they suffered. Not Qianwei, of course—I thought he was dead, anyway—but the others. And the reason why they suffered . . . oh yes, don't try to deny it, it was one reason . . . was that I'd been released. I got out. I became a capitalist running hyena. I missed the, what do you call it? The . . . main event. But I didn't just 'survive,' oh no. I married one of the wealthiest men in Hong Kong and lived happily ever after."

"Jinny—"

"Sorry. Sorry. But don't tell me it's got nothing to do with being Chinese. Just . . . *don't tell me!*"

She had scarcely raised her voice; none of the other diners would have realized that the Youngs were facing a crisis.

"You want me to decide," Simon said, after a pause. "You want me to take the decision for you, don't you?"

"I don't know."

"Remember the old Chinese saying: 'Of the thirty-six ways of dealing with any problem, running away is best'? Is that what you're doing?"

"And you say this has nothing to do with my being Chinese!" She knew a moment of resentment. "You're more Chinese than I am, sometimes. You know all these famous sayings; I don't."

"But still, you want me to decide for you?"

"I don't *know!*"

"If you ask me to decide, I'll try to bargain with Qiu for their release. Unless you actually forbid it."

"Oh, Simon . . ." She hung her head. "You're so kind. So patient. I know I'm behaving badly, that this is no way to repay you for all you've done. Most men would have beaten me for the lies I told about my past."

"I'm not the beating type. And there weren't any lies, not so much lies as . . ."

"As what?"

"Silence. Not speaking when you might have confided in me." He managed a smile. "That's all."

For a long time she said nothing. How hard it was to tell the truth! And the hardest thing of all was to make a clean breast to the one you loved best, because then you put everything on the line and had most to lose. It wasn't as if you gambled exclusively with your own happiness, either, although that would have been irresponsible enough. No—you risked your beloved's peace of mind as well.

When at last Jinny spoke again it was only to ask, "What's the timetable for tomorrow?"

"I have to meet Qiu . . . your brother, at ten o'clock. Tang has asked me to see him at noon. He'll have his answer ready by then, so I've got to have mine. In the afternoon, branch HQ for a high-profile meeting with Dicky, to give myself an excuse for being here. Dinner with the local board at the World Trade Centre.'

"How much of that involves me?"

"I'd like you to come with me to see Qiu. Moral support."

She lifted her chin, but submitted.

"Then, if you could perhaps have dinner with all of us. Is that asking too much?"

"Of course not. I have to visit the *Straits Times* sometime tomorrow; I daresay the afternoon will be all right."

"Oh?"

"They want to commission an article on the Red Cross work for Vietnam refugees in Hong Kong and I've said I'd write it."

"That's very flattering."

"Someone has to do it. We've been wanting to extend the work to Singapore for years now, they're so racially integrated here, and the chance of getting an article published is too good to miss. I meant to palm it off on Dr. Lim, but he's too clever to fall for that."

"I'm very pleased."

"Thank you. If I have any time left over, I'll try to track down some *limianhua* for you."

"Wonderful."

She tossed her napkin onto the table. "And now, if you'll excuse me, darling, I think I really ought to have an early night . . . no, please don't feel obliged to come." He half-rose to his feet but she stopped him, laying one hand on his shoulder. "Honestly, I have a headache—a real one. I think I might find it easier to sleep if there was no one else in the room for a bit." She gave him a tight smile. "Go for a mooch, why don't you? I do so love that word *mooch*—it sounds so much more exotic than going for a walk." For a second a little of the former gaiety showed through; then it faded and Simon was left to stare thoughtfully after his wife's departing back.

The next day Simon encouraged Jinny to walk with him from the Goodwood, past the Far Eastern shopping complex and the Dynasty Hotel, to the boundary of the Central Business District. He was hoping to pick up a cab whose driver had already purchased his city license for the day. This represented a matrimonial compromise. Simon did not feel able to ask Jinny to travel by bus, nor did he intend to lay out four Singapore dollars unnecessarily. As they were preparing to bundle themselves into a taxi they heard a squeal of brakes behind them.

"*Si*-mon! Hi-ee!"

A silver Mercedes had pulled into the curb, its front bumper just touching the cab's rear fender. The sunlight on the windscreen prevented Simon from seeing the driver's face, but the voice and the multibangled wrist frantically waving at him through the far window were more than enough to identify Maudie. Jinny, already halfway into the taxi, at once swung her feet back onto the pavement.

"We must thank her for the champagne, darling. And I am so dying to meet your hungry lover . . ."

But it was not to be. A blue-clad Malay policeman strode across Orchard Road, one hand unbuttoning the top pocket of the shirt where he kept his notebook. Maudie saw him. As Simon and Jinny came level with the Mercedes she raised her hands to her cheeks in a gesture of mock terror, looking between the looming policeman and the Youngs with ever increasing speed.

"They know me," she hissed. "They *all* know me—that's the trouble. See you."

Her hands dropped; next second the Mercedes lurched back from the cab and shot out into the main thoroughfare, narrowly missing the outraged policeman. He blew his whistle and waved, but Maudie had gone.

"You know that lady, sah?"

Simon said nothing for a moment. He stood looking after the Mercedes, puzzled to know why Maudie needed to have a two-way radio on the front seat of her car. He couldn't be sure, but it seemed to him that as she'd pulled into the mainstream of traffic she had raised the transmitter to her mouth.

"Sah?"

Simon put his reflections aside and shook his head at the policeman. "Younger sister, you understand," he said gravely.

"What was that all about?" Jinny asked as they finally settled themselves into a cab. "Younger sister, I mean?"

"Something Ng said. It's kind of hard to imagine her as anyone's elder sister, isn't it?"

"It was hard to imagine her at all, from your description. I think I'm starting to get the picture now, however."

The car turned right at Singapore Airlines' Orchard Road office and a few minutes later was pulling up outside the mansion where Simon had first met the bankers from Soviet Communal. Mr. Ng himself was waiting to receive them. He addressed Jinny in Cantonese.

"Welcome, welcome, Mrs. Young. So pleased you were able to come."

"The pleasure is all on my side, Mr. Ng. Wonderful place you have here."

"You're too kind. Come this way, please—Mr. Qiu is waiting inside."

On the way through to the living room Simon gently took Ng's arm. "Are we still secure?"

"I believe so. It is hard to keep secrets these days, but—I believe so."

Everything looked just the same as on Simon's first visit. Qiu was seated at the dining room table. When the Youngs entered, he stood up and went forward to shake Simon's hand, curtly addressing a few words in Hokkien dialect to Jinny. Her face at once molded itself into an expression of polite boredom.

"So, Mr. Simon Young," Qiu said, resuming his seat. "Have you decided?"

Simon waited until Ng had sat down before pulling out chairs for Jinny and himself. "I am very pleased to see you again, Qiu Qianwei," he said deliberately, using Mandarin. "Are you well-not-well?"

"Well." Qiu gnawed his lip. "And are you?"

"We are. We *both* are. Have you eaten this morning?"

Qiu made an almighty effort. "I have. Have you and Elder Sister eaten?" He looked across the table at Jinny, a hint of amusement in his eyes. Jinny's lips twitched, but she said nothing. Simon saw the exchange and felt frustrated by his inability to interpret it.

"We have eaten. We are making you travel a lot. You must be very tired, with so much flying. I hope you are well rested."

"I am." Again that humorous, almost conspiratorial glance in Jinny's direction. "But you and Elder Sister must also be tired after your journey."

"The hotel is very comfortable, thank you. We slept well." Simon held his gaze a moment longer. "Perhaps it would be convenient to proceed to business now. If you are not too tired."

"Only if you are quite ready." This time, the look he directed toward Jinny was sullen. "Does Elder Sister wish to rest upstairs?"

Jinny met his look with an almost imperceptible shake of the head. This nettled Simon. She was unintentionally weakening his authority in a way too subtle to be challenged. "Elder Sister will remain here, thank you," he said firmly.

"If you insist."

"Then in answer to your question: yes, I have decided that I am prepared to initial heads of agreement with SCB, on the assumption that an offer will definitely be forthcoming. I say that, because a few days ago I received a visit from Zhao Yi Qiang, one of your front men in Hong Kong."

"And so?"

"It will save time if we forgo the tactical maneuvers. I have made inquiries. I am satisfied that Zhao has been approached by an independent consortium consisting of more of your Hong Kong front men, with alternative proposals for the construction of this desalination plant. You have placed me under pressure, Qiu Qianwei. Gentle pressure—but I shall not forget. I understand the message, however: There is more than one entrepreneur in Hong Kong."

Qiu gave a little squirm of embarrassment. He still never quite knew how best to deal with Simon. "I have no knowledge of these matters, Mr. Young," he said.

"I think you do. That, however, is not important. I have already told you that I intend to proceed, but only to the stage of heads of agreement for the moment. In other words, I still reserve the right to withdraw."

"And you require an inducement not to withdraw—is that it?"

Simon began to speak but Qiu held up a hand, relieved at last to find himself in an area where he had been properly briefed. "We have thought about this. We understand very clearly that there is not one contract here, but two. You will make an agreement with the bank. But you also have to make an agreement with us first. So we come prepared to deal. We have already told you of our plans for promoting Ducannon Young to front-rank status after 1997. Those plans must—will—be reduced to writing; and it will be done long before the lawyers have finalized their drafts."

"You are prepared to give me that in writing?" Simon was incredulous.

"Of course, as long as you undertake to keep it confidential. And there is more."

Simon looked at Jinny. "More?"

"The People's Republic will also guarantee your servants, the Luk family, permanent Hong Kong residence with freedom to travel abroad at will, together with a full amnesty for their past crimes. But you must stand security for their future good conduct. Do you agree to this?"

Simon shot a questioning glance at Jinny, who nodded. "We agree," he said. "But there is more on our side, too."

"I don't understand." A frown distorted Qiu's face. "We are being generous with you, Mr. and Mrs. Young. Please do not provoke us needlessly."

"Nevertheless, I have a term. One more term."

Qiu darted a furious look in Jinny's direction and rattled off half a dozen words in Hokkien to her before Simon stopped him. "Speak a language we all can understand." His voice was rough. "Don't think you can split us. There are two sides to this negotiation, not three. There never will be three. Do you understand?"

Qiu turned back to face him. His smile was more than usually unpleasant. "Do *you* understand, Mr. Young?"

The question floored Simon. He knew that there was a tacit point of reference between the two Chinese siblings but he couldn't grasp it. And it maddened him. When Jinny lowered her head and stared at the table he wanted to shake her by the shoulders, forcing her to side with him openly no matter what the cost . . . but then the anger passed and Qiu's face had once more become a mask.

"Please state your term," he said.

"I think you know what it is."

"I think so too, but I would wish to hear it from your own lips."

"Jinny's sister, Kaihui—"

"*My* sister; not only hers."

"And your brother, Mingchao."

"What of them?"

"They must be free to decide whether they continue to live in the PRC or go outside. That is all."

Qiu's right leg had begun to jiggle up and down, causing the table to vibrate. For a long time he said nothing. When at last he did speak his voice was speculative, as if he had not quite foreseen the whole of Simon's term after all.

"What are they to you, Mr. Young?"

"They are my wife's relations."

"So? You have never met them. Why should you care whether they live or die? If they come out, they will become a financial burden on you, is that not so?"

Simon quelled his rising anger. "A burden which I can afford to shoulder."

Qiu appeared not to have heard. "She has asked this, I suppose."

This was too much for Jinny. Anger conquered her fear of Qiu. "You bastard!" she spat. Her face had flushed dark brown. "If you think—"

"Shut up," said Qiu.

Simon jumped out of his chair. "How *dare* you tell my wife to shut up in front of my face! Apologize. First to her, then to me!"

"No, Simon—" Jinny rose and grabbed her husband by the arm, terrified by the consequences of her momentary lapse. "Leave it!"

For a second fear showed in Qiu's eyes and was gone, to be replaced by a look of blank astonishment. "She's my sister!"

Simon shook off Jinny's arm. "She's my *wife! Apologize, damn you!*"

Qiu shrank back in his chair. To Jinny, the physical contrast between the two men was remarkable: Simon, seemingly tall enough to touch the ceiling and vibrant with rage; Qiu small and wizened and sulky. "I am sorry," the Chinese said at last.

"To *her!*"

Qiu swiveled until he was facing Jinny. "I apologize, Elder Sister. Please forgive me."

Jinny nodded in silence. "Nothing to forgive," she said mechanically. She would never forget; but that was not important. Her husband was vulnerable. He had no conception of the people he was dealing with, no idea of the danger in which he stood. Her duty was to protect him, subjugating herself to that one vital need.

Simon sank back into his seat very slowly. The process reminded Qiu of a long cobra recoiling itself after a fatal strike, and inwardly he trembled.

"Your term," he said at last, "must be considered in Beijing. I will report this." His eyes strayed to Jinny with a hint of their earlier malevolence. "All of it."

"Good. I want an answer in plenty of time before the lawyers produce their engrossments for signature. Do you understand that?"

"Yes. But I must repeat—do *you* understand?"

For an instant Simon was tempted to pursue the question, put thus oddly for the second time, but something held him back. To probe would put him at a disadvantage, yes, but there was more to it—by asking, he would place himself in jeopardy of being told the unwelcome answer, the wrong reply. Qiu was like a dragon. The fire reposing deep in his throat might merely be a dull spark, but perhaps it really was capable of bursting forth into flame. No one would poke the dragon with a stick just so as to find out that truth! "Who *are* you?" Simon wanted to ask; but it was Qiu who spoke.

"When is Tang coming?"

"The appointment's for noon."

"Then I must complete my arrangements. I shall be here, upstairs. Be very sure to wait for me after the meeting is over, please."

"I will wait."

"Elder Sister, what are you going to do now?"

"I will go now."

Simon turned to Mr. Ng, who had been watching the scene with total impassivity. "Mr. Ng, would it be possible for me to call a cab for my wife?"

"Surely, surely. Help yourself. You should find a list of numbers by the phone, among them taxi numbers."

Simon arranged for a radio-cab to collect his wife and waited with her on the front step until it came. As it reached the road he was already turning away when he thought he saw a silver Mercedes flash past the house, its driver's right arm casually draped along the far window ledge. Something glittered in the sun; it might have been a bangle. Or a radio aerial. Or not. By the time Simon had focused on the road the Mercedes had gone and Jinny's cab was slowly turning after it. He knew a moment of disquiet; and when he went back inside the house his face was thoughtful. There was no sign of Qiu.

"You want me to stay, hah?" Ng's face gave nothing away but Simon sensed that he would like to be about other, less emotionally charged business. The Englishman shook his head. "It is not necessary," he said. "Please don't think I am driving you out of your own premises, Mr. Ng. We have abused your hospitality enough."

"No abuse, please. But I think you can manage without me from now on. Mr. Qiu has a set of keys, he can lock up. Glad to have been of service. Any time, just ask again."

"Thank you. Oh, Mr. Ng . . . ?"

"Yes?"

"Have you seen Maudie this morning?"

"No. May I give her a message from you?"

"It's not important."

Simon hesitated an instant before deciding to commit himself. He liked Ng. "I am grateful to you for arranging my introduction to Soviet Communal Bank; I owe you a favor," he said quietly, watching how the man's face lit up at the loaded term. In Oriental business philosophy the word *favor* was regarded as *gui*, costly: you used it at your peril. Ng inclined his head, letting Simon see the appreciation in his eyes. "Thank you, thank you. I will not forget you, Mr. Young." Nor will I forget how you spoke of favors, he was saying.

Once Ng had left the house, time passed slowly. Simon wandered about the cluttered room, occasionally pausing to study a framed photograph or examine an ornament. He was starting to find Qiu oppressive, and he felt he was falling into the age-old trap of assuming too much, of deluding himself that he knew and understood the Chinese mentality. "Always remember that they're the enemy," Tom Young had remarked in one of his more savage moods. "Them and us, us and them. Kipling knew." "How can the chairman of the Corporation believe that?" Simon had remonstrated; but his father only laughed: "You can't be chairman and not know it!"

Did he trust Qiu? No, not entirely; perhaps not at all. Could the Chinese deliver what he promised about Ducannon Young's favored trading position after 1997? How could he be so sure that the mortgage over Simon's Founders Shares would be unenforceable? As Simon walked up and down the room he shook his head. But it was too late to think of withdrawing, and Qiu's participation was essential to the scheme's success. There was no choice, no alternative.

At last he heard the sound of a car pulling up outside and he went to the front door to greet Tang. The banker came quickly up the steps, hand outstretched. He was alone.

"Good to see you again, Mr. Young."

"It's mutual, Mr. Tang. Will Mr. Goh and Mr. Borisenko be joining us?"

"No." Tang sat down at the dining room table and opened his briefcase. "I am starting to worry very much about security. If Goh leaves the bank with me, it invites comment. We risked it once, but once is enough."

He took out a tissue, using it to dab the sweat from his forehead before wiping his hands. He was very tense. "I have some good news for you," he said. "Your loan has been approved in principle."

For all his self-control, despite all his inner doubts, Simon could not suppress a small puff of breath. Tang heard it and smiled. "Yes. I will let you into a little secret. For us, this is something of a record. Lot of money, hah?"

"Yes. A lot."

"But also, very good business for SCB." Tang blinked seriously through his thick spectacles. "I do not see any point in trying to conceal that. We are a comparatively new company. This is a major breakthrough for us." His gaze dropped to the briefcase and for a moment he seemed embarrassed. Simon felt a twinge of sympathy. Tang did not work for the KGB; he was merely a conscientious, hard-working Singaporean banker who had pulled off a major financial coup.

"A breakthrough for Ducannon Young also," Simon murmured. "I would like you to know that we see it in identical terms. May this be the first step of a thousand-mile journey together."

Tang smiled up at him with real gratitude. "Thank you."

"Do you have anything for me to look at?"

"Yes, we have prepared some draft heads of agreement, in the usual way. The size of the loan does not involve a change in our standard procedures, although I must tell you that these are the only copies in existence. We are leaving nothing to chance." He extracted another tissue and again wiped his forehead. "The thought of any of this coming out terrifies me."

"I'm pleased to hear that. It makes me afraid as well."

"Perhaps we could start by looking at the draft?"

Simon pulled a chair up to the table and quickly skimmed through the documents. "This seems to represent what we agreed," he said at last. "I'm delighted to see how you've been able to meet me on the third-year option with regard to deposits."

"We thought the compromise a reasonable one."

"It is. But I'm still at a loss to know why you want to take a charge over any Founders Shares to which I may become entitled in the future. I would not like you to proceed under a misapprehension. There is not the slightest reason to suppose that I shall ever own any more of those shares than I do now."

"Mr. Young, that form of words is the bank's standard drafting in these cases. I accept what you say, of course."

"Very well, then. As to the detail—you understand, naturally, that my lawyers may have other ideas."

"Yes. This is an agreement in principle only. There is a specific provision to the effect that the document is not to be legally binding on either side until formal exchange."

"Ah yes, I see."

"How long do you need for examination of these documents before signature? I must tell you that we on the bank's side are now very pushed for time." He hesitated. "Very pushed indeed."

Simon looked him in the eye. "If you can give me half an hour, and assuming no pitfalls, I'll sign now."

Tang sat up in his chair. "*Now?*"

"Mr. Tang . . . the man who holds the position of managing director of Ducannon Young is never hesitant by nature. We both know what we agreed and what we didn't agree. We both know the English language equally well. Just let me read this through, will you?"

Tang inclined his head, appreciative of the graceful compliment. Simon sat back from the table, laid the documents in his lap, where the banker would not be able to read any notes he made, and began to read. The drafting was clear and concise. Soviet Communal Bank had gone a long way to accommodate him. As soon as he'd finished he turned back to the first page and started to annotate the text, taking his time.

"Well, Mr. Tang," he said at last, "it seems it remains only to dot the i's and cross the t's. The name of the borrowing company, which we must now fill in, is Mandarin Salt Limited. Mandarin Salt was incorporated in Hong Kong last week, with a share capital of one thousand Hong Kong dollars issued and fully paid up for cash. Its registration is perfectly in order. It is a wholly owned subsidiary whose ultimate owner is a Liechtenstein *anstalt*. I hope that need cause no problems."

"None. Just as long as we have adequate collateral, as agreed."

"Of course. For your information only, the *anstalt*'s deed is in the possession of the trustees of a family settlement to which I am the sole investment adviser. The trustees are resident and domiciled in Grand Cayman."

"I understand."

"Now. I must ask you to warrant formally to me that you have the bank's authority to initial these heads of agreement between us."

"I do so warrant."

"For my part, I also warrant that I have authority on behalf of Mandarin Salt to proceed." Simon reached into his breast pocket and took out a large Mont Blanc fountain pen. Tang watched him curiously.

"Big pen, Mr. Young."

"It is a big contract. But I always use this pen to sign business agreements. It has been lucky for me."

"Your luck continues, I think." Tang hesitated. "Is it really lucky?"

"Oh yes."

"Then . . . may I please borrow it?"

Simon handed it over with a smile. "Do." Tang took it from him and rapidly initialed each set of documents. Then he stood up and silently offered Simon his hand.

The Englishman watched from the veranda until Tang's car had disappeared, then he returned to the house. He found that Qiu Qianwei had come downstairs and was standing with his palms on the table, looking at the papers spread out in front of him. As Simon swept them up and shuffled them together he heard Qiu mutter something and eyed him warily. "What?"

Qiu looked up with his by-now familiar smile. "Got you," he repeated.

10

Although Simon Young was a seasoned businessman, he could never quite suppress the nervousness that overcame him whenever he visited Ducannon Young's official bankers. He tended to take financial matters in his stride—except when it came to dealing with the Pacific & Cantonese Banking Corporation and its chairman, his own father.

The directors' floor of the Corporation's Victorian headquarters building in Des Voeux Road was not designed to have a steadying effect on the nerves. Visitors were escorted by two white-uniformed security officers (known, irrespective of age or status, as "boys") down the center of a long, oak-paneled corridor with heavy-framed portraits of luminaries long since dead adorning its high walls. The corridor's narrow strip of red carpet, which in the course of the average day bore countless well-shod feet, was replaced every six months whether it needed renewing or not. A heavy, never-fading smell of wax furniture polish suffused the upper part of the building. Each of the doors leading off this main passage bore a brass plate on which was etched in Gothic script the name of the director who sat behind it. If a member of the board resigned, the boys removed his plate before he had a chance to clear his desk, while no newly appointed director of the Corporation could enter the building without finding his name already perpetrated in brass on the door of his office. It was a convention. The Corporation resembled the British Constitution in that much of its routine was dictated by unwritten understandings, which had little need to rely on the statutes for their iron authority.

At the far end of the corridor the red carpet ended on the threshold of the Corporation's boardroom, where Tom Young habitually worked. As Simon approached the huge double doors he found himself wondering about Qiu Qianwei's last words in Singapore. Who, exactly, had Qiu "got"—SCB, or Ducannon Young? Or did he mean Simon himself?

Half an hour from now, he would know. For the immediate present, however, the important thing was to concentrate on giving his father one last chance to avoid delivering Ducannon Young into the clutches of Soviet bankers. And somehow he had to do it without letting Tom Young divine what was in the wind.

The Corporation's senior boy rapped three times on the left-hand door and flung it open.

"The managing director of Ducannon Young!" he cried. It was another convention that only kings and princes came to the Corporation's boardroom; ergo, everyone who was admitted must be treated as such, irrespective of his true origins.

"Morning, father."

Tom Young did not look up. He was seated at one of the marvels of the colony: a round table, manufactured to the Corporation's order in the year of Queen Victoria's jubilee. There was only one other like it, in the Naval & Military Club, Piccadilly. The table comprised a number of oak sections that could be made to expand or contract, depending on how many of the segments were employed. At its smallest, with only four of the sections in use, the round table could accommodate half a dozen people dining together in comfortable intimacy; at full stretch, however, it nearly filled the boardroom so that, with guests ranged along its inner, hollow ring as well as on the perimeter, it could seat a hundred.

Invitations to a Corporation banquet, of which there were three a year, inspired very nearly the same kind of response as royal commands. People went for the food, which was stupendous, but also to see the legendary table. Today it occupied about a third of the available space. Tom Young sat inside the ring. Papers and files were spread out at nicely spaced intervals along the table's glasslike surface. Tom's chair was on casters, so that as he proceeded through the day's business all he needed to do was edge his way around the inner ring until he had completed his tasks. On an average day he circled the inner ring one and a half times. Occasionally, however, he indulged in what his staff called "three-circuit days"—intolerable workshifts extending far into the night, during which the chairman of the Corporation appeared to lose himself in a frenzy of application. Three-circuit days were dreaded by everyone except Tom Young; mercifully, they were rare.

At the far end of the room stood a much smaller, square table laid out in readiness for a game of Mah-jongg—Tom Young's one weakness, his Achilles heel. By way of contrast to three-circuit days, it was not unknown for him to abandon work halfway through the afternoon and summon three of the Corporation's boys to play for whatever stakes they would. Some people affected to see in this an idiosyncratic departure from Tom Young's deep-rooted dislike of the Chinese race, evidence that he had human qualities after all. They were wrong. He played Mah-jongg with the boys because he despised them and he liked beating even those he despised. If a boy chose to lose a month's salary to the chairman at one of these sessions, that was no concern of Tom's; such behavior merely reinforced his belief in the essential worthlessness of the Chinese. It would never have occurred to him to forgive the debt.

A number of chairs were ranged against the wall opposite the window overlooking the harbor; Simon pulled one of them from the rank and went to sit on the outside edge of the table, opposite his father.

"I gather this is business," Tom Young said.

"Yes, please."

"I'm listening."

"You're not."

"Just because I'm capable of doing several things at once and you aren't, that doesn't give you the right to contradict me."

"Would it be possible, just for once, for us to have a reasonable business conversation?"

"Why break the habit of a lifetime?" Tom smiled bleakly.

"Something special, is it?" But he did push the current file away and replace the top of his fountain pen. "Forster's not with you?" he observed.

"As you see, I came alone."

"But this is a Ducannon Young matter?"

"Yes."

"Ah. So it's one of your private projects. You want money, of course, that goes without saying. Not desalination, I hope?"

"Yes."

Tom unscrewed the top of his pen once more and pulled the discarded file toward him. "Sorry."

Simon counted slowly up to five and began again. "I promise you, this is the last conversation we'll have on the subject, father."

"If I may correct you . . . the last conversation we had on the subject *was* the last."

Simon chose to ignore his father's rudeness and proceed with methodical patience. "You know the project inside out, just as I do. You've studied it—there was a time when you studied everything I put in front of you."

"That all ended with Ko Shan."

"Oh, for heaven's sake, father! Do we have to dredge that up every time we meet on business?"

"It's a useful reminder of the differences between us. I was right, you'll recall."

"You were right about the downward market trend. As for the Ko Shan project itself, you were as hopelessly wrong as it's possible to be."

"That's just your opinion, isn't it? And I can see it still rankles, I don't have to ask about *that*!"

"I refuse to be drawn into this nonsense again. You only bring it up because you feel guilty and you can't leave it alone."

Tom Young laughed, putting all the offense he could muster into the sound.

"You've studied the proposals," Simon repeated. "I don't have to brief you."

"No." Tom Young looked up from the file. "I know the score. It's you who's ignorant."

"I want to borrow one hundred million pounds sterling in order to go ahead. All I need is the money. And I need it quickly, before the whole thing goes off the boil." Before Tang gets his hands on my Founders Shares, he added savagely to himself.

"What collateral can you offer me?"

"Fixed and floating charges over all DY assets."

"I already have that."

"Not over all the undertakings."

"Over most. There certainly isn't anything like enough surplus to cover a loan in the sum you mention. And you know I don't do favors for family. Family, in my experience, is just as capable of losing money hand over fist as Mr. Won Ton Soup."

"My Founders Shares, then."

Tom laughed. "Christ, that's funny. The best shares in the world, the most valuable things you own or are ever likely to, shares for which you didn't turn a shovelful of earth in your life . . . and you're actually prepared to toss them overboard for a tankful of seawater. That's rich. Wait till I tell them that down at the club. No, on second thought, I don't want them to know I've got a moron for a son."

Simon swallowed bile and forced himself to be patient. "I still don't understand your objections."

"Good God, I've spelled them out for you often enough." Tom laid down his pen and said nothing for a while. The silence was eventually broken by the ponderous tolling of a large grandfather clock beside the double doors as it struck the hour of eleven. Tom glanced up at the clock, waiting for the chimes to cease before he spoke again.

"Sometimes," he said at last, "a good customer of the Corporation comes to me with a scatterbrain scheme and asks for money. I know he's going to lose whatever I lend him but I don't try to persuade him of that; instead, I take a look at the security on offer. If it's good security, I lend. If it's duff, I don't. Conversely, it does just occasionally happen that a good customer comes along with no security worth the name, but a really solid, twenty-two-carat project up his sleeve, and then again, I lend. You've got the worst of both worlds, Simon—no security and a worthless scheme."

"I've got collateral but you won't look at it."

"It comes to the same thing, doesn't it? When someone goes down to the pawnbroker's to hock his last piece of jewelry, the trinket in his hand doesn't have a value in any objective sense; it's worth exactly whatever the man behind the counter reckons it at. I won't let you throw away your Founders Shares on a useless scheme. I know I'm boring you, Simon, but I'll say it anyway: one day you'll be grateful. Or my grandchildren will."

"Suppose you're right, and the plant flops. You'll get the shares. What's wrong with that for a deal?"

"*I* won't get them! The Corporation will. It'll have to sell them, sell outside the family. Don't be a bloody fool."

"The scheme is sound. It represents an investment in DY's future here—insurance, if you like. It'll take a little time to bear fruit, that's all."

"It is *not* all!" Tom pushed his chair back from the table and stretched out his arms along its inner edge. "We've had this conversation before, over Ko Shan and a dozen things since. My personal view is that Hong Kong's finished." His face turned purple. "But you breathe one word of what I've just said outside this room and I'll smash you, God help me I will."

"Do you think I'm insane?" In spite of his resolve, Simon felt himself growing heated. It was intolerable to be back in short trousers again, listening to his father rant and rave. "You're so selfish, so self-centered, you don't even know what you're saying anymore. If the Corporation packed up here you wouldn't just ruin me, you'd ruin tens of thousands of people. Ordinary, hardworking people who've managed to save enough money to buy a few shares; people looking to the Corporation to show the way, inspire confidence in Hong Kong. No, I won't say anything, I'm not in the mood for suicide. Why, even a rumor of what you've just said would knock DY back twenty points across the world. And the Hong Kong & Shanghai Bank, and Hong Kong Land . . . where would they all be if you left?"

Tom's face twisted in a smile. "What a prig you sound. You know the answer to your question perfectly well—they'd go down the chute and end up where most of them belonged years ago."

"Don't give me crap like that. I'm an adult, capable of forming my own assessments."

Tom's face darkened. "I'm not so sure," he said. "Only a child would come up with a damn fool scheme to build a quite unnecessary desalination plant in Hong Kong twelve years before takeover."

"I've got Chinese cooperation."

"Oh, have you now?" Tom's sneer filled his son with rage, but he managed to hold himself in check. "And what exactly do you think *that* will be worth when the People's Liberation Army marches in?"

Simon was silent. "Got you," he heard a voice say somewhere inside his head. Got you.

"No, Simon . . . I've told you before—Singapore's the coming place. We have to talk about this sometime; now's as good a time as any. You should consider moving out while you still have the chance. I've been meaning to mention this to you. I want to bring you in on our plans, here at the Corporation . . ."

"You're bluffing. You'll never take the Corporation to Singapore, or anywhere else. You're locked in. Face it, father, there's no running before this storm, not for the famous Corporation."

Tom smiled. Simon thought he knew all his father's many moods but that smile chilled him. The old man had a secret to confide. Suddenly Simon knew what it was. He knew with the most perfect conviction that the Corporation was going to leave Hong Kong and his stomach heaved.

"I'm not bluffing," Tom said. "I'm one-hundred-percent serious. I've got a self-imposed deadline to meet. In 1988 I'll be sixty-five, I want to be in a position to make the move as soon as possible."

"Your last act," sneered Simon. "The one they'll all remember you by. Christ, what a monument!"

"Last act?"

"Before you retire."

"*If* I retire."

"You can't avoid it. Under the articles of association—"

"They can be changed."

"What? By act of Parliament? Don't be so ridiculous."

"Haven't you heard? The board of the Bank of China have asked the Politburo to sound out the British government as to the possibility of my staying on." Tom's voice was resonant with pride. Simon felt numb. "Nothing further to say?"

The son could not reply at once. His guts churned violently again. The Corporation was leaving Hong Kong . . .

"I suppose it hasn't occurred to you," he said at last, "that the only reason they're asking you to stay on as chairman is because they assume the Corporation'll be staying on here as well?"

"Of course." Tom's face betrayed signs of impatience. "Don't be ridiculous; I fully intend to postpone the move to Singapore until after my term of office has been extended."

"In other words, you're going to betray them."

Tom merely laughed.

"You won't lend to me?"

"I won't lend long-term to you or to anyone else who hasn't got the sense to see where this place is going. And don't tell me what I can and can't do. That's always been your weakness—you like to preach. Preachers are all very well, as long as they don't suffer from double standards."

"Don't talk rubbish."

"*I'm* not talking rubbish, it's you! All you care about is looking good, PR, call it whatever you damn well like. Perhaps you can afford to be priggish, strike attitudes, I don't know. What I do know is that I've got profits to make, shareholders to worry about."

Simon bit back harsh words and looked down at his hands. They were trembling slightly. He had wanted to avoid this, would have done almost anything to prevent it, but now he knew he had no choice. The Corporation was planning to abandon Hong Kong. His father, the old man, had gone over to the real enemies—not the Chinese, not the Orient, but cynicism and despair. And he, Simon, must now make contingency plans to deal with the crisis.

He raised his eyes and looked at the face across the table, willing his father to believe the first deliberate lie he'd ever told him. "I'm going to call an extraordinary general meeting of the holding company," he said flatly. "I want the shareholders' authority to investigate alternative sources of finance."

"Do it." Tom's voice was raised in anger now. "You just do that! If I won't lend to you, nobody will. *Nobody!*" His voice fell to a whisper. "If a father doesn't trust his son to see sense . . . who will, eh? *Who will?*"

Simon stood up and made for the door. Even before he reached it his father had already turned his attention back to the file in front of him. "By the way," he said, without looking up. "I can block you in the holding company."

Simon paused with his hand on the door handle. It felt ice-cold to his touch. "What?"

"I don't like traitors."

Simon released the handle.

"Traitors within the gates. So I've been taking precautions. I have share-voting agreements, tying up more than half the participating capital. I think you'll find those deals will stick."

Simon turned around very slowly, keeping his face impassive. "Traitors," he said quietly. "That's your policy on traitors, is it, father?"

"It is."

"Then tell me . . . what is your policy on rats, father, rats who desert the ship when it's not yet sinking, because they're greedy and ruthless and scared . . . what is company policy on liars, who tell the Chinese government one thing while planning to do the opposite . . . what's your policy on *cowards*, father? On people whose only concern is to get the money out if they have to blow up the foundations of Hong Kong to do it?"

"You talk to me like that and I'll—"

"You'll *what*? Ruin me, is that what you were going to say? But you'll ruin me anyway, won't you?—today, tomorrow, sometime. In revenge for my being right over the Ko Shan project, or for being successful, or for marrying a Chinese, or any excuse will do."

"Be quiet!"

"And all the others you hate so much: you'll bring them down because you're so afraid of losing half a cent to the Reds, so desperate that you'll stop at nothing to get out of Hong Kong, isn't that right? Well I'm staying. So is Ducannon Young."

"Get out of this room." Tom Young's voice was quiet and matter-of-fact. "I never want to see you here again."

Simon slowly shook his head. "You never want to see anything. It was the same when mother was alive. You never saw her. Then she died. Then, too late, you saw. Always the bloody same. Uncle David, locked up in a Manila hospital ward, swept under the carpet, left to die raving. You were sorry when he died, weren't you, but it was too late. Always too late. You bastard. You bloody bastard."

Tom Young was on his feet, his face contorted with fury. "Get . . . *out!*"

Simon wrenched open the door. The senior boy was waiting, his expressionless face just visible to Tom Young at his son's shoulder. "Throw him out," he snapped; and the senior boy's lips parted in shock.

Simon turned in the doorway. "Mother once told me you were a swine," he said quietly. "She was wrong. You're a shit, father. Just a shit."

The double doors closed behind him, leaving Tom Young alone at the round table with only the tick of the grandfather clock to mar the sudden silence.

11

Simon was dressing for dinner when Ah Kum knocked on the bedroom door and whispered hoarsely, "Boss! Honorable father is here!"

At first Simon thought she meant her own father, until he remembered that Ah Kum's parents were both dead. But surely she couldn't mean . . . He opened the door a crack. "My father? Here?"

Ah Kum nodded vigorously, keeping a sharp eye on her master's expression. By now all Hong Kong knew that banker Young had fallen out with his son again; the hot money said that this time the break was final. Tom's arrival at the Youngs' Repulse Bay home was therefore an event of some importance. Simon opened the door wider. His outward show of calm accorded ill with the turmoil he felt. "I'll be down at once," he said. "Please ask him to wait in the study."

But when he came down a few moments later it was to find his father sitting in Jinny's day-room, her boudoir as she self-mockingly called it, drinking whiskey and talking to his daughter-in-law as if rifts and rows were no more than the stuff of rumors. Tom registered his son's entrance but continued to talk to Jinny, who was nervously munching her way through a bowl of melon seeds much as another woman placed in the same awkward situation might have chain-smoked.

"Good evening, father."

"Evening, Simon."

Jinny looked unusually flustered. In spite of her reputation as one of Hong Kong's most relaxed hostesses, she did not find it easy to converse with her father-in-law.

Tom spoke again. "I was passing so I thought I'd drop in with something I meant to give you the other day." He waved his hand at a cardboard box standing on Jinny's favorite blackwood Chinese table, inlaid with mother-of-pearl. Simon opened the box to find two bottles of MacPhail's malt and he whistled.

"Generous. Thanks." But his voice was cool.

"Well. I thought perhaps you deserved a treat. Going out, are you?"

Jinny knew that she had just listened to an apology, or the nearest thing to it of which Tom Young was capable. She knew, because once or twice she had witnessed him saying sorry to Simon's mother in very much the same way. Jinny realized that between the two men the gesture was small enough; but Hong Kong would not see it like that. Hong Kong would see the chairman going out of his way to bring his son a gift. Hong Kong would explode into a million rumors, like a firework rocket disgorging myriads of highly inflammable sparks; on Monday the Corporation would open five points down on the stock exchanges, while Dunny's would romp ahead by lunchtime. Or the other way around. Simon's house servants would back DY, of course, and make or lose five hundred dollars by Monday evening; Robert Zhao, in a more sophisticated display of sporting spirit, would probably sell the Corporation short at ten, buy back in just before the last exchange closed and make a million. Or kiss it good-bye. Never mind, tomorrow was another day . . .

"We're going to Luk Yuk Tong's annual bash."

The muscles of Tom's right cheek twitched but he kept silent. He had come to be reconciled with his son, not pick a fresh quarrel.

"You don't approve?"

Jinny wondered if Simon meant his words to contain such a deliberate note of challenge, and was relieved when Tom merely shrugged. "This is our twentieth year," she said quickly.

"It's a long time to be hobnobbing with the same Chinese. They must think a lot of you."

"Y. T. is senior member of the Luk family here in Hong Kong," said Jinny. "When our two came out of the PRC, Simon agreed to take them on as servants and sponsor them with immigration. Y. T. never forgot."

Of course Tom knew the story, he had heard it often enough, but tonight what counted was keeping alive a conversation, any dialogue, no matter how stilted.

"Still. Twenty years is a long time."

"Yes," said Simon. "Y. T.'s official birthday falls about now. He gives a dinner to celebrate; we always get an invitation."

"You're the only Westerner who does, I imagine? Or at least, the only one who accepts."

"Yes."

Tom Young was in his daughter-in-law's room under his son's roof. He said nothing out loud; but that didn't prevent them all hearing the words, "Each to his taste . . ."

"Enjoy yourselves, then." Tom stood up. "Can't stay: dinner with the financial secretary."

"Social?"

"Not quite. H.E.'s had some telex or other from Cradock in Peking—the usual flap. They're finalizing the personnel of the Joint Liaison Group. Have you had an approach yet?"

Simon shook his head, astonished, and Jinny gasped.

"You will. 'Night, Jinny."

Simon saw his father to the front door. "Are you serious?" he asked in a low voice.

"Oh yes. I thought I'd mention your name, since you seem to like it here so much." Tom's lips briefly formed a smile. "Better than taking the salt out of water, I think you'll find."

Simon began to speak, then checked himself. His father affected not to notice. "Are you *really* going out to dinner with your own servants?" he asked dryly.

"Of course."

Tom shrugged. "I know how Ducannon Young has a public commitment to the Chinese population here. Inverse employment discrimination and so forth. It was just the same in your Uncle David's time. That's one thing. But people notice. People talk."

"Let them."

Tom almost smiled, then grunted instead. He inclined to Simon's point of view where gossip was concerned. "I'm surprised your club hasn't expelled you for dining with old Luk."

"You're twenty years out of date."

"Am I? Say ten, maybe." Tom's face became serious again. "Business and pleasure just don't mix here in that way. They're like oil and vinegar. And you know I detest French dressing."

"I like it, actually."

"Good night."

Simon closed the front door with a thoughtful expression on his face. He was still troubled by the knowledge that for the first time in their difficult relationship he had told his father a deliberate lie—he'd lied and then not set the record straight when Tom offered an olive branch. Simon did not really intend to give his father advance notice of his plans by calling a meeting of the Ducannon Young holding company. Under its articles of association he had the amplest possible powers and he proposed to exercise them without reference to anyone else: What Tom Young didn't know about, he couldn't prevent—share-voting agreements or not. But Tom was his father; and as Simon closed the front door his mouth was sour with the taste of self-reproach.

He turned around to find an entourage waiting for him. *Lao* Luk, as befitted the senior house servant, wore a dark suit. His wife was clad in an elegant emerald green *cheongsam*, while Lennie, their teenage son, sported a beautifully cut brown jacket over dark cream slacks. Simon smiled. "So smart," he said. "I feel I am underdressed. Should I change?"

Luk's eyes beamed with possessive pride. "Looking very fine, Boss. Very fine."

Jinny emerged from the "boudoir" and went to her husband's side. "I agree," she said cheerfully. "We mustn't keep Y. T. waiting. The driver's here."

On this evening of the year, at least, there were no economies. The Ducannon Young Rolls-Royce was already at the front door. There was no need for Simon to give his driver directions, because Y. T.'s birthday dinner was always held at the same restaurant, near Food Street in Causeway Bay. The elderly Chinese was waiting on the pavement of Gloucester Road, the nearest point at which the car could set down its passengers.

"Honorable Mr. Young," he said, beaming. *"Wah*, never absent, never late. Example to us all." He shook the Englishman's hand and Simon blushed. It embarrassed him to know how much he looked forward to this evening in the year. For a few hours at least he was a real citizen of Hong Kong in a way he never experienced at other times: accepted, welcome, no longer a *tai-pan* camping on the edge of China, but instead an honorary member of a community whose ancestral origins extended back into ten thousand years of history.

While Y. T. greeted the other occupants of the Rolls Jinny looked about her, enjoying the scene. It was nighttime, but only the sky was black; the street pulsated like an outdoor discotheque with light and color and noise. The pavements were far too narrow to accommodate the hundreds of Chinese swarming about in every direction like so many locusts; they spilled over into the roadway, causing cars to brake and hoot, into the neon-lit shops, all packed, all still doing brisk trade at eight o'clock with at least another two hours of turnover to rake in before their owners retired for the night. And the smells! Duck roasting, noodles frying, garlic, gingerroot, spice . . . Jinny's stomach bubbled gently, reminding her of how hungry she was. She had not eaten since breakfast: you had to bring your appetite with you to one of Y. T.'s dinners, for to leave a dish untasted would have been unthinkably rude.

As they began to walk down Food Street's covered arcade, Simon placed a hand on Y. T.'s shoulder. The Chinese, immensely flattered, drew himself up to his full height and looked around to make sure that everyone had noticed this token of esteem. People scattered in front of the odd pair, making way for the Western giant and the Chinese, a dwarf by comparison, whose friendship the Englishman so ostentatiously claimed. Some of the bystanders turned their heads, murmuring that the boss of Ducannon Young must be a cool one, *wah*, if he could go out to dine when his father was against him, but then the English were unfathomable devils.

"Family are how?" Yuk Tong asked. "Children are well?"

"Yes, thank you. And yours?"

"Well, yes, very well." Yuk Tong had been at war with the English language since adolescence, but nothing could have induced him to speak Cantonese to a guest such as this. "You have one son, one daughter, right?"

"That's right."

"Daughters very good, in my opinion."

Simon was surprised. "I thought all Chinese wanted sons."

"Yes, sons good also, but daughters look after you better in old age. Every man needs some daughters."

Jinny, walking a step or two behind, caught these last words and made a face. In her home village on the mainland, daughters were as welcome as a flood or a typhoon. Daughters were uneconomic. Only in Hong Kong and places like it did they become luxuries: unpaid geriatric nurses for their wealthy fathers.

But she continued to walk as if she had not heard, one hand resting gently on Lennie Luk's proud arm like a piece of jade on a velvet cushion. She cast a sideways glance at the boy, the sight of his tense face making her feel warm and liquid inside. So young, so idealistic . . . a quiet sigh escaped her lips and at once Lennie looked at her inquiringly. For Jinny to take his arm bordered daringly on the realm of the impermissible, so he was flattered and scared at the same time. Why had she sighed like that? Lennie, who ought to have been enjoying himself, felt wretched instead.

In fact, she was thinking that she had never taken a lover of her own race, had never felt the need; did Lennie sleep with many girls, she mused? Was he vigorous? Was he strong in bed? Or was he like so many Chinese men—interested only in personal pleasure, quick, easily spent, absorbed with the dubious virtues of powdered rhino horn and girly magazines? For although she had had no lovers, she knew many Chinese *tai-tai*s who were not slow to talk of their experiences.

Her eyes strayed to Simon's back. Englishmen who took local girls as mistresses were said to suffer from Yellow Fever. Did she have White Fever, then . . . ? She *tchah*'d and tossed her head, suddenly perturbed by her reflections and anxious to dispel them.

The restaurant was noisy—in Mandarin, *renao*, frenetic. But as Y. T. escorted his charges through the crowded dining room to the private salon beyond, the level of conversation and laughter quieted a little for long enough to allow the other diners a chance to absorb the new arrivals. Simon and Jinny were briefly aware of a hundred pairs of eyes digesting their progress along with the food before waiters slid the partition closed behind them and they became guests at a private party.

The Luk clan in Hong Kong numbered about fifty and this evening all of them were present. It was Yuk Tong's sixty-third birthday. The family members were sitting at circular tables but as the Youngs entered they stood up and crowded around with affectionate cries of welcome, eager for the favor of the rich Westerner's eye. Y. T. placed the Youngs on his left in the seats of honor, took the host's traditional place facing the door, clapped his hands and beckoned to the headwaiter.

"*Yu-sheng,*" he said importantly; seconds later, half a dozen waiters poured in from the kitchen bearing the ingredients for the marinated fish. Simon watched intently while the huge plate of raw vegetables and oil was mixed with large chopsticks before the fish and crispy topping were added. He loved raw fish. *Yu-sheng* was traditionally a New Year's dish, but Yuk Tong believed in having what you liked when you fancied it.

Simon munched on his helping of fish and surveyed the salon, content to see so many well-remembered faces. These were ordinary people: a few worked in factories or other men's businesses, but most of them were engaged in one or another of the family's modest concerns. Luk Yuk Tong was not a particularly rich man by Hong Kong standards, although he had his own small textile factory, a construction firm and a couple of restaurants in Wanchai. The family gathering brought together under one roof a fairly typical cross-section of the territory's five million Chinese inhabitants; and Simon was very fond of them.

"Cognac, *Tai-pan?*" Yuk Tong's words amounted to an invitation in form only. Simon, who would have much preferred to drink tea, accepted the essential command with good grace. Yuk Tong raised his glass. "To you, *Tai-pan.*"

Simon grinned and nodded. "And to you," he said, raising his own glass, "*Lo-pan.*"

Y. T. looked at him with real affection in his eyes. "You remembered!"

"When did I ever forget anything you told me, Y. T.? *Tai-pan,* literally translated, can mean the mama-san in charge of a dance hall. No wonder you Chinese used to love to use it to our faces so much."

"And *lo-pan* means . . . ?"

"*Lo-pan* means old wooden-plank. 'The boss.' Why d'you call yourself that, Y. T.?"

"*Lo-pan,* when written another way, is also the god of builders. Very good god. Use him a lot."

"*Use* him?"

"Oh yes. Gods very amenable to old Y. T., especially this year."

"I'm glad to hear it." Simon made a rueful face. "You must

put me in touch with a god who favors *tai-pan*s. Goodness, it's years since anyone called me that. You always did, in the old days. Until I stopped you."

"Thought you liked it. English very funny that way. Some of them," he added hastily, lest he cause offense.

Jinny laughed heartily. *"Very* funny," she agreed. "You can fix me up with a good god, too. Maybe then I'll take up Mah-jongg, after all these years."

"Mah-jongg god is hard to find. If I find, I keep for myself." Yuk Tong leaned across the table to exchange toasts with Jinny. When the drinking was over, Simon said: "I'm glad it's been a good year for you. What's the next one going to be like?"

"Next year, who knows?" Yuk Tong shrugged. "I get along while I have to—'As long as I am a monk, I go on beating the gong.' But maybe next year I try different god, just for change." He glanced up shrewdly at the Englishman. "Not such a good year for the dance-hall men, eh?"

"Mixed. There's what we grandly call a crisis of confidence."

"Which mean running shit-scared. When not? Please forgive me, I do not mean to be rude. Me the same: I got most of my money in Tokyo and Kuala Lumpur now. Can always bring back some day. Don't trust the Reds."

"Yet they have made written promises . . ."

"Pah! One time they promise no troops in Hong Kong. Then Deng Little Bottle says, 'Yes, there will be troops.' And there will be, too."

Simon tossed his head. "We should have a little faith, I think."

Yuk Tong finished his fish and aligned his chopsticks on their stand. He did not want to presume to debate with the Englishman, but dignity required that certain points be made. "Honorable Young, forgive me for say this, but you put too much confidence in bits of paper."

"I do?"

"Yes. Article thirty-five, People's Republic of China constitution guarantee freedom of speech, press, assembly, association and demonstration. Tell me please, you ever see spontaneous demonstration in the mainland?"

Simon poured tea for Jinny, his face thoughtful. "What do you really believe will happen here, Y. T.?"

"You've asked me that before."

"And had different answers over the years."

"Oh sure." He shrugged again. "This year, think everything okay for while. They slowly bleed place white, filter off profit to other regions of mainland. Then shut Hong Kong down."

"I do hope not."

"Many apologies for speaking out of turn. Have some more noodles, good for longevity."

"Thank you."

"Hah—Yu Chan!"

An attractive teenage girl sitting opposite the old man looked up from her bowl with an inquiring gaze. "What is it, Uncle?"

"How come a pretty girl like you don't have no husband yet?"

Yu Chan blushed. "No one's asked me."

"Got to look around, sow a few seeds. Find yourself a rich *taipan*—like this one here, next to me!"

When the girl laughed shyly Yuk Tong smiled and turned back to Simon. "Half population here under twenty-five, know that?"

"Yes."

"What all those damn kids like her going to do after changeover?"

"Find work. There's supposed to be full employment in China."

Y. T. banged one hand on the table and laughed out loud. " 'Scuse me, please. Anyway, we cannot change anything. Governor holds all power here. On mainland, insult to suggest cadres will destabilize Hong Kong in 1997. Here, insult to suggest we Hong Kong Chinese cannot manage our own affairs. Governor soon grow tired of insulting all peoples, go back to UK. Like Corporation. Like you."

Simon was shocked by this shrewd reference to the Corporation's supposedly secret plans. "I am sorry, Y. T., but I think you are wrong," he said at last. "Many of us will go, yes, although I hope to stay. China wants to keep this place going strong."

"Oh, really?"

Jinny had been listening with a troubled expression on her face. "Yes, really," she said suddenly. "I believe that. We all have to."

"Jinny's right," said Simon. "Look at the projects under way, even now. When the Shenzhen nuclear power station is finished it's going to sell about seventy percent of its output to Hong Kong. You can't just pretend that sort of thing isn't happening. Perhaps the Chinese will learn from the Hong Kong experience, extend our Western commercial ideas into the mainland itself."

"They learn, all right. Useful practice for takeover of Taiwan, which in my humble opinion is next item on agenda. Please, Mr. and Mrs. Young, no offense meant. Talking of projects, Mr. Young, you going to do this desalt thing? Forgive my presumption, please."

"Possibly." Simon stared down at the tablecloth. "I hope so."

"Advice can?"

"Of course."

"Sure? I don't want to offend you."

"Go ahead."

"Well, then: should save your money."

"Ah. Desalination is a project fit only for dance-hall keeper?"

Yuk Tong's face turned glum. "Please excuse, did *not* intend that."

"Nothing to excuse. I'm sure my father would agree with you."

The party was breaking up. The last course had been cleared and a respectful inner core of Luks now gathered around Y. T. while he studied the bill. At last he seemed satisfied. "Five thousand over . . ." he announced grandly.

He drew out his wallet to the accompaniment of admiring "*wah!*"s and began to finger bright red banknotes onto the tray beside him. At last the ritual was complete and he rose. There was a little applause as he made his way to the door, pausing every few paces to exchange greetings or merely pat someone on the back. Simon stood up and smiled at Yo Chan. "I must say thank you."

He found Jinny in the foyer with Y. T., who was engaged in the lengthy process of lighting an oval-shaped cigar. "Well," said the old man, "you going to do this salt thing, hah?"

Simon smiled at him. "Thank you for a wonderful evening, Yuk Tong. As usual, wonderful, but this year better than ever I think."

"Me too. *Good* birthday. Six pairs of long trousers given, to make sure I live a long time. Also, a lot of red packets, plenty dough. Should I use it to buy Dunny's, or should I sell?"

Simon fixed him with his eye for a long moment. "I should buy," he said quietly at last. "First thing Monday morning."

"You going to buy?"

"Yes. I'm going to buy."

As Luk Yuk Tong searched his face Simon wondered what he could read there. It must have been satisfactory, however, for at last Y. T. said, "It's right what they say—you trust too much. But you also a good man."

Jinny had come to stand behind her husband. "I think so," she said.

To the surprise of the others, Simon ordered his driver to take them to the Peak lookout. As they climbed up through the Mid-Levels the chattering died away until by the time they reached their destination the car was in total silence. The Luks wanted to go home. They had eaten and drunk; now they wanted to sleep. That was how life should go. Not even twenty years of dealing with Simon Young had quite reconciled them to the Englishman's eccentricities.

He got out of the car and they followed him, a little uncertainly, down the stone stairway to the lookout. Simon stood with his hands folded on the ledge, resting his cheek against one of the cold stone lions that guarded the vantage point. All Hong Kong was spread out below him, like the glossy original of the even glossier travel brochures: a thousand and ten thousand lights of infinite colors, some still, some in restless, constant motion, and the famous tower blocks pointing up to the sky like artificial jagged rocks in a sur-realistic landscape.

Simon's eyes strayed to where he knew the Ducannon Young building to be. Five years ago he would have been able to see the edifice, because in those days its ghostly green glass used to be illuminated from within like a glowing emerald. But that arrogant advertisement cost a great deal of money to maintain and he had abandoned it without regret.

By turning his head a fraction he was able to look at the solid Victorian pile of the Corporation's headquarters, its spires lit up by a single spotlight, and he frowned. He had told his father a lie. A major, massive lie . . . Not the first falsehood of his business career, by no means, but the first he had ever told his own father.

Movement distracted his gaze. A Cathay Pacific Boeing drifted ever lower on the western approach, the harsh shriek of its engines rising and falling in keeping with the night wind. Simon followed its lights all the way down until the plane's tail disappeared from sight behind the tangled mass of Tsim Sha Tsui. Moments later, another plane took off; through some quirk of the breeze its engines were inaudible so that it seemed to lift into the darkness like a huge, ominous bird before turning north and disappearing above the clouds.

So much majesty. So much beauty.

It was a moonlit night. The air scarcely seemed to move. Simon was conscious of many scents—the noxious smells of a teeming city, yes, they were there; but also the gentler aromas of the East: orange jasmine, frangipani, even a whiff of incense from far, far away; and—in his imagination only, this—the well-remembered scent of the Bauhinia flowering trees whose perfume gave point to Hong Kong's name.

"Incomparable," he breathed. The others did not hear him. Each was lost in his or her own ruminations; and Simon knew that although his companions were looking at precisely the same view, they saw different pictures made up of countless tiny ghost-memories superimposed upon the glory. When he retraced his steps to the car they took a little time to follow him. Lennie came up the stairs last and in the glow of the car's interior light Simon caught a glimpse of a young face, as yet scarcely touched by life, which nevertheless for some unguessable reason radiated sadness.

"Home," he said. It might have been a command, or just a statement.

When they arrived at Repulse Bay the Luks discovered that their master was still not quite ready for bed. He made them promise to wait in the kitchen while he went to collect his briefcase from the study. Ah Kum poured juice, but when Simon returned he waved away his glass and addressed himself to Luk Seng Kay.

"*Lao* Luk," he said gravely. "I would like you, please, to witness my signature."

"No!" cried Jinny.

He turned to face his wife, surprised. "What's the matter?"

Jinny felt hot with anger. It amazed her to hear him ask what was the matter. "That is not right," she hissed. "You cannot involve them in this thing." She smacked the table with her palm. "You cannot!"

Simon picked up the briefcase again and rose. "We will discuss this," he said evenly, "outside."

In the hall he rounded on her, furiously angry. "How dare you cross me in front of the servants?"

She folded her arms and lowered her eyes, the very picture of dumb insolence. When Simon reached for her hand she shook him off. Inwardly, though, she was trembling. She had never once stood up to Simon in this way. Her heart beat wildly, her eyes burned, but she would not, could not withdraw.

"I need Luk's signature," Simon said urgently. "I've reached absolute deadline, Jinny. I left it as long as I could, hoping father would see sense, but this is the crunch. The papers have to be with Tang in Singapore tomorrow or the deal's off."

"Good. Let it be off, then."

"Don't be ridiculous. D'you seriously think I've come all this way just to abandon it now for want of a witness?"

"You should have thought of that before." Who was this strange man, she wondered? What suddenly possessed him to shed his character and behave like all the other foreign devils? Tonight, it seemed, he had presumed to take food with the Luk family as a base prelude to their manipulation. Insult, willful insult . . .

"All right, I should have thought of it, but I didn't!"

"Let me sign, then. Don't involve them."

"No."

"Why not?"

"Because—" Simon paused. He had been on the point of saying, "Because you're my wife, I love you, you matter too much . . ." Instead he said, "Because legally a wife can't witness her husband's signature."

"I don't believe you."

"Jinny!"

Then it was her turn to pause. It was not only Simon who puzzled her. Who was this strange woman, defying ten thousand years of Chinese convention and debasing herself in the process? Had she really said that?—called her husband a liar to his face? Could she survive the shame of it? Yes. She could. She must. "I . . . I'm sorry. I shouldn't have said that. I'm sure that what you've just said about the law is correct. But I think that also you have another reason."

"What reason?"

"I think this thing is dangerous. It is a dangerous deal to be linked with. If so, you're making a big mistake. You heard what your father said—they're going to invite you to be on the liaison group. You can't afford any scandal. And yet you don't want to involve me, because you believe I need protection." When her husband said nothing, she went on: "But the Luks need protection also. They ran away from the mainland. They don't have the security I enjoy. You should think of them. You should."

"You're wrong, Jinny," Simon said quietly. "I've thought of them. There's no danger. None whatsoever. But I need to be sure of my witness. I need to know that, if the matter is ever tested in court, he will be available to give evidence."

"There, you see! Court, law . . . you know already that this deal will mean trouble."

"Be sensible. This is the biggest single thing I've ever undertaken. I can't afford to run the risk of the witness disappearing. I will not."

"You're wrong, Simon. You're as wrong as it is possible for a man to be. You'll be sorry one day."

"No, I shall not. I shall only be sorry if I use a witness who can't be trusted, or traced. It must be Luk. Now I want you to come back to the kitchen and tell him that."

"I won't!" But she felt the beginnings of despair.

"You *will*! You will obey me in this thing, or . . ."

"Yes?" She almost spat out the word. "Or you'll do what?"

Simon did not reply directly. Instead he took her by the arm, using such force that she could not resist, and steered her toward the kitchen. Only the utter impossibility of shedding tears in front of the servants kept her from crying aloud.

Simon sat down in one of the chairs and the Luks came to stand at his shoulder, wondering at this extraordinary, unprecedented dispute between Young and his *tai-tai*. He opened his briefcase and began to spread out papers over the table, sorting them into two apparently identical sets. For a moment he continued to stare at them, ensuring in his own mind that he understood fully what he had to do, so that there should be no risk of confusion.

At last he looked up and saw that Luk Seng Kay's eyes were fearful. Patiently he explained. "When I sign these papers, *Lao* Luk, I have to do so in the presence of a witness, who must then sign them also. The witness does not become bound by what is written. Do you understand?"

"Yes." But it was clear that Luk did not relish his signature going on the paper for all to read. Papers lasted. Papers had a habit of turning up when you least wanted or expected them to. Simon knew exactly what was going through the servant's mind and decided to take a chance.

"You don't have to do this for me," he said. "But it is fitting that you do. I would prefer you to do it."

"I think maybe Mrs. Young . . ."

"I would prefer you."

Luk looked uneasily from Simon to Jinny, who smiled a brittle smile and said, "You hear the master. Better you." She no longer wanted to weep. She wanted to be revenged, to prove herself right, to prevail.

Simon, ignorant of the crisis that overwhelmed his wife, stared into Luk's eyes again and this time saw only implicit trust. He pointed to the first of the documents before him.

"This is a memorandum of deposit of some shares." He hesitated, as if rehearsing the next words in his mind. "I would like you to sign two copies." He pulled the next document toward him. "This . . . is a power of attorney. I will sign it; you must watch." He picked up his Mont Blanc pen and signed the deed beside the red paper wafer at its foot. "Now you. Here . . . use this."

Simon laid a sheet of paper across the documents so that Luk would not be able to read them. The servant took the proffered fountain pen and neatly wrote his signature on both copies of the memorandum and the power of attorney.

"And this"—Simon picked up the last of the papers from one of the sets lying on the table, a bulky book of a document—"is a loan agreement. I sign it . . . so. Now you. Good. Thank you. And the other copy . . ."

They continued the rigmarole of legal execution through to the end. When the ink was dry, Simon swept up one set of documents and placed them inside a thick brown envelope that he took from the briefcase. As he went out to the hall he fingered the papers inside the still-open packet, until he found the copies of the memorandum and pulled them out. There, at the very foot, underneath Luk's scrawled signature, was a rubber-stamped rubric authenticating it as that of a duly appointed magistrate of Hong Kong. Simon gnawed his lips. Another massive lie, this time told to a servant who trusted him implicitly . . .

Business was business; sentiment was a waste of time. He reached a decision, pushed the papers back inside their envelope and sealed it. Now, in accordance with Qiu's precise instructions, there were two sets of documents; one for Simon; and another, identical set, contained in this envelope addressed to Soviet Communal Bank. With a single exception, both sets were genuine. Only the memoranda of deposit, charging Simon Young's Founders Shares in the Corporation with repayment of one hundred million pounds sterling, only they were forgeries. For they had been witnessed by Luk, and not the magistrate.

Then he went out to the drive, where his chauffeur was still waiting, and unwittingly did the precise opposite of what Major General Krubykov had predicted he would do. He handed the package containing the forged memorandum and other documents to the chauffeur and said, "Please take this to Kai Tak at once. Security Couriers International will be expecting it by the time you get there."

Simon watched the taillights of the Rolls disappear down the hill, then slowly went back inside the house. Suddenly his heart felt light; because on reflection it seemed to him inconceivable that the bank would fall for such an obvious trick. If they pointed out that the memorandum was defective he would apologize, promise to rectify the error . . . and then find some excuse to withdraw from the transaction altogether. The peril was too great. For Simon knew in his heart that he could never, never bring himself to put his Founders Shares at risk.

So as he reentered the kitchen, he had no qualms. It seemed to him that, on any footing, he had done the right thing.

Jinny and the Luks were sitting around the table. The servants looked at him, as if searching for an explanation, but Simon merely picked up the wet, frosted glass of fruit juice and raised it to the level of his eyes. When he spoke his voice carried a sternness none of them could remember ever having heard from him before; the Cantonese phrase rang through the house like an enchantment.

"To the Fragrant Harbor!"

And after a moment's hesitation they chorused: "To the Fragrant Harbor! To Hong Kong!"

12

Qiu needed a key with which to open a safe. If things had gone according to plan it would have been easy; but Mr. Tang, the branch manager of Soviet Communal Bank's Singapore branch, who owned the safe in question, was taking longer than anticipated to make up his mind about which side he was on. Qiu soon found what he wanted, however. His key came in the shape of a girl: she was five feet four inches tall, young and extremely pretty. Her name was Wei Shasha.

They had recruited her in Hunan when she was still only sixteen. The middle school's physical training instructors had singled Shasha out for her agility and precise judgment; they suggested a career in gymnastics, but the local Party secretariat had other ideas. She was summoned to headquarters and given what all Chinese youngsters dream of: a *hu-kou*, or household registration certificate, conferring the right to reside in a city: in her case the capital, Beijing. Shasha left Hunan, bidding farewell to her parents with tears in her eyes but joy in her heart.

Now, seven years later, she had attained the status of the Nine Sticks and was one of the Mah-jongg Brigade's most valued servants. They used her only for security penetrations. She was small, light and double-jointed; the perfect burglar. She also had unrivaled experience of the job. So when Qiu needed to open the Soviet Communal Bank's safe his thoughts turned at once to Nine Sticks Wei. He wanted only the best.

Red Dragon brought her down to Singapore by easy stages, anxious to avoid arousing suspicion. He made her spend a night in Hong Kong, a day in Manila and a few hours in Kuching, the capital of Sarawak, where she assumed her final identity as the sister of Mr. Tang's secretary on a visit to her relatives. She landed at Changi a little after three o'clock in the afternoon and went straight to the bank's headquarters building in Singapore's central business district. She gave her name to the receptionist, who rang up Mr. Tang's secretary and said that her sister was downstairs. Although the secretary was an only child, she did not protest. She had been told to expect Wei Shasha and she knew what she had to do. A little while ago she had made a mistake, just one, but it involved dishonest handling of her employer's money and Qiu knew about it. He had been waiting for her to make that mistake. From behind the scenes he had encouraged her to make it. If her parents ever found out what she had done they would disown her. Now she belonged to Qiu. She was also terrified; certainly biddable enough to tell Red Dragon the moment Simon Young's half of the executed loan agreement arrived at the bank and to indicate precisely where Tang had put it.

The security officer gave Shasha's briefcase a perfunctory search, after which she was invited to go upstairs to the ninth floor. There she was met by her "sister." It was nearly the end of office hours for the day; no one was interested. The two girls chatted, or rather Shasha prattled gaily on while Tang's secretary nodded in tense silence. Then they walked out of the suite of offices together, making for the lifts. The "down" arrow flashed. Tang's secretary stepped in; Shasha turned and walked the few steps to the nearest washroom. It was empty. Beside the line of basins was a plain blue door bearing the figures 1184. Shasha took a key from her briefcase and looked at its number tag. It matched. She opened the door, which gave onto a cupboard full of cleaning materials, and wedged herself inside, locking the door behind her.

Shasha had done this before. She was well used to waiting out silent hours of lonely darkness until it was time to move. The routines of the SCB building were locked into her mind: security patrols every two hours, starting at seven, one time even-numbered floors, next time odd-numbered floors, no cleaners until four A.M. She was not expecting any trouble.

She emerged from the cupboard on the stroke of midnight and padded down the dark corridor to the outer defenses of Tang's suite. It was protected by an electronic combination of a fairly rudimentary kind. The laser beam of Shasha's torch soon picked out the lock. From her briefcase she took a small box about the size and appearance of a pocket calculator. She pointed the box toward the door and pressed one of the keys. The tumblers slid back noiselessly. As she entered the suite she thought she heard a faint hiss. She stopped dead. The sound was not repeated.

It took her less than two minutes to work her way through the other doors that separated her from Tang's inner sanctum and find his personal safe.

The hiss came again, but this time she ignored it. Her intellect told her that the noise could safely be attributed to faulty air conditioning and all her instincts commanded maximum speed.

First, however, it was necessary to take some simple precautions. Shasha backed away from the safe and opened the door to Tang's private bathroom, keeping it behind her as a possible place of concealment in the unlikely event of her being interrupted. Then she returned to the safe and quickly opened it, using the numbers which her "sister" had supplied. She removed the documents she was looking for and laid them on the desk. A quick check sufficed to show that they were in order: one numbered set, exactly as Qiu had described them to her.

No, not quite. As she flicked through the loan agreement a sheet of rice paper fluttered out from between the pages. Shasha smacked it down with her palm and peered at it. The square of paper bore a Chinese character and some Western-style numbers split up by hyphens. A phone number? She squinted at the ill-formed character, evidently scribbled down by someone in a great hurry. What could it be . . . Zhao?

Another hiss, closer this time. Wei Shasha realized that she had dithered long enough. She laid the documents carefully in her briefcase and replaced them in the safe with another set, which looked the same but were not. What to do with the flimsy square of rice paper? The girl bit her lip. Better put it in the safe, she decided. Then she closed the door, remembering to turn the combination lock to precisely the same point on the dial from which she had started.

Up to that stage she had been alert but relaxed. Everything had gone, was going, perfectly. Then she realized that the mysterious hissing sound had become constant. Suddenly it didn't seem right. She wanted out. For a second her attention deviated from the safe's combination lock and there, perhaps three feet away from her, no more, was the Bushmaster. Shasha looked at the snake and the snake looked at her.

Then, simultaneously, they moved.

Obedient to the precepts of her training she had mapped out the office in her mind and memorized its topography before starting work. Eight feet behind her and a little to her left was the open door to Tang's bathroom. She got through it only just in time, for as the door slammed shut there came the dull thud of something hurtling against it.

The girl's heart was somewhere up behind her eyes. Shasha had never in her life been so frightened. She squatted on the floor and desperately tried to think.

She realized dimly what had happened, because she had studied and understood security in all its infinite manifestations. Instead of a noisy, expensive Doberman you slip a venomous snake, or even an insect, into the room as you lock up. An intruder can drug a dog because he knows it's there—it barks and it's expected. But how many burglars foresee a snake? How many spies know how to deal with it? A remarkably effective system—as long as its existence remained totally confidential. Certainly Tang's secretary could have known nothing about it, or she would have told Qiu.

Shasha was trapped.

The snake in the office was about one meter long and she sensed it was deadly, but beyond that the girl was ignorant. She did not know that it was a Bushmaster, *Lachesis Muta*, which can stalk its prey for hours, guided only by the body heat of the victim, before it finally strikes—and kills. No human being can hope to beat its reflexes. The Bushmaster's bite is always fatal. The creature slays its victims not for food, not to survive, but because mankind is its enemy. The KGB bred them as cheap substitutes for guard dogs.

Shasha raised herself from the floor and put on the light. She couldn't stay in the bathroom forever. The security patrols did not worry her; they would have been ordered to stay out of Tang's suite at all costs. But eventually someone was going to come along and round up the deadly guardian before admitting the cleaners. That someone would know at once that there had been an intruder: Shasha had closed all the doors behind her but her briefcase was still on Tang's desk.

No matter what happened, she knew that she must remove the briefcase and get its contents to Qiu. Everything depended on that. He had left her in no doubt that the future of Hong Kong, its security, its very existence, depended on her retrieving the documents that she had taken from the safe. And she must do it without leaving any signs of entry.

Think, she must think.

Her eyes scanned the tiny room to see what weapons were on offer. The cupboard under the washbasin revealed nothing of use: a lavatory brush, some soap, a safety razor, aftershave . . . a packet of spare razorblades. Shasha's eyes narrowed. A weapon, of sorts. What she needed now was some kind of lever, a stick.

Up and down she paced, round and round, stopping every so often to listen at the door. The beast was moving out there.

She knew she would have only one chance, one split second in which to act. The girl had faced danger bravely before now, but the prospect of grappling with the snake terrified her. All reptiles filled her with loathing.

At last Shasha opened the pack of razorblades, spilling them into the basin. Six of them. Then she picked up the lavatory brush, which was made of soft plastic. Slowly, being careful to avoid touching the edges, she inserted the blades one by one into the brush, forcing them home with all her might. Even so, they refused to penetrate more than a few millimeters. Shasha waved the brush gently to and fro. One blade slipped off and fell to the floor with a tinkle of metal on tile. She picked it up and refixed it. Her breath was coming very fast now. She knew it was almost time.

Her hand closed around the door handle and slowly she began to turn it. It took her a good half minute to clear the latch. Shasha swallowed hard but her mouth was dry and her throat hurt. She could feel the blood pounding through the artery in her neck. She flicked the brush a couple of times, ensuring that she had judged its weight correctly. One microsecond. One tiny flash of time . . .

This was her only chance. When she opened the door, she would be standing behind it. The snake would have to get itself into the bathroom and turn before it could attack. For a split second, she would be on the creature's blind side.

Shasha wrenched open the door.

The Bushmaster was waiting. It writhed through the gap, head up and curling round to bite the terrified girl, knowing her exact position from the heat she exuded. Shasha's right hand whipped down once, twice, three times, before her vision dissolved into tears and she could no longer see to strike. She drew in great choking breaths, fighting back the hysteria which threatened to overwhelm her senses. She couldn't see. *She couldn't see.*

Shasha raised her sleeve to her face and wiped away the tears. The Bushmaster lay at her feet. It was dead: she had sliced off most of its head with her first hacking stroke. The girl suppressed a scream and shrank away from the hideous coils on the floor. She wanted to run as fast as she could, but her training held. She knew what she had to do.

She made herself wrap the snake's mutilated body in reams of toilet paper before depositing it in her briefcase. Then she swabbed up all the blood, traversing every inch of the room on her hands and knees until she was satisfied that no trace of her butchery remained. And right at the end, when everything was tidy, she wrapped the blades in more paper and threw them into the brief-case to join the snake.

In the morning they would find no guardian, a lavatory brush bearing strange indentations and a mysterious dearth of spare razorblades. But they would find nothing else. Shasha would have preferred to do better, but she knew it was beyond her. She took a last look around and collected the briefcase from Tang's desk. Then she picked up the phone and dialed. This was an emergency procedure, to be used only as a last resort. It took all her remaining shreds of courage to do it. She had been taught six terse phrases, each signifying a different emergency. Shasha was tempted to use them all, but when someone answered the shaking girl merely said, "Sorry, I seem to have a wrong number," and at once replaced the handset. Now the Mah-jongg cadres on the outside knew that she was incriminated ("sorry") and needed help in covering her retreat ("wrong number"). Shasha trembled at the thought of what the consequences might be. To use any one of the six phrases meant failure. Then, at last, she departed, relocking the electronic combinations behind her. The outer corridor was deserted. She crept back to the broom cupboard and locked herself in. Even though she knew the snake was truly dead, she had to fight down the revulsion that possessed her at the thought of its loathsome body so close to her own. The hours dragged slowly by. At long, long last, however, she heard the distant sounds of people coming to work and she risked a peek at her watch in the light of the pencil-torch. Eight-fifteen. Another quarter of an hour. Would the Mah-jonggs rescue her? Shasha was shut up in total darkness, with a briefcase full of gruesome evidence. If Qiu abandoned her now . . .

A quarter of an hour; nine hundred seconds. To her they seemed like ninety thousand, but at last they were over. She waited until she was certain that the washroom was unoccupied, then let herself out, clutching the briefcase as if it were a life-support system. She hastily attended to her makeup in one of the mirrors and made for the lifts, walking like an automaton. No one challenged her.

As the lift doors opened at ground-floor level, Wei Shasha saw that the banking-hall was crowded and she shrank back. About thirty meters separated her from the main entrance. Uniformed security guards scrutinized whoever went in or out. She could not run the gauntlet of their piercing stares, *she could not*. In her feverish state of nerves it seemed to her that everyone was looking toward the lifts, that brows were already starting to crease in frowns. Her legs began to shake uncontrollably. A great wave of blood rose slowly through her body. She knew that when it reached her head it would overwhelm her and she would drop.

Shasha was on the point of collapse when there came a sudden commotion.

"Dar-*ling*!"

Her eyes flickered open. She was alone in the lift; the doors were already closing.

"Dicky, lah! Come and give Maudie a kiss."

With a second to spare, Shasha stabbed her hand down on the "open" button and the doors obediently slid back. Now no one was looking at her. All attention was focused on a large Chinese woman, daringly dressed in a screaming turquoise crepe de chine blouse and a white skirt slit as far as the upper thigh. She advanced down the hall toward a hapless man, who seemed incapable of movement.

Heads turned, tongues chattered. The larger-than-life woman reached her prey, theatrically threw her arms around him and planted a noisy kiss on his forehead.

As Maudie clasped her beringed hands behind the man's back her eyes narrowed and flashed in Shasha's direction. The petrified girl drew a deep breath and emerged from the lift. One step toward the exit. Two steps. Three . . . The security guards loomed closer. Their attention was divided between the doors and the extraordinary scene opening up on the banking floor.

Slowly, slowly, Shasha narrowed the distance between her and escape. Ten meters. Five. One of the guards glanced at her taut, white face, did a double-take and peered closer. Shasha froze.

"Ai-*ya!*" The sound of a slap resounded through the hall, overriding the buzz of nearby conversations. The guard's head whipped around. Shasha did not look back to see what was happening. She ran toward the door. "How *dare* you! Call the manager, yah!"

The guard moved. Shasha recoiled. But he brushed right past her, heading for the Chinese woman and the man she'd called "Dicky." As Shasha pushed through the swinging doors the last thing she heard was a loud female voice shrieking something about an assault.

Qiu had a car waiting in Collyer Quay. Shasha stepped lightly into the back seat, pulled the door shut and fainted.

Her memory became confused after that. Much later she was to recall Qiu pulling her up by the hair and screaming into her face; her gasping out what had happened; Qiu proceeding to have apoplexy. His voice squealed louder and louder in her ears; the car picked up speed along the East Coast Highway, she could dimly see its roof bob up and down, to and fro, above her throbbing head; then they came to a halt at Changi Airport, where Qiu evicted Wei Shasha from the car into the arms of a couple of waiting henchmen who pitched her onto the first plane out, going to Shanghai. She remembered hearing the wheels come up with a satisfying "clunk," the sweetest sound she'd ever heard because it meant that the aircraft had gone beyond recall, and at last she fell asleep.

13

Hong Kong people remembered and talked about the stone-laying ceremony at the site of the desalination plant for years afterward. Even by the exacting standards of that heady colony, it was an event.

Simon Young's day began at four o'clock in the morning on Friday, October 25, 1986, when, according to Dunny's *feng-shui* specialist, spiritual powers were likely to be most intense. Simon was secretly relieved, because it would have been embarrassing to confront China's first deputy prime minister later in the day with a superstitious ritual as part of the official dedication. He stood with his co-directors in the warm, predawn half-light, watching the geomancer methodically set up his equipment: a yellow lacquered wooden compass on its tripod; the *bhat gwa* hexagonal mirror to ward off evil spirits; and his leather-bound copy of *The*

Water Dragon Classic, geomancy's bible, a work more than twelve hundred years old. Then one by one the banners were unfurled: green for harmony, gold for heavenly glory, red for joy and fertility, white for purity, blue for the meditation of heaven. At last all was in readiness. The geomancer lit joss sticks, first a bundle to the north, then one to each of the other cardinal points of the compass, and began to chant.

When the *feng-shui* exorcism and other rites were complete a Taoist priest stepped forward to the edge of the foundation trench to mutter prayers, followed by a Buddhist monk in his saffron robes. These days hardly anyone kept up the old ceremonies, or at most they made a token gesture in their direction, but the directors of Ducannon Young were leaving nothing to chance. They had a work force to pay and they knew that their Chinese laborers might be reluctant to work unless they were satisfied with the site's auspices. So they waited in the semidarkness, patient and understanding, with their foremen ranged in front of them to witness the propitiation of the earth and its gods.

When the ceremonies were finally over Simon called the three celebrants before him and paid them one by one, using brand-new red banknotes issued the day before, their serial numbers thoroughly checked for unlucky combinations. He added lavish bonuses for work well done, much to the approval of the foremen, who regarded this as a favorable omen. Then he addressed himself to the geomancer, making sure that his words could be heard by all.

"You found no red earth?"

"None."

That was essential. It meant there was no blood in the land. The geomancer did not know that Dunny's had arranged for the foundations to be quickly dug by unsuperstitious Koreans, so that now all the red earth was safely covered up.

"And the dragon?"

"Nowhere near the tail."

"The site?"

"Excellent. There are mountains to the north, the front door faces south, streams encircle it. It has river access. To the south lies a plain big enough for a mighty troop of horses. It wants only trees growing on the north."

"They will be planted."

"Then by all the gods, may the building house you and your descendants for a thousand and ten thousand years!"

"The turn of the century should see me right," George Forster muttered to Simon as they climbed into the waiting helicopter. "I'll settle for that and a pension."

"Then you're a pessimist, George."

"So the market tells me. We closed at two hundred and sixty-four last night. Year's high. A thousand says we hit two-seventy by dinner."

"Done."

"Although if the punters knew what that little lot just cost us . . ." He looked out of the window at Tsim Bei Tsui, now fast diminishing below and behind them. "Priests, sorcerers, breakfast . . ."

"And compensation for disturbing the Mong Tseng Wai village's *feng-shui*."

"You'd think H.E. might have done something about that."

"The law's the law, George. The village headman has a right not to have his *feng-shui* disturbed. Dunny's does at least try to keep on the right side of the law . . . barring the odd accident."

"And the day's only just begun."

"Oh yes, you're right—the price gets higher along with the sun. But we'll touch two-seventy today. I took your bet for luck; but I know it'll be the best thousand I've ever paid anyone."

The helicopter clattered along the coast, heading southwest for Tuen Mun. It was going to be a beautiful, cloudless October morning; the nearest to an English autumn day that Hong Kong could produce. Far away to the other side of Deep Bay they could just see the Bao-An Peninsula, a pale mauve strip of the real China, while to the left lay the paddy-fields of the New Territories, spread out below their flight path like a checkerboard.

After a while Simon closed his eyes and let his mind drift back over the events of a frantic summer. Things had moved so quickly that he could still hardly believe it. First came the money—for a moment it occurred to him to wonder how Luk Seng Kay's signature had missed the scrutiny of Soviet Communal Bank's directors, but then everything else came in a headlong rush, all at once, extinguishing doubt: the agreement signed by the Governor and by China's prime minister, the land, the subcontracts, the licenses, the essential spark. Anglo-Chinese cooperation was suddenly the rage; and Dunny's began its steady climb to near the top of the Hang Seng basket of shares, while the Corporation wavered and fell.

Tom Young saw the point very early on. Early in the summer of 1986 he held a moist forefinger up to the prevailing wind, saw that it was blowing out of China and thought hard. Then, without any public explanation, he grudgingly began to change tack. That was why today the Governor of Hong Kong and the first deputy prime minister of the People's Republic would sail to the ceremonies at Tsim Bei Tsui on the Corporation's yacht, that flagship of Campers' mastery, loaned for the occasion free of charge. For the first time in Hong Kong's history the *Pacific Star* would fly the colors of mainland China from her mast; Thomas Edward Young knew that merely by setting foot on her well-scrubbed deck he could raise the bank's stock half a dozen points. He did not like what was happening, but he was a pragmatist first and always. When the *Pacific Star* put out from Ocean Terminal, he would be on the bridge for all Hong Kong's brokers to see.

There was no stopping that day, no time for rest. Simon raced from the helicopter to the car and on to Dunny's, where Mary Street had his favorite quick breakfast of *char-siu-bao* ready for him while he scanned the morning's telexes, initialed the minutes of the last board meeting and signed some post left over from the night before. Then Jinny arrived, gorgeously attired in a jade-green Cardin dress with matching hat, and they were off to the terminal, there to greet the dignitaries from both countries who had been invited to attend the official stone-laying ceremony. The approach to the dock was well policed but many of the nearby streets were thick with crowds. Until that moment Simon had given very little thought to his own role in all this. It was only when the Rolls drew up for a security check at the gates and the crowd surged forward with a burst of cheering that it began to penetrate his brain that he might actually be popular.

He looked at Jinny in astonishment while the Royal Hong Kong Police wrestled furiously with the human hydra that suddenly materialized to surround their car. She smiled back at him. "Didn't you know?"

Simon shook his head.

"You should read a paper sometime, darling. Now there's one less thing for which these people depend on the mainland's goodwill. They can't have political independence, but at least they have their own water supply."

"I knew the markets loved us, but this . . ." He shrugged it off with a smile, for today at least able to establish some kind of equilibrium between the double motives of commerce and civic benevolence that drove him. "I wish Diana and Mat could be here to see."

Then they were through the barrier, which clanged shut behind them, and in the comparative peace of the terminal they drew up outside the shimmering whiteness of the *Pacific Star*. Tom Young himself stepped forward to open the door.

"Morning, *Tai-pan*," he said ironically.

"Father."

"Rather a good win for you, I thought. Congratulations."

"Thanks. But isn't it mutual? I gather the Chinese request for an extension of your term of office has been referred to Downing Street."

"It has." Tom smiled thinly. "Well, mustn't keep you. Have a nice day, as the Americans say. You never know when your next one'll come along." He paused. "Where *did* you get the money from, Simon?" But when his son did not reply at once he quickly turned to Jinny and kissed his daughter-in-law on the cheek. "Come and meet the Corporation's directors."

The Governor's protocol secretary was waiting at the foot of the gangway, clipboard in his hand. Suddenly a nearby policeman's radio crackled into life.

"They're coming, gentlemen. Places, please . . ."

Outside the terminal's gates went up a tremendous roar; a sound comprising car horns, children's toy trumpets, whistles, an infinite variety of human voices from many races. As the gates swung open the bandmaster of the Royal Greenjackets raised his staff and the trumpeters slowly, gracefully presented their instruments to their lips. The huge Daimler, its paintwork reflecting the bright morning sun like solid black diamond, eased silently to the ship's side, a Union Jack pennant fluttering in the sea breeze. Another car flying the red and gold flag of the People's Republic pulled up behind it and officers of the Royal Hong Kong Police stepped smartly up to the doors. First to emerge was the Governor, closely followed by the diminutive figure of the wife of China's first deputy premier; then the second car disgorged the premier himself, one arm gallantly extended to the Governor's wife.

"Gen-er-al saa . . . *lute!*"

The trumpets sounded in fanfare. There was a moment's silence, followed by the two national anthems. With one exception everyone looked straight ahead to the front. Not Simon. His eyes were elsewhere. For out of the second car, apparently unheeded by all save him, had stepped another man, his exquisitely cut morning suit a very model of how these things should be; and as Simon found himself staring at Robert Zhao Yi Qiang, so unmistakably part of the official Chinese delegation, the air about him seemed suddenly to turn cold.

Because Simon's attention was fastened on Zhao and his party he saw something else he might otherwise have missed.

The anthems were concluded; the Governor moved forward to shake hands with Simon, who manufactured a smile from somewhere and falteringly spoke a few words. But still he could not quite distract himself from Zhao; and as he continued to stare in his direction he noticed the chauffeur getting out of the second car. An undersized Chinese chauffeur, who blinked in the sunlight through heavy-rimmed black spectacles, like an animal awakening from long hibernation. A chauffeur whose all-too-familiar smile came and went in a flash, the lips turning up-down, up-down, with no warmth in the eyes . . . Qiu Qianwei.

Simon felt light-headed. Somehow he managed to effect the well-rehearsed introductions, his smile intact, but the world around him lacked reality. There were gaps in his comprehension. One moment he was presenting a Ducannon Young executive to the Governor; the next, he found himself in the middle of a conversation with the deputy premier's wife; then he was somehow at the top of the gangplank, looking for Jinny, who had disappeared, while the *Pacific Star*'s captain repeatedly asked him a question.

"I said . . . are we ready to cast off, sir?"

What was happening? What in the name of God . . . ?

"Ah . . . quite ready, thank you. Is everyone aboard?"

"Very nearly, sir."

"I can't find my wife."

"I saw her on the quay a moment ago, Mr. Young."

Simon leaned down over the ship's side and saw Jinny standing with one foot on the plank. She was talking to Qiu Qianwei.

"Jinny!" Simon cried.

She looked up, said something to Qiu and stepped onto the gangplank. "Coming, darling."

Simon meant to wait for her, but the Governor's equerry came to his side and said, "You're needed" in a tone that brooked no denial. Simon took a last anxious look over the side to see that Qiu had laid a hand on Jinny's arm. The equerry tapped him on the shoulder and hissed, *"Now!"* Simon banged the rail with his clenched fist and nodded reluctantly. "Please ask the chairman for permission to sail," he said to the ship's captain.

What was Jinny doing?

Deep inside him the fragile construction of trust that had begun to renew itself over the past few months tottered and heaved. Somehow he found himself standing on the bridge, his father on one side, the Governor on the other, looking down at the band on the quay. *Where was Jinny?* There were a lot of multicolored streamers and he could not remember having ordered streamers. Simon craned his neck, looking to right and left. *Where was she?* Then the vessel's siren uttered three immensely long blasts, answered at once by a cacophony from Victoria Harbor that seemed to go on forever. The band was receding into the distance now; the tugs had done their work; bells clanged on the bridge and with a shudder the huge yacht began to move ahead under her own power. As she eased through the bobbing sampans out into the main navigation channel Simon could once more hear the sound of cheering from the streets. Three Very lights, red, white and blue, soared into the air from HMS Tamar, closely followed by three more, this time two red and one gold.

Tom Young led the way to the vessel's port side and pointed. As if at his unspoken command, huge columns of water spurted into the clear air from fire tenders ranged on the Hong Kong side of the harbor and cannon roared out their salute. The Governor waved, gently encouraging the shy deputy premier by his side to do the same. The *Pacific Star* was well under way now, engines turning at half-speed, and the last tug slipped her one remaining line. Harbor police cutters flanked the ship, their sirens roaring out a steady *whoo-ooOP, whoo-ooOP, whoo-ooOP*. Bells rang again and Simon heard the terse command, "Full ahead; midships." Hong Kong began to slip past Simon Young's eyes, faster and faster now; something made him turn back to the starboard side of the bridge, from which he could still just see the two Daimlers parked on the dockside. Of Qiu there was no sign; it might have been an illusion, but he thought he saw a flash of jade green at the nearside window of the Chinese delegation's car as it slowly glided away toward the terminal's gates. "Jinny!" he shouted as he ran down the nearest ladder, the official guests almost forgotten, only to find his way barred in most unexpected fashion.

"Simon, dar-*ling*! Of all the unlikely people, fancy seeing *you* here."

For several seconds Simon Young just gawked at Maudie in

silence. She was wearing a dazzlingly cut dark blue dress with a gold pendant at her throat; on her elaborately coiffured hair perched a tiny hat that seemed to be composed only of net and tiny peacock feathers. The overall impression was of extreme simplicity bought at one almighty price.

"Maudie! What . . . why on earth . . . ?"

"Well, darling, I waited and waited and when you didn't ask me to your beano, I sulked, isn't it? So then I rang up H. E. and wangled myself an official invitation. Dear Edward . . ."

Simon cast a desperate glance toward the shore. The Daimlers had disappeared. Behind him someone cleared his throat and he wheeled around.

"Excuse me, Mr. Young . . ." It was the chief steward.

"Yes?"

"I was wondering if we should serve the champagne now."

"You should ask—"

"Mr. Young Senior says I'm to take my orders from you today, sir."

"But *dar*-ling," Maudie interposed. "There's only one answer to a question like that, yah." She placed both hands on her hips and looked the chief steward up and down. "What are you waiting for, baby?"

Simon caught the man's eye and nodded before turning back to his unexpected guest. "Have you seen my wife anywhere?"

Maudie spread her hands in an elaborate shrug. "Noo-lah. It's no good asking me about wives, darling. Wives aren't Maudie's specialty at all. Now if it was *husbands* you were interested in, I could tell you a few stories about this boatload of buccaneers that would make you shiver your timbers." She frowned. "Was your wife wearing a jade-green dress?"

"Yes."

"I heard a lady complaining of feeling ill. She was wearing a dress that color."

"Excuse me, Maudie, I must go—"

"So rude, lah!"

Simon looked down. Maudie's hand had closed around his wrist and was squeezing it hard enough to make her knuckles show white. He could not move. She was detaining him. For a second his brain refused to believe the truth, but then he was forced to accept that she was actually, physically detaining him. He jerked his head up to find her eyes filled with resolution, her tight-lipped smile now almost nonexistent. "Excuse me," he repeated stupidly.

"Stay and talk to Maudie, Simon. So long since we met."

He yanked his hand away but she grabbed it again and this time he could feel her nails digging into his skin. His eyes darted desperately to the brass-mounted clock over the nearest door. Even as he looked the minute hand jumped to the hour and his eyes switched back to Maudie's face in time to see her register that it was eleven o'clock precisely. Simultaneously, as if preprogrammed, she dropped his hand.

"Sorry darling," she murmured, her smile quite restored. "Maudie mustn't keep you."

The sound of footsteps on the companionway behind Simon distracted his attention. Then the equerry rematerialized at his elbow and the official party once more became his personal responsibility.

"*See* you," sang Maudie as she disappeared into the saloon, pausing just long enough to intercept the single tulip-shaped glass that the chief steward was carrying on a silver salver toward His Excellency the Governor of Hong Kong.

Ah Kum opened the door to see Qiu standing on the step, right arm linked through Jinny's left, and her eyes widened in shock. "*Ai-ya!*"

Qiu and Jinny came over the threshold, closely followed by a shifty-looking Robert Zhao. Ah Kum knew from the way her mistress stared at Qiu's hand that she was under duress.

"Mrs. Young is a bad sailor," snapped Zhao. "She will join the celebrations later." Qiu led Jinny through into the living room that overlooked the sea and pushed her down into a chair. Ah Kum tagged along behind. The door to the kitchen opened a fraction to reveal *Lao* Luk, his lips parted in fear, and at once closed again. The house seemed strangely silent, as if it were swathed in soundproofing.

"When first I entered this house," Qiu said, "I thought of the old saying . . . 'If a man becomes an official, even his dogs and chickens will ascend to heaven.' " He wandered around the room, inspecting its furnishings with jealous eyes. "How true it is." As he spoke the word *true* his malevolent gaze lighted on Ah Kum, who retreated a couple of steps. "Listen to me, Ah Kum. You have not seen Mr. Zhao here today. You have not seen me. Now get out. And if you want to beat the firing squad that's waiting on the other side of the Shamchun for you and all the other capitalists, don't let me catch you listening." Without warning or transition his voice rose to a scream. "You hear?" Ah Kum fled.

Qiu walked across to the windows and lowered the venetian blinds, shutting out the hot white sky. The room quickly became stuffy but he did not seem to notice. He sat down in a wicker chair opposite Jinny's, never taking his eyes from her face. Robert Zhao hitched himself onto a table and thrust his hands into his pockets. Whenever Jinny looked in his direction she found him staring at her through brooding, speculative eyes.

"Why have you chosen to shame me?" she asked suddenly. "My husband is waiting for me on that ship. As long as Hong Kong lasts, my shame will be talked of in connection with this day."

"Why have you chosen to shame us?" Qiu replied. "You have grown above yourself, Wang Linhua. You have grown very high."

"You speak of 'us,' " Jinny muttered. "What 'us' is wide enough to embrace both you and Robert Zhao?"

There was an uneasy pause, while each man waited for the other to speak. "We have certain things in common," Zhao said vaguely at last. "But I am here to watch your interests, Jinny. To see fair play."

"What need have I of fair play? Here, in my own home?"

"It will cause less comment if I am seen to be accompanying our friend Qiu."

"He is no friend to me. You are not welcome, Robert Zhao. You should be ashamed."

"*I* should be ashamed? I have deceived a friend, perhaps, but you have deceived a husband."

"You are insolent. I do not trust you. I have never liked you. After today, do not ever enter this house again."

He blanched and looked away; but before very long his gaze slid back to her face, as if drawn to it by a magnet. Qiu made an impatient gesture.

"We've been kind to you," he said. "Too kind, perhaps. We rescued you from semistarvation in rural Sichuan. Then as if that were not enough, we educated you. We sent you to Hong Kong to work; when you sought our permission to stay here, we gave it— on our terms, to all of which you agreed. Never forget that you were part of our annual emigration quota; the number we let go each year is less than that of all the Middle Kingdom's emperors."

"You had your reasons."

"We did. There was a time when we had much respect for you. Who else married a mighty *tai-pan*? Who else afforded us such great opportunities as you?"

"I performed all my obligations. It was hard to live apart from my brother and sister, hard to live with a man who trusted me, knowing that I deceived him daily." And now I regret it, she thought bitterly; I shall not repeat the error. "Yet I did what you required."

"At the beginning, yes. But it is many years since you earned your rice. I correct myself. Your *family's* rice—you yourself are well provided for."

"My family. Not our family any longer, I notice."

"Have you told him the truth: that I am not related by blood to you in any way?"

Jinny shook her head.

"Good. At least you have learned something. But why do you not obey us any longer when we give you instructions?"

"Because it was not part of the bargain. I informed the cadres that I loved my husband and they agreed that I should be released. You know it."

"Do I? Perhaps you confuse me with someone purged in the Cultural Revolution, when so many people were lost and papers destroyed."

She looked up at him and knew from the set of his face that her cause was hopeless.

"Let me remind you of your situation, please," said Qiu. "You have a brother and sister in the mainland. They depend on you for their lives. In an extreme case of disobedience on your part, we would not hesitate to execute them and present you with a bill for the bullets we used. This you know the comrades have done, in Shanghai and elsewhere. The cost of a bullet"—he paused, as if calculating—"is fifteen fen. Tell me, Wang Linhua, do you have thirty fen to spend?" He waved his hand in an arc, delineating the room's finery. "Does he, who has so much, have enough to spend on *that* extravagance?"

Jinny's face had turned white. The airless room seemed to bear in on her, stifling such resistance as she had left. She glanced at Zhao, but there was no help to be had there. He wore the slack look to be found only on the faces of the very rich or the irredeemably poor—the expression of one who has no one to please but himself. His eyes alone spoke of something more specific. Jinny looked into them and for the first time acknowledged to herself that he wanted her sexually. She could have laughed, it was so ridiculous: she was in her forties, hardly beautiful, married, with two children. She looked again and the laughter died. Sex recognized no rules. Zhao was consumed by lust.

Qiu spoke again. "Yet even now, we are prepared to grant you one last chance. We will not shame you, as you express it. You pretended to be sick, you played the part well. Now you can meet the yacht when it anchors off Tsim Bei Tsui. All will be forgotten in the excitement of the moment."

Jinny dragged her eyes from Zhao's face and gazed defiantly at Qiu. "What is it you ask of me?"

"Just this. We will go now to your husband's study. He has a wall safe there. Do you know the combination to that safe?" She looked away, giving him the confirmation he sought. "Good. Inside the safe is one copy of his contract with Soviet Communal Bank. You will open the safe and allow me to inspect the contents. Then you will close the safe again. That is all."

"Why must I do this?"

Qiu pursed his lips and hesitated. It was no part of his plan to exclude her from complicity in the assignment; quite the contrary. But he had to consider Zhao. Qiu was at one with Jinny in neither liking nor trusting Robert Zhao. "We have two versions of the contracts now," he said. "The bank's, and ours. We need to be sure that your husband possesses the correct version. So we will open the safe in the next room and make an inspection. Then, Wang Linhua, then truly, you can be released."

Qiu shot a quick glance at Zhao, but could learn nothing from the businessman's face. If the woman complied, it would be necessary to distract Zhao's attention while Red Dragon effected the switch, substituting one set of papers for another, and Qiu had prepared a number of stratagems to meet that eventuality. Now, however, as he redirected his attention to Jinny, he sensed that this was likely to be academic.

Jinny let the silence go on for a long time before she lifted her chin and said, "No."

Her face was the same color as a death mask. She reminded Qiu of an ill and frightened child but the comparison inspired no pity in his heart. "You refuse?" he asked.

"I refuse."

"Why?"

"Because I have a husband now. A man I love and respect and will honor all my remaining years. The debt I owe him is too great: he has forgiven me everything. I must reward him somehow, even if only by remaining loyal to him. The things you talk of are past. They belong to another lifetime."

Qiu looked at his watch. "You can take a few minutes yet to think it over."

"I don't need to think. I refuse."

Qiu turned to the other man. "You asked to come. You suggested—I quote your own words—that it might be better if you came. I presume you wish to say something?"

"I would like to, yes."

"Proceed, then."

"My dear." Zhao spread his hands in a disarming gesture. "My very dear Jinny, have you thought about this? About the consequences for you? For Simon? After all, he's fully committed to this assignment. In it up to his neck, you might say. And if you refuse to cooperate, who can say what might happen, eh? Now come along. If I—"

Jinny listened with disbelief. At last she could bear it no longer and she rounded on Zhao, her face alight with anger. "What's your connection with Qiu?"

"Connection?"

"He's a spy. What does that make you?"

"My affiliation with the People's Republic of China is well known. If I can be of some assistance to them—"

"Yes! Yes! I see it now. You, too, belong to the Mah-jonggs. You told them you had influence over me."

"Please be calm." Zhao was becoming agitated. "It doesn't help if you make such wild accusations—"

"You told him you could persuade me! How dare you! Did it mean so much to you to gain access to my house one more time?"

Zhao began to stutter something and fell silent.

"Did you think *he* would leave you alone with me, perhaps? Hah? Did you intend to exercise your powers of persuasion in the bedroom, Robert Zhao? As you tried to do once before, on your yacht? Yes, I remember that!" Suddenly the contempt she felt for him bubbled over in a white-hot flood. "Only this time it was to be on my husband's bed, Zhao *xian-sheng*, is that it?"

Zhao leaped up and stormed across to the window, where he stood sightlessly facing the drawn blinds. His shoulders were shaking. Qiu decided that Zhao had had his chance. The outcome did not surprise him, but nothing was lost. Indeed, Red Dragon had learned much. "You are aware of the consequences?" he asked Jinny.

"Yes. I cannot do this thing. It is not within my nature. 'As you are made, so will you always be.' "

"What of Mingchao? Of Kaihui?"

Jinny raised her hands to her ears. "Don't speak to me of them," she cried. "I won't hear it!"

"Their fates are in your hands . . ."

She jumped up and ran to the door. "Be *quiet!*"

"Your brother . . . your sister."

"*Wo mei mei-mei,*" she shrieked in the language of her childhood. "*Wo ye mei zui-xiao-di!*"

For a long while Qiu said nothing. At last he stood up and made as if to take her by the arm. She jerked away but he caught her viciously.

"I agree," he whispered. "You are very right. Now you have no younger sister. Now you have no youngest brother." With his free hand he opened the door and stepped aside for her to pass through it. "Mrs. Young, shall we go?"

II

THIRTEEN
ORPHANS HAND
1988

14

The summer of '88 began with a few small dust swirls on the floor of the Gobi desert: evil djins of yellow powder that penetrated even the thickest walls or the heaviest clothes before mingling with the skin's sweat to make a mask of astringent mud. Overnight, these djins grew and sprouted, multiplying a hundredfold in the course of their gusting journey to the southeast. By the time they crossed Inner Mongolia into Shanxi and Hebei they had combined to form a rippling wave of heat riven with fine-blown, gritty loess, a wave that could be seen ten miles away as it shimmered relentlessly on toward the Yellow Sea—and Beijing. There was a suspenseful pause between the end of spring and the onset of summer proper, while torrential rains washed the city's alleys clean of a year's accumulated muck and debris; then the wave of heat came down like a blast from the door of a furnace that suddenly yawned wide. The Mah-jongg cadres manfully stuck it out for a week before they prepared to pack up their belongings and move to Beidaihe, on the blessedly cool coast, 180 miles to the northeast of the sweltering capital.

Qiu Qianwei foresaw the relocation and summoned a departmental meeting after normal working hours, determined to make sure that everyone knew his duties in the coming transfer. Schedules were drawn up, lists were made, and earnest cadres pored over them by the dim light of single bulbs in the hope of winning advancement through the detection of omissions or weaknesses in the organization.

But Qiu's organization was excellent. He had grown a good deal over the past two years, learning many new practical skills. The physical education instructors had toughened him into a more formidable figure than the frail waif who'd inherited the Red Dragon tile. And he had grown inwardly, also; for this the army took the credit. With the army he'd learned about pain thresholds, calibers, tactics; but it went much further than routine training. The PLA honed his resources of self-reliance and self-sufficiency to the point where Qingqing no longer felt quite sure that this was the man she had married.

"You will take good care of yourself?" she said to him on the morning of the move.

"I will."

Qiu, engrossed with baby Tingchen's attempts to prize the badge from his father's cap, spoke absently. He was about to leave his home in Beijing for the best part of four months, but there were important things on his mind and the unshed tears echoing in his wife's voice were not among them. When the driver rapped on the front door Qiu snatched the cap from Tingchen's hands. Halfway down the drive he seemed to remember something, for he stopped short, turned and said to Qingqing, "You'll be all right by yourself, hah?"

She nodded.

"A pity my mother is no longer here. . . ." Qiu, aware that he was entering the realm of the contentious, broke off unhappily and looked away. Guilt pricked him. After a second of hesitation he trotted back up the path, led his wife inside the house and kissed her gently on the mouth. "Good-bye," he muttered sadly. "I wish you could come to Beidaihe with us."

"Yes. Oh, so do I!" Qingqing put her arms around his neck

and pulled him close to her, rubbing the tip of her nose against his earlobe. But she, like her husband, had learned much over the past three years. Qingqing was a good army wife now, and knew better than to detain a colonel, any colonel. "Good-bye," she choked; and gave him a push, laying her clenched fists against his chest in a courageous little gesture of exhortation.

He was early, so he made the driver stop at Tiananmen and strolled through the gardens of the Chairman Mao Memorial Hall to the southern entrance. As he entered the central chamber he removed his cap and approached the crystal coffin on its black marble base surrounded by flowers. He stood in silent contemplation of the body for a few moments before raising his eyes to the white marble south wall on which was inscribed, in gold characters, ETERNAL GLORY TO THE GREAT LEADER AND TEACHER CHAIRMAN MAO ZEDONG. It occurred to him that the word "eternal" had ceased to have a definitive meaning in the Chinese language and he left in somber mood.

The car dropped him off at headquarters, where he took command of his ninety-strong contingent, and the convoy of minivans and coaches set out for Beidaihe. Before they had gone very far Qiu found himself in an exceedingly bad temper. The weather was hot. For this special occasion he had decided to wear his new People's Liberation Army uniform, still crisp from the tailors, with its smart red tabs and newly reinstated insignia to distinguish him from the enlisted men; but after the first fifty miles he was reduced to the same state as the other dozen occupants of the van: all were equally sweaty, crumpled and thirsty.

To add to Qiu's difficulties, the woman driver assigned to his minivan proved to be an independent-minded harridan who persistently queried his references to the map on the grounds that it was out of date and anyway she thought she knew a shortcut. Red Dragon eventually lost patience with this constant niggling and ordered a halt at one of the roadside teahouses. The driver tried to insist on their traveling another ten miles to the nearest garage, so that she could combine the van's needs with those of its occupants and fill up with petrol at the same time, but Qiu Qianwei would have none of it; and one look at his face sufficed to assure the driver that she had better comply.

The break was refreshing but it put them behind schedule. Qiu knew that Sun Shanwang would be awaiting their arrival at HQ, and as the van entered the outskirts of Beidaihe he became increasingly tetchy. He felt that the members of his staff were having altogether too good a time; their faces wore broad smiles and they were looking out of the windows, pointing, giggling and chattering. Beidaihe was lost on Qiu. It was a pretty place, having large, well-watered public gardens, many teahouses and some good restaurants, with a sprinkling of comfortable clubs and hotels where foreigners were allowed to congregate with China's favored VIPs. Mao Zedong used to summer here, a historical association that still clothed the resort with a certain cachet. At this time of year it was also full of smartly dressed young people, who could stay at the local youth hostels for three yuan a night. As the minivan raced along the promenade, its occupants, according to sex, cast many an appreciative glance at the girls in their billowing, flowery summer dresses, or at the young men wearing expensive mirrored sunglasses. For people in Beidaihe had money; only the wealthiest cadres could afford to holiday there.

Qiu, oblivious to all these enticements, rose from his seat and turned to face his staff. "I think it would be an excellent thing if we demonstrated our enthusiasm for our arrival now. Please join me in song."

The cadres' faces instantly turned glum, but it did not occur to them to disobey. Red Dragon was Red Dragon. When Qiu Qianwei cleared his throat and began to beat time with his forearms they sat up straight and made ready to follow his lead.

"To the frontier, to the country,
Where the Revolution needs us most . . ."

The other occupants of the van felt self-conscious at being asked to wade through such old hat, but three years of watching Qiu's progress had left them in no doubt as to who was master. They sang.

"Great Party, beloved chairman,
We are ready at your command . . ."

So that when the van came to an unnecessarily violent stop in the courtyard of the Summer Residence overlooking the sea, Sun Shanwang was treated to a perfect exemplar of noisy and patriotic enthusiasm.

". . . To the frontier, to the country,
To the harshest places in the land!"

Qiu clambered out of the van, his eyes blinking against the
glare of the sun, and greeted his superior with an equal's smile.
Sun Shanwang surveyed him thoughtfully. "I sometimes wonder,
Qiu Qianwei," he said at last, keeping his voice low so that no one
else could hear, "whether you are quite sane."

Qiu's smile faded.

"To the frontier, to the country . . . pah! You want to return
to the days of living in the bitter sea, is that it?"

Qiu took offense and let it show. "I wished merely to keep up
morale."

"By singing the songs of the Cultural Revolution?" Sun shook
his head, a look of genuine sorrow on his face. " 'The tall tree is
crushed by the wind': don't try to stand out. Come with me. I have
things to say to you and no mistake."

Qiu followed him inside the cool building, which had once been
a hotel; its thick, cream-colored walls and terra-cotta roof spoke
of prosperous and more gracious times. When the two men crossed
an archway giving onto the sea Qiu caught a glimpse of youngsters,
clad in white and wearing straw hats, as they sauntered along the
promenade on the other side of the hotel garden. He would have
liked to join them; but instead he trotted obediently behind Sun
Shanwang until the latter suddenly pushed open a glass-paneled
wooden door and began to descend a dark stairway to the base-
ment.

The transition from heat to coolness was immediate; Qiu could
feel the sweat drying on his skin. At the foot of the rickety stairs
Sun rapidly forged ahead until at last they came to a square room
with a concave roof which had evidently been decorated recently,
for it still reeked of fresh paint. The only means of ventilation was
provided by a metal grill in the far wall. Qiu, who had eaten nothing
but a biscuit for lunch, began to feel queasy.

The room contained only two chairs—one on either side of a
basic wooden table—an ashtray and a plug-in telephone. That was
all. The concrete floor and stark white walls were otherwise completely bare. Sun pointed to the chair in front of the table and Qiu
sat down. He was cold now; cold and nauseated. The harsh smell
of turpentine pricked the back of his throat. It seemed to be rising
upward into his head, via his delicate sinuses. Sun took the other

chair, lifted the phone and spoke a few quiet words. For a while nothing else happened. The two men stared mutely at each other across the table. Eventually Sun took out his cigarettes and lit one. Qiu did not react. Somehow he knew, without having to ask, that he was not at liberty to smoke. After his superior had taken two drags, however, he tossed the pack across the table in a careless gesture accompanied by a brief smile. Red Dragon pushed the packet back with a shake of his head but no corresponding words of thanks. By now he was very cold.

Five minutes passed.

Then the door was flung open and Qiu, startled, swung around just in time to see a human figure pitched headfirst into the room: a girl. Two men quickly followed. Their rough hands dragged the girl up from where she had fallen and made her kneel on the concrete floor. They did not find it difficult. She was little more than a skeleton covered with skin.

"Head down!" cried one of the men.

"Hands behind, arms stretch! Wing position!"

The second voice brooked no denial. The girl obeyed; and, as she did so, Qiu Qianwei realized with a start that he knew her. She was thin as a cane, her greasy hair stuck to her scalp in patches, there were bruises on her arms, her face, her legs, but still he could just dimly recognize Wei Shasha.

Even in the midst of the mental turmoil provoked by the girl's unexpected appearance, Qiu could perceive, with a curious kind of empathy, what was going through her mind. For the rules were the same whoever you were; the same for Qiu and for Wei, even the same for Sun. Like every inhabitant of the People's Republic of China, Shasha had always anticipated that this day might come. Now that it was here, she knew exactly what was expected of her. Her only course was to submit; and do it with good grace. Keeping her head bowed, she extended her arms straight out behind her, while the strange voices embarked on an unholy litany.

"Ghost . . . !"

"Demon . . . !"

"Freak!"

"Look up." Shasha raised her head to gaze into the impassive eyes of Qiu Qianwei, who stared back as if nothing were happening. *"Speak!"*

"I am sorry."

"There, see! She admits it at once!"

The two newcomers were standing on either side of the table. As the initial shock wore off, Qiu's eyes focused; he could see them clearly now, their faces contorted with rage, hands clenched into threatening fists. He had never met either of them before but he knew who they were. They belonged to Unit 8341, Chairman Mao Zedong's praetorian guard which, under its former leader, Wang Dongxing, had usurped responsibility for all matters relating to internal security and discipline. Even Sun Shanwang, the deputy controller of Central Intelligence, was indirectly subject to their jurisdiction and control.

These men wore white shirts, open at the neck, over black trousers. Their hair was long, lank and unwashed; their hands were crude. The larger of the two was stocky, in his forties; the second man was younger, much thinner and half a head shorter than his companion. They were both peasants, men who had helped make the Ten Terrible Years of the Cultural Revolution; men without refinement, intelligence or sensitivity of any kind. Officially, they and all their kind were out of favor and under suspicion; their unit was no longer even recognized as having an independent existence. But in China, nothing ever worked quite like that. Nothing was ever thrown away. A policy might be put on the shelf to gather dust, but no shelf was so high as to be altogether beyond reach. Chinese civilization extended back into history for ten thousand continuous years. Nothing was new. All things had their turn.

Qiu trembled inwardly and was patient. He did not bang the table with his fist, shout that he was a colonel, goddammit, and just what the hell did they think was going on? This was the Middle Kingdom. Everyone in the tiny room knew his role, just as if they were all participating in a Chinese opera. Wei Shasha's duty was to acquiesce in whatever was done to her. She was under an obligation to submit. Red Dragon's role was different. He was meant to observe—and learn.

Sun Shanwang leaned forward to stub out his cigarette, turned to Qiu with a polite smile and spoke. "Difficulties have arisen," he said matter-of-factly. "You know this, Wei Shasha."

Although his words were nominally addressed to the girl, Qiu saw at once that they were meant for him alone. Everyone realized this. One of the men who stood beside Wei shook her shoulder and said, "Speak up, rightist!" but his eyes never left Qiu's face.

Wei Shasha whispered something and was silent. Red Dragon knew that the time had come for him to respond on behalf of the girl and of himself, but his brain refused to function with its usual efficiency.

"Difficulties . . . ?"

"It is an unfortunate fact that your people have not so far succeeded in retrieving Simon Young's copy of the contract. His wife, Linhua, is a grave disappointment to us. Also, the catastrophe in Singapore when this girl was nearly caught inside Soviet Communal Bank, undermined Baba's Hong Kong wall. You know this."

"Excuse me, but was it *really* a catastrophe?" Qiu returned Sun's polite smile. "And those things occurred more than two years ago. There were bound to be setbacks at the start of the project. Personally, I never quite believed that the Chrysanthemum had the kind of influence over Young Linhua that he claimed, but I saw no reason why he should not be allowed to try to persuade her."

"I see. He did not succeed, of course. But in over two years, nothing has been done by you to retrieve the situation. And only now do we face the full extent of our troubles. Linhua, Nine Sticks Wei here . . . they were your servants. And they have failed."

"Forgive my obtuseness, Elder Brother, but I do not understand."

One of the men from Unit 8341 leaned down, pulled Shasha's head up and, very deliberately, spat full in her face. "You intellectuals!" he cried. "Why, what is it our Great Helmsman called you? The stinking ninth!"

His colleague likewise brought his own face down to Shasha's level. "You are *fan-hua*. You are anti-China!"

"Traitor!"

"Yes, you are a smiling tiger, a hypocrite."

"We will put a cap on you, Wei Shasha—*dai-mao-zi!*"

"Yes, we will make you wear tight shoes." His voice rose to a scream. "It is time! Time to settle accounts!" He cuffed the girl's ear, as if to ram the dreaded phrase—*suan-zhang*—into the colonel's head. For now there were two, quite separate but linked, conversations going on: the men from Unit 8341 maintained their dialogue with the unfortunate girl, whose job it was to act as surrogate for Qiu; while the two "brothers" calmly continued to analyze the project's limited success as if they were alone in the room. But it was obvious to all concerned that Wei Shasha did not qualify for the label "intellectual." No one doubted the identity of the real villain.

Sun was speaking again. The other two men reluctantly drew back, as if barely able to restrain themselves.

"There were twelve numbered copies of the Ducannon Young contractual documentation with the Soviet Communal Bank. Only twelve. That includes drafts, everything. Patiently, and with great skill, our friends in the other world outside have been collecting those documents for us and returning them to Beijing. Clerks in solicitors' offices. Triads. Yes, common thieves even, but friends of China, all of them. One by one eleven of those twelve documents have been retrieved, and replaced with the substitutes you and I prepared. In nearly every case there has been no trouble. No one suspects. But in the case of Singapore, Little Brother, things were very different. And in the case of Linhua, I have to say, with deep regret, that your department failed outright."

He broke off to light another cigarette. This time he did not offer one to Qiu. The men from Unit 8341 folded their arms, never taking their hostile glares from Red Dragon's face. The stench of paint was in his nose, his mouth, his stomach; he wanted to be sick. But through all the hostile sparring and the intimidation at one remove, he kept hold of a simple fact: Sun continued to address him as Little Brother. It signified that this session would end and the world would go on as before. What happened in the room constituted a warning, but Qiu was to be given another chance. It was therefore necessary for the deputy controller to preserve an elementary façade of courtesy, so that next day the two men could face each other again. If ever Sun dropped that façade, Qiu was executioner's business. As long as Sun remained civil, however, he was safe. Relatively speaking.

"Singapore was bungled, Little Brother. Botched. Yet you chose personally to oversee the operation. It was your idea to send the Nine Sticks, not ours. You went down with her yourself. You supervised everything, just as you deliberately chose to supervise the removal of Young's copy of the contract from his safe in Hong Kong. Can you please very kindly explain yourself?"

"Certainly." Qiu was amazed to hear how calm his own voice sounded. "Those were the most important of the contracts, Elder Brother. The bank's own master copy, Young's personal copy, the ones they would, *will* use in court." He broke off as the memories of his last encounter with Jinny Young came flooding back. "I . . . I felt it necessary to take a personal interest, to ensure that when the Soviet Communal Bank comes to enforce its security it wins the case. So I took command of the individual assignments."

"Yes, you did. And of all the various operations mounted to retrieve these contracts, only those two failed."

"May I please very humbly suggest that they did not fail. In Singapore, the contract was taken from the safe. What else could this girl have done? The substitution was made."

"It was made. Unfortunately, we do not know if the KGB realize that. The Nine Sticks left signs. For one thing, she removed the snake's body. Its absence must have been noticed the next day."

Qiu shrugged. "Not necessarily, I think. There are always air vents, lift shafts, nooks and crannies. The disappearance of a reptile would not, I venture to suggest, have caused undue concern—not in a place like Singapore."

"Perhaps you are right. But that wasn't all. The loan agreement which she found in Tang's safe contained a scrap of paper, with the Chrysanthemum's name on it. Was it planted there deliberately? Was it left there by accident? These are things we do not know."

"There are many Zhaos in Singapore."

"You know, as I do, which Zhao was intended. Did you ever check out the telephone number on that piece of rice paper?"

"I tried." Qiu, aware that he was about to score a valid point, grew more confident. "I was told to stop—that from then on, what happened in Singapore was none of my business."

Sun frowned. "I did not know that. Sometimes these things happen. But in any case, let it be said that the number was checked. When you dial it you get only an answering machine, never a person. The machine has been traced: it is in an apartment in Singapore, a bare apartment with no furniture, not so much as a mat. Zhao—Chrysanthemum Zhao—goes there once a month."

"But may I please suggest an explanation? I thought that we were to approach Tang and try to bring him over? Perhaps the Chrysanthemum had already made a start—"

"We were and are interested in Mr. Tang. But the Chrysanthemum is no part of that scheme. It was not his business to interfere."

Qiu's mouth fell open. "That's terrible!"

"Not terrible. It is a matter which we are weighing, that is all. Mr. Zhao does a lot of legitimate business with Soviet Communal Bank. It is natural that someone of his stature should deal with Mr. Tang, the chief executive of the branch. The slip of rice paper proves nothing by itself. It may have got into the Ducannon Young loan documents by accident. The Chrysanthemum has managed to overcome the many financial difficulties which beset him two years ago. He is once again a rich man, secure in his position. We have no reason to mistrust him now."

"But in the past you implied that his financial speculations were leading him into areas of temptation—"

"Yes, there were times when we feared for his loyalty. Those times are in the past. But do not, please, concern yourself with this. You have other worries. As I have said, the paper was only one thing: Wei Shasha left signs of her presence."

"She left signs. But the bank did not detect them."

"How can you be sure?"

"They would have raised the question with Simon Young, asked him to reexecute the documentation. They did not do so."

"It might not be in their interest to do so. Although there's still time for them to do so. And it leaves untouched the question of your own failure in Hong Kong, with Young's wife."

The room became silent. One of the Unit 8341 men unfolded his arms and Red Dragon saw that his right hand held a long knife. Qiu swallowed, but his mouth was dry of saliva and his throat hurt. Shasha twisted her head around to look up and uttered a moan. The man disappeared behind her; next moment she could feel a point pressing against her neck. She lowered her arms. She was panting like an exhausted dog, with yelps of terror. Suddenly she retched, choked and was sick on the floor. The edge of a man's hand chopped at the nape of her neck and Shasha collapsed into a puddle of her own vomit.

"You must mend your ways, Little Brother," Sun said. "In some respects you have improved, in others not. You muddle through from day to day. Also, you are overconfident in your own abilities. This is not what we require. The organization has higher expectations than that."

The organization; in other words, the Party. Sun's message was very plain: Qiu was in imminent peril of losing not, perhaps, his life, but his Red status, of becoming "capped" as politically unreliable. Sun continued to address him from behind the table, affecting unawareness of his subordinate's blue-lipped pallor, only once again his words were nominally addressed to the girl.

"Wei Shasha, remember what the women tell their daughters-in-law when they have borne a girl child: 'You had flowers, next time bear fruit.' If you fail, we will handle you. We will give you more than a big demerit. Lift her up, please."

The larger of the two Unit 8341 men bent down to pull Wei upright by the neck of her army tunic. She swayed but remained on her feet, while Sun Shanwang continued to address the room in the same quiet tone. "The Nine Sticks has just returned from Qinghai, Little Brother, where she has undergone reform through labor."

Qiu shuddered. *Laodong gaizhao* might stand for many things, but in popular parlance it meant quite literally working a person to death. Qinghai was China's equivalent of Siberia: few of those sent there ever came out again. Wei Shasha had been lucky, then.

"You should take heed," Sun went on. "We are 'killing the chicken to scare the monkey,' so-not-so?"

Qiu hung his head. "So."

"We have reached a watershed. Hence the point of this meeting. You are a fortunate monkey, this time. The Nine Sticks was an opportune chicken. You should take heed of this. 'A dead pig doesn't care about being scalded'; but for you there is still much to live for. Do you understand?"

"I understand." Qiu lowered his head in shame. He felt dreadful. It was he who ought to be there on the floor, not Wei Shasha. But that knowledge didn't prevent a part of him from feeling glad that she had suffered in his place.

"Good, good. There is also much to be done. Now, however, I think you need to reflect on some things. Perhaps we were wise to choose you for these tasks, perhaps not. You are still too much of a theorist. You must complete your transformation into a man of action. And as I say, you must not be so confident of knowing all the answers in future."

Sun Shanwang turned to face the girl. "As for you . . . for now it is merely appropriate that you write a final self-criticism. I will not cost you face by making you read it aloud to the cadres— this time. It is between you, me, Red Dragon and these two comrades." He indicated the men from Unit 8341. "They will assist you. They have . . . experience of such matters."

The shorter of the two men picked up the table and carried it out of the room while his colleague removed the chairs. Sun Shanwang unplugged the telephone and tucked it under his arm. As he reached the door the other two were returning; Qiu saw how Sun hesitated for a second before pushing past and knew a second of gritty satisfaction. Then he lowered his gaze to what they had in their hands and he winced.

"Look *up!*"

As Wei Shasha threw back her head the first man poured a bucket of ice-cold water over her while the other sluiced the soiled floor. Then the larger man gave her a shove, sending her toppling backward onto her coccyx.

"Here . . . paper!" The second man tossed a pile of loose sheets in the general direction of Shasha. Many of them landed on the floor where they sopped up water but she managed to retrieve about half a dozen and keep them more or less dry. "Stand up! You can write on the wall, can't you?"

"I can."

"*Ai-ya!* You capitalist! How long have you been plotting, eh?"

Sun spoke from the doorway. "I think, Colonel, that it would be as well if you were to stay here and help Wei *tongzhi* with her essay."

Qiu swallowed. "Certainly."

"Perhaps you would like to suggest an opening sentence for her consideration?"

Qiu's features shaped themselves into an expression of sub-servient humility. "Let us begin with . . . 'I deeply regret my incorrect attitude.' " He looked away, unwilling to meet Shasha's eyes.

"Good, good. Write that."

Shasha tremblingly held a sheet of paper up to the wall and began to write. Sun watched for a moment, then addressed himself to Qiu for the last time. "When you have assisted Wei *tongzhi* to attain a more correct attitude, there is much work to do. You can prepare some further proposals for retrieving Young's copy of the contract. Then, please do an analysis of the Ducannon Young loan documentation, with particular reference to the mortgage."

"The mortgage? You mean the memorandum of deposit?"

"Whatever!" Sun frowned. "We are missing something, Little Brother. The . . . memorandum charges not only Young's existing Founders Shares, but also those to which he may become entitled in the future. Tell me, why was such a clause introduced into the memorandum? It was unnecessary. It was wrong. And we are missing the significance of what has been done. It is important. I do not know why, but I know it is important. So—prepare for me an analysis."

"But Elder Brother, that is no more than standard banking practice."

"I sense that there is more to it than that. You will write the analysis."

"I will, I will."

"And finally, you will please notify Assistant Commissioner Reade that the Mah-jonggs are about to play the hand. On July 31, 1988, eight years and eleven months before we resume control, the hand will commence. It is now your responsibility to ensure that Simon Young makes default on his loan repayments at the earliest possible opportunity. Got it?"

"Zhidaole." Got it.

The stocky Unit 8341 man grabbed Wei Shasha's few remaining hairs and used them to bang her head against the wall. *"Xie!"* he said. "Write!"

15

The recently completed desalination plant was a long, low building that nestled in a cove just beneath Tsim Bei Tsui headland. Its site had been chosen only after protracted debate between structural engineers, who were worried about the subsoil's ability to support the foundations, and Hitachi Zosen's marine experts, with their meticulously drawn graphs of irregular wave patterns thrown up by the shoals of Deep Bay. The result was a compromise; but Qiu Qianwei, studying the scene through the submarine's night periscope, thought it an admirable one for his purposes.

He handed the scope back to the first officer and turned to the captain. "There is no moon, but the plant is lit by eight floods. The white walls are the only problem. As background, they will show up everything." He looked at his watch with a frown. "It is all a question of timing."

"How long do you need?"

"One hour. After that, assume we are all dead and proceed to base."

"*Zhidaole.*"

Qiu hesitated a moment longer, weighing up what he had seen through the periscope. "We go."

Two men were in the Ducannon Young boardroom, overlooking Victoria harbor. It was nearly eight o'clock at night, but neither of them minded that. Simon Young habitually worked long hours. Mr. Ng, who was semiretired, did not; but he didn't come to Hong Kong very often either. On his rare visits, he never complained at having to wait to see his good friend Simon Young.

Ng had made many inquiries about the Englishman after their first meeting two years before. He liked what he learned so much that he did his first, cautious piece of business with Ducannon Young: a joint venture that paid off. Ng began to buy Dunny's shares and now he owned a substantial minority holding. He was attracted by the group's wide spread of activities: insurance to construction to electronics to general trading. Above all, he had a nose for success; and Simon Young fairly reeked of it.

So Ng was no stranger to this boardroom. He sat on a sofa next to the plate-glass windows, quietly sipping a cup of tea while Simon finished signing his late mail. With one exception, the room looked to Ng exactly as it had always looked. Scattered pools of creamy light illuminated its principal features: the long table, Simon's stand-up desk, the telephone . . . and the one feature that was new.

On a table beside the desk stood an ordinary microcomputer keyboard topped by a larger than usual video display unit. The keyboard was light gray in color, its keys picked out in charcoal; the screen's casing was jet black. Ng liked the design. He thought it all looked very purposeful, very efficient. He put down his empty cup, rose and went across for a closer look, running his fingers over the microcomputer's keyboard with an expression of awe on his face. "So small," he commented.

"Yes." Simon Young replaced the cap on his pen and came across to join the Chinese. "Small is the name of the game where those things are concerned. The idea has always been to bring modern chip technology onto the desk of the average middle manager. Market research shows that he can't adjust psychologically to a big machine. And above all, he's got to be able to make himself believe he isn't sitting at a typewriter, he's not a mere secretary."

"This middle manager sounds like a difficult man."

"Very. What he wants is a large, prestigious calculator."

"I see." Ng tapped the casing. "This is not our machine, however?"

"No. This is a prototype Chinese-language graphics computer. Ducannon Young Electronics has been working at it for years, in an on-and-off kind of way. I'll tell you a funny thing: it didn't really start to make any headway until the son of my house servants joined the team. An extraordinary man called Lennie Luk. He's a genius, or so they tell me. We're going to beat the IBM 5550, and they've spent $50 million on research to my five."

"Ah! I've heard of these machines, but never seen one." Ng chuckled. "I couldn't even operate a Chinese typewriter. You would need about twenty thousand characters—but, there aren't many keys . . ."

"No. The secret is graphics. It derives from the Cang Jie method. You assign a basic character element to each key on the standard board, like the one you're looking at. Then you construct the ideograph with up to five keystrokes. Only we're getting it down to four keystrokes maximum."

"It must take a long time."

"A good typist can learn to do sixty characters a minute."

"Very fast."

"It will get faster, with practice and improved software."

"But our machine is to be different?"

Simon drew a deep breath. "Very different. If our joint venture succeeds, it will make that micro on the table so much junk."

Lennie Luk's team had made a major breakthrough with artificial neural nets; and Ducannon Young Electronics was going straight for Sixth Generation, a vocal computer that could not only recognize Mandarin words but also distinguish between the various tones of speech. If it worked, the day would come when every office in China, perhaps in the Far East, had a console; and then Simon Young would rank as one of the five richest men in the world. In Beijing, they were confident enough to have invested seventy million yuan in Ducannon Young's research. Mr. Ng had sufficient faith to warrant a personal investment of five million Singapore dollars. That was why he had come to Hong Kong—to sign a joint venture agreement with Ducannon Young Electronics.

Ng shook his head in wonder. "Junk, you say—but an impressive piece of junk."

"Not impressive enough, I'm afraid. So out of the window it goes. Would you like to sign now, Swee Kam?"

The task force—Qiu Qianwei and five men from the Mah-jongg Executive Unit—landed a hundred meters southeast of the plant, well into the mouth of the bay, where it was darkest. They swam ashore, hauling their equipment behind them in buoyancy bags fitted with short-range radio transmitters that would enable the cadres to relocate them in the darkness once the mission was over. Two men carried Stechkin pistols and twelve spare magazines, while another three towed concentrated high explosives together with a selection of detonators. Qiu himself was responsible for the compact, high-voltage generator.

"Down!"

Qiu's command scarcely carried, but the five men heard. One second they were standing up, the next they lay like black shadows on the sand. The engines of a Royal Hong Kong Police cutter throbbed far away in the distance, a single light at its masthead clearly visible to the task force on the beach. The light continued to move against the darkness without deviating to port or starboard. Qiu waited for the noise of engines to subside. "On!"

The shadows came alive. In total silence the six men made their way along the beach until they were in the lee of the concrete raft that supported the desalination plant. Six feet above their heads the raft gave way to white wall. They crouched with their backs to the concrete. To their left was the sea; to the right the beach sloped gently upward to the road, and the main entrance to the plant.

Qiu closed his eyes and reviewed the layout in his mind for the last time. The long side of the rectangular plant facing the sea housed the inlets. On the landward side, working from southeast to northwest, lay the powerhouse, the control room overlooking the hydraulic seagates, staff daytime quarters and—in a separate compound encircled by a fence—the acid tanks.

Qiu tapped the cadres on either side of him. At once they leaped to their feet and dissolved into the darkness.

Qiu began to count.

One of the two men felt his way along the edge of the concrete raft where it adjoined the sea until he found the first of the inlets. He packed it with high explosive. As he began the delicate task of attaching detonators and fuses, the other cadre reached the telephone pole nearest the road and began to climb, walking straight up it, hand over foot; seconds later the lines were down.

Qiu's count reached one hundred. He stood up.

The four remaining Chinese edged away from the sea, along the lip of the raft. Eight floodlights mounted on masts fifty meters high illuminated the bare expanse in front of the plant. About thirty meters away, to the left of the task force and parallel to the sea-shore, was a high perimeter fence topped with outward-facing strands of barbed wire. It curved round to come between the beach and the forecourt. Qiu pointed at the fence. One of his cadres pulled out a pair of wire-cutters and made a neat hole wide enough to admit a man. The four of them picked their way through the gap and silently lay flat.

Qiu reached for his Zeiss night glasses. There was a lawn in front of the building, with flowerbeds on either side of it. The semicircular driveway connected two gates in the outer fence. Everything was just as the aerial photographs showed. Nothing moved. Where were the watchmen? There should be three of them, if the reports were correct. He swept the face of the building, stopped in midscan and made a minute adjustment to the focusing ring. Yes, there—a solitary light in the staff quarters. But no one was patrolling the frontage.

"Go!"

Two men leaped over the edge of the raft and sprinted toward the acid-tank compound. The first one to reach it began to cut a hole in the wire-mesh fence that surrounded the tanks. Metal clanged against concrete and Qiu winced. The second man ran up to join his colleague. They clambered through, making the fence rattle for about ten seconds. Qiu ground his teeth in frustration. "*Shit!*"

"Who's there?"

Qiu jerked the binoculars back to his eyes and scanned the forecourt. A man had emerged to stand in the driveway with his back to the building. He was old and skinny and he wore a holed vest over baggy shorts. Qiu focused on his face. Yes, an old man, his head shaved in a razor cut.

The watchman caught sight of the two invaders working at the base of the nearest acid tank. "Hey, you!" he cried; but they took no notice. The watchman went back inside the building and reemerged holding an Alsatian dog that strained against its leash, sniffed the air and suddenly began to bark.

Qiu tapped Ye Youmei, his second in command. "Up!"

As the man hurtled across the forecourt, Qiu drew his Stechkin and fired three shots. The first missed. The second killed the dog outright. The third caught the old watchman in the stomach; he doubled up and fell to the ground with a howl.

"Kill that noise!" yelled Qiu.

Ye Youmei reached the old man, prodded him over onto his stomach and put a single bullet into the base of his skull. After that the silence was eerie. All the members of the task force stopped what they were doing and listened intently.

Nothing. The breeze. The waves.

Nothing.

Ye raced toward the door to the plant. He had half a second in which to assess the situation. He flung his back against the outside wall and unwound himself through the brightly lit rectangle, absorbing the interior with a glance. Small room, table, chairs overturned. Rice bowls on the table. Man, indeterminate age and appearance, frantically jiggling the hook of a wall-mounted telephone. Another man, young, active, possibly Filipino, shotgun . . .

Ye dived into the room, sliding under the table on his stomach. The shotgun fired, one barrel splintering the doorjamb where he had been standing a bare millisecond before. Ye rolled onto his back and thrust his hands and feet against the underside of the table, forcing it up like a shield, second barrel coming any moment . . .

The flying table knocked against the gun, sending its blast harmlessly through the ceiling. Ye grimaced with the shock of the noise but managed to stagger to his feet. He threw himself into a horizontal dive, pounding the table toward the far wall like a piston. It hit the man as he was trying to reload his gun, hurling him backward. The Filipino recovered enough to raise the gun by its stock, waving it like a club. Out of the corner of his eye Ye saw the other man drop the phone and come at him, did he have a knife . . . ?

The Stechkin spat once, hitting the Filipino in the neck. Ye was in the act of turning even before the first bullet hit—yes, knife, coming down in a clumsy arc, jump left and forward, work around beside the assailant, *that's* right, one foot out, trip . . .

Ye kicked the knife out of the flailing man's hand, knelt down for maximum leverage, put him in a half nelson and executed him with a single bullet.

Qiu Qianwei appeared in the doorway. He took in the scene with a glance and made a face. "Was all that necessary?"

" 'No witnesses,' Colonel—those were the orders."

"Armed combat against untrained civilians . . ."

"Very unpleasant. We are ready to go now."

Qiu Qianwei wiped his brow. "I left the generator out front when that dog barked."

"I'll get it."

As Ye Youmei sped off, Qiu raised his head. What could he hear? Inland . . . no, seaward side. He ran out, to be joined by the cadres from the acid-tank compound. One of them said, "You hear that, Colonel?"

"Yes. What—?"

"Ship's siren. Police cutter."

Qiu raced to the perimeter fence. Long before he got to the beach he could see that the cadre was right. The ship's masthead light seemed only a few meters away from the spot where he stood. Qiu wasted less than a second on assessments. He turned back to the plant, cupped his hands to his mouth and shrieked, *"Run!"*

Simon Young looked up from the joint venture agreement he had been studying and raised his eyebrows. "Not different?"

"Not really, no. I was expecting to see greater changes since my last visit."

"Which was when? Remind me."

"Just over one year ago." Ng put aside his own copy of the contract and folded his hands on the table in front of him. "The London-Beijing agreement has been signed and ratified for a long time now. Takeover is scheduled for nine years hence. It was my belief that all the so-called 'smart' money would have disappeared and Hong Kong would be half-empty."

"A few companies have gone," Simon agreed. "But I'm still here. Dunny's made it very clear some years ago that it wasn't going anyplace. Oh, I won't pretend we haven't made a few contingency plans, like everyone else. But now we've done that we've gone back to concentrating on doing what we do best, what all true Hong Kongese do best: making money. Nine years is a long time in trade."

"But after that?"

"I'm confident. People aren't so much frightened about their money—for the most part, they've salted it away somewhere safe."

"So what is troubling them really?"

"They're frightened about the quality of life when the mainland Chinese take over. They've really woken up to the fact that the

Brits are going. No more habeas corpus, no more Caucasian detective inspectors to complain to when the Chinese traffic cops make trouble. English laws, yes, for a while at least, but enforced by the PRC."

"And of course, it's the enforcement that counts."

"That's right. Mainland morality reinforced by mainland muscle. When I said people are waking up to these things, I meant it. You said it all looks the same and I know what you mean. Tomorrow I'll take you to a restaurant and you'll start to see the differences."

"Surely that's the last place where anything would change?"

"You'll see. And hear—you won't need your ear-plugs, for a start. Talk in Hong Kong is muted now—can you imagine that? People don't know who's sitting at the next table. The PRC's here. Their presence is being consolidated at every level."

"Was that not always so?"

"It was. But now they're coming out into the sunlight. Take banking. There are thirteen banks in the Bank of China group. Their presence here is literally massive. They have their own stock-broking subsidiary—Chung Mao. And have you heard of a company called Conic, which they bailed out? Last week we had one of their vice chairmen down here, Chang Yanging. He was telling a seminar of businessmen—"

The intercom buzzed. Simon pressed the switch. "Yes, Mary?"

"You asked me to remind you at eight-fifteen, Mr. Young."

"Ah, thank you."

"Will there be anything else tonight?"

"No, thanks. You can go now, Mary. Good night. Oh, leave a line through, will you?"

"Of course, Mr. Young. Good night."

Ng made a rueful face. "I could not get my secretary to work for me on a Sunday night. No one in Singapore could, I think. I suppose that is why Hong Kong is such a success story."

"Yes, people do work here; but even so, Mary's an exception." He smiled apologetically. "I'm terribly sorry, but I have to go on to a reception at Government House. There's a trade delegation from London . . ."

"Please excuse me. I've kept you for far too long."

"It doesn't matter in the slightest; I'm only sorry that I have to leave you now. Look, why don't we defer signing the agreement until tomorrow? We oughtn't to rush it."

"If you still have a few moments, I'd prefer to sign now. Then tomorrow we can socialize with clear consciences!"

Simon laughed and took out his pen. "Good idea." He pulled his copy of the computer joint venture agreement toward him. "Shall we date it with today's date?"

"Certaily." Ng looked at his digital watch. "July thirty-first."

They signed both copies of their agreement and Simon placed his in the office safe for the night. Then the two men rode down in the lift together, still talking about the future of Hong Kong.

The lift reached the ground floor and the two men emerged into the reception area. As Simon went to sign them out in the security guard book his eye lighted on a copy of a newspaper that someone had left lying beside the receptionist's telephone.

"Have you seen that?" Simon tapped the headline. "About my father? I knew a couple of days ago, but I see it's gone public now."

"So the bill passed into law," Ng said, studying the report.

"Yes, late Thursday night, London time. A two-clause bill to extend Thomas Edward Young's tenure as chairman of the Corporation for another decade went through its final stages in the Lords. So now he's stuck here for the duration."

"Are you pleased for him?" Ng asked.

"I think it serves him bloody well right. It illustrates the point I was making earlier, though—the future may not be safe, but it's certainly no more risky here than it ever was."

Qiu flung himself down on the sand to await the rest of his men and raised his binoculars. The cutter was creaming its way toward the desalination plant at twenty knots. A spotlight lanced out, searching the waters of Deep Bay in a broad sweep. Qiu cursed.

"Be quick!"

Ye Youmei was feverishly connecting wires to Qiu's portable generator. He gave the nuts a final twist: all secure. The cutter was less than a quarter of a mile away.

"Into the water! Wait—gun?"

Qiu threw the Russian-made Stechkin up the beach. It lay in full view under the glare of one of the floodlights. By now all his men had reached deep water. But the police cutter lay directly between them and the submarine lurking in the channel. The next sweep of the searchlight couldn't fail to detect the helpless frogmen.

Qiu backed along the shore, paying out the wire, until he felt the sea rise around his ankles. Ye Youmei was waiting for him. Qiu thrust the last remaining buoyancy bag into his hands and snapped: "Dive."

Qiu gave Ye ten seconds to clear the beach. He wound the portable generator to prime it and was about to press down on the plunger when a thought struck him. The cutter was plowing inshore. If it came close enough it was bound to be damaged by the blast and its crew would have no time to worry about frogmen . . .

The cutter's spotlight swept the sea, connected with the men in the water, homed in. A loudspeaker crackled.

"Hold quite still, or we shoot. Stop swimming. You will be picked up."

Qiu let go of the generator. He ran up the beach, grabbed the Stechkin and fired two shots at the cutter's light. Before the crew could react he had dropped the gun and regained the shoreline. A quick burst of automatic fire raked the sand by his right foot. In the same second he jabbed his finger down on the generator's plunger; a huge wave of hot air picked him up as if he weighed no more than a feather; and Qiu Qianwei was flung forward into a boiling sea that suddenly glowed a mysterious shade of coral-pink.

16

The helicopter came in at five hundred feet. Simon persuaded the pilot to circle the blaze three times. Even at that height he could feel the heat radiating upward through the rolling clouds of orange and black smoke. The flames, blazing against a dense backdrop of tropical darkness, looked much worse from the air than they really were, but even so Simon was left in no doubt as to the size of the disaster facing him.

"What's that?"

Simon pointed downward and the pilot dipped to the right. "Looks like a ship. Police cutter, I think. Christ, she's drifting. What the hell—?"

"Take us down now, please."

As the helicopter landed in a field opposite what remained of the plant, a man ran forward at the crouch to open the passenger door, and Simon recognized Reade.

"Peter—thank God you're here."

"I came as soon as I heard. Wear this and keep your head down." Reade thrust a yellow hard hat into Simon's hands. "They're fighting to save the last acid tank. If it goes, hit the deck."

They began to run toward the plant. Simon could see that the main structure was holed in several places, although the building itself still stood. Flames flickered at the windows and doors but they were dying down now. A heavy shower of water from the seaward side deluged the site from on high. Simon stopped short and pointed. "What's that, Peter? Rain? Can't be—"

"Seaborne tenders. Stroke of luck—they were on their way back to Victoria from a gas explosion on a supertanker. We diverted them."

"What are they doing about the acid tanks?"

"Nothing. They're out of range of the hoses. We've got men fighting it on the ground, but it's hellish dangerous. Come on."

They ran past the front entrance and turned left up a low rise topped by thick bamboo. Two jeeps were parked side-by-side in a clearing, a table between them and gaslamps on their hoods. Various uniformed figures bent over the table to examine plans; other men stood in groups and talked; troops came and went; but Reade wasted no time on unnecessary introductions.

"Right," he said. "Situation. A police cutter cruising in the bay heard suspicious noises coming from the plant."

"Noises?"

"Shots."

An army lieutenant came up to Reade, saluted and said, "Sorry to interrupt, but we're evacuating the villagers from Mong Tseng Wai. Any problems with that your end?"

"None. Why bother, though?"

"Because if we don't, and this thing spreads, London'll eat the Commander British Forces Hong Kong for breakfast."

"Right, get on with it. Sorry, Simon. The cutter came inshore and found men in the water and another on the beach. He fired; they fired back. Next thing they knew, the plant went up in flames. Hell of a shock wave: the cutter damn near turned turtle. They've still got two men unaccounted for."

"What about the men they saw?"

"No sign."

"So what the hell—?"

"Come." Reade led the way to the makeshift table. "Look at that—no, don't touch it."

He pointed to a pistol lying on the table, a brown label attached to its trigger guard by a piece of string. "They found that on the beach. It's a Stechkin. Russian."

"Good God." Simon leaned against the table, his legs suddenly feeling weak. Reade laid a sympathetic hand on his shoulder. "Sorry, Simon, but I can't begin to puzzle out what's going on here."

"I can." Simon shook his head. "It's incredible that they should get away with it. I thought you had the Soviets nailed down tight here."

"Don't remind me. Are you saying you know what happened?"

"Isn't it obvious? Soviet Communal Bank really doesn't intend for me to repay the loan. They want the shares. And they know that if I can't bring this thing on stream soon, I'm in trouble." Simon lowered his voice. "What are you going to do about this, Peter?"

"Do?"

"*Yes*, dammit, do! I went into it on your say-so, remember."

"Let's talk about it in the morning."

"Now *look*—"

"The morning."

Simon was about to protest but he was interrupted by cries from the road. A Chinese policeman ran up the rise, "They're bringing out bodies, sir. Sergeant Pearson says would you come?"

Simon and Reade sped down the slope. In the middle of the road, under the glare of an arc lamp, lay three long shapes covered by white sheets. Reade knelt down, pulled back the nearest sheet and grunted. "Want to look?" he said to Simon. "I don't advise it."

Simon took a step forward. For a moment he couldn't quite understand what he was staring at—it was unusual to see a black man in Hong Kong. Then a horrible smell hit the back of his nose and he retched.

"Oh, God," Reade said wearily. "Features melted, we'll need the teeth. Sergeant!"

"Sir."

"This is now a murder investigation. Contact Central and get a surgeon out here pronto."

"Yes, sir. The man over here has been shot."

"What?"

"Shot, sir. In the neck. Small-caliber bullet, by the look of it." The sergeant bent down low so that he could talk to Reade without being overheard. After a moment, Reade rose to his feet and took Simon's arm. "Talking of shooting—did you know that your night watchmen had a shotgun on the premises?"

"Shotgun? Of course I didn't! You know damn well I'd never—"

"Then that's something else we'll have to discuss in the morning."

Another policeman came up. "Excuse me, sir, but Mr. Young is wanted."

"Oh? Who wants him?"

"His family, sir. Three of them, in a car."

"You'd better go, Simon. I don't want Jinny anywhere near this lot."

Simon needed no prompting. Apart from anything else, he had not seen his children since their arrival. "Where are they?"

"We stopped them a hundred yards or so down the road."

He found Jinny's red Porsche parked off the road on the verge. As soon as he entered the headlights' beam the doors opened and three people hurriedly emerged.

"Da! Oh, Da—"

He ran to take his daughter in his arms. "What a homecoming," he murmured in her ear. "Sorry." They hugged; then he held her at arm's length, to see how she had changed.

She was still wearing her traveling clothes: a pretty tailored blue dress with a white collar that set off her lightly tanned face. Her hair was dark brown with tints of rust red, taking nothing from either parent; it fell in tresses around her face, still slightly chubby from too much school food, somehow accentuating the generous sprinkling of freckles that nature had allocated her. She hated those freckles because she thought they impaired the purity of her skin, at seventeen not yet awake to the knowledge that allure can take many forms. Simon thought of his daughter in precisely that way: still not quite awake, but stirring in her sleep.

"Da, how awful for you. How horrible, hateful. I am so sorry." She had grown up. She realized there was a crisis and was serious but quite composed. No one meeting Diana for the first time would have known that she was of mixed race; only on closer acquaintance did a trace of Oriental blood show through. If the lineage showed anywhere, it was in her voice: the girl's intonation owed everything to Canton and nothing to Roedean, where she was educated. Although she spoke perfect English, it was with an intriguing foreignness that would one day bring men to her side.

Simon released his daughter and half-turned to greet his son. He held out his hand and was surprised when the boy embraced him. "Hi, Da." Mat sounded embarrassed, as if conscious that although at eighteen he was nominally an adult, yet he lacked the means to cope with this disaster. The boy was nearly as tall as his father and had Simon's piercing dark brown eyes, but his thick, straight hair was jet black, the principal sign of his semi-Chinese ancestry, and when he moved it was with an athletic ease which the older man now lacked. He was dark and lithe and in Mat's face his mother's East met father's West, but on good and equal terms.

Simon held his son close, feeling the tension in him and wondering what caused it. Jinny came up to them slowly, giving them time to adjust to one another, but Simon released Mat and took her in his arms at once.

"Are you all right?" she murmured. "I am so very, very sorry."

"It's all right. Thanks, but I'm okay."

"I just don't know what to say, I—"

"No, don't talk." His next words came out in a rush. "Oh my dear, I am so very glad you've come."

"How could we stay away? The children just had to see you."

He gave her a final squeeze and gently disengaged her hands from his shoulders. "You mustn't come any closer, though. There are . . . awful things back there."

"Bodies?" said Mat.

"Shut up, Bean Sprout." Diana's voice sounded firm.

"I was only asking."

"Bodies," said Simon. "Very badly burned bodies. Peter Reade is—"

The last explosion came without warning. They all heard a high-pitched whistle lasting less than a second, followed immediately by a blue flash and a bang that seemed to reverberate on and on, but there was no corresponding shock wave.

"What was that?" asked Jinny.

"The last acid tank. They were trying to save it. They . . ." Simon turned away his head, not wanting them to see him battle with the tears that rose to his eyes.

"I've brought you some food," Jinny said after a while. "Soup, bread. And there's whiskey."

Simon drew a deep breath. "We'll all have some whiskey," he ordained. He made a great effort to sound normal. "Bad news, yes, but good news too. Both my children on one day. Too much."

Mat caught his mother's eye. "Girl child, thousand ounces gold, boy child, ten thousand ounces gold," he teased.

"Oh, blah," said Diana, "you can be such a tactless pig at times." Her anger dissipated as quickly as it had arisen. "Da, what's it all mean? How did it happen?"

"They don't know yet, Diana. It will take them ages to find out, I imagine."

Jinny brought a flask of whiskey and some plastic glasses. Simon raised his and said, "To us. To the Youngs."

"To us!"

But it was a sad little toast. None of them could think of anything else to say. After a while, Simon drew Jinny aside. "You should take them home now."

"What about you?"

"I can't leave yet. I'll come when I can."

She squeezed both his hands between her own. "I want to stay."

"There's nothing you can do. Go home, get some rest. I'll need you all later, when this is over."

Reluctantly she nodded. Simon had already turned away from the car and was walking back to the bamboo grove where Reade had established his temporary base, when, to his surprise, he felt a hand pluck his sleeve.

"Da."

"Why, Mat—what is it?"

"I need to talk to you. Okay, I know this isn't the best time, but . . ." He faltered. Simon looked at him questioningly.

"It isn't the best time," he agreed. "But if it's that important to you . . ."

Mat's face wore an anguished look. "No," he mumbled at last. "It can wait."

"You're tired. We're all bushed. Wait until you're fresh, mm?"

The boy nodded and backed away from his father for a few paces, before he turned and ran to the car. Simon stood and watched the Porsche drive away until he could no longer see its taillights.

The fire was more or less under control by now, although the last explosion had done nothing to make the firefighters' task any easier. Simon sat in the front seat of one of the jeeps, impotently listening to the shortwave radios crackling, conferring with Reade, waiting for news. At last daybreak came, bringing some answers, but also posing fresh questions.

The main structure of the one-story building was badly affected but not devastated. There had been four charges: one planted next to the acid stores and the other three in the water inlets. The latter were destroyed or blocked and the control room had been taken out completely. Army experts, quickly on the scene, estimated that altogether three hundred pounds of high explosive had been used; and Reade, grimly conscious of an unparalleled threat to security, ordered an inquiry into how the stuff had been smuggled into the New Territories.

Simon Young had other, more personal concerns.

As he wandered through the smoking, sodden wreckage his mind wrestled with the potential disaster that stared at him. The plant had been due to come on stream in less than a month. At that point, two things should have happened simultaneously: the interest payable on his loan from the Soviet Communal Bank would increase dramatically to a full commercial rate; while the plant itself started to generate an income from which to pay the bulk of that interest. Now the first event was still going to happen but the second was not. The differential was vast.

And Soviet Communal Bank would not wait. That thought was uppermost in Simon's mind as he stood in the remains of the plant's control room, watching the first boatload of workmen disembark. The bank would not wait.

A refined English voice carried easily through the drifting smoke. "What a grim picture. I'm sincerely sorry." Simon, startled out of his reverie, looked down and saw Robert Zhao standing on the jetty beside his long white launch, which today flew a Union Jack at its stern.

"I'll join you," Simon said.

As he approached he saw the Governor disembark from the launch and sourly acknowledged to himself that over the past three years Zhao had managed to make some awesome friends. His Excellency was accompanied by the Commander British Forces Hong Kong, as if to underline that this was no mere courtesy trip. The four men made a quick tour of the plant, their faces heavy with shock. When the Governor asked for an assessment of the damage, Simon did a mental calculation and reckoned that it might cost anywhere between two and five million pounds to repair the structure and make it fully operational. He said nothing about interest repayments.

The Governor and Commander British Forces soon departed; but Zhao remained. Simon looked at him in surprise. He was not in the mood for company.

The Chinese shook his head a great many times, as if wanting to deliver a lecture but afraid to speak. At last he said, "I saw this coming, you know. Taiwanese terrorists, of course."

"Thanks for the warning, then."

"Simon, Simon . . . things are changing here. In some ways it's a pity this wasn't a Chinese project."

Zhao sounded sincere. Today he made no pretense at being a mannered, slightly eccentric English gentleman.

"It is a Chinese project," Simon said.

"I mean exclusively Chinese. We could have dealt with the bandits in Taipei. We have ways."

"That's as you wanted it. With Ducannon Young laying the pipes. Or lending the screwdrivers—which was it, Robert, I forget?"

"Bitterness between us won't help." Zhao's voice was reproachful and sad. "We have to be constructive."

Simon turned to look at Zhao. He was not inclined to be polite. "What the hell does constructive mean?"

"Well, we have to consider what can be done to salvage the plant. It was for the good of Hong Kong. It was the most popular thing anyone has done for years. People will be outraged; they'll crowd around to help you rebuild."

"I doubt it. They'll say this place is bad joss and stay away in droves."

"Not at all. But in any case, you must be insured against this kind of thing. It is a setback, not a disaster. It doesn't even dent you." He paused. "Does it?"

Simon was almost moved to tell Zhao the truth, but he checked himself and said nothing.

"I'm sure you'll find the most massive support in town today. Massive." Zhao smiled. "I myself have a number of positive suggestions to make. Let me take you to lunch; you look as though you could use a break from all this."

"Make your suggestions. I'm listening."

"Well, if you're really in a bind I might as well make the most outrageous suggestion of all—"

"I'm not in a bind."

"And offer to buy the whole thing off you." Zhao laughed in his easy, well-mannered way.

"I see. I see. For how much?"

"Goodness me, Simon, it's early days yet. I mean, I'm only making a proposal in principle to help you out."

"You have a figure. I'm sure of it. Please give me the figure."

"Well . . ." Zhao's voice had suddenly become sharp. "Why don't we cover your costs with Soviet Communal Bank, plus a few thou' over for finder's fee, or management, or something? We can lose it in the accounts somehow, I'm sure."

Another boatload of workmen had arrived. The foreman had already organized them into gangs and they were starting to clear up the lighter items of flotsam and jetsam that littered the site. A lot of things were still too hot to touch. It would be weeks before rebuilding could start. Simon Young considered Zhao's proposal against a background noise of planks being thrown one on top of the other. It was the saddest sound he had ever heard.

"How did you know about Soviet Communal?" he asked.

"Oh, come on now. This is Hong Kong."

"It was totally secret. Not even my father knew. How did you know, Robert?"

When Zhao said nothing, Simon went on. "Tell me something else. Do you know a man called Qiu Qianwei?" He was studying Zhao's face closely as he spoke the words, but the Chinese remained inscrutable.

"Doesn't ring a bell at all. Why—should it?"

Simon turned away from him and shook his head. "It doesn't matter. So that's one suggestion. What are the others?"

"Sorry?"

"You said you had a number of suggestions to make. A number."

"Ah. Well, that is the main one to have occurred to me so far."

"I see. You're not even trying to be subtle, are you? Tell Qiu that the answer is no. Have you got that? No."

"Look, just who is this Qiu?"

Simon raised his eyes to the sea. Zhao's high-powered launch, having delivered the Governor and Commander British Forces to Hong Kong island, was approaching across the flat gray water. The glare of its bright paintwork under the white sky made him wince and he looked away.

"You must be going," Simon said.

Zhao studied the Englishman's haggard face and sighed. "I suppose I must. I don't like leaving you here. You look all in. Can I offer you a lift?"

The morning was bakingly hot. Humidity had reached its seasonal peak. Simon's body dripped with sweat; he had been wearing the same clothes for twenty-four hours and they reeked of smoke; he desperately needed food and rest. But he was damned if he was going back to Hong Kong with Robert Zhao.

"There's a lot to do here. Good-bye."

The deliberate omission of thanks was an insult and Zhao's face hardened. "As you wish," he said, not bothering to offer his hand. He ran down to the jetty, picking his way lightly through the wreckage, and hopped aboard his launch. As the boat pulled away, heading for the open sea, he did not look back. Instead he went straight to the day-cabin and ordered his captain to set a course for Guangzhou. Then he poured himself a drink and settled down in one of the sofas, opposite his guest.

"How did it go?" asked Qiu Qianwei.

"Not too well." Zhao frowned, stung by the memory of the recent interview. "He rejected the offer out of hand."

"Of course."

"But that may only be because he's in a state of shock."

"No. Even when he recovers from the shock, he won't be interested in your offer. May I have a glass of water, please?"

"Help yourself."

Qiu poured water from the chilled flask and resumed his seat opposite Zhao. "I have some further instructions for you, Chrysanthemum. From Baba himself."

"Haven't I done enough? There's nothing else in the contract."

"What contract? You forget, I think, how much you owe us. Owe us in money and also in other things more valuable than money. Life, for instance."

"That's what *you* say. I think the account is running quite strongly in my favor, but we can discuss it some other time. Why don't you just tell me what Baba wants so that I can consider it."

Qiu pursed his lips. "You understand the position we have reached?"

"What do you mean?"

"Soon the Russians will call in the debt. Young cannot repay. So the bank will sell his Founders Shares."

"Of course."

"It is now Baba's wish that you buy them with money we shall provide, and then transfer them to us."

Zhao had been toying with his glass. As he heard Qiu's words his hand closed around it with such force that the knuckles turned white. Red Dragon observed with curiosity how the man's whole body was shaking, but he held his peace and waited for Zhao to speak.

"I see." He did indeed see, all too clearly: he was now under an obligation to transfer the same set of Founders Shares to the Russians *and* the Chinese. For a moment he felt so frightened he could not breathe.

"You will do this for us." It was not a question.

"I had not appreciated that this was what you wanted, Red Dragon. I thought the plan was very different—to bring down the bank. It was on that basis, on that understanding alone, that I consented to become involved."

Qiu shrugged. "What can it possibly matter to you, Chrysanthemum?"

"The plan was—"

"Do not worry about the plan. Just consider your instructions, please, and prepare some proposals for giving effect to them. Soon, too—very soon."

Zhao stood up and went across to refresh his drink. He felt he needed alcohol to stay alive. As he dropped ice into his glass he heard Qiu say, "You will do this thing."

"Oh yes," said Zhao as he turned away from the bar, drink in hand. "Whatever Baba wants, of course. Oh yes."

17

Simon spent most of the rest of that day in the Ducannon Young boardroom, making phone calls around the world. At tea time George Forster brought in the first set of provisional figures. Unless they could raise in excess of one and a half million pounds sterling within the next twenty-seven days, Ducannon Young would default on its interest payments to Soviet Communal Bank.

Simon slumped in an armchair at the head of the table and pointed to the seat on his right, nearest the window. As Forster sat down Simon asked him, "Can we borrow that kind of money? Surely we can."

"It's come at an awkward time, but I think so," said Forster. "We have the insurance to fall back on. I spoke to the lawyers at lunchtime: they say the underwriters must indemnify, although not necessarily yet. I can take the policy to the big lenders and try to borrow against it."

"Where do you suggest?"

"Go big, go respectable. Let me talk to Nomura in Tokyo. They're among the best friends we've got, they'll put something together."

"Perhaps—but how soon?"

"We have nearly four weeks. That should be long enough. Do you want to involve your father?"

"No. He's the last person. And don't let's get overconfident. Remember how hard we tried to raise finance initially without going to the Russians? Why should people be any kinder now? It was difficult enough to interest investors in Hong Kong in 1985. Now it's ten times worse."

"You're insured. That makes a big difference."

"So you say. I rang a hell of a lot of people today. No one wants to know, insurance policy or not." He sneered. "So much for Robert Zhao's 'massive support.' "

"Leave it with me, Simon. I'll talk to Nomura tomorrow. They'll come up with something, I'm sure of it."

"So am I, at bottom. It's bad, but we'll weather it. Have you tried Beijing?"

"What?"

"The PRC dreamed up this scheme in the first place. Why shouldn't they bail us out now?"

George Forster shook his head. "You'd be asking for a vast commitment. There's nothing in writing. They'll say you've had bad luck, that's all."

"Then what about Reade and his crowd? He backed this, backed it all the way—though you wouldn't think so, to hear him talk last night. I used to trust Peter Reade; now I'm not so sure. Let's test it. Let's send the bill to HMG."

"By all means ask. But the British government didn't plant those bombs. Terrorists from Taiwan, it had to be."

"I suppose so. That or the Russians."

"You're not making sense. I know the business with the pistol was odd, but never in a million years will I believe that Soviet Communal organized that explosion. It's a preposterous thing to allege. International banks just don't go in for that sort of thing."

Simon stared at him through bloodshot eyes. "It's my Founders Shares we're talking about here. Twenty of the most valuable shares in the world. A fortune in themselves. Anybody would do anything to get them. And just whose side are you on?"

George Forster was tempted to remind his managing director

that in 1985 he had advised against pledging the shares on any terms, but he bit back the words. "Your side. The company's."

Simon's gaze slid away. "Sorry."

Forster, hurt, was silent for a moment. "Have you spoken to Soviet Communal yet?" he said at last.

"Yes. I managed to get through to Tang after lunch. He was very formal. Said he'd have to refer the matter to his board on Monday."

"To Moscow, in other words."

"Damn right. Borisenko. The KGB. I just can't believe this is happening! You say that international banks don't go in for this sort of thing and on the whole I believe you—but we've never dealt with a KGB-backed organization in our lives before. Who knows what they'll do?"

"We have a few resources of our own, remember."

"How do you mean?"

George hesitated. "Well—I'm still not sure I've got all this right, but . . . as I understand it, you very carefully made sure that the documents you sent down to Soviet Communal in Singapore were irregular on their face."

"Yes. To be valid, they should have been executed in front of a magistrate, who would then authenticate my signature with his own."

"But that didn't happen. The authenticating signature, so-called, was written by Luk Seng Kay—"

Simon had been nodding his head with increasing impatience during Forster's speech. "Yes, yes, I know what you're going to say: If the documents are technically forged, the bank can't sue on them."

"That's right."

"But I'm not sure that it *is* right! Bankers never part with a loan until they've checked and double-checked their security. So why did they lend the money in the first place?"

"Sorry?"

"Cast your mind back to the day when the first part of the Soviet Communal's loan came through; didn't it all seem artificial to you then? How could Tang have missed such a glaring defect in the security documents? Was it just carelessness?"

"What else could it be?"

"I'll tell you. Suppose there'd been a switch, before Tang had a chance to examine the documentation I sent him. Suppose Qiu and his gang got there first."

"Qiu?"

"Who else could it be?"

"But—but he has no possible motive. It was Qiu's idea in the first place to have forged documents. You said so! You told me that the very day you came back from Beijing: 'Qiu suggested putting up forgeries,' those were your words—"

"Yes, all right—but who else do we know who'd have the slightest interest in fiddling with the documents? I tell you, this is starting to drive me mad." He banged the table with his fist. "If we're losing Peter Reade's support, we're in real trouble. Real trouble . . ."

Forster saw the worn expression on Simon's face, "It's nearly six now; you can't do any more tonight. You've had a shock, you're all in. Go home, eat, sleep."

Simon's brain was exhausted, like his body. He knew that there was an answer to George Forster, there had to be, but it wouldn't come to him. When George picked up the phone and called for the car he did not protest. Suddenly all he wanted to do was crawl home to his family and eat the first proper meal of the day.

They were already gathered around the dinner table when he came in. It was Mat, sitting immediately opposite the door, who looked up first and saw his father's tired face. "Ah, the *tai-pan* returns," he said cheerfully. "Back from the money mill."

"You don't want to make money, I suppose." Simon managed a smile.

"Oh Christ, yes. I'm a Young, aren't I? A *Ducannon* Young. I want to make money, a lot of it."

"Do you think you'll succeed?"

"Yes. I've got your business brain, your streak of ruthlessness and none of your high-mindedness. What an awful drawback that must have been, by the way."

"You're welcome. I've had it up to here with Hong Kong."

Mat crowed with laughter. "Stuff Hong Kong! I'm off," he said; and—Ah, thought Simon, how brutal are the young.

"Da, how's your day been? What's the news?" Diana sounded concerned.

"No news." He smiled at her; there might have been no explosion, no bodies, no commercial disaster staring the family in the face. "You know the rules. No business at dinner."

Diana pouted but kept her mouth shut. Tension had always been part of the atmosphere in this house. The children were used to it by now.

Ah Kum brought Simon a dish of sizzling prawns. "There's fish, chicken curry, baked liver and green vegetable. Some of everything?"

"Yes, thanks. And fetch me a whiskey, will you?" He smiled at Jinny, who sat opposite him at the round table, and said, "Long day."

"You look exhausted." Her face was almost as tense as his own.

"I am. Don't let it get you down." He indicated, with a little shake of his head, that he didn't want to talk about it in front of the children. "We'll survive."

"Survive!" Ah Kum had brought the whiskey. "Boss, you should talk 'survive' to your daughter, here."

Simon struggled to put his cares behind him. He turned to Diana on his right. "What have you been up to now?"

"Nothing."

"You're not eating," Ah Kum insisted to Diana. "Thin as a wire."

"Thin as a bean sprout, that's Mat you're confusing me with. I'm getting huge. I'm fat."

"Fat, pooh! What man will ever desire you, so thin and tall? You want Chinese husband?"

"Definitely. And some more of your black bean sauce."

Ah Kum hesitated in the doorway, exploiting her twenty years' license as a servant in the family household. "Chinese husband very good, can be very rich. Marry older than yourself, though."

Jinny caught Ah Kum's eye and frowned. "What do you want? Hanging around there listening, as if nothing to do."

"All right, all right," Ah Kum grumbled. "When you are old, you'll maybe want to rest too, now and then. Listening, indeed!"

Diana ran around the table to kiss her father. "Early night. Jet lag."

"Good night. Sleep well."

"Coming, Bean Sprout?"

"Uh—in a mo."

Simon looked at his son inquiringly. The boy was dressed in jeans and a T-shirt, as if for relaxation, but his face was drawn. "Dad, can I have a word with you and Ma?"

"What's it all about?"

He meant to sound interested and kind, but somehow succeeded in conveying only impatience. Mat was discouraged at once.

"Um. It's about my future, and things."

"I see. About Cambridge. I've been meaning to write to your housemaster to see what he thinks of your chances. Any ideas?"

"No." Mat hung his head. "Look, this is going to take some time. Maybe tomorrow night."

Simon felt that his son wanted to be made to yield up his message under pressure; he needed milking. It was the wrong time—Simon longed only to go to bed.

"Perhaps tomorrow would be best," he agreed.

"Yup." Mat sounded relieved. "Well. Think I'll go to bed. 'Night."

"Have you any idea what that was about?" Simon asked as the door closed behind their son.

"I have an idea, yes. But he hasn't confided in me, if that's what you mean. I should wait until he's quite ready, if I were you."

"Come and sit here."

Jinny came around the table, collecting Diana's empty chair on the way and pulling it close to Simon's. She put her arm around his neck, took one of his hands in her own and hugged him tight. "Bad day?"

"Not good. Better now, though. It's lovely to have them both back."

"I am sorry about Mat. It wasn't a good way to welcome you. He's still not very sensitive."

"Mm? Oh." Simon shook his head. "Never mind that. I don't want the children worried about things. I'd much rather they weren't sensitive."

She kissed his cheek. "You were right, in what you said."

"What's that?"

"We'll survive." Her voice sounded fierce. "It doesn't matter about the money. It does not matter. We're together."

Simon's smile was rueful. "I don't want us to be poor. I don't think we'd be much good at it."

She squeezed his hand. "We'd become good at it. Don't fall into the trap of thinking that I've loved you for your wealth. I love you as a man. Qiu Qianwei either didn't understand that, or he forgot it. Please don't make the same error."

He gently pushed her away until he could look at her properly. Then he brushed a strand of hair off her forehead and ran his fingers down her face, pausing for a second on the tiny mole, marveling to find so much beauty beneath his hand. "I love you," he said abruptly.

"Yes. And for me it's the same."

Next morning saw a miraculous break in the weather. Humidity dropped, the seemingly perpetual summer blanket of cloud disappeared and a hot sun shone down on the inhabitants of Hong Kong.

Simon awoke shortly after seven. For a long while he lay staring at the ceiling, unable to move. His body felt rested but heavy, as if the effort of swinging his legs off the bed would cost too much. His mind was strangely empty. Several times he tried to concentrate on business problems, but his attention invariably slid away and he ended up focusing on the pattern of the bedroom curtains, or the flicker of light reflected off the sea onto the wall opposite.

Jinny was still asleep. He managed to shower and dress without waking her. He went out to the garage and took the Porsche. There were people to see, things to be done; the sun was already high.

The rest of the household awoke about an hour later. Jinny announced over breakfast that she was going to the shops. When she asked if anyone else wanted to come, Diana said that she was still too tired and Mat had already arranged to play tennis with some friends. By nine o'clock, Diana was alone in the house except for the servants. As she sat in the lounge reading the paper she heard the front doorbell ring; a moment later Ah Kum put her head around the door and said, "Surprise for you."

Diana looked over Ah Kum's shoulder and with a cry of pleasure recognized her grandfather.

"Diana . . . how marvelous. My, but you're looking well."

"Thanks, Gambs. You look fantastic yourself. Like an ad for old age!"

"Thank you indeed. Just what I needed to hear. May I come in?"

"Of course. You're in the papers, did you know?"

"Oh, *that.*"

"Congrats. Fancy having an act of Parliament all to yourself. What does it feel like, having your tenure extended? It sounds like a nasty operation you have in hospital, doesn't it?"

"It feels a bit that way, too."

"Come and sit down."

Tom made himself at home in the living room. He half expected Jinny or Simon to enter, but when the door opened again it was to reveal only Ah Kum bearing a tray of tea. "The house is so quiet," he murmured. "Where is everyone?"

"Ma's gone shopping and Bean Sprout's playing tennis." Diana sat next to him on the sofa and poured his tea for him. "Da's gone to work, I think."

"It was your father I came to see, actually. Oh dear, that does sound rude, doesn't it? I'd forgotten you were due home, to be frank."

"That's all right. You must have masses to do." She reached out to stroke his hand. "Lovely to see you."

Tom sipped his tea. "Excellent." He drained the cup and held it out to her wordlessly. Diana understood without having to be told that he wanted it refilled, not removed, and picked up the teapot.

"How's your father feeling, do you know?"

"Pretty shattered, I think."

"How's your mother taking it?"

"Bearing up. We all are, really. It's sort of . . . unreal. Sometimes I think it's just another one of Da's business problems, you know, and then at other times—can I ask you something?"

"Of course."

"It's a silly question I know, but . . . do you think, well . . . is there anything I can do? Anything *any* of us can do?"

He shook his head. "I don't think so."

"Do you mind talking?"

He considered the question calmly, as if he had been asked for his views at a board meeting. "No." He could see what was coming, and concluded that his granddaughter was old enough to cope with trouble.

"Is it bad?"

"It could be. The company can rebuild the plant quickly, I should think. And of course they must have been insured against things like this. But your father will have to find some money very soon."

"A lot of money?"

"A lot."

"More than I've got in my piggy bank?"

It was her way of offering Simon all she had, which was not inconsiderable, and Tom knew it. "More."

"What happens if he can't get it?"

He was silent. After a while Diana said, "Are you going to lend it to him, if he needs it?"

"We'll have to see. I would need to have the answers to a great many questions before I could consider that." His face set into a hard expression. "And when I say many, I do mean many."

"I see. I need to know something. I've been thinking, and I really do need to know. It's not just prying."

"Go on."

"You won't be cross, or anything?"

"I'll try not to be."

"What went wrong between you and Da?"

Tom smiled uneasily. "Why do you need to know, as you put it?"

Her answer came out pat. "Because I'm a member of this family too, and the family's in trouble and I want all the information I can get. I want to assess our chances."

"I see. And you believe that knowing about your father and me will help?"

"Yes."

"You're wrong."

Diana jutted out her chin. "I think you should let me be the judge of that."

Tom sighed and was silent for a moment. Then he said, "Do you know what people mean when they describe me as a money man?"

She shook her head.

"They mean I'm someone who lives for money. Not personal spending money, not that. I'm not obsessed with the desire to make money, any more than I'm consumed with a lust for pretty women or drink or power. But money's my life. I like to manage it. I like to make it grow: a vast oak of money growing from one tiny acorn of investment." He grunted. "You're bringing out the corniness in me."

"No, I'm not. It's fascinating. Go on."

"Well . . . your father's not like that, of course. He's very different. He doesn't succumb to the fascination of money. Or at least, he does, but he's always got to have a double motive, another reason for doing something apart from the financial profit involved. Have you noticed that?"

"Yes."

"A long time ago, we fell out about our different conceptions of money, of business. Your father wanted to do a housing development called Ko Shan. I wouldn't lend him the money because I foresaw, correctly, what was going to happen to the property market here in Hong Kong. And he got very upset. He's never quite forgiven me."

"But—you were right, weren't you? I mean, property here is a bad investment, isn't it?"

"I thought so, yes. But Ko Shan was eventually built by Hong Kong Land, and they made a fortune out of it. A fortune that your father might have had. They bucked the trend. But it was worse than that, in a way; worse for Simon, I mean. The government here held up Ko Shan as a model for others to follow. Somebody, the architect I think, got an MBE for it."

"Da wouldn't have cared about a medal."

"I know. But he'd have liked the thought that he'd done something right for Hong Kong."

"Well, at least it wasn't your fault that they bucked the trend, was it? Anyway, Da could have borrowed the money from someone else."

Tom shook his head with a smile. "Hong Kong isn't like that. Out here, when a father won't lend to his own son, no one else will."

"You sound . . . sad. Almost as if you regret your decision."

"Wouldn't you? Wouldn't you regret it if something like that poisoned the whole of your relationship with your own son?"

The bitter question brought Diana up short. "I don't know," she said at last. "I'm not sure. But I do know one thing, Gambs."

"What's that?"

"I'm glad you told me. And . . . and I hope you and Da find a way of, of . . . well, sorting things out."

Tom sighed, patted his knees and stood up. "I must go." His voice had turned cool.

"Business?"

"Yes, business. A meeting, then lunch."

"Ooh, sounds nice. I bet you don't have to queue for tables. I bet you've got fantastic restaurant presence."

Tom laughed. "Business lunches always sound nice to people who don't have to attend them."

"Where's this one?"

"Ocean Park. There's a high-level trade delegation out from London and it's been decreed that we should take them to lunch somewhere *different*." He snorted with derision. "Extremely boring, if you must know."

"I've always loved Ocean Park. I hear they've finished the funfair. Is it true?"

"It's true."

"Will you take me with you? Not the lunch, of course, but to the funfair?"

"I've no objection to giving you a lift. As long as you realize that we'll have to separate as soon as we get there."

"Of course. Give me some rough idea of when you'll be leaving, and I'll meet you at the cablecar: then you can take me home as well."

"What cheek!"

"Oh, go on."

Tom considered the proposition. "All right," he said at last. "Why not? You go and get ready, I'll meet you outside."

A few moments later he emerged from the house with Diana and began to walk toward his car. "Fabulous," she cried excitedly. "You've brought the Rolls! Do you still drive yourself?"

"I do. I can't abide chauffeurs."

"You're so terribly sixties. Never mind, I still think you're terrific."

"I'm glad you approve. I've had this now for—hey! Hey, you!"

As Tom went around to the driver's side a youth who had been lurking behind the car jumped upright and stared at the two of them, as if undecided how to react. Tom, thoroughly startled, saw that he was a surly Chinese with the expression and general appearance of a Hakka. For a moment the two men just stared at each other. A huge gold ring dangled from the Hakka's left ear. The ornament attached to it was unusual and large enough to attract Tom's notice: a molded ideograph representing the Chinese word for "I."

"What the hell d'you think you're doing?" Tom said angrily at last. Without bothering to reply the Hakka spat at them and raced for the gate. Tom Young was too surprised by the youth's unexpected appearance and dramatic departure to see him signal to another man waiting on the other side of the road; but Qiu Qianwei, who had been keeping the Youngs' house under surveillance for the past twenty-four hours, missed nothing.

Hong Kong's Ocean Park occupies a large, hilly expanse of land at Repulse Bay, overlooking the East Lamma channel. It is built on two levels. As the visitor enters he can either explore the zoo immediately in front of him or he can take the cablecar up the steep hill to the funfair, aquarium and dolphinarium. Diana wanted to visit the funfair and "see the fishes," as she used to say when she was little, while Tom Young's meeting was due to take place in the upper-level restaurant; so the two of them proceeded straight to the cablecar and in a quarter of an hour were carried aloft, high above the bay, to the top of the hill.

They parted at the terminal, with Diana promising to be back at the cablecar no later than three o'clock. She bought herself a hot dog and a Coke and then set out for the aquarium. Ever since she was tiny, she had loved to buy a cardboard cup of scraps and toss them to the sea lions and dolphins, watching in awe as they came bounding out of the water to catch their dinner.

Diana walked slowly along the concave outdoor gallery, watching the sea lions glide through the aquamarine water as the complex machinery behind the scenes produced waves of differing depth and force. She tossed her scraps, leaning as far out over the five-barred railing as she dared, before going to sit in the auditorium to watch the high-diving display.

While she sat, she thought over what her grandfather had said earlier, trying to make sense of it. The undercurrent of hostility that ran constantly between Tom Young and her father used to frighten her, because she had never understood it. Now it no longer seemed frightening; just inexplicably silly. But, she realized, that didn't make it any easier to resolve.

When the diving was over she visited the funfair and scared herself rigid on the roller-coaster, before strolling back to the terminal, ready to meet her grandfather.

The weather began to fail: clouds once more overlaid the sky and the afternoon was sultry with the pressure-cooker steam heat that typified Hong Kong at that time of year. Diana was glad when Tom came to their rendezvous on time. She wanted to go home for a bath and a long siesta.

"How'd it go?" she asked. "Who took who to the cleaners?"

He guffawed. "You ought to think about a business career. You have the right instincts."

"Thanks, but no thanks."

"What do you want to do with your life?"

"I haven't got a clue. Isn't that dreadful?"

"Well, it's not wonderful."

As they joined the queue for the cablecar there were only

about a dozen people ahead of them. Tom rested his back against the white safety railing and for the umpteenth time vainly tried to work out how the system worked. The cars were little round plastic bubbles just large enough to accommodate six people sitting around a central hub. Each bubble was separated from the next by about fifty meters of cable; but as the cars arrived at the terminal they somehow reduced their rapid velocity and bunched up together to make a fat, disjointed caterpillar. This caterpillar never quite stopped, but while it completed the necessary U-turn it slowed to the pace of a gentle walk; so that, as a bubble passed by, the intending traveler had to hop in quickly and sit down before the doors automatically closed and the car once more began to accelerate out into the void.

They had reached the head of the queue. Tom stood aside to let his granddaughter enter the car and quickly followed her in. Immediately behind them was a family of five; as was customary on these occasions, none of them made any attempt to enter the Youngs' bubble, being content to await the next one and travel together. But as the doors were on the point of sliding shut a young Chinese male thrust his way past them and insinuated his way into the car, twisting his body sideways through the narrowing gap.

Tom knew a moment of alarm. Queue-jumping was far from unknown among the Chinese, but this young man had shown unusual determination to push his way to the front of a line that by now had grown long. He was wearing a shabby, off-white shirt, black jeans and sandals. It was obvious that he had not shaved for at least a couple of days. His long hair hung across his forehead in lank, unwashed rattails. Tom Young didn't care for the look of him.

Tom became aware of a commotion on the terminal which they had just left. A second Chinese had pushed his way to the head of the by now outraged queue and was standing on the very lip of the deck, looking after them with an expression of anger on his face. As Tom watched he turned and ran back, beyond the range of his vision.

Diana was looking out of the round perspex pod at the rugged coastline below and did not appear to have registered the intruder's unsavory appearance. There was a long, lonely stretch of rocky terrain to be traversed before the car climbed once more to breast the last hilltop and start its descent to sea level. With a shiver Tom realized that the three of them were isolated from the outside world, cut off from help of any kind.

He told himself not to be a fool. The two men sat opposite each other, facing inward. The Chinese, far from posing any threat, slumped in silence, with his knees almost touching Tom's. Diana, in the seat next to her grandfather's, sat twisted round so that she could look out and see where they were going. As they passed underneath one of the steel pylons built into the side of the hill there was a clank and the pod swayed slightly before resuming its even, quiet progress. Tom groped for something to say to his granddaughter, anything just to end a silence that was becoming ominous.

He turned his body so that he could face Diana and touched her arm. As he opened his mouth to speak, the youth suddenly pulled something from the top pocket of his soiled shirt. Tom heard a rustle and could not check an instinctive desire to look around. The youth's eyes moved rhythmically from the thing in his hand to the face of the Englishman opposite. Tom realized that the boy was holding a square of cardboard. And simultaneously he deduced, with horror, that what the youth held was a photograph of him, Tom Young.

"My *God*! Look!"

He twisted back to look out of the front of the car. Diana had half risen and was staring fixedly through the perspex. He followed her gaze but could see nothing. "What? What is it?"

"There! You see . . . that man climbing up the pylon, the one nearest. No, *two* men. And look—can you see more of them on the further pylon? The pylons . . . they're swarming with people."

Tom looked over her shoulder and saw that what she said was true. Even as he watched, one of the men on the nearest pylon swung himself off the steel ladder and on to a cross-strut, where he hung precariously over the void beneath. A second man was still climbing quickly up the ladder. In the distance he could see other, antlike figures manning the next pylon.

For once his mind let him down; and in so doing, nearly cost him his life. He perceived the men on the pylons as assailants. All his attention was concentrated on evading the attack that, he anticipated, must come as their car passed underneath the pylon which they were fast approaching. He forgot completely about the Chinese youth sitting behind him. It was only when Diana looked over her shoulder, into the car, and screamed that he woke up to his mistake.

What happened next was over in little more time than a camera shutter takes to click, but to Tom it seemed like a slow-motion movie. First he was conscious of an odd squeezing sensation throughout his body, as adrenaline poured into his system and his natural defenses organized themselves for the coming assault. Muscles tensed, blood prepared to congeal, white corpuscles multiplied. Then he looked down to see the long, silvery blade sliding toward his stomach and he bent at the waist, seeking to avoid its thrust. At the same time his hands lanced out toward the face of the Chinese, fingers poking straight for the eye sockets.

It was a standoff. The youth jerked his head backward and to one side, stumbled but quickly recovered his balance. The knife blade, deprived of momentum, stopped a millimeter short of Tom's suit. There was a clank and a loud rattle as the pod ran under the first of the pulleys that supported the cable away from the pylon. Diana shrieked. The youth swung his arm back sideways and drove the knife toward Tom's torso. Then came a crash as something heavy landed on top of the bubble; the car swayed dangerously to and fro, sending all of its occupants sprawling. The diverted blade drove through perspex, developing a huge rent and forcing open the doors, through which a pair of legs plunged down into the car. Diana pushed the youth off her; in the same flash of time a fourth person thrust his way through the doors and almost simultaneously Tom heard one short, sharp scream, a man's this time: a cry cut off with terrifying suddenness. Blood spurted everywhere: over the perspex windows of the bubble, the floor, Diana's face and clothes, over his own face and hands.

His body, long out of training, began to send out urgent messages. The heart was laboring under protest, the inside of his head seemed to split open with pain, sending blinding flashes of purple light across his eyes. Then the film speeded up again. The Chinese youth once more sat slumped on the seat opposite, only now around his throat there was a jagged red line from which blood still pumped in an ever lessening flow. His eyes were glazed in death. Diana held clenched fists to her cheeks and screamed as if she were never going to stop. The fourth person, a man, paid her no heed. He too had a knife and now he used it to cut a larger hole in the plastic wall of the pod, through which he heaved the dead body with one effortless-looking shove. The dead assailant fell fifty feet onto the rocks below, bounced once and rolled all the way down to the distant seashore.

Tom heard the rattle of pulleys and knew they had reached the next pylon. He tried to see the face of the man who had saved them but, apart from registering that he was Oriental and very tall, he was unable to identify the features. The banker's vision was blurred; his hands, covered in blood, were shaking; he couldn't think. Then the savior departed as swiftly as he had arrived. He leaned backward through the yawning gap in the car's wall, reached upward and pulled himself through. Next second Tom had his hysterical granddaughter in his arms; as he tried vainly to comfort her he saw a figure launch itself into space from the side of the car and swing from the pylon they had just passed.

Tom shook Diana, without producing any visible effect: she continued to scream and struggle, oblivious to his presence. He fought back a rising desire to vomit, and slapped her face. At once she fell silent. Suddenly her eyes opened wide; for a moment he knew she recognized him, then her gaze strayed wildly around the blood-soaked car, her hands pushed against his chest and she fainted.

The pod was descending quickly now. It came down over the coarse, rust-colored grass of the zoo, crossed a road and slowed to walking pace in the terminal. Policemen were keeping a large, excited crowd at bay. As the door slid open Tom half fell into the hands of a uniformed inspector, who assisted him gently to the ground.

"My granddaughter," he croaked.

"All right, sir. We're taking care of her. There's an ambulance."

"My God, my God . . ."

"Don't try to talk, Mr. Young. You've had a terrible experience. We're going to get you to hospital just as soon as we can."

"I'm all right. There was this man in the car with us. He . . . he . . ."

"We know what happened to him. And the other one."

Somewhere in the background a policeman with a loudspeaker was repeating a litany. "There is nothing to see. I repeat, there is nothing to see. Please clear the park now. I repeat, please clear the park now." Tom struggled to sit upright. The world rippled up and down but at least he could see. "What . . . other one?"

"He had an accomplice, Mr. Young. I really think you should rest, sir."

"I'm all right, I tell you." His head was clearing now. "Where's Diana?" The inspector, who had been kneeling, rose to his feet and looked over his shoulder. "They're taking her to the ambulance now, sir. She's in shock. Can you walk?"

"Yes . . . yes, I can walk. Inspector, listen to me—what other one are you talking about?"

The inspector surveyed him doubtfully. "We'd like you to take a look at him later. When you're fit, that is. But that can wait. Look, the doctor's arrived, I really think you should come to the ambulance."

"I've told you, I'm all right. Let me see Diana, will you?"

The doctor and the policeman helped Tom to his feet. He watched while the stretcher bearers carried Diana to the ambulance, before reaching in to stroke her blotchy, blood-marked face. She felt his touch and stirred with a little moan.

"Try not to worry. The doctor says he can't find a wound anywhere. It's just a severe case of shock. Will you go with her, Mr. Young?"

Tom massaged the base of his neck with his fingers. He felt very old. "I suppose I'd better. The parents . . . Do you need me here, Inspector?"

The policeman shot a glance at the doctor, who shrugged and nodded. The inspector studied Tom a moment longer before he spoke. "We'd like you to do a quick identification. It needn't be now, but . . ."

It was plain that he wanted it to be now. Tom stared at him. "The body of the . . . the man who attacked us?"

"No, sir. Some of my men are recovering that one from the sea now. No, someone else. We found him first: in fact, we found him before we even knew about the attack on the cablecar. He's in . . . in rather a strange place. If this was a perfect world, we'd ask you to look at him before we moved the corpse."

"Let's get it over with."

Ocean Park was empty; the police had cleared everyone out. The three men walked through the zoo in silence until at last they came to the distant enclosure where the walruses and sea elephants were housed. The inspector led the way to a low wall and pointed. Tom followed the direction of his finger. At first he could see nothing except an artificial rocky pen containing a pool of water, slowly and noisily replenished from a spout. On the largest rock a huge black walrus was lying contentedly asleep, regardless of the fact that he had some unusual company. At the base of the rock immediately below the walrus a man lay spreadeagled on his back; it was obvious from the state of his naked body that he was dead. Tom had seen nothing like it since the liberation of the Japanese prison camps in the war. When he was able to focus again he saw that the inspector had been joined by a plainclothesman who coughed apologetically and spoke.

"Morley, Triad Bureau. Sorry about this, Mr. Young."

"Who did . . . that?"

"Hard to say, sir. *Hak shea wui*, of course. Black Societies, triads, whatever you like to call them. Whoever did it wants us to believe that it's classic Hong Kong work: Hung Obedience Hall of the Golden Orchard, and so on. But some of those wounds you can see are Green Pang ritual cuts." Morley began to warm to his theme. "The way the heart and intestine are laid out, penis slit lengthways—"

"Yes, yes, all right. Green Circle?"

"Shanghai, sir."

Tom stared at him. "Shanghai?"

"Yes. Do you recognize . . . that?"

"I don't."

"Are you sure, sir?"

"Quite sure. Who was he?"

"A low-grade villain. Until now the only thing special about him was that he did odd jobs for the KGB."

"Oh, come off it."

"Mr. Young, I wouldn't dream of telling you how to run the Corporation. Please give me the credit for knowing a Russian legman when I see one."

Tom was silent. The inspector's eyes bored into his. "Can you think of any reason why the KGB might want to see you out of the way?"

"None whatsoever. The whole thing's absurd."

"Who knew you were coming here today?"

"Who *knew*? Well . . . my secretary, I suppose. Lots of people knew; I was coming to meet a trade delegation, it's been in the papers."

"I see. Anyway—you're sure you don't recognize him?"

"Positive."

"Thank you. Then we needn't trouble you further. I'm sorry about all this. You've had a very lucky escape."

Tom took a final look at the mess spread out on the rock. Something about the body held his attention. A vague memory insisted on forcing itself into his mind across the hideous panoply of events he had recently lived though. Something about this man, his flat face . . . a Hakka. Tom Young stared at the remains of the left ear, where metal glittered in a dark pool of congealed blood. Gold . . . The Chinese all looked alike, of course, but that metallic object . . .

"Just a minute. He's wearing an earring, yes?"

Morley's eyebrows shot up. "We haven't got that far, to be honest with you."

"At my son's home, this morning, when I picked up my granddaughter. There was this man, this Hakka, I think he was a Hakka . . . he was hanging around my car. He looked like a petty thief. He was wearing an earring. The Chinese character for 'I' was on it."

Morley nodded. "We'll check that out. We needn't detain you anymore, not now."

"Thank God for that. But listen, I can't . . . I can't follow this. Who saved us? Was it you?"

"It wasn't anyone connected with the Royal Hong Kong Police. We had a tip-off at two o'clock that there was going to be an incident here. We assumed it was something to do with the trade delegation. It didn't give us nearly enough time to organize anything, let alone a full-scale rescue."

"Tip-off? Who from?"

"*Xinhua*. New China News Agency."

Tom stared at him, reluctant to believe. "The mainland . . ."

"Yes. So it seems."

"Then who rescued us?"

"I'd give a lot to know the answer, sir. Seems to me that this afternoon the colony was invaded by two sides fighting a private war. A war over you. The Soviets versus the Chinese. And we don't like it. You might care to think about that. Is there any reason why those people should want to fight over you?"

There was a long silence while Tom looked from face to face. The two policemen were polite but not overfriendly. "No," he said at last. "And now if you're quite finished, I'd like to go home."

Morley nodded and the group began to walk slowly toward the Park's exit. But the afternoon still had not quite exhausted its stock of terror. As they left the enclosure, Tom suffered a momentary hallucination. Placed beside the path was the flat wooden figure of a penguin. A hole had been cut in its face, so that children could peer through it and be photographed. As Tom walked past he looked straight at it and for a second thought he saw, framed in the wooden penguin cut-out, a small, bad-tempered, adult Chinese face wearing thick spectacles and a deep frown.

He rubbed his eyes and looked again. The Chinese face changed. The corners of its mouth quickly rose and fell in what might have been an eerie apology for a smile. Tom blinked—and the hole in the penguin's face was empty. He began to divert from the path but as he walked toward the wooden figure he felt his legs crumple; the ground seemed to be coming up toward him with terrifying speed; he was aware of hands grasping him; then nothing.

18

Simon went berserk. Mat had finally plucked up the courage to tell him that he was leaving school—for good, he said. He wasn't interested in Cambridge anymore. He wanted a job, any job, which couldn't on any account be with Ducannon Young but which his father must nevertheless arrange through his business contacts. Something in the Far East or, preferably, Australia, involving software development. Tell you what! Simon shouted: I'll give you ten thousand Hong Kong dollars and you can spend the rest of your life programming the world! Mat struggled to escape, but his legs wouldn't carry him. Then it was too late. His father drew a gun and fired it, *bang, bang* . . .

The boy sat up in bed, rubbing his eyes. His heart pounded furiously. A dream . . .

The house seemed deathly quiet. The noise that had awakened

him was not repeated. Mat swung his legs off the bed and gave his head a brisk rub, examining the flakes of dry skin left on his fingernails. Shit. Must get back in condition. Why was it so quiet?

He stood up and slouched across to the bedroom window, overlooking Repulse Bay. He had the best view of anyone, because he slept on the top floor. Beneath his window was the terrace outside his parents' room; below that lay the swimming pool and the steps down to the beach. There wasn't much of a view today, however; the sky was overcast and the sea looked as flat and gray as a stagnant lake.

Mat sighed and allowed the curtain to fall back into place. Poor Di, being attacked like that. What an awful experience. She'd be home today, though; that was something.

He embarked on an intensive study of his bedroom. The location might be great, but the decor needed work, he decided. During last year's summer holidays he had decorated it to suit himself, but this year it all looked so . . . well, juvenile. The Duran Duran poster. The huge flag of the USSR that adorned most of one wall. Last year's cassette tapes, last year's videos. Boxing gloves he'd never wear again. The Sony Walkman that didn't work.

He threw himself down on the floor and did twenty push-ups in quick time, then flipped onto his back and stared at the ceiling. Shit. He'd have to tell Da soon, but when? The man was so uptight about that plant of his. Perhaps he'd tell Ma first, and she could tell Da. Yeah, great idea. Shower first, though.

Mat donned his bathrobe and made for the door. As he headed for the bathroom, something made him look over the banister, down the stairwell. A man was standing in the hall, a Chinese, hands on hips. Mat didn't recognize him. He had short black hair and wore a white, short-sleeved shirt, not tucked into the waistband of his black trousers. He was in his forties, Mat guessed, but you couldn't deduce much from the top of a guy's head. Delivery man, maybe. Friend of *Lao* Luk.

Mat was about to pass on when another Chinese wearing identical clothes emerged from the dining room and joined the first. The boy glanced at him and did a double-take, unable to believe what he saw: for this second man held a gun in his right hand. Mat gasped and backed against the wall, swallowing hard. As he moved, the first Chinese looked up directly at him and spoke a few words to his colleague.

Then they began to climb the stairs.

As the second man placed his foot on the lowest step he pulled a magazine out of his hip pocket and loaded the gun—Mat clearly heard the *snap*. He backed into his bedroom, slammed the door and turned the key, fighting for breath. Sharp pains radiated from the base of his spine and he recognized one of the symptoms of shock. Then, mercifully, his brain cleared.

Mat threw off his bathrobe. He snatched up his sheets, knotting them together and twisting them into a makeshift rope which he attached to one of the legs of his bed. He lugged the bed under the window and threw back the curtains. Twelve feet to the terrace below . . .

Miraculously, the sheets held together under his weight. Mat scrambled out of the window and down the face of the wall to land, panting, on the terrace outside his parents' bedroom. The french windows were ajar. He stole inside and made for the door to the passage, pressing his ear against the panels. He could hear footsteps outside; quite close, he judged. His hand instinctively went to the key, hovered . . . no. That was stupid. If the two Chinese continued to climb to the third story, he could duck out through the bedroom door, along the passage, down the stairs and out.

Where was Ma? Where was Diana? Of course, in hospital—and Ma was going to collect her.

Mat's eyes strayed to the bedside telephone. Risky. What was happening on the landing? He pressed his ear to the door again, but outside all was silent.

The boy quietly locked the door, tiptoed across to the telephone and lifted the receiver. No! He knew he was trapped. He knew they had a gun.

Think, *think*! The Luks. Where were they?

He stabbed his finger down on the bedside intercom. No response. The men he'd seen on the stairs must have reached his room by now. What if there were more downstairs? What if—Mat froze—what if there were others and they were in the kitchen and had heard the intercom buzzer? Then they'd know he was still in the house.

The boy raced for the door and unlocked it. As he eased it open, the first thing he saw was a close-cropped Chinese head less than a foot from him. One of the men had stopped on the second landing, his back to the bedroom door, while the other went on up . . .

Mat slammed the door and locked it, no longer caring how

much noise he made, before racing to the french windows. There was nobody on the terrace. He ran to the guard rail and clambered over. There was a drainpipe on the wall below. Mat scrabbled for a hold on it with his hands and knees, and he began an awkward descent. When his hands scraped themselves on one of the rusty metal brackets that fastened the pipe to the wall he yelped in pain; next second, he barked one of his knees against the wall, lost his grip and slithered all the way to the ground.

Mat heard a voice high above his head. He looked up to see the two Chinese intruders at his bedroom window, pointing toward him. The boy wasted no more time. He fled.

But now he had a plan. At last he knew where he was going. The boat.

The Youngs' cabin cruiser was moored to a jetty beneath the house. A steep flight of wooden steps zigzagged to the beach. Mat flew down them two at a time, caught up in a relentless rhythm, knowing that if he broke stride he was going to fall. Faster and faster he ran, his breath coming in agonized gasps. He leaped the last half-dozen steps, landed on the pebbles with a scrunch, fell to his knees, and for a moment could not move. But there was no time to waste. He managed to lever himself upright and turned to face back the way he had come. Nothing. Yes! There, at the very top of the steps, one figure, two figures.

The Chinese began their descent. Mat wasted a valuable second trying to work out why they didn't run. He knew there had to be an answer, but then everything was swallowed up in panic. He turned back toward the sea and loped off along the jetty.

The white cruiser was moored by two lines. It took only an instant to cast them off. Mat jumped over the side and made for the cabin, trying to remember how the controls operated. What if his father had taken the keys? *Shit!* No, it was all right, they were there: the boy scrambled into the cabin, hoisted himself onto the captain's raised chair and managed to stop his hands shaking for long enough to fire the twin ignitions. Once. No response. Twice. Nothing.

He flung himself sideways off the chair and leaned out of the port window. The two Chinese had reached the foot of the wooden stairway. Now he could see that the second man was stubby and fat, with part of his stomach protruding between two of his shirt buttons. His eyes were lost in rolls of blubber, but his mouth was set in a vacant grin. He looked like a harmless simpleton, but there was nothing harmless about his gun. As Mat watched, he set foot on the jetty and began to lumber toward the boat.

The boy climbed back onto the chair, prayed and turned the keys a third time. The engines fired. He moaned aloud in relief. Now. Half-ahead . . .

The cruiser began to move. Mat looked out of the cabin window again. As he saw the jetty disappear, leaving the Chinese stranded, he lowered his head onto the control panel in front of him, drawing in great gulps of air.

Both his hands were firmly clutching the wheel. But—Oh my God, he thought—the shoals, I haven't got a chart, I don't know where to steer. But it didn't matter. All he had to do was maneuver the cruiser away from the shore, into the bay, and he could radio for help . . .

It didn't work out. Suddenly Mat saw another pair of hands close around his own. For a second he just stared at them, dazedly wondering whether he was still asleep and his earlier dream had somehow resumed. Then, as someone pulled a cloth bag over his head and wrenched his hands away, Mat's last conscious thought was that, of course, there must have been four intruders; not two, but four . . .

Jinny parked the Porsche on the forecourt of Queen Mary Hospital and got out. She went around to the passenger side to lock the door. As she came upright again a hand plucked her arm. "Good morning, Elder Sister."

She wheeled around. "What do you want?" she hissed.

"What I want," said Qiu Qianwei, "is very simple. You will smile. You will not make a fuss. And you will come with me inside the hospital where together we shall make one phone call."

"Get away from me, before I scream!"

"Look." Qiu pointed. Jinny followed the direction of his finger and drew in a sharp breath. About fifty meters away, Diana was sitting on the forecourt in a wheelchair. She looked as pale as a corpse. Two Chinese porters were preparing to hoist her into an ambulance. Jinny opened her mouth to shout "Stop!" but when Qiu tightened his grip on her arm, she could not do it.

"Your daughter is heavily sedated," he said quietly. "She cannot help herself. This morning, you called the hospital authorities and asked that she be taken home by private ambulance."

"I did not!"

"Of course. But the hospital believes that to be the truth. They received such a phone call. A private ambulance arrived: there it is. And so Diana has been made ready to leave. Do you follow me?"

Jinny said nothing. Her face had turned the color of old parchment. Qiu, seeing the state she was in, pressed his advantage. "Come inside, phone and then attend to the formalities of discharging your daughter. If you obey, you may yet see both your children alive. If not . . ."

Jinny knew she could not ignore his threats. He might be bluffing, probably was; but she declined to participate in a game where her own children were the stakes. She allowed him to lead her into the main administration building, where there was a public phone. Qiu handed Jinny the receiver. "Dial your home." She hesitated. *"Do it!"*

Jinny dialed. The phone rang three times before someone answered.

"Wei?"

"Who is that?"

There was a pause at the other end of the line. Then an unknown voice said in Mandarin, "It does not matter who, Mrs. Young. We have your son. He has not suffered any harm. Now let me speak to Red Dragon."

Jinny dropped the receiver. Qiu grabbed it and muttered a few words into the mouthpiece before replacing it on the hook. "You heard?"

Jinny nodded. She could not speak.

"Good. Come, then. Sign the necessary papers and let the ambulance leave."

He walked her to the clerk's office, where he introduced himself as Mrs. Young's brother.

"Oh, yes," said the clerk, a pleasant, gray-haired English lady. "Doctor Chan would like to see you for a quick word, Mrs. Young. His office is just along the corridor, I think he's in."

Jinny gazed at the woman, a glimmer of hope in her eyes. "Of course," she said quickly. "I would like that."

"Good idea," agreed Qiu. "Linhua, why don't you just sign the papers and then we'll go and see Dr. Chan?"

Hope died. Jinny stared at Qiu's smiling face but saw only the waxen, listless features of her daughter. "Yes," she said mechanically. "Let's do that." Qiu waited patiently while she signed the forms. Jinny looked at the bored English lady sitting behind the desk and wanted to shout, "My children are being kidnapped! *Do something!*" But she did not. Instead, she signed.

"Where are you taking me?" she said as they came out of the office.

"To the car."

"You heard what she said—we ought to see the doctor first."

"Too bad."

"Where are we going, then?"

"Home. There you will do what you refused to do last time, and open your husband's safe."

"I will never do that. I told you so then."

"Last time was different." Qiu's microsmile briefly disfigured his face. "Your children were in England. Then."

Jinny's mouth fell open. Her lips worked, but no sound came out. When they emerged into the parking lot she saw that the ambulance was already driving toward the exit, its right indicator winking. "Where are you taking Diana?" she whispered.

"Home. Not yours—home of another sort."

It was an enigmatic answer, but she guessed at once what he meant. "Oh, please no!"

"It's out of my hands."

"She'll never survive it!"

"Be quiet," said Qiu Qianwei. "Unlock the door. I've always wanted to drive a Porsche."

Before leaving the office on Tuesday, Simon had convened a board meeting of DY Trading International Ltd for noon the following day. Trading International was the holding company that exercised control over the Ducannon Young empire, subject only to the ultimate sanction of its shareholders. The six other directors accepted short notice of the meeting as a matter of course. By eleven forty-five they had assembled in the Ducannon Young boardroom, anxious for an opportunity to discuss the extraordinary assault on the chairman of the Corporation which that morning had provided the lead story for nearly all Hong Kong's seventy-odd papers.

As Simon rode up in the lift he felt uneasy about facing his co-directors. He seemed to have aged ten years in a weekend. The bombs, Zhao, Soviet Communal Bank, Tom and Diana . . . there were limits to human endurance. In the course of his career he had fought many battles. Some he had won, some he had lost. But now events seemed to have involved him in a campaign with no resolution.

He nodded wearily to Mary Street, who was speaking on the telephone, and walked across to the boardroom doors. As he reached out for the handle Mary said, "Mr. Young . . . I think you ought to take this one."

"I'll phone back later."

"I really do ask you to take this call."

He stopped and turned. Mary Street's face wore a strained expression he could not remember having seen before and certainly her words were unprecedented. He resisted the urge to snap at her. "Who is it?"

"The Corporation."

"Tell my father I'll speak to him later."

"It's not your father. It's the registrars' department."

"What in hell's name do they want?"

"They won't tell me. But they say it's urgent. It's the chief registrar. He says I'm to find you and interrupt you, no matter what you're doing, and somehow get you to a phone."

Simon's face set. He strode quickly across to Mary's desk and snatched the phone from her hand.

"Young."

"Anson, chief registrar. We have a problem, I need your instructions." There were no preliminaries, no social niceties. Simon realized that the man at the other end of the line was in the throes of a crisis which to him looked every bit as serious as the one confronting Ducannon Young. He stuggled to fit a face to the name Anson.

"Go on."

"I have a lawyer waiting outside in the corridor. He turned up ten minutes ago with a power of attorney bearing your signature, demanding that we transfer your twenty Founders Shares into the name of a company registered in the Bahamas."

"*What?*"

"He claims to act for Soviet Communal Bank's Singapore branch. As well as the power of attorney he has produced a contract, a memorandum of deposit of the shares, a share transfer form, again bearing your signature, and a certificate of default signed by a man called Tang. The manager of SCB's Singapore branch is called Tang, I checked that."

"This is outrageous." Simon struggled to find the appropriate words, but his brain was tired. "Mr. Anson, you're to do nothing. Send this rogue packing."

"Mr. Young, you don't seem to understand my position here." Anson's voice had risen in pitch. "I'm looking at documents which on the face of them are genuine and regular."

"There has been no default, I tell you. What this man is trying to do is a breach of contract between me and his bank. Send him away."

"I *can't* just send him away! Mr. Young, do you deny that this is a power of attorney which you executed?"

Simon said nothing.

"Mr. Young. *Mr. Young.*"

"How can I know? I haven't seen the document, have I?" It was a feeble response and he knew it immediately; the kind of response that answered far more questions than had ever been posed. "Look, Mr. Anson . . . wait. Stall. Hold him off for a few minutes longer while I talk to my own bank." He placed his hand over the mouthpiece and snapped at Mary, "Get me Hillaby on line two."

"I can't hold him off much longer, Mr. Young. I really *cannot.*"

"I understand that, Mr. Anson. Just . . . *hold on.*"

Mary held up another phone and he snatched it from her. "Hillaby! What the devil's going on? Soviet Communal says I'm in default . . . what? What d'you mean, 'oversight'? . . . Well, pay it, man, *pay it now.* . . . How much? . . . *How* much? You must be joking. Look, never mind that now, just *pay it,* do you understand me?"

He slammed down one phone and picked up the other. "Mr. Anson, are you there?"

"Yes."

"I've spoken to my bank. It seems that through an oversight last month's payment was twenty thousand dollars short. That's what this is all about—twenty thousand dollars. I've given instructions for it to be paid immediately."

"There was a default, then."

"Yes. A technical default. Twenty thousand Hong Kong dollars, two thousand pounds, my God, you call that a default?"

Anson said nothing. Simon strove to keep his temper and modified his voice to a more reasonable tone. "Mr. Anson. Read the contract. Read it again. It provides for the loan not to be called in for twenty years after signature. The twenty years are not up yet."

"Except in case of default . . ."

Simon raised a clenched fist to his forehead and silently prayed for strength. "Mr. Anson. *Please!*"

"The contract I am looking at provides that in case of default for any reason the entire loan, capital as well as interest, shall forthwith and without more . . . I'm quoting now . . . automatically become repayable."

"I know that. I understand that." Simon drew a deep breath and jumped into the void. "But the contract is unenforceable."

"What did you say?"

"There was a mistake when the documentation was executed. We have been meaning to set it straight but somehow never got around to it. The signature on the charge, the signature of the witness, is not that of a Hong Kong magistrate."

"I'm sorry, but . . ."

"Please listen, Mr. Anson. The charge, look at the charge for a moment, will you?"

"I'm looking at it."

"It's witnessed by someone called Luk. Luk is my house servant, not a magistrate. There was a mistake."

"This charge is witnessed by Magistrate Hua. His official chop has been affixed next to the signature. There can't be any doubt about it, Mr. Young, that's the first thing I thought of. Magistrate Hua witnessed this charge."

Simon very slowly lowered his hand until the telephone he was holding landed on Mary Street's desk with a clunk. As if across a vast distance he could hear Anson's voice humming and whispering to the unresponsive wood. It seemed to bear no relation to him or his problems. The conversation he had been having with Anson was an aberration. A mistake.

He lifted the receiver to his ear and said, "I will bring my copy of the contract to you at once. In the meantime, I instruct you not to effect this registration, which is based on an application fraudulently made." He heard Anson's sharp intake of breath but paid no heed. "In the event of your effecting registration pending my arrival, I shall forthwith issue a writ against the Pacific & Cantonese Banking Corporation and against you personally, claiming exemplary damages for negligence and the tort of fraudulent conspiracy. Do you understand?"

"I hear what you say." Anson's voice had turned bleak and cold. "I will expect you here within one hour. After that, I shall have to use my discretion."

"You do that, and see what happens. Good-bye."

Simon replaced the phone on its rest and stared across the desk at Mary. He felt sick. "Lawyers," he said at last. "Alan Sanditon, here, now. Tell him I may want an injunction in a hurry. You've got the gist of it, Mary, you can fill him in when he gets here, but don't do it on the phone." He paused, calculating. "Put the board back to three o'clock, with my apologies. Shut yourself up in private with Sanditon, explain what's happened as far as you know it; then shunt him around to the Corporation's registrars, fast. I'll meet him there. God *damn*, where are they?"

"Queen's Road Central."

"Above the corporate finance division?"

"Yes."

"I know it. I'm going home now, then on to the Corporation. I'll be back here before three, God willing."

He drove fast, pushing the Rolls to its limit and praying that Hong Kong's traffic cops were all asleep or at the races. Less than twenty minutes after leaving Mary Street's office he swung in through the gateway of his home.

Something was wrong. He knew it the moment he stepped out of the car. The house, silent and odorless, seemed dead.

Jinny, he knew, had gone to collect Diana from the hospital. But she should have been back by now, surely? And where was Mat? His son liked to sleep late during the holidays, but by midday he could usually be found in the kitchen, preventing Ah Kum from doing her work. Simon cocked his head and listened. He could hear no voices, no clattering of pots and pans. He stood in the driveway, indecisively tossing his keys from hand to hand, loath to enter. For it was wrong.

He did not know what he meant by that, but he felt it intensely. The setup, everything, was wrong.

His eyes lighted on the front door and immediately he saw that it was open a crack. His right hand froze around the bunch of keys. No one in Hong Kong left an outer door open, ever.

Simon approached very slowly, as if drawn against his will, and gently pushed. The door swung open, revealing the entrance hall and, beyond that, the half-open door to the kitchen. His mouth was dry; he swallowed several times, forcing saliva into his mouth. "Hello," he called.

No reply. The walls seemed to absorb his voice and rob it of all resonance. Simon reached behind him and closed the front door, debating his next move. Something told him to get out fast and call the police from a neighbor's house, but he dismissed it as the reaction of a coward.

While he dithered in the hallway a faint smell drifted into his nostrils, a sickly fragrance reminiscent of the recent past. He raised his head and sniffed. The odor had unpleasant connotations for him, but he couldn't identify their source. Not cooking, not sweat, not excrement, but something that nevertheless partook of all three. The harder he sniffed the more his olfactory nerves accustomed themselves to the smell and the fainter it became.

Simon made an effort to shake off the oppressive atmosphere surrounding him. He moved rapidly through the various living rooms, his study, the kitchen, dining room and den. For some reason he needed to satisfy himself with regard to every room in the house. He bounded upstairs and swiftly searched the bedrooms. Nothing, no one: he was alone.

He came down the stairs very slowly. The smell was still hanging around. It seemed stronger on the lower floor.

Why was nobody in? Where were the Luks?

Simon realized he had neglected to examine the servants' quarters. He went back into the kitchen and knocked on the door of the Luks' room. There was no response, but the door gave under the rap of his knuckles and swung open. Suddenly the smell was overpowering and Simon stepped back. He hesitated for a second longer before deciding he had had enough of procrastination. It was time to know.

He went into the tiny lobby and turned to his left, where the Luks' bedroom was. The door stood half open. Through it he could see the bottom of their bed, and on it four human legs. Two of them wore trousers, two wore stockings. Simon advanced into the bedroom like a man under hypnosis, already knowing what he would see.

Luk Seng Kay and Ah Kum lay face down on the bed. Someone had tied their hands behind them and shot them in the nape of the neck, but they were still alive. No, that wasn't right—look again. The impression of life derived only from the writhing black mass of flies that covered the wounds. The heavy aroma pervading the house was the smell of death.

There had been a struggle, that much was obvious. *Lao* Luk's face was covered with lesions. He had died trying to protect his master's home.

Of Lennie there was no sign—but, of course, he was at work. Simon barked a short laugh. Working for Ducannon Young Electronics, how priceless, while his parents lay on the bed, murdered, butchered. Nine-to-five, good pay, excellent prospects—what a marvelous opportunity for a young man with a future.

But no parents.

Simon walked out of the bedroom, took out his handkerchief and used it to close the door. He went back to his study and, still using the handkerchief, telephoned Reade. It surprised him when the Assistant Commissioner said what all good policemen say: "Don't touch anything. I'll be right there."

Simon replaced the receiver and sat staring out of the window at the distant point on the horizon where sea met sky. He felt a strange sense of calm begin to steal over him. The more he was beset by horrors, the more his body's reserves rose to the occasion. But he knew there would come a moment when he must start paying for that.

Reade came quickly. Together he and Simon went back to the scene of the slaughter and stared down at the bed, saying nothing. A thought struck Simon and it was this: an almighty gulf separated him from Reade. The Luks' former employer looked at the bed and was reminded of a thousand memories, incidents, scenes, rows, all part of the process of living in the same house with other people. Decent people. People you almost grew to love. Whereas Reade looked at the same grisly sight and saw only two dead middle-aged Chinese lying on a bed. There was no way in which Simon could communicate his emotions to Reade. As Lennie might have said, their data banks were incompatible. They could not interface.

"I must tell the son. I must do it myself."

"You're not fit." Reade's voice was courteous but firm. "Too much has happened to you. Where are Jinny and the children?"

"I don't know. Jinny was supposed to go and collect Diana from the hospital. She must have taken Mat with her."

"Let's check if she did." They went back to the study. Reade picked up the phone and dialed. At the same moment two squad cars arrived, without noise or fuss, followed by an ambulance. Simon admitted the first of many strangers who were to intrude in his life from that time on. When he came back it was to find Reade standing by the window, a peculiar expression on his face.

"What's the matter?"

"Jinny arrived at the hospital, but without Mat. Diana left in an ambulance about an hour ago. So where is she? And where's Mat?"

"I don't know. He's not in the house, I checked."

Reade picked up the phone again and commenced dialing. "If they're in the colony, we'll find them."

Simon stared at him. "Why the panic? They're out shopping, or visiting friends . . ." But Reade held up a hand and spoke urgently into the phone.

Suddenly Simon remembered: the contract . . . He got up and went across to the wall by the window, where the safe was concealed behind a Constable landscape. He swung back the picture and reached up to the recessed combination.

"Don't touch that!" Reade slammed down the phone. "Here, let me . . ."

The safe was unlocked; it opened at a touch. Simon gaped. "That . . . that's extraordinary."

"You always lock it?"

"Yes."

"When did you last have it open?"

Only when Reade impatiently repeated the question did Simon's brain supply the answer. "Two nights ago."

"And you locked it afterward?"

"Yes. I know I did. Oh my God . . ."

He'd kept his copy of the contract with Soviet Communal Bank in the wall safe. And as Simon recalled that, another thought struck him: a memory of something that had happened more than two years ago now. He seemed to hear Jinny telling him that he could not involve his servants in the forgery. Because it was too dangerous . . .

"Does anyone else know the combination?"

"Only Jinny. I make sure she always knows it."

"Why?"

Why? Because it was a way of showing her that he still trusted her, that's why. But he couldn't tell Peter Reade that. "In case of emergencies."

"Is it written down anywhere? Could anyone else find it, if they searched?"

"No. I memorized it and burned the manufacturer's only copy. Besides, I change it every six months or so. I never write it down."

"When did you change it last?"

"Oh . . . say last May."

"Let's look inside, then."

Simon reached up and rummaged around in the safe. His hand lighted on the Soviet Communal Bank loan documents. He pulled them out of their envelope and scanned them quickly. They seemed to be in order. But before he could turn to the last page, where the signatures appeared, Reade pointed into the safe and said, "What's this?"

Simon followed his gaze and saw a cheap manila envelope with his name typewritten on the face of it. "I don't know what that is," he said dully. "I've never seen it before."

"Right. Then we'll wait for someone with gloves. Sergeant!"

When a uniformed NCO answered the call Reade explained what he wanted. The sergeant came back a moment later with a pair of thin, transparent plastic gloves and gingerly opened the envelope. It contained a single sheet of paper covered with neat handwriting.

"English," said Reade. "Addressed to you, Simon. Sergeant, hold it so that Mr. Young can read it."

Simon squeezed his eyes tight shut and opened them again. The writing was a blur. He blinked and reached out to grasp the sergeant's forearm, bringing the paper closer. Now the letters seemed to coil and writhe, as if reluctant to yield up their message. He closed his eyes again; when he opened them, he could see.

"My dear Simon . . ." He read aloud, very slowly. "For many years I have deceived you. Now you must learn the truth. My first loyalty could never be to a foreigner. My task in Hong Kong is ended. I must return to do my duty where I belong. I am sorry."

Simon's hand began to shake uncontrollably. The sergeant's forearm vibrated with it, making the paper rustle.

Reade had been holding his breath. Now he released it in a long, low whistle and shook his head. "My very dear chap . . ."

Simon looked at him; and to Reade's astonishment he saw that the managing director of Ducannon Young was smiling. Reade's eyes narrowed. "I think," he said lightly, "that we ought to get you to a doctor."

"I have an appointment." Simon's voice was equally light; it sounded almost happy. "With the Corporation's registrars."

"Don't be ridiculous, Simon."

"Are you arresting me?"

Reade looked at him and for a moment was tempted. In his present state, Young obviously needed to be protected from himself. He had been found alone in the house with two corpses, two murder victims. But—"No, I'm not arresting you," he said at last.

Simon picked up the bundle of documents relating to the Soviet Communal Bank's loan. "Thank you. Then I'll be on my way."

As Simon went through the front door Reade signaled to the sergeant and spoke. "Don't lose him. Not unless you fancy directing traffic between now and retirement."

19

At a little before five o'clock that same evening Simon Young
applied to Mr. Justice Ang, sitting in the new Supreme Court
building, for an injunction against Soviet Communal Bank.

For half an hour beforehand Qiu sat on a bench in Admiralty
Gardens with a bag of curried fishballs for refreshment, occasionally raising his head so as to keep an eye on the court's entrance.
He knew exactly what to look out for. A few days previously the
Mah-jongg Brigade had unobtrusively moved into Hong Kong with
a mandate from Beijing to show strength and take whatever was
needed. The fine network of intelligence that overlaid the colony
even in normal times had been tuned and stretched to breaking
point. None of the other players at Red Dragon's Mah-jongg table
could move without him knowing.

Qiu felt cautiously optimistic. Sunday's exercise in Ocean Park had been executed brilliantly, under extreme pressure of time. The Luks' deaths, unfortunate operational necessities, were skillfully effected by agents who vanished. The Mah-jonggs were ready for the time when they would take command of Hong Kong. The apparatus was perfect.

Through the grapevine that was part of that apparatus Qiu learned how one of London's best Chancery barristers, Richard Hearn QC, had been stopped at Kai Tak on his way back to England and returned post-haste to the Peninsula Hotel for an immediate consultation with Young and his solicitor, Alan Sanditon. There had been a hurried exchange of messages between the hotel and Hearn's chambers in Lincoln's Inn; a fee had been agreed; Qiu knew exactly what it was, for the hotel's telex manager had told him. In his pocket Red Dragon had a sheaf of notes compiled by the floor boy who looked after Hearn's suite. Qiu found the content of these notes interesting. It seemed that Hearn's initial reaction toward his client had been one of hostile skepticism.

From where he sat Qiu enjoyed an uninterrupted view of the Supreme Court building: a tall, square, pale gray tower built out of the side of a hill. The only touch of color on its drab façade came from a solitary Union Jack floating above the roof of a low wing that extended along the front of the edifice at first-floor level. Next to the stately green architecture of the Ducannon Young building, its nearest neighbor, the Supreme Court looked stunted and dowdy. Qiu much preferred the old courts in Statue Square, with their dignified palladian façade overtopped by a dome the shape of the pontiff's tiara. After 1997 there would still be a need for carefully scripted show trials, and the classical, off-white stone building in Statue Square would provide a much more majestic setting for them than these new courts in Queensway. After changeover, the Party would have to try the thieves who had been bleeding Hong Kong for many years: the so-called entrepreneurs, the businessmen, pirates all, whose morality involved an unbridgeable gulf between laws to which they paid lip service and the facts of their worthless lives. Men like Young . . . Qiu shrugged, uncomfortably aware that Simon Young did not fit into this mold quite so easily.

Red Dragon looked at his watch. Time to make a move.

He rose and left the gardens, making for the stairs to the shopping plaza and the pedestrian bridge that spanned Queensway's six lanes of traffic. The plaza was thronged with people bustling in all directions, tourists in search of their last bargain of the day, office workers at the start of the evening rush hour, students on their way home from class; but none of them paused to look at Qiu as he strolled along, munching his fishball. He was an insignificant, almost invisible speck on a frenetically busy landscape.

As he descended the steps to the south side of Queensway he caught sight of a group of men huddled together in tight formation, walking along the short stretch of pavement between the Ducannon Young building and the courts. Simon Young; Sanditon, his lawyer; two assistant solicitors and Hearn. Qiu quickened his pace and ran up the steps to the court entrance, where he took the lift to reception. As he emerged from the lift a Chinese man who had been sitting in one of the black vinyl-covered chairs folded his newspaper and rose to his feet. Qiu nodded in recognition. "Where?" he asked.

"Twelfth floor, court twenty-eight."

"Wait here."

Qiu turned to his left and walked through the main smoked-glass double doors that led to the vehicular access at the side of the building. He took a quick look around. On his right, two fountains played noisily into green pools; the drive was deserted. Qiu turned left and went to stand on the terrace overlooking Queensway. He placed his hands on the gray-tiled ledge, then raised them slowly above his head in a long stretch. The gesture was noted by many pairs of eyes. Quietly and without overt fuss, the configuration of human beings in and around Queensway rapidly changed. Now it was impossible for anyone to approach the Supreme Court without being detected by the brigade.

Qiu rapidly returned to the interior of the building, took his guide by the arm and said, "Show me. Be quick."

The two men rode up to the twelfth floor. They emerged into a deserted central area. On their right, gray-tinted glass windows stretched from floor to lofty ceiling; on the left were the entrances to three courts and an interview-room, the latter a mere recess separated from the central area by a partition of black glass. Two rows of low dark-brown chairs in cream metal frames occupied the central floor area, which smelled of stale smoke.

Court twenty-eight was at the other end, farthest from the lifts. Qiu took a look inside and frowned. "Difficult," he said: for the courtroom was brightly illuminated, its honey-colored pinewood furniture heightening the impression of light and space.

"If you sit well down in the back row, no one will notice you. Young and his party, the lawyers, everyone, must sit in front."

Qiu nodded. "Good. Go now."

He scuttled into the very last row of seats, seeking out the far corner where it was darkest, and studied the scene before him with curiosity. He had never set foot inside a Western court before. It was very different from what they had back home. For instance, there were no large signs in front of the seats to indicate the identities of the principal characters: judge, prosecutor, accused and so forth. And for some unaccountable reason the judge's seat was up high, behind a kind of barrier, as if to suggest that he was in some way superior to those brought before him, instead of being merely hardworking and lucky enough to stay out of trouble.

He heard voices outside and slunk even further down in his seat. The court began to fill up. There were two "camps": on Qiu's right sat one group of men, the bank's lawyers presumably, their heads huddled together to preserve confidentiality.

Qiu turned his attention to the left-hand side of the courtroom, where Simon Young was sitting with his lawyers. The Englishman occupied a place at the far end of the first row of seats, with Sanditon next to him. Hearn sat behind with a Chinese lawyer wearing the same extraordinary clothing: black robe over a dark suit, stiff-collared shirt and two white rectangles of cloth dangling from beneath the chin. Qiu had once heard a rumor that some foreign lawyers wore wigs made from the hair of horses and he was astonished to find that this insanitary practice did, after all, prevail. Extraordinary! The two assistants, both English, spread themselves and their papers in the row behind. Qiu disapproved of such waste of space; they could all have fitted quite comfortably into the first row.

Simon Young sat with his back ramrod stiff, staring in front of him. Qiu slid a little further along the bench so as to get a better sight of his profile. The Englishman's face was white and taut with strain. How peculiar, he thought to himself, that a person can be that color and still remain on his feet. When Sanditon spoke to his client Young responded with a snap.

There was a commotion as the judge appeared through a door behind the bench and the occupants of the court rose. When the judge sat down, so did everybody else except Richard Hearn, who placed a blue-covered notebook on the lectern in front of him and began to speak. Qiu leaned forward, trying to follow the proceedings, but it was difficult for him to hear and anyway the language was highly technical.

He found his eyes straying to the judge's face. Mr. Justice

Ang, in his early sixties and soon due for retirement, still wore a sprightly air. His half-moon spectacles were allowed to rest on the tip of his nose, their owner seeming to have little use for them. Qiu had never seen such a deeply wrinkled face, not even in his home village on the mainland. When Ang spoke it was in a sharp, high-pitched voice which reminded Red Dragon of a familiar Chinese opera character, the scholar—courteous and persuasive but at the same time a touch too deferential. Qiu made a mental note to research Ang's background, thinking it improper for a Chinese judge to adopt such a humble demeanor in front of English advocates.

Mr. Justice Ang, for all his politeness of manner, obviously found it difficult to follow the story Hearn was telling. Slowly, almost imperceptibly, the expression on his face began to turn from puzzlement to irritation. After Hearn had been speaking for about twenty minutes the judge nerved himself to ask a question. Hearn said something about an affidavit and turned around to rummage through a file in the keeping of one of the assistant solicitors. Qiu had his first proper look at the barrister: a short, rotund man with chubby red cheeks, flat nose and tortoiseshell bifocals. When he found the paper he was looking for he began to read aloud in a fast monotone, making it impossible for someone sitting at the back of the court to distinguish the words. Qiu's attention started to wander. But suddenly the judge tapped on the bench with his pen and Hearn stopped in midsentence, his head cocked at a questioning angle.

"Your client is there stating that a magistrate did not witness the document."

"Yes, certainly."

"Meaning the memorandum of deposit which charged the Founders Shares?"

"Meaning that."

"Show it to me, please. No, not the photocopy with the affidavit." The judge turned to the bank's coterie of lawyers. "Do you not have the original?"

It was handed up. Mr. Justice Ang turned to one side and held the memorandum to the light, squinting at it ferociously over the rims of his spectacles. "Mr. Simon Young swears that this is not Magistrate Hua's signature—is that correct, Mr. Hearn?"

"Yes."

"And therefore it is not, cannot be, his own signature either, because he in fact witnessed the memorandum, not in front of a magistrate, as the articles require if the document is to be valid, but in front of a servant called Luk?"

"Indeed yes."

"Who has now been murdered?"

"Yes."

"Please take instructions. Does your client have a document here, anything, perhaps a credit card, with what is undoubtedly his signature on it?"

Sanditon plucked Simon's arm. The Englishman spoke a few curt words to the lawyer but then reluctantly reached for his wallet. Qiu observed the judge closely, saw how his lips pursed in disapproval, and was well satisfied.

A credit card was handed up. Mr. Justice Ang subjected the back of it to critical study. "It is my opinion," he said at last, "that these signatures appear to be indistinguishable."

"That would, of course, be a matter for expert evidence on both sides at trial." Hearn made an effort to conceal his unease.

"Quite. If there is to be a trial."

"I'm sorry, your Lordship has lost me."

"I said . . . if there is to *be* a trial."

"Be a trial?"

"Yes. If your client persists in these . . . these rather strange and very serious allegations, there will, I suppose, have to be a trial."

"My client has sworn his affidavit, my Lord. The allegations stand." Hearn's voice now matched the judge's for coldness. "They will stand until resolved one way or the other."

"Well I wonder about that, Mr. Hearn. Do you have your copy of the memorandum of deposit of shares?"

"I have it."

"As I understand this matter, the articles of association of the Pacific & Cantonese Banking Corporation provide that no charge or other disposition of its Founders Shares shall be valid unless executed in the presence of a magistrate of Hong Kong who shall then and there attest the charge or disposition . . . have I the wording right?"

"Not quite, I think, my Lord, but the substance is undoubtedly the same."

"To the same effect . . . very well. Tell me, Mr. Hearn, just why was all this rigmarole involving magistrates thought to be necessary?"

"Because Founders Shares are bearer shares, my Lord. They

belong to whoever can produce the share certificates. Charging such shares is difficult, because both lender and borrower naturally wish to have or to retain possession of the certificates. Hence this compromise, designed to protect both sides—the borrower retains possession of the share certificates, but the lender has the added protection of an authenticated document which, in the ordinary course of events, could not be challenged."

"Yet your client is challenging it! He says that this memorandum was not, in fact, executed before a magistrate of Hong Kong but before a servant, now dead."

"Correct. As I said, in the ordinary course—"

"But then, why did he not execute this document properly? Why did he go through the solemn farce of signing a piece of paper which he knew to be worthless on the one hand, while he was only too pleased to lay his hands on the one hundred million pounds sterling which the bank was prepared to offer him on the other? He says: 'A mistake was made.' So be it. Why was this mistake not corrected later? Is that an act of commercial probity?"

When Hearn said nothing the judge went on. "Would you like an opportunity of taking instructions on that point, Mr. Hearn? It seems to me that the bank's only legal remedy reposes in its right to be registered as the holder of Mr. Young's Founders Shares and to gain possession of the material certificates. It has no other."

"The bank could sue on the covenant to repay—"

"Sue a worthless company, without assets?"

"In our submission, that is one of the many matters which will have to be explored at trial." The barrister's voice was bland but there was no disguising the note of despairing self-skepticism that it contained.

"You may be right. Incidentally, I happen to be familiar with the signature of the magistrate who purports to have witnessed the memorandum of deposit in this case. It looks authentic. I suppose you would say, Mr. Hearn, that that too is a matter for the trial judge after pleadings, discovery and so forth?"

"I would."

"And even if I adjourned this application until tomorrow and invited Magistrate Hua to give evidence before me with leave to you to cross-examine, it still would not get over the difficulty that your client is, in effect, alleging that one of the material documents was, without his knowledge, tampered with. Switched is perhaps the word?"

"Switched, yes. So that the document before the court today is, in effect, a forgery."

"But which forgery, as you term it, he apparently *ought* to have signed. I see." Mr. Justice Ang turned toward the lawyers appearing for Soviet Communal Bank. "Mr. Li . . ."

"My Lord?"

"Looking at it from the bank's point of view, I can see the problem here. But it is hardly realistic of you to suppose that the Corporation's registrars are going to put you on the share register now, in light of the evidence which Mr. Young has sworn in support of this application."

"Perhaps not." Li sounded reluctant to concede the point.

"Is not the proper course then for you to start your own action claiming repayment of the debt in full? Or perhaps you could counterclaim in Mr. Young's action? If you undertook to issue and prosecute a counterclaim with all reasonable dispatch, I could direct a speedy trial, restraining you from applying for registration in the meanwhile."

"That would all take time, my Lord."

"Three months. The state of the list is good. I could offer you a trial date at the end of three months from today."

"But Mr. Young's evidence is so flimsy . . ."

"I know. I hope I will not cause undue offense if I say that I find it barely credible. But he has sworn what he has sworn, Mr. Li. If he has lied, then he must answer for those lies. But still, I have to accept today that his affidavit could be the truth." The judge looked at his watch. "It is late. Do you want to address me further, Mr. Li?"

The advocate shook his head and sat down.

"Then I order as follows. On the usual cross-undertaking as to damages from Mr. Young and upon the bank's undertaking by its counsel to issue and actively to prosecute a counterclaim for the debt, restrain dealings with the shares until trial or further order. What is the exact form of words you want, Mr. Hearn?"

The advocate picked up a sheet of paper and said, "In terms of the notice of motion, if your Lordship wouldn't mind."

"From selling, pledging, parting with possession of . . ."

"That's right."

". . . all Founders Shares to which the defendant bank is now or may at any time in the future become entitled. . . . What is all that about, Mr. Hearn?"

"My Lord?"

"Your client charged only his twenty shares, did he not?"

"He charged the only shares he has at the moment, certainly."

"Then why the reference to future—"

"Because it follows the wording of the memorandum of deposit, my Lord. That's what the document says."

"That's what the document says, is it?"

"Yes."

"I find that strange. However. Very well, that is the injunction. Speedy trial. Now, timetable." The judge rapidly gave directions for pleadings and trial, started to rise, thought better of it and sat down again. "Mr. Hearn."

"My Lord?"

"What I am about to say is meant in a kind spirit. I may say, a compassionate spirit." He hesitated. "I know your client. Everyone in Hong Kong knows the managing director of Ducannon Young. He is in court, I have observed him. He does not look well. There is time in which to reflect. Do you understand me?"

"I do. And I thank your Lordship."

Ang nodded and quickly left the court. Qiu, satisfied with the result, waited until everyone else had risen and was bowing to the departing judge, then used the opportunity to slip out quietly. As he scampered toward the emergency stairway next to the lifts he could not resist glancing back over his shoulder. The bank's lawyers were first to leave the courtroom and although their faces wore serious expressions Qiu could see that they were not unhappy with the outcome of the day's proceedings. Young's party emerged some minutes later. Red Dragon concealed himself in the shadow of the stairway and watched avidly as Sanditon turned to speak to his client. Even at twenty paces' distance Qiu could see how the Englishman was livid with rage. "Arrogant, interfering old fool!" he heard Young exclaim. "What the hell does he know about Hong Kong's commercial probity . . . ?"

Sanditon tried to calm him but when his words appeared to have little effect he reluctantly went over to join Hearn. The barrister's face was tight with strain; sweat stood out on his forehead in large drops and his voice had taken on a taut, metallic tone. As he approached the lifts Qiu heard him say to Sanditon, "Those are some of the most horrific allegations I've ever made in a court. Forgery, conspiracy, fraud—"

"I know, I know."

"Simon Young, managing director of Dunny's, accusing Soviet Communal Bank of . . . it defies belief."

"How long can you stay, Richard? We desperately need you here at the moment." The two men passed beyond earshot. "Oh for God's sake, I'm all right," Qiu heard a familiar voice say; he peeped around the wall of the stairwell to see Simon pushing away a hand offered to him by one of the two assistant solicitors. "Of course I'm all right."

He did not look all right, but the young men exchanged glances and shrugged. They were frightened, Qiu could see that. Long before morning, news of what had happened in court would travel throughout the colony. Sanditon's firm was assuming professional responsibility for some of the most outrageous claims ever made against an apparently respectable bank, claims with which ambitious, upwardly mobile assistant solicitors practicing in an incestuous, close-knit community like Hong Kong had no wish to be associated.

"There's a car waiting, sir," one of them murmured.

"I don't need a car."

"It's waiting at the front entrance, Mr. Young."

"Are you deaf? I said, I don't need it!"

The hapless solicitors withdrew. Simon was left standing alone in the central area. He wiped a hand across his forehead and stared at the floor, swaying slightly, like a man who has had too much to drink and knows that if he tries to take a step he will fall down. At last he was able to summon a lift. Qiu waited until the Englishman had disappeared before emerging from the shelter of the stairs and pressing the "down" button to call another lift for himself.

He had heard Young say he didn't want a car. That suggested he was going to walk, which in turn meant he would descend all the way to street level. Qiu did the same and found he'd guessed correctly. The managing director of Ducannon Young leaned against the tiled wall flanking the stairs to Queensway. He looked like a man defeated; and Qiu, to his mild surprise, experienced a momentary desire to stretch out a hand toward him. But instead he slowly edged away toward the tropical dusk, passing unnoticed within feet of the Englishman. Once again, the configuration of people in Queensway changed. The intangible human cordon disbanded, shuffled and regrouped. Qiu was about to turn on his heel and disappear when Simon Young unexpectedly raised his head and stared straight at him.

"You!" he said. His voice vibrated with rage, making heads turn. For a second Qiu was tempted to flee; but then a feeling of calm stole over him and he knew the kind of peace that derives from acceptance of the inevitable. Simon Young might be the man they judged him to be or he might not. What followed in the next few seconds could advance or retard the building of the wall. What mattered was that it should happen: that, one way or the other, the Mah-jongg Brigade should know this Englishman for who he really was.

Simon Young very slowly bore down on Qiu, standing at the edge of darkness, without once taking his eyes from Red Dragon's face. Qiu returned his gaze without expression. When the Englishman was only a few paces away, Qiu spread his hands and spoke a few words in the Hokkien dialect, guessing correctly that Young would not understand. Simon's forehead screwed itself up into a frown. "I know you," he said.

Qiu was surprised. He had imagined that Young would be in no fit state to recognize anyone. "But I do not know you," he said in Hokkien. "Please go away now."

"I know you," Simon repeated. It was as though he could not put a name to the half-familiar face of an acquaintance. "You did this. You switched one set of forgeries for another. And that silly old man had the nerve to lecture me about commercial *probity*. My God!"

When Qiu said nothing, Simon came even closer and bent down to peer at his face. "Qiu Qianwei," he said at last; and now his voice was quiet, controlled. "That's who you are. My wife's brother." He shook his head; and—"Qiu Qianwei," he repeated.

The Chinese knew his position to be unassailable, but for some reason as he heard his name pronounced a second time he experienced a tremor of unease. Things were not working out as they should. He knew that if *he* ever faced ruin and discovered that Qingqing had defected to the West, all on the same day, he would be devastated. Yet here was Young suddenly in full control of himself, his face alight with recognition and purpose.

"I have done nothing," Qiu said defensively, still in Hokkien. Over Simon's shoulder he caught sight of two policemen eyeing the pair of them, suspicion on their faces. One officer turned to the other for long enough to speak a few words; then they began to move toward the ill-matched couple standing at the entrance to the courts.

"You did this," Simon repeated; only this time he spoke in Mandarin. "I have not the time, or the energy, to deal with you now. But I shall not forget what you did. We shall have an opportunity of discussing this—elsewhere."

For an eerie moment Qiu could not move. He stood motionless, hypnotized by the light burning in the Englishman's eyes, marveling at this unexpected display of power. But then he spread his hands again and risked one last glance at the advancing policemen. "Do you not trust me, Mr. Young?" he said quietly in English.

Simon's jaw dropped. He reached out to touch Qiu, as if afraid his hand might pass right through the phantom standing in front of him, but before he could make contact Qiu inclined his head in the direction of the two constables, by now only a dozen steps away, and Simon made the mistake of turning around to see what had apparently attracted his attention.

The human Mah-jongg tiles who guarded Queensway rearranged themselves for the last time. When Simon turned back it was to find a small, bespectacled, somehow familiar figure standing in the space that Red Dragon had occupied; only it wasn't Qiu, it was a different person, a woman carrying two large shopping bags, who stared at him rudely before going about her business.

"Here!" Simon cried. "You! Stop!" When one of the policemen laid a hand on his shoulder he roughly shook it off and began to run toward the woman. But the officer, used to dealing with would-be escapers, was faster. He deftly shot out his foot, catching Simon under his raised heel. The Englishman's legs buckled at the knees and he sank to the ground.

From the top deck of a tram crawling along the brilliantly lit carriageway Qiu caught a quick glimpse of a foreign devil kneeling on the pavement, one policeman holding him by the shoulder, and for a second knew a pang of disappointment. Then an uncomfortable, elusive memory brushed against his conscious mind. Suddenly he identified the faint echo and his face hardened: a high-ranking Party cadre watching his trusted agent kneeling in her own vomit while the men from Unit 8341 deprived them both of all pride, all face; stripped them, in short, of all the qualities that make a man human and raise him above the beasts. Or, which in Qiu's eyes amounted to the same thing, above the *guai-lo*, the foreign devils of Hong Kong.

Above most of them, anyway.

20

The woman squatted by the side of the road, arms clasped around her knees, and stared into the middle distance where a heavy cloud of dust heralded the approach of a vehicle. She had spent half an hour doubled up in the same position, but she was used to squatting and it caused her no discomfort. The weather was hot, well into the nineties, with humidity on the high side, and the flies troubled her greatly; but waiting by the roadside was better than work in the paddy-fields. Almost anything was better than that.

As the cloud of dust drew closer the woman saw that it was generated by an old, beat-up black Shanghai sedan—the only kind of car she knew. She recognized it because the secretary of the local production brigade drove the same model, although his looked rather better cared for than the one that now pulled onto the side of the road and expired with a splutter. For a moment nothing happened; then the nearside front door opened and one of the passengers got out, lifting his arms high above his head in an exaggerated stretch. The woman, recognizing him too, noisily hawked and spat. The cadre from Beijing was back, then: may the gods shit on him and his kind.

Then the rear doors of the car opened and the peasant woman unsteadily began to ease herself upright.

Jinny was the first to emerge. She was still wearing the dress she had chosen before setting off to collect Diana from hospital; but now it was stained and moist with perspiration. The peasant woman eyed it curiously, wondering how much it had cost. A lot, of course: that went without saying. Since she had never seen anything remotely like it, however, assessment was difficult. The face above the dress was soft and pretty, but the eyes were ringed with black and it was obvious that the stranger had been crying. She looked around her slowly, a look of disbelief on her face, and the woman by the roadside followed her gaze in an attempt to see what was so shocking. The winding road ran through low, wooded foothills on the fringe of a red-soil plain carpeted with the remains of this year's spring rice crop, for the most part already harvested. The air, heavy with moisture and heat, clung to the skin like an oppressive garment; the gray sky above was bloated with rain; all the world was like this. Wasn't it?

"Come," the cadre shouted to the stranger. "Come and see your sister."

The well-dressed lady obeyed, but with reluctance, as if truly she had no will of her own in the matter. She approached the peasant, keeping her face expressionless. For a long moment the two of them just stood and stared at each other.

"Kaihui?" the stranger said wonderingly.

"Yes."

Jinny very slowly shook her head from side to side, making herself believe. "He told me you were dead," she croaked.

"Well, you see I'm not dead." Kaihui spoke Mandarin with a thick Sichuan accent but Jinny could understand what she said. "You don't want to believe all *he* tells you." She jerked her head toward Qiu, who frowned a visual reprimand.

"He said he would shoot you. And Mingchao."

"Mingchao is quite well, and about to become a husband. You're in time for the wedding, Eldest Sister." There was a long pause, during which the two of them continued to stare at each other. "Suppose I should feel glad to see you."

"Too many years."

"Yes. It's hard to start again."

They made no attempt to touch.

"How long will you stay, Linhua?"

Jinny, startled by the sound of her old Chinese name, said nothing for a moment. Then she turned towards Qiu, her face suddenly contorted with hatred and fear. "Ask *him!*"

"No good asking him. All lies. All lies and upset. Him and his family."

"His family?"

"Yes. They came too. Father, mother, child. A boy. Boy's not bad." Kaihui raised her voice so that Qiu could hear. "But father and mother are not so good, they need to be reeducated. No May Seventh School, so let's send them to Chaiyang." She reverted to her normal tone. "Your children came as well?"

"Yes."

"And your husband?"

Jinny wiped a tear from the corner of one eye. "He didn't come." Kaihui saw how it pained her sister to speak and she nodded phlegmatically, as if that was the answer she had expected. "Where are my niece and nephew?"

Jinny made an effort and turned. The children had got out of the car and were standing a little distance behind her. She saw them and pitied them but did not know what to say. Their young faces were still ravaged by the shock of the past twenty-four hours. It had been a wretched journey. The drugs had finally worn off and they awoke as they were being driven out of Chengdu, the provincial capital of Sichuan. The three of them had been very sick. They were given a little water but no food. Jinny understood what had happened and accepted it as accomplished fact. As yet the children neither understood nor accepted.

"There they are." Jinny gathered her few remaining reserves of strength and spoke to them in English. "This is your aunt, my sister, Kaihui. She does not speak any language but Chinese." The children said nothing; she was not sure if they had even heard. They stared at Kaihui as if she were an alien. Jinny sighed and turned back to face her sister. "They do not speak Chinese."

"That will be hard for them in the village. Why did you not teach them?"

"I tried. Their nurse tried also. But when they went to England, they soon forgot."

Kaihui frowned. "Where is England? Near to Hong Kong?"

"No, Younger Sister. Not near." Jinny swallowed back the tears that were gathering in a hard, tight ball at the back of her throat. She knew what had to be done, knew she could do it, but the children. . . . Don't despair, she told herself. You are their bridge, their only support.

"Hello. *Ni hao.*" It was Diana who spoke. Jinny looked down in surprise to see that her daughter had extended a hand toward Kaihui. It was trembling. Kaihui smiled and took the hand. "*Ni hao,*" she replied cheerfully. Diana felt her aunt's rough touch and for a second she wanted to jerk her hand away. How could this woman be related to her? She was fat and dumpy, wearing baggy overalls of some faded gray material peppered with patches and small, unmended holes. Her round, yellow, wrinkled face was that of an old woman, but Diana knew that Kaihui was younger than Jinny. Aunt Kaihui was a peasant. Her life was hard. That was why she looked so old. The only soft things about her were the eyes; and they were kind. Diana liked her aunt's eyes.

"We must walk now." Kaihui looked at Qiu. "Any luggage?"

"No luggage."

"Good. Are they fit enough?"

"Enough."

Kaihui took another long look at the newcomers and saw three worn-out souls, barely able to stand. "Sure?"

"*Yes!*" said Qiu.

"Come then."

Kaihui led the way up the hill into the trees, following an ancient path trodden out of the soil by a hundred generations of bare feet and then another hundred wearing wooden clogs and then yet another hundred shod in sandals like Kaihui's. Walking was always difficult in the oppressive heat of rural Sichuan, but to the three sick Hong Kongese it seemed like torture. Mat was the first to complain. "Why can't we take the car?"

"No road," said Qiu. He had conceived an intense dislike for Mat, who appeared to have inherited none of his father's admirable qualities. The boy was weak. Well, a sojourn in Chaiyang would harden him.

"Why isn't there a road? I knew this country was backward, but Christ . . ."

"There will be a road one day. Chaiyang is not important enough yet."

"Where are we? Where are you taking us?"

"Sichuan province. You are going to a peasant village called Chaiyang, where you will stay."

"Stay how long?"

"All your life."

Qiu was walking in front of Mat when he spoke these words and so could not see the boy's face, but he heard his exhausted sob and felt gratified.

"Why are you doing this?" asked Mat.

Qiu merely smiled grimly and trudged on in silence. The track wound around the side of the hill and began to climb more steeply. After about forty-five minutes of slow progress the group was starting to fragment. Kaihui continued to lope on at the same even pace, with Diana doing her best to keep up and Jinny not far behind. But Mat was tiring rapidly. He had eaten nothing for many hours, his head ached. Suddenly he stumbled across a tree root and fell. Qiu prodded his inert body with a plimsoll-toe. "Get up," he said.

"I'm tired. Leave me alone."

"Impossible. We must go on now. You can rest in the village."

"Leave me *alone*, I said!"

Qiu looked down at the boy and saw nothing worthy of sympathy. Mat wore the clothes thoughtfully packed for him by his kidnappers—faded blue jeans and a T-shirt that once had been white but now was gray. He looked slovenly. Who in his right mind was rich but strove to look poor? Qiu asked himself savagely. And that face! Mournful, pathetic . . . He gave the teenager a kick in the ribs. Mat yelped with pain.

"Listen to me, English boy." Qiu made no attempt to keep the malice out of his voice. "Do you think I wish to be here with a weakling like you? No! I do not! Have you heard of something called the Long March? Eh? When a hundred and thirty thousand men, women and children started out, but only twenty thousand arrived? Our fathers left one hundred and ten thousand where they fell, in the ice, in the desert, on the plains. Where are they now? They are dead! *Dead!* You must learn *zili gengshang*. You do not understand? Then let those be the first Chinese words you learn. *Zili gengshang*. Self-reliance. Repeat them!"

"*Zili jinshang* . . ."

"*Gengshang, geng, geng!*"

"*Zili gengshang*."

"Better. Now up, *up!*" He kicked Mat again and again, until at last the boy staggered to his feet and groggily began to stumble along the path to where his mother and Diana were waiting. Their faces showed distress but they could offer him no comfort.

"I'd like to kill that man," Mat hissed as he limped along beside his mother. "We could do it, too—he's not so strong, there are three of us . . ."

"Don't talk rubbish." It was Jinny who spoke. "We are a long way from anywhere. If we touched him, we would be caught and they would punish us. There is nothing we can do."

"There must be omething. There must!"

"There is nothing," said Diana. She had developed a blister on her right heel and dreaded that it might burst before they reached their destination. It cost her an effort to talk, but her brother's feebleness only served to underline her own pain. She wanted to shut him up. "Let's just hope we reach the village soon. Maybe there'll be food for us. Save your breath."

Now Diana and her mother were walking side by side. "You've grown up," Jinny murmured. "Suddenly you talk like a woman."

Diana produced a wan little smile, but lacked the strength to reply. The woods were thinning out. Ahead of them, Kaihui had breasted a rise and was standing, hands on hips, looking into the distance. One by one the stragglers caught up with her and flopped to the ground.

"Chaiyang," she said with a touch of pride.

Immediately in front of them the hillside sloped away to the open plain where a cluster of houses nestled on the very edge of the rice fields. The foreground was colorful: tall green trees bounding the village, ochre-red soil and white buildings underneath roofs made of mossy ridged tiles. But the village itself was only about a quarter of a mile square, no more; and on the other side of it the panorama began to shade into pale browns and grays: they could see tiny figures in pointed straw hats laboring up to their knees in the flooded paddy-fields, harvesting rice, and beyond that the dim foundations of agricultural terraces rising up the far side of the plain. Then the woods took over once more, shrouding the distant hillside with drab olive green until at last the eye lost itself in heat haze, no longer able to distinguish between the tops of the hills and their humid cloudcaps.

Kaihui looked at her sister and asked, "You remember?"

Jinny hesitated a long time before answering. "It is bigger," she said at last.

"Yes. And richer. When you left us, only four hundred *mu* of agricultural land. Now, six hundred. And each family has a tenth of a *mu* of their own. A small school. Piped water in the square now." She spoke complacently, like one who knows her home's true worth, but then her face clouded. "Eldest Sister, is it so that in some places there is water brought in pipes into the house?"

"Yes."

"I'm not sure. It sounds all right. But what if the pipe should break in the night?" Kaihui shook her head. "Better to bring the water to the square and leave it there, where it can do no harm. Come. We'll go on now."

As they came down the path to the first houses, Jinny saw that a reception committee awaited them. A group of women, children and scabrous-looking dogs . . . but of course at midday the men were all in the fields and only the women had come back to the village, to cook. About thirty of them formed a wall of faded gray, a human barrier across the entrance to the village. They did not smile or give way at the approach of the strangers; Kaihui pushed straight through them, looking neither right nor left, and the others, after a moment's hesitation, followed her through the breach. Even Qiu seemed slightly apprehensive: he knew that he was an important official, that any insult to his person would be avenged—but only *afterward* and perhaps a long time afterward at that.

"This place stinks," Mat moaned. "What is it?"

"Human excrement," said Jinny. "Eight hundred million Chinese have to live off the land. There isn't enough fertilizer to go around, so they use what's available."

"You mean they use . . . *shit?*"

"Yes. And please don't use that word."

"Oh Christ. Oh Jesus Christ."

"You'll get used to it after a while."

"I'm not staying here long enough to get used to it."

"When will you wake up? *There's nowhere to go!*"

"And the people . . . look at her over there. I'll bet she hasn't washed her hair for a month!"

Jinny sighed. She was exhausted, but she knew that once she lost patience with her son she might not easily regain it. "People don't wash their hair in the countryside," she said, very slowly. "Only when swimming."

"What, never?"

"That's right. Because you see, there's nothing to wash it with.

And please, please be careful how you act. I know these people." She hesitated. "I am one of them."

They had reached the square. For the first time in a long while, Diana raised her eyes from the road and looked about her. She was tired and unhappy but she had enough reserves of strength to be alive to her surroundings. She knew that no foreigner had ever seen this village. And somewhere deep inside, that part of her that was ten thousand years old began to stir. For this was the village. *Her* village.

Kaihui marched up to one of the mud-brick houses, plucked a washing tub from its hook on the wall, upended it and climbed onto her makeshift podium. The village women closed around it in a silent circle.

"Hah, please attend. Production brigade has given instructions. These people are guests of the village, for now. She is my eldest sister . . . she is my eldest sister's youngest child . . . he is my eldest sister's eldest child. All will work, but now they must rest."

At the words "all will work" the impassive faces of the village women lightened somewhat; and Jinny realized that Chaiyang, although more prosperous than she remembered it from childhood, was nevertheless still poor. Poor to a degree that two rich children from Hong Kong could not even begin to imagine. There they stood, towering over the villagers, so obviously well fed on milk and meat despite their fatigue. They were the equivalent of landlords' children, of cadres' children. How could they hope to survive here?

Kaihui clambered off her tub and went to hang it back on its hook. "Come now," she said.

Once off the concrete square the going was difficult, because it had rained recently and the path was no more than a muddy runnel. Jinny walked, mesmerized. The village was laid out haphazardly but she knew every turning, every kink in the road, every house they passed. Then suddenly there it was, the last dwelling to the east of Chaiyang, home.

"But . . . it is bigger!"

"Oh yes. Mingchao has built on, for himself and his wife-to-be. They will marry soon. Now we have a proper courtyard, as in the old days." Kaihui sounded very happy. "This is partly thanks to you, Eldest Sister. We used the money you sent every year. Also, now we have a bigger allocation of responsibility land. The family earned over two thousand yuan, last year. This year, more."

Then her face darkened. "All's well, except that cadre and his family now occupy the new part of the house. They must move before the wedding can take place."

Jinny turned to look over her shoulder. Qiu walked behind the children, keeping a close and malevolent eye on them both. "Why is that one here?" she hissed in Kaihui's ear.

"I do not know. Very big man, according to the Party secretary, but if you ask me he's in need of reeducation. *Xiafang.* Go-down-to-countryside. Under the shadows. I am guessing, you understand; but what other reason could there be? His job is to look after you. More than that I do not know, except that he and his wife and child live in *our* house. Pah!" She hawked and spat again. "Boy's good, though. Tingchen."

They came up to the two-story house where Jinny had spent the first years of her life. Hesitantly she laid a hand on the wooden front door, newly painted, and pushed. It swung open with a creak to reveal the main room. Everything looked the same, exactly the same. Chairs, stained table, picture of that Red Sun, that Great Saving Star, Mao Zedong; and beside it her sister's set of twelve framed photographs of the legendary youth-hero, Lei Feng, each print showing him engaged in yet another good deed. Her eyes strayed at once to the kitchen doorway from the jamb of which hung a little chopsticks box. It had been her job to wash and count the *kuaizi* after every meal before dropping them back in their box with a clatter. All just the same . . . all different. Older, yes, but also more comfortable—there were red cushions on the crude wooden chairs and the oilskin tablecloth of her youth had been replaced by a blue and yellow cotton one. The cast-iron stove stood in its usual place, but next to it stood a modern oil heater. A thick rug covered most of the floor: not a plain rug but one with a picture of a brown bear on a bright green background.

"Concrete floor, I see."

"Yes. Most houses have them now. The earth was so damp, in winter."

Another figure appeared in the doorway, wiping her hands on a cloth, and Kaihui beckoned. "Sister-in-law, this is my eldest sister, Linhua. Linhua, this is Zhaodi, wife-to-be of Mingchao."

The two women, thus introduced, smiled and bobbed. Zhaodi was very thin and tiny but she had a lively manner and her wide eyes looked intelligent. How like Mingchao, thought Jinny, to choose a wife with a name carrying such bitter overtones—for Zhaodi meant "Call-in-younger-brother," suitable only for a daughter whose parents had wanted a boy and didn't care who knew it. But then, that was Mingchao all over: no head, warm heart.

"I have one son," said Kaihui. "Very fortunate. He's out at work now, but he'll soon return for rice. Mingchao also will return." Kaihui gestured toward Jinny's children. "They must get to know their family, eh?"

"Yes."

Qiu entered the house, slamming the front door behind him. He stalked across the room in silence and for the first time Jinny noticed a new doorway set in the farthest wall, surrounded by an uneven border of raw cement. As Qiu pushed through it she caught sight of yet another woman holding a child, a pained, apprehensive expression on her face; then the door closed and she saw no more. Kaihui sniffed expressively. "Neighbors!" she scoffed. "Come, we'll eat now. Sit, sit."

Jinny needed no further bidding, but lowered herself into the nearest chair and at last gave way to exhaustion. Mat had already sunk down onto the floor. Diana slumped apathetically against the wall.

"You sit too, future sister-in-law," said Zhaodi as she bustled in with a tray bearing cups and a teapot. "You have worked enough this morning."

"Thank you." Kaihui poured tea and handed around the cups. The flower patterns were faded and the enamel was cracked but to Jinny they spoke of the past like nothing else she had seen that day. She cradled her cup in the palm of her hand, turning it around and around as if hypnotized.

"Kaihui," she whispered.

"Yes?"

Jinny hurriedly put down her cup and closed her eyes against the rising flood of tears. "Oh, Kaihui . . ."

Kaihui took one of Jinny's hands in hers. "What is it, Eldest Sister?"

Jinny clasped her sister's hand to her cheek. "I've missed you so," she breathed.

"Yes. For me the same." Kaihui saw that Jinny was losing her battle with the pent-up tears. She knelt down and tried to offer comfort, but Jinny needed physical release. She wept quietly. At last she wiped her eyes. "It is strange, but—part of me is so glad to be home."

Kaihui, however, had little time for emotion. Seeing that Jinny had recovered, she redirected all her attention to the practicalities.

"We must talk," she said. "Eldest Sister, there is trouble, isn't that so?"

Jinny put away her handkerchief. The tea was beginning to restore her. "Yes."

"You came here against your will, because that cadre from Beijing wished it."

"Yes."

"Your husband is where?"

Jinny shook her head. "I don't know."

"This is very bad."

"Very bad."

"Will he come?"

"Don't know."

"But that cadre next door knows."

"He knows."

"What are we to tell the children?"

"Don't know."

"You have nothing? No clothes, no possessions?"

"We were taken by force. We have nothing."

Kaihui sighed. "The daughter," she said, nodding in Diana's direction. *"You-mei-you dao-mei?"* The question, literally meaning, "Does she have rotten luck?" signified "Is she old enough to menstruate?"

"Yes."

"Pity. I have a spare belt, and can provide rags, or toilet paper if she prefers. Tell her to let me know when she wants."

"No tampons?"

"What is that?"

Jinny tried to think of a way to explain but soon abandoned the attempt as hopeless. *"Mei guanxi."* It doesn't matter.

"Clothes I can provide. The cadre has money and chits for them. You are to be allotted work points on the same basis as the rest of us. But this is for the future. There is one thing I would ask of you, Linhua."

"What is that?"

Kaihui nodded in the direction of Diana and Mat. "Tell them why the cadre next door has brought you here. You should do this. Please excuse Younger Sister speaking so bluntly."

"You're right." Jinny raised her head and said to the children, in English, "I must talk to you."

Diana at once directed her questioning gaze back to her and, after a few seconds of indecision, Mat dragged himself upright.

"We must talk now. You should know why we're here."

They looked at her expectantly, but she had difficulty in finding the words. Her brain was tired. . . . "When I was young," she said at last, "I was taken from this place. I was given a great opportunity—to go out. To leave China. But there was a condition. I had to agree to work for them, always."

They stared at her in astonishment, as if a total stranger had suddenly arrived among them. Diana struggled to understand what her mother was saying. "Them . . . ?"

"For the Mah-jongg Brigade. Also called the Seventh Department of the Central Control of Intelligence."

And then they did understand. "You were a spy." Mat's voice was perfectly calm. He did not appear to find the proposition difficult either to grasp or to accept. For Diana, however, it was not so easy. Her face turned white, and her mouth opened but no sound came out.

"For nearly twenty years I was not asked to do anything. I had no duties. Then the man next door, Qiu Qianwei, came to give me an assignment. He wanted me to open your father's safe and remove a document. And I refused—then."

"You . . . refused?"

"Yes, Diana. At that time, I told him the past was dead for me. Even though it meant"—she swallowed painfully and went on—"it meant the death, I thought, of my brother and sister. They were my hostages, you see."

Diana digested this with an expression of horror on her face. Then she said, "Why did you refuse?"

"Because I love your father. I couldn't betray him." Jinny placed unintentional emphasis on the last word and simultaneously her guilty eyes strayed to Kaihui. "My family does not know these things."

"You said—'at that time.' Why?"

"Because at first, I was strong. You and Mat were away at school in England. But when you both came back to Hong Kong, and Qiu threatened you, I had no choice. Either I obeyed him, or you would die. . . . So I gave in, I opened the safe. I wrote . . . a letter—" Jinny broke off, her lower lip trembling.

The kitchen door opened to admit Zhaodi, laboring under the weight of a fully laden tray, but Diana ignored her. "If you helped him, if you gave in, why are we here?"

"I don't know the answer, but I can guess. Just as my brother and sister were hostages for me, so now the two of you, and I myself, are hostages to guarantee the behavior of your father. As long as they hold us here, they can control his actions."

"But why on earth should they want to control father?"

"It's complicated. Later, when I've rested."

Now it was Mat's turn to ask, in an accusing tone, "How long are we going to have to stay here?"

"I don't know."

Zhaodi put down the tray and began to pass out bowls of rice with mixed vegetables. Suddenly Diana jumped up, causing Zhaodi to draw back in alarm. "Where's my father?" the girl shouted, while Kaihui and Zhaodi looked on in amazement. "Mother! Did you hear what I said? Where's Da?"

"I don't know."

"Is he alive? Is he dead?" When Jinny did not react immediately she clenched her fists. *"Mother!"*

Jinny felt sick. She looked down at the bowl in front of her and with a weary gesture pushed it away. "I don't know."

21

It was the day after the disappearance of Jinny Young and the children. From the first-floor window of Government House Simon would have enjoyed an excellent view of the famous pink azalea beds, if only he'd cared to look. But he had other, more pressing concerns.

He found himself in a peculiar physical state. At certain times his vision seemed fuzzy, at others abnormally acute; likewise his hearing. In the course of the past twenty-four hours he had eaten and slept little and by now the strain was telling. His problems continued to mount.

Every hour he telephoned Reade, seeking news of his family, but the answer was always the same: we'll be in touch the second we hear anything, there are still about thirty unverified sightings to investigate . . .

Ducannon Young had to be run, too. Business didn't stop just because the managing director suffered a personal tragedy. There were board meetings for him to attend, contracts and checks to be signed, telephone calls to be made or received. And at the back of it all there was always the nagging memory of red figures on a statement, one hundred million pounds sterling with interest accumulated over two years, debit to you, payable by you.

Simon paced restlessly around the room, a victim of his own unpleasant thoughts. Had Jinny continued to deceive him for those two years? *No!* No, he couldn't believe it. But—she had opened his safe. It must have been she; there were no signs of a break-in. *Why? Where was she?*

He caught sight of the day's English-language newspapers, laid out on a table by the window, and went over to snatch one up. The court case. He threw the *South China Morning Post* back onto the table and picked up another, but the lead story was identical. All the headlines followed the same pattern: DUCANNON YOUNG MD IN COURT STORM, BANK TO SUE FOR HK $1000 MILLION, DIRECTOR'S STORY 'BARELY CREDIBLE'—JUDGE.

Behind him one of the double doors eased silently open to admit a secretary. Simon did not turn around, did not even hear her quiet cough.

"Excuse me, Mr. Young."

"God damn!"

The woman primly adjusted her pink wing-rimmed spectacles, using the thumb and second finger of her right hand to push them up the bridge of her nose. In all her repertoire, this was the nearest thing she had to an indecisive gesture. "I'm sorry . . . ?"

Simon wheeled around from the window. With the light streaming into the room behind him he looked like a vampire: a walking, white-faced corpse with two deep, dark holes where the eyes should be. "The press," he said softly. "I'd forgotten the press."

"The financial secretary will see you now, Mr. Young."

Simon came to himself and followed the woman out of the room, along the corridor and into an oak-paneled office made more gloomy by the presence of thick heat awnings over the windows. This was normally reserved for the use of the governor. Today, however, it contained Sir Martin Burney, Hong Kong's financial secretary, approximately equivalent to England's chancellor of the exchequer. Burney rose to shake hands. As he did so Simon became

□ 316 □

aware of another occupant of the room, standing by the window looking out, with glasses dangling from his hand. Something about this man's arched back spelled outrage. Then he turned around and Simon recognized his father.

"Good morning, Simon."

"Father." There was a frigid pause. "That business in Ocean Park, I . . . I'm glad to see you're all right."

"Yes. Thank you. You're coping?"

"Just about. What brings you here?"

"I'm here at the invitation of the government."

Simon rounded on Burney. "I asked for a private appointment," he said. "What I have to say is none of the Corporation's damn business." But Burney's lips merely curled in a smile and he pointed to the Louis XV chair in front of his desk.

Tom Young moved away from the window, glasses still swinging from hand to hand. He did not look at his son or speak again. The formal preliminaries seemed to have exhausted his conversation. He began to inspect the room's gilt furnishings, as if he were a bored visitor at a waxworks, indifferent to the Young-Burney tableau by the desk.

While Simon surveyed his father, the door through which he had entered opened again to admit Assistant Commissioner Reade, who walked across to the desk and took his seat beside the financial secretary without waiting for an invitation. He did not greet Simon Young or even look in his direction.

"Do sit down, Simon." Burney's voice matched his manner: both were deep, rich and cordial; honed and shaped by years of cautious supping with a necessarily long spoon. He was in his late fifties and it was obvious that his career could not hope to outlast British suzerainty over Hong Kong. A finished man, then, in every sense of the phrase.

Simon lowered himself into the proffered chair, relieved to have his father behind him, out of sight. Burney resumed his own seat and pushed a silver cigarette box across the desk. Simon shook his head.

"Well, now . . . could I just begin by saying, on the personal level, how extremely sorry I was to hear about this frightful business over your family." Burney leaned forward to rest his elbows on the desk and lowered his voice a semitone. "His Excellency himself has made a point of asking me to assure you that everything . . . *everything* humanly possible is being done to trace them."

Simon was uncomfortably aware of his father padding around the room behind him. "Thank you." He turned toward Reade. "Thank you, Peter. I know I've been demanding, yesterday and today. But I do want to say how grateful I am."

Reade smiled tightly, inclined his head and said nothing.

Burney leaned back in his chair, evidently well satisfied with his opening shot. "I understand, however, that that's not why you requested this meeting—"

"This private meeting."

"Ah . . ." Burney apologetically expelled a little puff of air and raised his hands a fraction off the desk. "I'm sorry that you feel so strongly about your father's presence. I really would like him to stay and hear what the position is."

"I don't see what the Corporation has got to do with any of this. Reade's another matter. I'm glad you're here, Peter."

The ACP did not respond, so Burney smoothly picked up where he had left off. "But my dear chap, the Corporation has everything to do with this." His voice had shed a little of its engaging good humor. " 'This' is all about big money. In Hong Kong, big money comes back to the Bank, Standard Chartered and the Corporation. With the kind of figures you're dealing in, who else can we talk to?"

"London."

"Doesn't want to know." Burney looked over Simon's shoulder and frowned at Tom Young. "We are not wholly blind to the problems which exist between Dunny's and the Corporation. If there was an alternative—"

"What about the Bank, then? Why can't Hong Kong & Shanghai help? Or Standard Chartered?"

"They say they would prefer not to become involved. The economic climate is such that—"

"Well, kick their arses until they *do* want to be involved. What's the use of living in a dictatorship like this one if you can't even bring your bloody banks into line?"

"Typical," he heard a cold voice say behind him; and he swung around angrily in his chair.

"You stay out of this."

"I intend to." Tom Young walked around to stand beside Burney's chair, laying one hand on its headrest as if to underline where his loyalties lay. "Martin's too nice to spell it out for you, so let me do it instead. The Bank, Standard Chartered, they won't do business with you anymore. Do you know why? Because they think you're mad or bad, and they can't make up their minds which."

Simon started to speak but Tom cut across him. "You have about three months, no more, to think of a way of staving off payment of a debt that by now, even in Hong Kong terms, is astronomical. If you fail, twenty of the Corporation's Founders Shares will pass into Russian ownership—Russian, by God!—and we all know what that means!"

"Oh, come on—SCB's a legitimate Singapore bank."

"Legitimate! I'd rather you borrowed from the devil. I suppose you'd say that was past history, but you're wrong. You'll find out how wrong you are when you next try to do business here. *If* you ever do. And as the result of the terrorist attack on your desalination plant, it can't possibly come on stream in time to save you."

"It's not my fault that someone blew up the plant."

"Perhaps. I really couldn't comment on that without knowing a good deal more than I do about your security arrangements. I understand the reinsurers are rather unhappy about them, too. Something about a shotgun, is that right? An illegal firearm, a clear breach of the policy conditions?"

Simon said nothing. What his father said was true. The underwriters, while not actually repudiating liability, were taking far longer over their inquiries than he'd ever anticipated they would. All because of a watchman's shotgun that he had never authorized and would have forbidden if he'd known about it . . .

"Now you maintain that the Soviet Communal Bank is relying on forged documents. Of course, I'm only going by what I've read in the papers. You've seen today's papers, I take it?"

"Yes."

"Then let's see if I've got it right. One. You had the money. Two. You 'mistakenly' signed false documents in such a way as to avoid having to repay it. Three. All Hong Kong knows about these things because you had the nerve to swear an affidavit which was read out in open court."

He paused, expecting a response. When one was not forthcoming, he continued. "Tell me, Simon. Who, who *exactly* is going to pick up the pieces? Who is going to queue up for the privilege of doing business with the managing director of Ducannon Young?"

"I should just continue to worry about your own affairs if I were you."

"I see. Not a thought for your children, it seems, or their futures. Not a thought for Jinny—"

"That's rich, coming from you," Simon exploded. "She's Chinese, remember? No hypocrisy, please. Not now."

"Don't be offensive. I've never held it against Jinny that she was Chinese. You've never heard me utter an unkind or rude word to your wife."

"No, you're right," Simon sneered. "I always felt it must have been difficult for you, being nice to her all these years: son marries a Chinese wife, has half-breed kids—"

Burney, sensing that the meeting had begun to slither out of control, cleared his throat. "This isn't very profitable, gentlemen. Tom, I think you overstate Simon's difficulties. This is Hong Kong, not London. Our rules are somewhat laxer here. Your son's a respected man and memories are short. His reputation may be dented for the moment, but he'll recover. We've got to hope and pray that he'll recover, because if Dunny's goes down—"

"If Dunny's goes down," snapped Tom, "I and a lot of other people are going to want to know the hows, whys and wherefores."

"Then ask him." Simon jerked a contemptuous finger at Sir Martin Burney. "Ask H.E. They put me up to it." He swiveled angrily in his chair. "Peter, if I signed fake documents, you know why." He turned back to face Burney. "Ask him and see what he says."

Burney looked up at Tom Young and the two men exchanged unhappy glances. "We have asked him," the financial secretary said. He seemed reluctant to face Reade.

"And?"

"And . . . I think it would be best if Peter told you himself."

"Well, Peter—go on, man!"

Reade smiled. To Simon, there was something sadistic in it. "I spelled it out to you very clearly at the time. If you approached us and said that you had the money for this project, Her Majesty's Government would not ask awkward questions about where you got it or what the terms were, as long as the lender was financially respectable, solvent and untainted by Communist connections."

"But that's a *monstrous* distortion of what you told me!"

"I disagree."

"You actively encouraged me to deal with Soviet Communal because you said it tied in nicely with your own plans—which you weren't prepared to discuss, I need hardly add."

"Now it's your turn to distort."

"That's a lie! A damnable lie. You all but told me that this was a joint operation between DI6 and the Chinese intelligence service."

"I said no such thing."

"But that . . . that's ludicrous!" Simon jumped up. "I've got witnesses. George Forster, he'll tell you—"

"Your finance director?" Tom Young's voice oozed scorn.

"Qiu, then."

"Who?"

"Qiu Qianwei. The PRC agent."

Sir Martin Burney spread his hands in a helpless gesture. "I'm sorry, but you've lost me. Peter . . . ?"

Reade shook his head.

"Tom . . . ?"

"I was lost a long time ago." Now he made no attempt to keep the bitterness out of his voice. "Sometime in Simon's childhood." Tom Young turned back to face his son. "Whatever the financial secretary may say within these walls, you're finished in Hong Kong. By some miracle you managed to keep Dunny's out of the Russians' hands. As soon as I can make arrangements, I'll have you removed from all the boards and put the company back on a proper footing—"

"It's always been on a proper footing." Now the gall was rising to the surface. "Ever since I rescued it from David, that loon of a brother of yours, before he could drink the entire profits and be damned—"

"Be quiet!"

"Only by the grace of God he died first, of tertiary syphilis—"

Tom's face had turned crimson. Now he started to come around the desk with fists clenched, but Simon stood his ground.

"—in that wretched little nursing home in Manila, that slum where you put him, hoping the papers wouldn't get hold of it—"

"Be quiet, or I'll—"

"—worn out, drunk, *worm-eaten*—"

"You say another word and I'll give you the leathering I ought to have given you years ago."

"You! You're not *strong* enough."

Simon saw Tom's eyes grow larger and knew that in another second his father would strike. A wave of sound reverberated in his ears, blotting out all extraneous noise. Then something very strange happened, something quite outside his experience. One moment he felt immensely tired, tired to the point of collapse; the next, he sensed an exhilarating flood of strength pour through his body like a magic elixir and deep inside his head, above the roaring, he heard a distinct *crack*.

Odd things appeared to happen, but with frustrating slowness. As if from a distance he saw a pair of hands—surely not his?—grasp the lapels of Tom Young's suit and wrench them forward, thus bringing the face of the other man to within a millimeter of his own; and in a flash Tom's expression seemed to change. Now he was no longer an angry patriarch, merely an old and frightened man.

The extraordinary wave of sound reached its apogee and Simon's eyes focused. Every line in the room seemed razor sharp, each object crystal clear.

Tom's mouth opened and Simon imagined he felt a great weight on his hands; then his father seemed to fall to a kneeling position and tip over against Burney's desk, cutting his head against its edge.

The roaring in Simon's ears died away; his vision blurred, refocused; the peculiar hallucination passed. Tom Young stood in exactly the same place as before. Simon looked at Sir Martin Burney to find him still frozen behind the desk, an equally strange look on his own face: a look in which were mingled sympathy and apprehension and, yes, contempt as well.

"Ask him," Simon grated, "ask the chairman-by-act-of-Parliament how far he's got with his plans for moving the Corporation to Singapore."

He took a long, last look at Tom Young, as if trying to imprint the memory of his face for all time, and—"You're the one who's finished in Hong Kong," he said. Then, without another word, he turned and left the room.

22

When he came out of Government House the chauffeur held open the door of the Rolls-Royce for him and awaited instructions. But Simon had no clear idea of where he wanted to go or what he should do.

Somehow he had managed to involve himself in a nightmare of which this was merely the latest installment. First the plant destroyed, then the murder attempt on Tom and Diana, then the debt called in, then the disappearance of his family. And now, at a time when he needed all the support he could muster, he had finally broken with his own father.

"Where to, sir?"

The Chinese driver gazed through the windscreen, studiously avoiding the sight of his employer's tortured face in his rearview mirror. Simon hesitated for a moment while he thought things through.

Qiu.

Qiu held the answers to everything. How to contact him? Reade wouldn't help. That left . . . whom did that leave?

Only one possibility. One last hope.

"Kai Tak," he said crisply. "Singapore Airlines."

He was in no mood for economies or gestures; he flew first class. But when he attempted to pass through immigration control, the duty inspector stopped him. Simon listened in a daze as the official read from a clipboard: "Emergency Powers Ordinance . . . self-protection . . . pending inquiries . . ."

Then another voice said: "It's all right, Inspector. Mr. Young is free to depart."

Simon wheeled around. "Well, well," he said. "Peter."

Reade was wearing an elegant double-breasted charcoal-gray suit with navy blue tie and matching handkerchief in the breast pocket. He stood with arms folded, one foot jutting out in front of the other and shoulders hunched. Simon thought he had never seen anyone look less like an officer of the law. Reade surveyed him for several moments before glancing at the inspector, "Let him go."

The inspector's face grew taut. "Sir, I have reason to believe that persons hostile to the colony may wish to abduct this man. His family have already disappeared."

"Oh yes, I daresay." Reade sounded indifferent. "He's over twenty-one, though."

"Mr. Reade, I have emergency powers to detain—"

"Of course you do, Inspector, of course you do. And in the case of this man, I override those powers. All right?"

The inspector took a last, hostile look at Reade, saluted with exemplary precision and withdrew.

"What was all that about?" asked Simon.

Reade spread his hands. "He was only doing his job."

"Never mind him. I meant you: Why interfere?"

Reade merely shrugged. As the assistant commissioner moved away, Simon shouted after him: "My God, Peter, I'm going to fix you when this is over."

Reade laughed, but his pace never faltered. "Have a nice trip," he said over his shoulder.

The first-class cabin was nearly empty. Just before takeoff there came a commotion. Simon, his mind elsewhere, vaguely heard the steward welcoming a last-minute passenger aboard, but he paid little attention until that same passenger lowered himself into the vacant seat next to his with a grunt.

"Evening, Simon."

Simon slowly turned his head. "Hello, Robert."

"Mind if I sit next to you?"

"Suit yourself."

The aircraft climbed rapidly through the cloud layer. Robert Zhao, still out of breath, seemed content to wait until the engines had throttled back before attempting to talk.

"Simon, I must speak to you urgently."

Simon registered that Zhao was not merely out of breath. For all his efforts at self-control, it was obvious that the Chinese was extremely agitated. Perhaps even—Simon took a closer look—frightened.

"Can't it wait? I've got enough on my mind at the moment."

"No, it can't wait. Why do you think I nearly killed myself to catch this plane?"

"How should I know?"

"Because I've been following you, looking for a chance—"

"*Following* me?"

"You want your family back, don't you? Of course you do, don't bother to answer me, just listen. I know where they are. I can help you get them back."

"You can—"

"Shh. Just *listen*! I need help, Simon." Zhao swept a lock of hair off his forehead and looked quickly around to see that they were still unobserved. "Christ, do I need help." He drew a deep breath and held it for a few seconds until he was calm.

"Your uncle David. He died raving, in Manila. Some people I know got to him before he died. They listened to him. He said a lot of interesting things. About the settlement. You knew about that?"

"What settlement? What are you—?"

"No, that's right, that's right, they said you didn't know about it. That's right, of course." Zhao chewed a sliver of nail from his thumb. "There was a trust. Your grandfather, Richard Young, established it in the thirties. He settled thirty of the Founders Shares. When Tom dies or ceases to be chairman of the Corporation, six of his shares pass to you."

"*What?*"

"Six shares come to you, under the terms of the settlement. You get a controlling interest in the Founders Shares. You can run the Corporation. Run it off the face of the earth, if you like."

Simon sat there speechless. He could not begin to absorb what Zhao was telling him.

"I . . . I was involved with some people who are known to you. I had worked for them before. They wanted my services."

"They? Who's they?"

"Qiu. And others."

"So you lied to me, about not knowing Qiu?"

"Yes."

"Why should I believe you now?"

"If you want to see your family again, you'd better! And I'll tell you something else—you're next to disappear. It's all plotted, all arranged."

There was a long pause. "Go on," Simon said at last.

"They told me what my role was. And I believed them, at first."

"What did they tell you?"

"That I was to force you into dealing with Soviet Communal by preparing an alternative scheme, making you think there was genuine competition."

"You succeeded, then. Go on."

"Also, I . . . I was to keep an eye on you. Report back anything you said."

"Spy on me, in other words."

"Yes, if you insist! Christ, Simon, we can have all that out some other time—what matters now is your family. Jinny . . ."

"Oh really? I thought you wanted my help."

"I do, I do. Look. Some other people found out about my involvement with Qiu."

"What other people?"

"It doesn't matter. You don't know them. But they're the ones who found out about your grandfather's settlement. They're the ones who tried to kill Tom at Ocean Park."

"But why, in the name of God—?"

"Don't you see yet? Tom's tenure was extended by the UK government. The shares weren't going to pass to you when he was sixty-five after all, because he wasn't going to have to resign his chairmanship then. It meant that under the terms of the settlement he could keep the shares until he—"

"Until he *died*."

"Yes!"

"But I still don't see why—"

"Look. These . . . these other people. They wanted to control a majority of the Founders Shares. So they set you up, made you sign a charge over all the shares which you either owned or became entitled to later."

"You mean these people knew, right from the start, what was going to happen?"

"Of course."

"The loan, the bombs at the plant—"

"No, not the bombs. But the loan, yes! It was all part of the plan. And"—Zhao's face suddenly assumed a shifty expression; he could no longer meet Simon's eyes—"and the attack on your father, that was part of it, too. At first they were content to wait for Tom to retire, but when it became obvious that he wasn't going to, they tried to kill him."

There was a long silence while Simon Young digested the story. His brain could not cope with the shock. "Why are you telling me this?" he said at last.

Zhao started work on his other thumbnail. For several moments he continued to stare at Simon over his knuckles, as if trying to assess how far he could go. "I said I need your help," he said at last. "Time's run out for me."

"Explain."

"These other people I was telling you about, they have a role for me in all this. When Soviet Communal come to sell the Founders Shares, I've got to buy them."

"You?"

"Yes. I'm the front man. I've been working on Tang, you know, SCB's Singapore branch manager. I buy the shares from the Russians, but as their nominee."

"Have you got that kind of money?"

"No, but I don't need it. It'll be provided."

"So what's in it for you?"

"The chairmanship of the Corporation."

"I see. That's nice. Congratulations. So why are you so scared all of a sudden?"

"Because there's been a change of plan in Beijing."

"I don't get you."

"At first, Qiu and his gang wanted only one thing—to ruin the Soviet Communal Bank."

"They told you that too, did they?"

"Oh, it was true. At first. They were going to blow up the plant to make sure you wouldn't be able to repay the loan in a hurry; then they'd engineer a default, prove that the bank's security documents were forged, bring down the bank."

"You say was—it *was* true. What's changed?"

"Qiu wants the shares. For the PRC."

"*What?* But—but how? The documents were forged, Qiu knew that, he arranged it all in the first place."

"Oh yes. You gave him a real headache. At first, Qiu planned for you to execute genuine documentation. He told you that he'd swap it around after the loan had gone through. But you were too clever to fall for it, so he had to let you sign forgeries in front of Luk and then make the switch *after* the bank had received your half of the contract."

"But . . . *what* did he switch?"

"Oh, for God's *sake!* He took away the papers you'd already signed, in front of Luk. In their place he substituted brilliant forgeries, prepared in Beijing, forgeries clever enough to deceive a court. Not only did they forge your signature; they forged a magistrate's as well, as witness."

"Qiu really did all that?"

"Yes. And it's that second set that everyone's been working on ever since. That's the set that was produced in court."

"And the default—did Qiu arrange that, too? The missing twenty-thousand-dollar payment?"

"Of course."

"So soon the shares are going to be up for sale to a Chinese front man—"

"And I'm the front man who's been chosen to buy them. As nominee."

"That's a lot of nomineeships you've got there, Robert. One too many, I'd say."

"You're right. I . . . I have to disappoint someone."

"So what am I supposed to do about it? And how does this tie in with my family?"

"We can deal. You and I."

"We can?"

"Yes. You've got to redeem the loan, buy back the shares. That way, I get off the hook."

"Yes, I see that. But there are two problems."

"What?"

"For one thing, I haven't got that kind of money. And for

another, it doesn't do anything to help me get my family back."

"It might. They're alive. They're in Sichuan. Qiu's people are holding them hostage for your good behavior. My God, the thought of Jinny . . ." He drew a deep breath. "But that's only temporary—they plan for you to join them. I'm prepared to stand up and say that, in public, if you like."

"Beijing'll just deny it."

"They won't. Not if you pay back the loan. At that point they'll see they've lost."

"So we're back to the loan. Where do I get the money from?"

"I can get it for you." Zhao's eyes slid away. "I think."

"Where from?"

"Half from me, half from Ng Swee Kam."

"Oh, you know about Ng, do you?"

"Yes. I was Qiu's man, remember."

"You're the one who doesn't seem to remember. Whose man are you now?"

"My own. Help me, Simon. For God's sake, help me!"

Simon thought. "Ng works for Qiu. Why should he help?"

"Qiu doesn't own him. Ng's free-lance. And you've done a lot of business with him over the past three years: he might turn out to be on your side, not Qiu's."

Simon remembered another conversation, this time with Qiu. Ng was strictly free-lance . . . Qiu had already implied as much. "I was going to see Ng," Simon said, almost unwillingly.

"Good. Go. Tell him he can contact me at the Shangri-La. Where will you be staying?"

"I haven't thought. Somewhere out of sight." Simon hesitated. "I might ask Ng to put me up."

"That's not a very good idea. Qiu knows you're on this plane. They know what you're up to. Remember—you're next to disappear."

"That's something else I don't understand. Why kidnap me? Why not just kill me and have done with it?"

"Insurance. They need you alive, in case something goes wrong over the next few months. They don't trust me. Until they've actually got the shares in their hands, they're not going to do anything they can't undo later."

Simon gave him a shrewd sideways glance. "All right—I'll find somewhere safe. As long as I can find you in a hurry, there's no problem."

When Simon said nothing more for several minutes, Zhao turned and saw that his eyes were closed. The Englishman's face was clammy with sweat. "Hey . . ."

"What?" Simon opened his eyes again.

"They could kill me. They're capable of that."

"Which side are we talking about now?"

Zhao licked his lips. "Both sides. Both."

The two men said no more. When the plane came down at Changi along with the dusk, Simon wasted no time on good-byes. He watched Zhao until the Chinese had been driven away in a taxi before going back inside the terminal to look for a telephone.

The monotonous single tone sounded in his ear for what seemed like a very long time before someone picked up the receiver. Then there came another pause, as if the person at the other end of the line wasn't sure what to say. Simon, in his exhausted state, did not notice anything unusual.

"Hello . . . hello?"

"Who is this?" A quiet, well-spoken woman's voice.

"Simon Young. I'm calling from the airport. Can I speak to Mr. Ng, please?"

Another longish pause. Then: "Si-i-i-*mon*! How wonderful to hear your voice again."

"Maudie?"

"Of course."

"Maudie, I'm sorry to trouble you but I urgently need to see your brother. Maudie? Hello, are you there . . . ?"

This time the pause went on for a very long time indeed. The line sounded muffled, as if Maudie had placed a hand over the receiver while she spoke to someone in the room with her. Simon's mind, no longer attuned to the passage of time, drifted.

"Simon, darling . . . of course, we would love to see you, isn't it? Please come now."

"To the house."

"Yes . . . oh no, wait a moment, Simon *dar*-ling, when I say the house I mean to the big house."

"The mansion, off Kim Seng Road?"

"Right, right."

"Give me the address, will you please. I never wrote it down."

"O-*kay*. Here we go, lah . . ."

Simon scribbled the address in his datebook while Maudie dictated. It dimly occurred to him that she sounded tired and distant.

"Simon . . ."

"Yes."

"Are you alone?"

Something about the tone of the question made him pause and for a moment he wondered whether to stall. Did he really trust these people? They constituted a direct link with the Chinese secret service; if put to the choice their loyalties might lie with the People's Republic. How could he be sure . . . ?

"I'm alone."

He'd expected Maudie to say good-bye but the line went dead with bleak finality. Simon came out of the phone booth and went in search of a taxi.

It was a rainy night in Singapore and the city's streets were jammed with cars. Simon's cab took nearly an hour to travel from Changi to the Ng mansion. The house was in total darkness, except for one red light burning behind a rattan blind on the second floor. A warm, wet wind blew the branches of the nearby trees to and fro across the façade of the building, giving it a sullen, haunted look.

Simon walked down the drive, wishing, too late, that he had thought to bring an umbrella. Squalls of rain lashed downward through the branches, drenching his clothes before he'd gone a dozen yards. He ran up the steps to the front door and to his surprise found it ajar.

"Swee Kam?" No response. Simon pushed on the door and it gave. "Swee Kam?" he called again. "Maudie . . . ?"

Silence hung oppressively in the room. Simon hesitated on the step a moment longer. Surely someone must have heard him. Had he understood Maudie correctly? He was so tired. . . .

"*Si*-mon . . ."

The soft, rich voice came from an inner room, beyond the entrance hall that housed the family altar. Simon advanced, banging his knee against a chair. Light flared and he caught sight of a yellow hand holding a candle at arm's length.

"Maudie? Is that you?" He peered ahead into the gloom. There were two candles now, one at each end of a long table. Simon entered the main room, cautiously picking his way between the myriad items of furniture that littered the floor. "Why aren't there any lights?"

"Power-cut. Please shut the front door, see that it's latched."

He stopped. Maudie was standing on the far side of the table, midway between the two sputtering candles. Simon registered, not for the first time, how beautiful she looked; never more so than in the ivory glow of the naked flames. Tonight she seemed to embrace all that was soft and feminine in a male-dominated world. He felt his way back to the front door and pushed it shut. As he returned and Maudie's face once more blended out of the gloom, he marveled at the incredible softness of her perfect skin, the flashing, bejeweled quality of her eyes, the silken, ebony hair . . .

"Simon. How nice. Come closer, where Maudie can see you."

But he stopped, suddenly unsure of himself. Maudie was attractive, yes, but he had never thought of her as beautiful before. And her voice did not sound quite as he remembered it. Tonight it seemed less raucous, lighter, almost too feminine. Something about that voice disturbed Simon. It wasn't natural.

Power-cut, she said. But there was a light burning on the second floor. . . . Simon knew there was a light switch on the wall behind him. He turned away from Maudie and moved toward it.

"Stop there, Simon."

This time there was no mistaking the change in the voice. It was vibrant, high; the voice of someone enjoying her kick.

Simon turned around very slowly. The person on the other side of the table looked the same in every respect except one. Her right hand held a gun. It was aimed at him.

Simon raised his hands. "Maudie?"

Then the woman changed in a second aspect also. She reached up and with a theatrical toss of the head she peeled away her wig to reveal close-cropped black hair.

"Eric, actually."

The boy was astonishingly beautiful, even by the legendary standards of Singaporean transvestites. Skin, makeup, figure; all were perfect enough to put many a real woman to shame. And he was enjoying his role, Simon could see that, enjoying it like a snort of cocaine. The boy's eyes glittered with malicious amusement reflected in the exquisitely shaped lips that now opened to display his white, even teeth, grinding in triumph. Simon could not think. He could not speak. This boy was a woman. He *was* Maudie.

"Good evening, Simon Young," said a new but nevertheless familiar voice.

A light came on. The Englishman's gaze shifted and he saw a man framed in the doorway. He too was holding a gun.

"Good evening, Qiu Qianwei." But Simon could not resist the

urge to look back at the transvestite. The fascination seemed mutual; for the boy was licking his moist lips in what might have been invitation.

"Mr. Young . . ."

Simon refocused his eyes on Qiu, who now held up the gun at arm's length and steadied his right wrist with his left hand. Simon looked at death approaching and felt only a curious emptiness. Nothing mattered any more.

"Mr. Young, do you remember me once telling you what we do to homosexuals in China?"

For a moment Simon did not understand. Qiu, his face at its most malevolent, was slowly swiveling his extended arms away from the Englishman, toward the transvestite. Simon found himself looking into the boy's eyes for the last time. He saw there a flash of precognition as Eric intuitively sensed what was about to happen and started to turn toward Qiu. Why? Simon wondered. To plead for mercy? A waste of time. To register one last forlorn protest against the fading of the light? To remember the face, so that one day he would be able to call his executioner to account before the gods . . . ?

The mansion reverberated with a terrible crash as flame spurted from the mouth of Qiu's revolver. The impact hurled Eric forward against the table. Both candles fell with a clatter and were extinguished, mercifully concealing the back of his shattered head. Simon took a step toward him, knowing it was hopeless, that there was nothing he could do for the beautiful, wrecked butterfly that lay sprawled on the floor; but as he moved, a pair of hands holding a cloth closed over his mouth from behind and he was briefly aware of an acrid, burning liquid splashing onto the fabric before he passed out.

Simon dreamed he was in an iron foundry. He had been there a long time. The heat, already unbearable, was increasing. Dust filled his nostrils. Somewhere close by they were beating panels: *bang, bang, bang.* He struggled to find a way out, but there was none. He wanted to throw off his clothes, but they stuck to his body. *Bang, bang, BANG!*

He awoke. The iron foundry was still inside his head; he moaned with pain. A heavy, liquid mass began to move inside him, traveling along his torso.

Simon struggled upright and was violently sick.

Slowly, his vision cleared. Hands. Hands holding a bowl beneath his chin. Hands wiping his face with a cool cloth. Beyond that, the gray early-morning light barely illuminated earth walls, wooden beams, a few sticks of rustic furniture.

He raised his eyes to see a familiar face smiling down at him. Jinny.

"Simon . . . oh, my love . . ."

The pain in his head faded away to a dull beat. He managed a smile. "Hello."

He lay back and stared at the rafters, trying to remember what had happened. Someone had been shot. That was in Singapore. But this wasn't Singapore.

"Where am I?" he said.

"Chaiyang."

"Chaiyang? But that's your village. That's in"—his mind worked slowly—"in China."

"Yes."

He stared at his wife in disbelief. "How did I get to China?"

"Qiu Qianwei brought you here."

"Qiu. He said . . ." Simon falteringly tried to clear his memory. "There was a letter . . . you wrote it."

"I had no choice. He had the children. I could not fight him as long as he had Diana and Mat."

There was a long pause while he digested that. Then: "Where are they? The children . . ."

"Here. In the village. They're at work now."

His mind still wandered. "But . . . the letter . . ."

"I had no choice," she repeated firmly.

She could see he did not know whether to believe her or not and her chest tightened. "I'll bring you tea," she said. "You are to rest, for a while."

"A while? And after . . ."

She hesitated, wondering how to break it to him. "After, you will have to work. As we all do."

"Work." The word seemed novel to him. "What kind of work?"

"In the fields."

His tired smile made her want to weep, so childlike it was. "Rice?"

"Yes. Rice."

For a long while he said nothing, but merely gazed up at the ceiling as if the answers to the questions that plagued him could be found in the beams. At last he said, "I know what they want, now."

"What?" When he did not reply, Jinny shook his arm, ever so gently. "Please answer me. What do they want?"

But he merely turned his head on the pillow, letting her see the suspicion in his eyes, and after a while she had no choice but to release him. They continued thus for a long time, quite silent, each engrossed in thoughts too fearful to communicate, while outside the rising sun inexorably dissolved the shadows that, until now, had veiled China from Simon's sight.

23

The house, built just below a peak of the Nine Dragons foothills near Ak Tai To Yan, commanded an unparalleled prospect of Guangdong Province. It was an odd structure to find in Hong Kong's New Territories. Robert Zhao had retained a Swedish architect who conceived it in terms of a lopsided, split-level chest of drawers, giving the walls a sandstone finish and topping off his handiwork with pale gray tiles. The edifice looked every bit as tough and functional as its owner. It also resembled him in managing to convey an air of distinguished, if idiosyncratic, style.

It was possible to approach this house by a narrow earth and stone track, which in the wet season turned to sticky mud, but hardly anyone did. There was a helicopter landing pad in a hollow immediately beneath the lowest terrace, and most visitors arrived by air. The inhabitants of the nearby villages had grown accustomed to hearing Zhao's Bell Jet Ranger clatter overhead between Kai Tak and the house, but for the most part the locals avoided the house and its occupants. They knew that Zhao's mistress, Lai Wan, lived there in permanent seclusion, but they considered this to be nobody's business except Zhao's and possibly his wife's. In the rural New Territories the rich were viewed with an interest that was never less than circumspect.

Robert Zhao stood on the upper terrace looking north, toward China. It was a warm and sunny morning, typical September weather. The hills of Guangdong showed pale mauve on the horizon, their tops sheathed in wispy cloud. Zhao lit a cigar and rested his hands on the rail in front of him. The view from where he stood, both literally and metaphorically, was breathtaking, but the beauty of the morning did not improve his mood.

The noise of the helicopter's rotors sprang out of the blue, causing him to turn and look up over his shoulder. The house was so situated that it was often impossible to hear the machine until after it had rounded Tai-Mo Shan and flown to within a mile of the house. This Sunday morning the pilot swung far out toward Fan-Ling before turning back in a broad, flat sweep that carried the Bell Jet Ranger down in a steady drift to land on the pad below. Zhao raised his hand and waved.

The passenger door opened to emit a pale-looking Chinese, carrying a briefcase. He blinked in the sunlight, unused to it after the protection of the helicopter's tinted glass. Then he caught sight of Zhao and smiled.

"Come up. The stairway's to your right."

His visitor, a tall man who walked with a stoop as if he were ashamed of his height, peered around until he discerned the flight of shallow concrete steps that led up to the house. He was wearing a suit and tie and he climbed slowly, obviously bothered by the heat. As he emerged onto the upper terrace Zhao walked toward him with a welcoming smile, hand outstretched.

"It seems a long time since last we met, Mr. Tang," he said, in Cantonese.

"Not so long." Tang shook his host's hand gingerly, as if worried about losing a finger. "The negotiations over the Taipei Leisure Complex, I think."

"You're right, that's when it was. Come, let's go in. It's cooler inside."

Tang gazed enviously at Zhao's outfit. He was wearing a plain cotton short-sleeved shirt, white yachtsman's trousers and rope sandals—the kind of clothes a shop assistant bought because he imagined they made him look like a millionaire, and a millionaire wore because they were comfortable and he liked them. Tang was a banker. Even on a Sunday he wore gray.

As the two men went inside, the Bell Jet Ranger took off and circled the house before disappearing in the direction of Hong Kong. Zhao placed one hand on Tang's shoulder and glanced skyward. "He shouldn't take long."

"Magistrate Ko has not yet arrived, then?"

"Not yet. I wanted to make sure you got here from the airport and then have a few words with you in private before he came."

"That means two trips for your pilot. I'm flattered."

"You shouldn't be. This is quite an occasion, Mr. Tang." Zhao sat his guest down on a stark Scandinavian chair which happened to chime in with his view of the banker's personality. "May I offer you tea? I was going to have a beer."

The banker pulled out a handkerchief and dabbed his forehead. "Beer would be excellent, thank you." While Zhao rang the bell and gave orders to the boy, Tang looked around him nervously. He was not used to houses with walls consisting mostly of glass. Even though the venetian blinds were down, he felt exposed. The room was built on more than one level: a square, black-carpeted well in the center, surrounded by a raised border of polished wood that resembled teak. Zhao saw him eyeing it and said, "You like my choice of timber?"

"Oh yes. The grain, it's very unusual."

"Iroko. From West Africa. I build it into all my boats now. The architect had never seen it, he was most impressed."

The beer came in two bedewed silver tankards. Zhao tossed back half his drink while Tang sipped more slowly, his eyes darting. "You have a wonderful place," he said.

"Thank you. I find it convenient to have somewhere out of town where I can entertain a few friends in peace."

"Yes." Tang's expression was strained and Zhao guessed that he was wondering about the absence of a hostess.

"I lead a quiet life. My wife spends most of her time in Paris, now. These ladies, eh?"

"Quite."

"Perhaps there will be a little more peace where you are going, Mr. Tang?"

The banker hesitated, unprepared for the sudden shift to business so early in the meeting. "Perhaps."

Zhao came to sit opposite him, putting down his glass on the blackwood table which occupied the center of the square. For a moment he said nothing and then, to Tang's surpise, he spoke in English. "Our mutual friends have done a sound job, wouldn't you say?"

"Oh, very."

"So now . . ." Zhao's voice softened to a whisper. "Now you have something for me, I believe?"

The banker hesitated a moment before reaching down to lift his briefcase. As Zhao watched him fumble with the combinations he could not quite manage to control his features. He had waited a long time for this moment. It should have represented the end of a lot of problems; only now it didn't. Now it meant only fear.

Tang opened his case and extracted a single, faded sheet of thick paper which he laid in the exact center of the table. Zhao could not take his eyes off it, but he did not pick the paper up at once. When at last he opened his mouth to speak, the words seemed incongruous. "The journey . . . I trust it was comfortable?"

Tang did not reply. Zhao looked up to see that the banker's eyes also were fixed on the sheet of white paper.

"Mr. Tang?"

"Mm?" Tang came to himself with a start.

"The journey," Zhao repeated softly. "Was it comfortable?"

"Oh yes. Thank you." Zhao's smile was still intact but Tang's face wore a guilty expression. His host had been gently reminding him of what civilized behavior, the "rites" of society, required. He did not, could not, know that Zhao was testing only himself.

"And your onward flight is all arranged, I assume?" Zhao's voice was cordial but there was an edge to it.

"Yes. I fly to Beijing this afternoon."

"I have not yet congratulated you. To become a vice chairman of the People's Bank of China is a great honor."

"It is, it is."

"Do you ever think of what the future holds? I think I would, sometimes. If I were in your position."

"No." Tang removed his spectacles and began to polish them with his handkerchief. "Moscow's arm does not extend to Beijing. And I have no plans to travel outside China ever again."

"Your former employers will be angry." Zhao's voice was uneasy; he appeared to be musing aloud. "*Extremely* angry."

"Yes." Tang's face betrayed quiet satisfaction. "Let us hope so."

"And it doesn't worry you?"

"No."

"You're brave."

"No. I'm a patriot."

Zhao looked up sharply, but it seemed that Tang was perfectly sincere. His face was composed and stern, the eyes showed no trace of humor. Zhao suddenly felt lost and had to grope for bearings. "I see," he said at last; and only then did he reach forward to pick up the paper.

It was folded into four. He opened it carefully, smoothing its surface, slightly roughened with time, against the tabletop. It was not white, after all, he noticed, but a color reminiscent of best quality vanilla ice cream, on which the black printing stood boldly forth. Instinctively his fingers moved to the bottom right-hand corner, where the seal had been affixed. "Real wax," he murmured. "Wonderful, wonderful."

"You have never seen such a share certificate before, I think?"

"Never." Zhao began to read aloud, taking his time over the legal jargon. "The Pacific & Cantonese Banking Corporation. Founders Shares. This is to certify . . ." His voice faded but he continued to read the document through to the end before allowing it to slip from his fingers back onto the table. "Incredible," he breathed.

"Yes. Worth in the open market one hundred million pounds sterling, at a conservative estimate."

Zhao closed his eyes and sank back into his chair, lost in contemplation of his own wretched position. To come so close to the verge of success and then to be—he sat up again, so that he could see the share certificate on the table—to be robbed of the earth and the fullness thereof . . .

"One hundred million," he breathed. "But in the closed market, much, much more."

"Infinitely more. I shall need certified copies of all the documentation, including the judgment, please. For Beijing."

Zhao shook himself, making a conscious effort to concentrate. "Magistrate Ko will have your copies with him. I've asked him to certify everything personally."

"Yes, I agree that will be best. Everything must be done in

such a way as to make these shares as marketable as possible."

"You're right. When Ko certifies the papers and witnesses the disposition of the shares into my name, a purchaser should have little to complain of. Incidentally, Mr. Tang, I haven't seen a copy of the judgment. Is there anything unusual about it, anything to cast doubt on its finality?"

"Nothing. It merely recites the debt and interest, and the fact that no defense was filed in the time allowed. It goes on to give formal judgment for the money. Then, of course, there is the declaration as to the validity of the bank's charge over the shares, and an order obliging the Corporation to deliver the certificate to Soviet Communal Bank."

"Was there any difficulty about enforcing delivery?"

"Not really. The Corporation's registrars waited until close of business on the very last day allowed by the court, but then they handed over the certificate to my co-director, Mr. Goh, without demur."

"Excellent."

"I am still not altogether happy about the court's order. A default judgment can always be set aside."

"Not unless the debtor applies to set it aside. Not if the debtor disappears. Young vanished weeks ago, there's still no sign of him."

"A strange occurrence. What do you make of it?"

"Suicide, perhaps."

"Perhaps. But that solution would still leave the mystery of his family. One thinks in terms of an accident, an air crash, yet there have been no such reports."

"No."

"Anyway, it's far too late for Young to do anything. Legally, no one else is in a position to repay the debt even if he had the resources to do so. There was talk of the Corporation coming to the rescue, but we made it clear that we were prepared to deal only with our original borrower. Since Young exercised total control over the borrower company, that was the end of that. The borrower has been made bankrupt, incidentally, on our petition. We thought we had better go through the motions of executing the judgment before we foreclosed on the Founders Shares."

"Were there assets?"

"Not so much as an office chair and typewriter."

"Excellent. So the shares were your only remedy; no one could possibly criticize you for selling them."

Tang sighed. "Already the bank has received offers. Nothing overt, you understand, just soundings. Some of the figures being bandied around in Singapore, well . . ."

"Tempted?"

Tang vigorously shook his head. "Not in the least. The shares belong to the People's Republic." His eyes glittered with uncharacteristic humor. "Like the money which now buys them. You have the check, I suppose?"

"I have it here ready. Magistrate Ko will of course expect to see everything done in proper form before he witnesses the instrument of transfer."

"No problem." Tang shrugged. "I have identification on me which proves that I am chief executive of the Soviet Communal Bank's Singapore branch. The certified copy of the judgment proves that the bank is owed money for which the shares are security. The memorandum and articles of Soviet Communal Bank authorize me to sell shares, receive money and execute transfers on its behalf. Ko will watch you hand a certified banker's draft for one hundred and fifteen million pounds sterling representing principal, accrued interest and charges to me in my capacity as the bank's duly authorized representative. In exchange, I will give you a validly executed transfer of the shares and that certificate lying on the table. You then become a bona fide purchaser for value and your title is unimpeachable."

"Even though the chief executive of SCB's Singapore branch office is shortly about to disappear for good and not a penny of this money will ever find its way back to the bank?"

"That does not matter. What counts is that the money is paid to an official of the bank, an agent acting within the scope of his actual authority. Nothing that happens afterward can undermine your position, which is in any case a strong one."

"Why do you say that?"

"Because you are a respectable businessman with no political overtones. Presumably that is why our principals decided to involve you in the first place."

"Yes, of course." Zhao smiled. "Incidentally, what will you do with the bank draft?"

"Do with it?" Tang was puzzled. "Take it back to Beijing, of course, where the money originated."

"Of course—I merely thought you might want to hang it in a frame on the wall of your new office."

"Oh. I see." Tang did not smile. "An interesting thought, Mr. Zhao."

"But one, I realize, that does not appeal." Zhao took a deep breath. There was something he had to do, something that he had been putting off for as long as possible. "What about this share certificate?" he said.

"Sorry?"

"My present instructions are to keep it here, but I feel very reluctant to do that. Would it not be best for you to take it back to Beijing until it's needed? For safety's sake?"

He closed his eyes for a second, unable to contemplate the possibility that Tang might actually accept. But—"I have no such instructions," said the banker. "Surely it will be safe enough here?"

Zhao opened his eyes. "Probably."

"Besides, you'll need it when you come to register the transfer into the name of our chosen company. The authorities in Beijing have still not quite decided how best to place these shares. Until the final vehicle is known, it will be necessary for you to be able to produce the share certificate so as to complete the formalities."

"True. Yes, indeed, I had forgotten that." Zhao was obliged to wait a long time before his heart stopped pounding. He knew that offering the share certificate was an essential step if he was to retain Beijing's confidence, that it would work, but still . . . supposing it hadn't? It would then have become necessary to kill Mr. Tang forthwith and Zhao had not been relishing the prospect.

At last he patted his knees and stood up. "I think I hear the helicopter. Shall we go and meet Magistrate Ko?" He looked at his watch. "And then you must be on your way."

"Yes. It would not do for me to miss the afternoon flight. I want to be in Beijing before my absence is noticed in Singapore."

It was on the tip of Zhao's tongue to say, "Before the absence of the shares is noticed," but he refrained. Instead, as the two men went through the sliding glass doors which led to the terrace, he gave vent to a genuine curiosity.

"What made you do it, Mr. Tang?"

"Do what?"

"Come over. Change sides."

Tang raised his head toward the sun, smiled and thought for a moment. "That's a difficult question," he said at last. "The man I answered to, Borisenko . . . he was difficult to satisfy. Sometimes he made that obvious, very obvious. And there were times"—

he broke off with a grimace as he remembered the disgraceful scene in the brothel—"there were times when he behaved as no man can behave and still call himself civilized."

Zhao, who had memories of his own, chuckled. "Anyway, I congratulate you on your timing."

"Why so?"

"Because if you hadn't decided to come in with us before the loan documentation reached Soviet Communal Bank, someone else might have inspected the signatures too closely and created problems."

"Ah yes, I see what you mean. But I must tell you that I had not finally made up my mind when the papers arrived in my office. I was still undecided where my loyalties lay."

Zhao very slowly swiveled on the balls of his feet until he was facing Tang. "What?"

"I examined those signatures for a long time, late one night. And do you know something? I looked through all the official registers, but I could not trace a Hong Kong magistrate called Luk Seng Kay. I really could not."

"Yet you said nothing?"

"No. I said nothing."

"You puzzle me greatly."

"Is it so hard to understand?" Tang shrugged. "The more I thought about it, the more clearly I saw that the scheme would certainly work. It was about then that you made contact and assisted me toward a final decision. But of course by that time your colleagues in the Mah-jongg Brigade had effected the necessary substitution without any help from me."

There was a long silence. At last Zhao asked, "What does it feel like, to be going home to our friends after all these years?"

When his guest did not reply at once, Zhao turned to see that the banker's eyes, now fastened on the distant, pale mauve hills of Guangdong, contained an expression that was not far removed from ecstasy.

"Indescribable," breathed Tang.

24

It was harvest time in Chaiyang: the shoots had turned gold and their heads hung heavily. A lot of work needed to be done. Anybody who wanted to eat had to earn his rice.

Simon Young bent double to cut the tender shoots, swinging his tiny semicircular knife from right to left in the rhythmical movement that had become second nature to him. Every so often he would stop to wipe the sweat from his brow, lifting his pointed straw hat and rubbing both hands through his hair to encourage the scalp to breathe. His back never ceased to ache, his arms were raw and red with sunburn, but he had crossed some kind of pain barrier. He knew it this morning, as he saw the pole-bearer come along the line of peasants up to their knees in muddy water—when, instead of experiencing mere relief, he felt a second's resentment at having his work interrupted. He could hardly believe it—but a moment later he realized the significance of what he felt. It meant he could survive, at least for a while.

He looked up from his task to see that the pole-bearer was Mat. "Hi."

"Hi, Da. Want a cup?"

"You bet."

The two of them exchanged tired smiles. "Do you have to go at once?" Simon asked, as he stretched his aching arms.

"I can take a break. You're last in line today." The boy eased the long pole off his shoulders with a sigh of relief. "Ow! My shoulders."

Simon grunted. "It'll pass."

"Yes." Mat hesitated, wanting to talk but unsure of his ground. "Look—I'm sorry about last night."

"Forget it. It hardly matters whether you still want to go on to Cambridge or not, now." Simon gestured wearily at the surrounding paddy-fields.

"I didn't mean that. I meant, you know—those other things I said. About you, your job. I shouldn't have said them. And I'm sorry."

"Don't be." Simon smiled at the memory of Mat's angry outburst the previous evening. "You just want to go. Like any other child who ever grew up. . . . Like me."

"You?"

"Yes. Of course. I didn't want to work for Uncle David."

"You didn't?"

"No."

"But I always thought you wanted to be a businessman from the year dot."

Simon lifted his hat and scratched his scalp. "Come on, no point in talking about it now. I'll tell you sometime. Back to work."

Mat looked around to make sure they couldn't be overheard. "Da," he said quietly. "What about the escapè? Anything new?"

Simon shook his head. "No. We *have* to wait for the right moment, there won't be another chance. And now let's get on, before they start to get suspicious."

But as Mat was replacing the pole across his shoulders there came an interruption. A long, shrill scream rang through the humid air, bringing work to a halt. Simon looked up to see peasants from all corners of the paddy-field running toward the main embankment where it adjoined the drainage ditch nearest the village. He and Mat were at the scene within seconds.

"Oh my God," gasped Mat.

Qiu Qianwei was lying on the ground, one trouserleg soaked in blood. His face was white, he seemed barely conscious.

"What happened?" Simon asked the nearest villager.

"A buffalo backed up the cart. The cadre tripped and got himself crushed against the wall."

Some of the peasants were already bringing a makeshift stretcher of sacks strung between bamboo poles. When they lifted Qiu onto it, none too gently, he howled with pain.

Mat nudged his father. "Where are they taking him?"

"House, I expect."

"Shall we go with them?"

Simon hesitated. "No," he said at last. "Don't risk it. Act normally. Let the villagers sort it out, it's their problem, not ours." But as some of the peasants carried Qiu away he stood for several moments looking after them, using his straw hat to shade his eyes from the sun's glare while his brain calculated and schemed.

Evening came; it began to grow cooler in the valley. Simon walked home slowly with Mat, not saying much, just savoring the lush scenery and the pungent scents of twilight. A faint mist had begun to weave its way among the rice shoots, softening the dreariness of the watery landscape. As knots of peasants overtook the two foreigners, some of them allowed their faces to break into reserved smiles, which were returned. There were no good times in the village; but evenings were the best of the bad times.

The peasants rose with the sun, went out to their toil, returned at lunchtime for two hours, went back to the rice fields and stayed there until it was dark. Even the women labored at harvest time, garnering work points in the paddies, alongside their menfolk. It was difficult work. Then the stalks had to be bunched and dried before the rice could be threshed, cleaned and husked. And all this in time for the next crop, when the whole process would begin again; for winter was short here, with scant frost and lots of rain.

Simon and Mat found Jinny waiting for them beside the house nearest the fields, as usual. She was the weakest of the Youngs— unused to exercise, let alone heavy labor—so for the most part she stayed at home, preparing food or looking after the livestock and the children who were still too young to work.

She took Simon by the arm and began to walk home with him.

"Tired?"

"Yes."

"Are you hungry?"

"Mm-hm."

She turned to look him in the face and saw his eyes full upon her—fond, but also questioning. She knew then that he still had not quite made up his mind about her. Well, there was nothing she could do about that, she told herself sadly, except wait and hope.

Simon entered the house and tossed his pointed straw hat onto the table. He did not want to relax, not yet. Once he sat down he would fall asleep, and he still had much to do before nightfall. Besides, he was curious to see what had become of Qiu.

A crowd blocked the doorway that separated the old section of the house from the new. Mingchao stood a little apart, hands clasped behind his back. Simon approached and linked an arm through his. The Chinese jumped, looked up timidly and smiled.

"Hah, Brother-in-law Simon . . . you have returned."

"Yes."

"Late tonight, hah?"

"Harvesting, Mingchao. Soon 'green and yellow don't meet' and we shall be between seasons. I can rest then."

"But you should rest now also. You work very hard."

"I came to see how our invalid was."

Simon smiled down at his brother-in-law, real affection in his eyes. He had never met an Oriental with so much warmth of soul, or a peasant who opened himself to strangers so fully and so soon. Mingchao was in his early thirties and very short, even by Chinese standards. He wore tattered gray trousers that stopped halfway down his calves, a white vest and round black-rimmed spectacles too small for his eyes. Now he returned Simon's look with a grin.

"The barefoot doctor has come. The cadre's wife radioed for her. Lucky, hah?"

Simon absorbed this new fact—Qiu had a radio—without any overt sign of surprise, but he felt an inward tremor of excitement. "You don't have a doctor living here in the village?" he asked.

"No, no." Mingchao smiled. "No bottle caps either!"

"Bottle caps?"

Mingchao raised his hands to his head and deftly outlined a peaked cap. "Bottle caps, police."

"Ah."

"No doctor, no police."

Mingchao grinned again and Simon understood what his brother-in-law was trying to say: you win some and you lose some. "What does the doctor think?" he asked.

Mingchao jerked his thumb toward the new part of the house. "Go on, take a look."

"Thank you." Simon lowered his voice. "Mingchao, have you had any luck with what I asked for?"

Mingchao's face darkened. "Yes, yes," he whispered. "I've got it. But please talk later, when the house is quiet."

Simon nodded and gently pushed his way forward to the front of the little group gathered in the doorway. As he emerged from the throng he saw that Qiu was lying on the floor stretched out under a blanket, his head supported by a pillow. He looked pale but at least he was awake.

Qingqing squatted at Qiu's head with a resigned expression on her face. The doctor was kneeling beside the patient, her right hand wrapped tightly around his left wrist. Simon was curious. He had heard much about barefoot doctors but he had never seen one before. The girl, scarcely more than a teenager, was questioning Qiu in a quiet but confident tone.

"What was your health like before this accident? Do you perspire a lot?"

"Not much."

"Do you fear cold, sleep curled up?"

He shook his head.

She sat back on her haunches. "You have a superficial, empty pulse and no mistake. There is a pattern of disharmony here, quite apart from the wound."

Qiu smiled wanly. "Maybe."

"I have stitched the cut, but that by itself is not enough. It is necessary to restore the imbalance. Your *qi* is most deficient. So is your blood. So is your *shen*. For the moment, I do not think the needles will help. You need to build up your constitution. I will try herbs."

She stood up and turned around. Then, seeing Simon for the first time, she froze and her mouth dropped open. When he smiled at her she blushed, avoiding his eyes. "Does the village have an herb patch?" she asked, covering her embarrassment with unnecessary curtness.

"It has." It was Kaihui who answered.

"Do you grow Dragon Eye Fruit?"

"What?" Kaihui's expression was blank.

"Longan?"

Kaihui shrugged. The girl pouted and picked up her canvas bag with a bad grace. She rummaged around inside it for a few moments before pulling out a large book, the Jiangsu New Medical Institute's edition of the *Encyclopedia of the Traditional Chinese Pharmacopoeia*. Kaihui came to peer over her shoulder while the doctor leafed through the tome in search of the herb she wanted. It took a long time. There were over five thousand entries and it was obvious that her familiarity with the work was less than complete.

"Here"—she pointed at a photograph—"do you have any of this?"

Kaihui's face brightened at once. "Hah, yes, plenty."

"Then you must make him a drink from hot water infused with this herb and some others which I shall give you."

Kaihui stepped back and leveled an accusing finger at Qingqing. "*She* will make the drink. I am not his wife."

Qingqing quailed, but nodded vigorously as if eager to please.

"Good," said the doctor. "I must go now. You"—she beckoned Qingqing—"Come here please and I will tell you how to make the drink and what other herbs to use. Also, how to dress the wound."

Simon stepped back to allow Kaihui to pass. She gave him a tense smile, having no time for the Qiu family. "We'll eat," she said. "Children home?"

As if in answer, Diana's voice was heard outside the house, talking to her brother. "Guess what," she said as they entered. "I caught a fish! In the paddy-field."

Diana's job was to clean and husk the harvested rice, ready for packing and transmission to production headquarters, under the eyes of the brigade's accountant. She worked long but irregular hours, with generous rest periods in between shifts, and she spent much of her free time exploring the village environs.

"Where is it, then?" asked Simon.

"She gave it to Comrade Wang's family," said Mat in a disgusted tone.

"Oh Bean Sprout, don't be like that! They're so hard up since Mr. Wang's been ill . . ."

Simon hugged his daughter, relishing the fresh smell of rice straw and alfalfa in her hair. "That was kind of you. Tired?"

"Yes, tired." She sank into the nearest chair with a sigh and bent down to massage her feet. "Oh, I nearly forgot." She reached for her straw basket and called, "Aunt Kaihui . . ."

Kaihui, recognizing her own name, poked her head out of the kitchen. "Look," said Diana, "I brought these for you . . . *gei ni, gei ni.*"

Diana thrust lotus flowers into her aunt's hands, relishing the smile of gratitude that she received in return. "From the ponds," she explained needlessly. Kaihui disappeared into the kitchen and a moment later came back with a small bottle, which she held out to Diana. "*Gei ni, gei ni,*" she mimicked her niece. "For you, for you . . ."

"Oooh, Seven-Up!" It was indeed Chishui, Chinese lemonade, a rare gift in the village. "Thanks."

Diana took a swig from the bottle and offered it to Simon as he sat down beside her. He took a sip of the warm, sticky liquid and made a face. Diana smiled and slipped one arm through her father's. "They met this morning," she whispered. "I saw them."

"Who met?"

"The happy couple—Mingchao and Zhaodi. They were up at 'great-uncle.' You know—the shrine! They put flowers down and I think they prayed together. It was very touching."

"And you saw them."

"Yes. I heard Mingchao get up very early and I went after him. Was I horrid?"

"Yes, a bit."

"Oh, Da . . ."

"Forget it. Listen . . ." He gripped her arm and looked around swiftly to make sure that they couldn't be overheard. "We've had a stroke of luck. Qiu's been injured."

"What's wrong with him?"

"His leg was gashed open by a cart this morning. The medic's stitched him up, but he looks bad. Exhaustion, if I'm any judge. He's sick, the wedding's tomorrow, Mingchao's managed to get hold of a map. It's tonight, Diana. It has to be tonight."

"Oh. But—I thought you were joking, when you said we were going to escape, I thought—"

"Would I joke about a thing like that?" His voice was fierce. "Do you think I intend to let us stay here for the rest of our lives? Get Mat and your mother; we'll meet in the bedroom."

A few minutes later the Young family assembled in the room they all shared. Simon wasted no time in needless preambles. "You're going out. Tonight." Seeing the blank looks on their faces he drew a deep breath and said, quite calmly, "You have to choose now."

"Choose?"

"Yes." Jinny stared at him in alarm. She knew her husband possessed a strong will, but suddenly there was an expression on his face she had never seen before. "The escape plan, it has to be tonight. Qiu's ill, the wedding's tomorrow, Mingchao's promised me a map. Everything's come together, there'll never be another opportunity like it. You are going out. Just like I told you. To-night."

"Out?" It was Mat who spoke, scarcely able to contain his excitement. "But, will it work? Will it really work?"

Simon brushed him off and seized Jinny's shoulders, forcing her to look at him. "I don't know. All I know is that it represents a chance, the one chance we have. You must leave now if you are to leave at all. Are you with us, Jinny?"

"Of course I'm with you! How can you ask that question?"

He subjected her to another of his long, doubting looks. "Good. Will you go with Mat and Diana, or are you staying here with me?"

Jinny answered quickly. Ever since Simon first proposed his plan she had known what she would do. "I'll stay with Father," she said. "Better so."

Simon turned to the children. "You, too, must choose. We all have to choose."

"What's to choose?" said Mat. "For God's sake, let's get ready."

Diana stared at Simon. "We're really going?"

"Yes." He took her hands and held them tightly. "I've seen things, these last few weeks. I know how you feel about this vil-lage—some of it, anyhow. Not everything here is bad. But I need your help. So much depends on you; the boy trusts you."

She studied his face in silence for a long moment. Then she said, "If it works, if we get away . . . will they ever let us come back?"

"Perhaps." His eyes clouded, as if he were contemplating a future long since marked out and determined. "I think so. I believe I understand a lot of things I didn't know before. There's hope." When still she hesitated Simon said: "Choose, Diana."

She continued to stare at him, searching his face for something she could trust; and then at last she said: "Let me pack now."

Simon released her hands. "Be quick," he muttered as he turned away. "We must have dinner, as if nothing's wrong. Be as natural as you can. Jinny, is the food and water all ready?"

"Yes. I've been keeping things back, a little each day, just as you said."

"Does Kaihui know?"

"She suspects. But she doesn't ask questions."

"Good."

Downstairs the table was laid for dinner. Kaihui served up *guo-tieh*, fried dumplings stuffed with cabbage and pork, of which she was justly proud. There was little conversation over the meal. After a day in the fields most people were too tired to talk or even to notice much of what was going on around them; which was just as well, Simon thought despairingly, or they could hardly fail to be struck by the unnatural tension in his children.

As soon as the meal was over Simon helped Diana clear away. "Go now," he muttered. "It's time."

She looked at him with uncertainty in her eyes, but his face remained hard. She wanted to kiss her father good-bye and found she could not: the steel in his eyes forbade it. So she contented herself with saying, "Have you seen the boy?"

"No. But he usually plays outside at about this time. Qingqing'll be fetching him in soon; be quick."

Sure enough, little Tingchen was squatting on the doorstep. As Diana and Simon came out he stared up at them with unblinking curiosity. The girl smiled and said in Mandarin, "How are you, Tingchen?"

The boy continued to gaze at her without speaking, until suddenly another voice said, "Answer, why don't you?"

Diana looked up to see that Qingqing had come to stand on the step next to her son. She gave them a quick smile before reverting to the boy. "You should answer when somebody talks to you."

"Hello."

Tingchen had spoken in English. Qingqing beamed proudly and addressed herself to Simon, knowing that Diana's Chinese was virtually nonexistent. "His first English word. Your daughter taught him." She paused. "Very kind of her."

"They're fond of each other."

"True, true." Qingqing looked on placidly as Diana picked up Tingchen and gave the solemn little boy a hug. "Want to come and see the fireflies?"

When Simon translated Qingqing frowned. "It's late."

"Not so late. Did he nap today?"

"Yes."

"I thought he looked lively. The fireflies are so pretty. You know the pool at the end of the alley? The village children like to play there in the evening. Diana will take him."

"Well . . ."

Simon turned to his daughter. "Don't lose sight of him," he said, translating the words for Qingqing's benefit.

"I won't. I promise."

Qingqing smiled. "All right. But just for a quarter of an hour."

"*Zhidaole*," said Diana, proud that she had understood Qingqing's last words.

As the two adults watched Diana pick her way down the lane Qingqing said, "Truly, Comrade Young, your daughter is very kind. The boy likes her a lot. Do you know, the other night I found him sleeping in her bed?"

"She'd been reading aloud to him. They both fell asleep. I hope you weren't worried?"

"Not worried, not at all. I knew he would be with Diana. If ever I can't find him these days, he's with her."

On the very fringes of the thickening dusk, Diana turned, waved and smiled. Simon raised his hand in a gesture that might have meant farewell or benediction, she could not be sure which; then she took another few paces forward and was lost from sight.

"Is your husband better?" Simon asked politely.

"A little. I must go back now, to see if he needs anything. Please do not let Diana stay out with Tingchen for too long."

"I won't."

As she went inside the house she met Mingchao coming out. He gave way for her with a smile and when he emerged onto the street at once plucked Simon's sleeve. "Hah, you want to come with me to Weidong's house?"

Simon smiled. Weidong's front room doubled as a small bar for the men of the village, where burning *maotai* liquor was in plentiful supply at bargain rates. "No thank you, Mingchao. I think I'll go to bed early tonight. But I'm grateful for the invitation."

"Well then, I'll go alone." He glanced shyly at Simon. "Tomorrow I'll be married, then no more bar."

"Zhaodi will be pleased to hear that."

Mingchao looked around him cautiously. "Please walk some of the way with me," he murmured.

By now it was nearly dark. Mingchao had brought his lantern with him but he did not light it. Instead he ventured a few steps down the alley and then pulled Simon into a doorway. "Here," he said, unbuttoning his shirt. "This is a map of the district. It is very old, I warn you—start of this century."

"It doesn't matter, as long as it shows the roads and the main towns."

"Oh yes, it shows that. The roads and towns have not changed for a thousand years, I should think so."

"Where did you get this?"

"The headman gave it to me."

"Was he suspicious."

"Yes, very." His face clouded. "Brother-in-law, I worry for you."

"Don't. I told you—it doesn't matter how suspicious people are."

"You're sure?"

"Certain."

"You *want* them to know you have this map?"

Simon smiled. "I want them to know; I want them to think I do *not* want them to know."

Mingchao sighed and shook his head. "You are very deep, Brother-in-law."

"Perhaps."

"The headman asked me . . . are you going away?"

"What did you tell him?"

"I told him I did not know."

"Good. Please continue to say that to whoever asks."

"But are you going?"

Simon raised a finger to his lips. "Don't ask."

"Well." Mingchao shrugged, seemed to be on the point of saying something, then changed his mind. And changed it again: "I shall be sorry if you go," he said. "I think it a bad idea."

"Why?"

"It's impossible to escape from this place. You can't disguise yourself as a Chinese. The countryside is open. This village is many *li* from the nearest border, I should think so."

"Seven hundred and fifty miles to Hong Kong. That's my guess."

"There, you see! Impossible!"

"Nothing is impossible. It's all a question of will."

For a long time Mingchao said nothing while he thought over Simon's words. Then—"I wish you good luck. Good night, Brother-in-law Simon. Good-bye, maybe?"

"Good night, Mingchao."

"Will I see you at my wedding tomorrow?"

When the Englishman did not answer Mingchao shrugged again, took some matches from his pocket and lit his lantern. In the glow shed by its sputtering wick he glanced up sharply at Simon, trying without success to read his eyes; at last he gave up and began to walk away, every so often pausing to look back over his shoulder and wave.

Simon watched Mingchao pick his way delicately along the lane until his lantern was out of sight, before returning to the house and spreading out his map on the kitchen table. It was as Mingchao had described it—very old—but it would serve. Simon rummaged around in Kaihui's kitchen drawer until he found a stub of pencil, with which he proceeded to draw a bold line between Chaiyang and Tunglun, the nearest town of any size, before carrying the line on southeast, in the broad direction of Hong Kong. The ploy was crude, but when Qiu found the map he should have no difficulty in deciding where the fugitives had gone.

Simon folded up the paper and stuffed it behind the dresser, leaving a tiny piece of it showing in a way that was not obvious but which would readily be noticed by anyone conducting a search. He was on the point of extinguishing the candle when he heard a noise and looked up to see that Mat had entered the room.

"Ready?"

"Yes. Did Di get off all right?"

"Yes. Have you fixed the bed?"

"As best I can. If you stand at the door it looks like Di and Tingchen cuddled up together. It's okay as long as you don't come any closer."

"I'll check it out. You know the way?"

"Of course. You drilled it into us often enough."

"I hope so. Frightened?"

"Nah! It's an adventure! Anything to get out of this place. Only . . ."

"Only what?"

"Well . . . the kid. Tingchen."

"What about him?"

"It seems kind of cruel."

"I know. Do you remember once accusing me of high-mindedness?"

"Oh. Yes. The night after they blew up the plant."

"You said I must have found it an awful drawback having morality, something like that."

"I remember."

"Still think so?"

Mat smiled but said nothing.

"Life's not a simple business."

"I guess not."

"What's more important—getting out of here, or refusing to put Tingchen at risk?"

Mat did not hesitate. "Getting out."

"Right. It's a question of goals, isn't it? Of priorities."

"I suppose so."

"Bear it in mind. Don't get overconfident; keep calm; remember all I've told you. Oh, and Mat—"

"Yes?"

"For God's sake, look after the little boy."

Mat did not go immediately. Instead he walked up to his father and put his arms around him. Simon fought down his surprise and returned Mat's embrace, hugging him close until his taut muscles begged for release.

"Good-bye, Da. Good luck to you, too."

Simon let the boy out by the back door and watched him slip away. His children were gone, he did not know when he would see them again and he hated it. Suddenly he felt terribly afraid. When Jinny came to place a hand on his shoulder she was surprised to find him trembling.

"Are you all right?"

"I'm a bit"—he shook his head brusquely—"a bit tired, that's all."

"What happens now?"

"We have to give them a start. Come on, let's go next door. You go first, I'll follow in a moment; it'll seem more natural that way."

But before either of them could move, the door opened and Qiu limped into the kitchen, leaning heavily on his wife's arm. Qingqing assisted him to the nearest chair and lowered him down gently. Qiu's face twisted in pain. His left leg stuck straight out in front of him; it was bandaged from calf to knee and in several places blood stained the white gauze.

Simon smiled pleasantly at him. "I'm glad to see you up, Qiu

Qianwei. But shouldn't you be resting?" He spoke in Mandarin, so that all could understand.

"I can rest in here. What matters is that the leg does not stiffen. That doctor was too soft. She would not be acceptable in the army."

His face was drawn with pain. Simon found it hard to understand how someone with such a small frame could withstand so much agony and yet still force himself to walk. "Can I get you anything?" he asked.

"Thank you. I haven't eaten. My wife will fetch me something. Qingqing, please . . . ?"

"Qingqing, there's some *doujiang* left over."

"Than you, Comrade Young." She went to the stove and poured some of the gruel from its pot into a wooden bowl, which she then placed before her husband. "Would you like some?" she asked Simon.

"Thank you."

Qingqing brought another bowl and handed it to the Englishman. "For you, Comrade Linhua?" Jinny shook her head.

"Can you sleep?" Simon asked Qiu.

Qiu picked at his gruel. "No. Everyone else is asleep but me. Us."

"Would you like some company, or do you want to be alone?"

The pause before Qiu answered was a little too long to make his eventual reply sound convincing. "There's no need to stay." Another pause. "You must be tired."

But instead Simon lowered himself into a chair at the side of the table, so that by turning his head to the left he could see Qiu's face. Jinny sat down opposite her husband. Qingqing pulled up a stool next to Qiu, who was sitting at the head of the table.

"What happened today?" asked Simon.

"I was crushed by some stupid peasant driving a cart."

Simon stirred his bowl of milky soybean soup. "Was it an accident?"

Qiu shrugged. "I don't think so, but I can't prove anything."

"Perhaps it's best that you can't."

Qiu smiled thinly and sipped a couple of spoonfuls from his bowl. "Perhaps." The attraction of talking to someone, anyone, was becoming steadily more apparent. "What did that doctor mean? *Qi* and *shen* . . . all such nonsense, if you ask me."

"She was going by the only authority she knows, the *Inner*

Classic of the Yellow Emperor. It's the source of all theory in Chinese traditional medicine. The *Nei-Jing.*"

"How do you know this?" Qingqing asked.

"I read. I listen. *Qi* is hard to define. It warms and protects the body against disease. *Shen* is spirit, vitality. A *yang* substance. I believe the doctor was correct to say that Qianwei's is deficient."

"You are typical of many Westerners." Qiu's voice was scornful. "You're in love with the East, yet to you it is all legend and romance. We who live in China know better."

Simon ignored the scorn. "I'm sorry to see you reduced to this," he said.

"Why feel sorry for me?"

"Sorry for your wife and child, then."

"Hah, yes. Always 'looking through the mist but can't see home,' both of them."

"I don't understand."

Qiu twisted his head around until he could see his wife. "Always crying for Beijing," he sighed. "That's not easy for them—or for me, either."

"Yet I think Tingchen is not so unhappy, from what I hear. Diana brought him back a few moments ago. They've crept upstairs together, I didn't want the boy to disturb Qianwei."

"That was very thoughtful of you. It's better if he doesn't have to see his father ill."

"That's what I thought too. He was very tired, poor little chap."

"I should think so!" Qiu showed faint signs of animation. "Do you know what they make him do? They take him out at dawn and make him pick up dog droppings! He's exhausted."

"All the other children do that." Jinny spoke, her voice gentle. "It's for fertilizer. The children think it's fun."

"Shocking!"

Qiu turned his face away and fell silent. Simon gazed at him with sympathy. At last he said, "Why do you think you're here, Qianwei?"

Qiu sighed. "I've made errors. I thought they were in the past, but I was wrong. I have to be corrected. Chaiyang is a good place for correction." He muttered something inaudible.

"I couldn't hear you."

Qiu turned back to face Simon and to the Englishman's astonishment said, "It is all one who does the planting and who does the watering and each will duly be paid according to his share of the work."

"You amaze me! I believe those words come from the New Testament of the Christian Bible."

"Why does that amaze you? I received a Western education. Once I was powerful and arrogant. Now I'm here in Chaiyang. It is fitting. It is right. I accept it. 'It is all one.' Do you not agree?"

"I agree. Although I think you've been corrected enough—I've seen how hard you work. But I also think this is only one reason. There's another."

"What?"

"Your masters observe that we're good for one another."

"*Good!*"

"Yes, good. We've become accustomed to each other's different ways. We're linked."

Red Dragon was becoming more and more puzzled. "We are?"

"Of course." Simon stretched out his legs and rested his hands on his thighs. "I don't seriously believe that your employers will leave you to rot in Chaiyang. You would be better employed elsewhere."

"You say that, yet you know nothing of me, nothing!"

"True. But I'd like to."

"Why? It's no concern of yours."

Simon took another spoonful of gruel and waited patiently for Qiu's anger to subside. After a while the Chinese began to speak in his former rational tone. "My mother died not long ago, before we came here. She told me a lot about my ancestry."

"I'm sorry to learn of her death."

"She was very sick, it was her time. As I say, she could remember much of the old days. My great-grandfather was a presented scholar at the age of thirty-four, can you believe it, so young? He became a magistrate. He ruled the *yamen* at Amoy. Then he was promoted to the imperial household, where he became a grand councillor under Emperor Tong Zhi. He was in charge of the imperial gardens and hunting parks."

Jinny exclaimed. Simon kept his face straight, but only with difficulty. It was an astonishing background for a cadre to have.

"Afterward, my grandfather held office under the Emperor Guang Sui, who was deposed by the Empress Dowager. When she returned from exile, grandfather offended her deeply. He supported her grandnephew, Pu Jun. So she had him exiled, but he left behind his eldest son, my father. He joined the Long March. I was born in Yenan."

"Yenan. Then you remember . . ."

"Oh, I remember everything. Mao Zedong. The caves. Above all, I remember the army. The army did not rape, or plunder or steal. They paid for whatever they took. Such an army . . ."

He was silent once more. Qingqing looked down at him with adoration in her eyes; but Simon was shaken. He was also immensely curious. "How did you escape?" he said at last. "With a background like that it must have been difficult for your family to win acceptance."

"In those days, the Party wasn't like it has become now. All they cared about then was where your heart was." He paused, as if astonished by his own temerity, but then the dam broke. "Now things are very different," he said in a rush.

"But you were educated abroad, weren't you? The Cultural Revolution . . ."

Qiu pushed away his half-finished bowl of gruel. *"Ma-mu-le."* His voice was matter-of-fact but he could not conceal the depth of emotion beneath. Simon had heard the old phrase many times— "I was stunned"—but the cadre's whisper conveyed more than numbness. It conveyed horror.

"Fortunately, I left before the worst began. Even so, I saw . . . many things. I managed to stay away for several years, going on from one Western university to another. My father had been highly placed in the Central Control of Intelligence, he was able to protect me. And of course, I was being prepared."

"Prepared?"

"For later. The time of peace, when China would once again seek her place in the world. Then, people like me with a Western education would win respect and play their proper part."

There was a long silence. After a while, Simon pulled his chair closer to Qiu's so that his face was almost touching that of the cadre and said, "I wish to talk to you."

"What about?"

"Would you prefer a time when the two of us can be quite alone?"

"That's not necessary. My wife is a good Party comrade. Her affairs and mine are the Party's also."

"For us it's the same." One of Jinny's hands was lying on the table. Simon reached out and took it, cradling it between his palms.

She looked at him in surprise, taken aback by this unusual public display of affection, of solidarity.

"Talk, then," said Qiu. "If you must."

"First, I'd like to know something. Why did you force my wife to write that letter and leave it in my safe?"

Jinny had been sitting with her eyes glued on Simon's hands. Now she raised her head and regarded him intently, while an expression of joy stole across her face.

"Have you any idea of the depth of suffering that caused me?" Simon went on. "Why, Qiu Qianwei? Why?"

Qiu scowled, but he did not answer. After a while Simon said, "I've had much time to think while I've been here. I think I know the answer. You never trusted me, you never felt confident that I would obey your instructions. Therefore, it was necessary to throw me off balance, weaken my defenses."

"Maybe," Qiu mumbled. "I had orders. I obeyed them."

"But then tell me—why was it necessary to involve my family? Why must they suffer for your conspiracies?"

Qiu snorted. "Is it not obvious? Your wife knew too much about us. Your son was a potential witness to the murder of your servants."

"But that doesn't explain why you had them brought to Chaiyang. You could simply have killed them."

"Hardly. They made perfect hostages, didn't they? We meant to use them to control you until we could bring you to China as well. Fortunately, it proved unnecessary to exert pressure through them—we took you in Singapore at the first attempt."

"I see. I'm glad."

"*Glad?*"

"Yes, glad. Because it has made me closer to my wife and children. Chaiyang is like that. It's a place of restoration."

Jinny squeezed his hands and turned away her head to hide the tears. Simon raised her hand to his lips and said, "I owe you much."

"You owe me nothing," she murmured.

"You stood out against them, when it would have been easy to surrender."

"Stood out at first," Qiu put in haughtily. "She opened the safe, in the end."

The pressure from Simon's hands was causing Jinny pain, but she gave no outward sign of it. There was a long silence. At last Simon asked, "Why did you refuse to open the safe at first?"

"Because of the debt I owed you. I told you many lies. You did not reject me. You did not reproach me. You were patient beyond endurance. Only when he took our children did I fail you."

"I know. And you didn't fail."

"You're so English," she murmured suddenly.

"Why?"

"Because of the way you love. Because you're so confused in your thinking about what you call morals. In China, we have no morals; only obligations."

"Am I confused?"

"Oh yes. You wish to succeed in whatever you do. Hong Kong is right for that. There, a man gets on however he can. But even though that's your world, you don't like to be thought of in that way."

"I try to be honest in my dealings. But I don't always succeed."

"That's not the Hong Kong way—to try to be honest. So you're English, you see, although you think you have Eastern ways. Also, you don't respect your father. For that, the Chinese dislike you."

Simon was startled. "Really?"

"Yes. They can't understand that at all."

Simon stared into the candleflame, meditating on his wife's words. Every so often Qiu would cast a sideways glance in their direction, curious to see the Youngs so intimate. When Simon suddenly turned to him, he jumped.

"It was you who rescued Tom and Diana that day in Ocean Park, yes?"

Qiu examined the Englishman's sudden question for tricks but could find none. "Yes."

"You saved the lives of my father and my daughter. You see, I said we were linked: once you save a life, you're responsible for it thereafter."

"You're too full of fantasies." Something of the old sneer had returned to Qiu's voice.

"For a long time I didn't understand Ocean Park. I thought it was you who tried to have my father killed. But if it wasn't you, who could it have been?"

"We're not sure."

"And why did they do it?"

Qiu's only answer was an irritated shrug. Simon raised his arms high above his head and stretched. "I think," he said at last, "that the time has come for me to propose some answers to the questions I asked you earlier."

But before he could continue, Qingqing rose. "I'll go to look in on Tingchen, see if he's all right."

As she moved toward the door Simon reached up to grab her by the forearm. She gasped with pain and surprise. For a long moment he looked between her startled face and that of his own wife, while Qiu quivered with mute offense.

"Yes, why don't you?" Simon said quietly.

She snatched her arm away and ran from the room. Qiu stared at Simon, hostility in his expression. "Why did you—?"

"Be quiet, Qiu Qianwei. We don't have long." Simon stood up quickly and Qiu was again reminded of a cobra uncoiling itself in readiness to strike. "There's a radio here; don't bother to deny it. Long ago I guessed they must have given you some means of communicating with the outside world; then today your wife used it to summon the doctor."

Qiu took refuge in sullen silence. Simon continued to address him at breakneck speed, not giving him time to think. "You'll make contact with Beijing. Tell them that on my way to see Ng in Singapore, immediately before you kidnapped me, Robert Zhao traveled on the same plane."

"Zhao!"

"Yes. He told me many things. He told me of a settlement created by my grandfather, under which six more Founders Shares will pass to me in the event of my father's death, thus giving me overall control of the Corporation—"

"*What?*"

"He also told me of your change of plan. You want the shares for yourselves."

"You're lying—"

"You want the shares, but there's a problem. Robert Zhao Yi Qiang is working for others who want them also. Only those others know that there is a controlling interest at stake and until this moment you did not."

"Lies!"

"And it doesn't take much imagination to work out who those others might be, does it? Who else has a vested interest in controlling the Corporation?"

The cadre was overwhelmed. He tried to struggle upright, wavered and sank back exhausted. He opened his mouth and was about to speak, when a heartbroken wail reverberated through the silent house. Qiu jerked his head upward in the direction of the terrible cry, they heard a clatter of feet on the stairs and Qingqing flung herself into the room with tears streaming down her cheeks.

"Tingchen. *Tingchen!*"

"What . . . where . . . ?"

"Gone . . . he has *gone!*"

For a moment nobody moved. Then Qiu swore and thrust his right hand into the pocket of his jacket. When he removed it again it was holding a revolver.

"You!" The cadre pointed his gun at Simon. "Where have you taken the child?" Qiu's voice rasped with fatigue and tension. Suddenly a phrase came into Simon's mind, a phrase he didn't like. *Trigger-happy . . .*

"He's safe." He spoke slowly and quietly, keeping his hands spread far apart on the tabletop. "I've sent him away for a time. Only I know where. My wife doesn't know. The boy is safe. Diana will care for him. They have food and water."

Before Qiu could answer, Qingqing pushed her way forward. "Please do not do this thing, I beg you, *beg* you! . . . My husband is sick."

"Be quiet!" Qiu shouted at her. "Are you out of your senses?" He swung back to face Simon. "Is your son with them?"

"Yes."

"I don't trust him. He is a bad element. He is anti-China!"

"He's my son. He has been given instructions to take good care of your son. He will obey."

Qiu used his free hand to wipe his forehead. Simon saw the look of desperation in his eyes and knew a moment's pity.

"I thought you had brains," said the cadre. "I thought you were a man of intelligence. How far do you think they'll get? Alone, without a map, hunted by the army?"

"They'll go where you'll never find them. Or if you do, it will be many, many days from now. And who knows what will happen in those days?" Simon allowed his gentle voice to harden somewhat. "Your son is very young. It's your duty as a parent to see that his ordeal is not prolonged."

"It will not be! It will not be! But *your* ordeal is just beginning." Qiu smashed his fist down on the table. "Many people will be subjected to ordeals here. Your plan has failed—my orders from Beijing are plain. In case of trouble, I have a free hand to exact whatever reprisals I please. Starting—here!" He pointed the gun at Jinny's head. Simon saw his finger whiten on the trigger. Without bothering to plan or analyze, he swept his wooden bowl along the table, sending it hurling like a discus. It struck Qiu on the forehead, leaving a residue of gruel which ran down his face into his eyes.

Before the bowl sped off the lip of the table, Simon had hurled himself after it. He landed on top of Qiu, one hand going for the cadre's throat, the other for the gun. The struggle was short: Qiu had no strength left for a fight. His chair went over backward, taking the two men with it. Simon was tall and relatively fit; Qiu was puny and ill. After a while Simon ceased to grapple with the cadre but merely lay on top of him, letting his weight do the rest.

At last he raised himself onto his knees and looked around for the gun. Jinny had picked it up. She was standing at the far end of the table, opposite Qiu.

"Jinny—give it to me."

But Jinny merely said, quite calmly, "You should kill that one."

"No."

"Then I will do it."

She raised the revolver, using both hands to steady it, until the barrel was pointing horizontally down the table at Qiu Qianwei.

"Jinny!"

But she did not take her eyes from Qiu's chalk-white face. "This is an obligation," she said slowly. "It concerns my brother, my sister, my son, my daughter, my husband. This obligation does not rest on you."

Nobody moved. No one else spoke. Jinny's lips tightened into a thin straight line as her finger took the gun's first pressure, and the hammer moved back. Seconds must have passed thus, perhaps even minutes. Then the barrel wavered slightly—scarcely more than a millimeter, but they all saw it.

Simon walked swiftly to the other end of the table and caught the gun as it fell from his wife's limp fingers. She was sobbing. As he lowered her gently into the nearest chair he murmured, "Forgive me for doubting. Forgive me, forgive me . . ."

Simon Young released his wife and stood up. When he once more addressed himself to Qiu Qianwei, his venomous whisper sounded abnormally loud. "You will establish contact with Beijing. You will tell them that the Founders Shares, like your son, are gone and that I, only I, can get them back. You will do it now. *Now!*"

25

China's controller of Central Intelligence had grown ever more
frail with the passage of time, so that now, in certain lights, his
face resembled little more than a collection of features etched on
glass: faint white lines standing out but dimly against the surrounding gray. When he touched Tang's arm the banker percep-
tibly blenched. Baba sensed it and smiled, but he said nothing;
having now lost his sight, he knew that Tang, like most Chinese,
was both awed and frightened by the legendary powers of blind
men who saw too much.

"Thank you, Comrade Tang." Baba's voice scarcely brushed
the atmosphere that separated the two men: the banker felt it
inside his head rather than heard it with his ears. "You've been
kind, very kind, to this old man."

"I've done nothing."

"You've done everything. Because of you, the ways of the Chrysanthemum are known. They are uncovered. You have provided figures which convince me that this man is selling all he has. You have traced his financial dealings for me in a way which no one here could do. My one regret is that I could not find the time to hear your report as soon as you arrived last week."

"Yet I've only used my"—Tang, on the point of saying "eyes," quickly changed his mind—"contacts."

"Which are extensive." The Old One smiled again and then, almost as if he had divined Tang's change of tack, said: "Now I would ask one thing more. Be my eyes. See for me the things which I cannot see."

"Anything." Tang's voice was hushed, to match that of his interlocutor.

"This house which you have described. It is very beautiful, is that not true?"

"Very."

"And very empty?"

Tang hesitated. "Empty?"

"From what you've said, I feel, I sense, that no other person inhabits that house."

"There was a servant . . ."

"I exclude him. The house was deficient in masters."

"This may be true, Baba. I too felt that."

"And yet . . . the man's concubine, Lai Wan, is known to live there also. Or perhaps I should say, she did live there."

"Yes."

"But you saw no sign of her?"

"No sign of her, or of Zhao's wife either."

"No women's voices in the distance, hah?"

"No voices."

Baba nodded slowly. "And throughout that house, were there indications of a woman's presence?"

Tang thought. "None."

"No hint of perfume. No feminine possessions. No photograph."

"Nothing."

"Hah . . . hah." The Old One sighed like a father who laments his daughter's passing. "Lai Wan has gone then. She is not in Hong Kong. She is in the world somewhere, but I do not know the place. Everyone in that house has departed. And the Chrysanthemum . . . perhaps soon he too will go."

"He said nothing of that, Baba."

"No, not to you." The old man sighed. "I'm glad to have met you, Tang *tongzhi*. It's always good when an overseas Chinese comes back home. I know: You were not always a friend of ours. But new friends are often the best."

"I hope so. In the past I was misguided."

"Yet if you had not been, you would not have worked for the Russians. And if you had not worked for the Russians, I could not have built my wall. The past is dead. Forget, forget."

"Thank you."

"But the Chrysanthemum . . . him I cannot forget."

Baba stared straight to the front, as if reading a message that was invisible to all but him. After a while Sun Shanwang realized that the interview was over and he made a discreet gesture to indicate that Tang should leave. The banker rose, pushed back his chair and hesitated, as if awaiting his formal dismissal by the Old One. But when no sign came, Tang eventually backed away from the table, keeping his eyes fixed on that ghostly face until he had groped his way to the door.

As it closed behind him Sun Shanwang asked, "Shall I put on more lights?"

"Is it night?"

"It is two in the morning."

"For me, it is always night." From the smile on the Old One's face Sun knew that this was not a complaint. Baba had long been content to occupy a twilight realm of perpetual shadows where he could wander at will and hearken to the stillness. "Please summon Hu Chuangmei."

"At once."

Sun left the room. A moment later the wall panel slid open to readmit Sun, together with a bowed figure leaning heavily on a cane. Hu Chuangmei limped slowly to the chair beside the Old One's and lowered herself down with a grunt.

"I cannot see, *Airen*. I see but do not see."

The Old One's whisper died away and there followed a long silence, broken only when his wife spoke. "Fetch the book." Suddenly the woman rapped on the floor with her stick and Sun Shanwang jumped. "Fetch the coins."

Sun went swiftly to the bookcase and reverently lifted the *I Ching* from its place. He laid the heavy book in front of Hu Chuangmei, then collected the chamois leather bag from its box.

"You are tired, Hu Chuangmei," said Baba. "I'm sorry."

"I am old, Baba. Almost as old as these coins." It was dark in the room but the woman had no need of light. She shook the coins from the bag and held them between her clasped palms, letting them feel the blood course through her veins. "What would you see?"

"Will the Chrysanthemum betray us?"

Hu Chuangmei grunted again. "A time would help."

"Hah, so difficult. Within a month. Within half a year."

Hu closed her eyes, squeezed the coins and cried, "Will the Chrysanthemum betray us within the next moon?"

The coins fell onto the table with a clatter. Again and again they fell.

"*Qian* above and below—the Receptive!" Hu raised her head and began to chant.

> "*The Receptive brings great success and benefits through the*
> *quality of a mare.*
> *The superior man leads an undertaking and goes astray:*
> *Later he receives guidance.*
> *Find friends in the south and west: forego them in the north*
> *and east.*
> *Peaceful perseverance. Good fortune.*"

She lowered her gaze to the table once more and said in her normal tone, "Open the book, Sun Shanwang."

Silently he obeyed. Hu Chuangmei leafed through its flaky pages until she found the entries she sought. "Six at the bottom," she breathed. "Hoarfrost underfoot; solid ice will follow." She slammed the book shut. "Misfortune is building up, no mistake."

" 'Friends in the south and west,' " Baba softly echoed. "A friend of China who is a Westerner . . ."

"Perhaps." Hu's voice sounded impatient. "Hong Kong lies to the east of here, east as well as south. Do not interpret too literally, Old One. Ask again."

"Advise me. What shall I ask?"

Hu Chuangmei studied the coins, her brows knotted together in a tight frown. "I think," she said at last, "that there is great danger here, Baba. Ask your question anew, but in regard to the next week."

"So, so. Will the Chrysanthemum betray us within the next seven days?"

Hu repeated the question aloud and began to cast the coins. "Increase," she said at last. "*Sun* above *Zhen.* 'Increase. Benefit in setting forth. Benefit in crossing the great water.' The time of increase will not last, so now is the time to act without hesitation."

"And the lines . . . what of them?"

Hu Chuangmei looked at the trigrams, consulted the book and gasped. "Nine at the top!"

"Well? Please tell me, what does that mean?"

The old woman sang:

"Nine at the top: increase to no one, someone beats him. His heart is inconstant. Ominous."

She went on in her usual voice: "The lines indicate treason, alienation and loss. Also, a time of retribution."

"Hah . . ." The Old One's sigh drained away into silence. "Thank you, Hu Chuangmei. I apologize for taxing you in this way."

"It does not matter. May I go now, please?"

"You may, you may."

The woman levered herself up onto her crooked feet, those two brittle, long-broken claws, and hobbled from the room. Sun Shanwang waited until the concealed panel had slid shut behind her before he said, "My orders are what?"

But Baba did not reply immediately. He continued to sit in silence, staring through his deputy's face, without moving. Then he raised a hand from the surface of the table and Sun stiffened.

"Hah, the coins, the book . . . please replace, Sun Shanwang."

The deputy controller of Central Intelligence quietly obeyed. As he returned to the table he said, "Baba . . . there is some connection between Zhao and the KGB. And it was the KGB who tried to kill Thomas Young and his granddaughter. I am sure of it."

"Perhaps."

"Who else could it have been? Soviet trash was used in the attempt; Soviet trash tipped us off beforehand. How else could those particular informants have known, unless their usual employers were responsible?"

"The Soviets may well have done it. But—for what reason?"

"I cannot begin to guess."

"Hm. We must see that Thomas Young is protected."

"Steps have been taken. But, Baba . . . suppose there's a link between Zhao and the Soviets. Suppose that link goes back a long time, to the days before Tang joined us. What then?"

"You are thinking of the paper the girl saw in Singapore?"

"Yes. When Wei Shasha opened the safe she found that paper with Zhao's name on it. What business had he with Tang, ah?"

"The Chrysanthemum has many interests."

"But—the timing! There are too many coincidences here. Why was Zhao traveling to Singapore on the same plane as Young, the night we took him?"

"Zhao may travel to anywhere he pleases."

Sun threw up his hands in despair. "Baba, please!"

Before either man could speak again there came a knock on the outer doors. Sun padded across to open them.

"Well?" he snapped at the young cadre waiting outside.

"There has been a transmission on the Chaiyang emergency frequency, Deputy Controller. Status Flashpoint."

"Give it to me." Sun snatched the sheet of paper from the cadre's hands and scanned it rapidly. The Old One raised his head in the direction of Sun's voice and said, "What has happened?"

"Excuse me, Baba, it is very long. . . . Shall I read it to you?"

"Please. Please read."

Sun Shanwang began slowly, but before very long his words were tripping over one another. When at last he had finished he tore the spectacles from his face and wiped his forehead. He was trembling. Only after a full minute had ticked by did he replace his glasses and say tersely, "My orders are what, please?"

But the Old One continued to stare into space without speaking, and although the first grays of predawn light were beginning to blend out of the darkness, yet they could not dispel the murk that now intensified and expanded to fill every cranny of the controllers' minds; until at last even Sun Shanwang, for all his sharp-sightedness and wisdom, was obliged to admit defeat.

26

The wedding day dawned not only dry, but actually sunny. By half past seven a light, early-morning mist had rolled away to reveal clear blue sky and the makings of a broiling hot day.

Cautiously, Simon drew aside one corner of the curtain that protected the Qius' room from prying eyes and peered out. "All quiet," he muttered.

The atmosphere inside the room was hot and stuffy. Qingqing lay half asleep on the pallet bed, her head jerking from side to side as some uneasy dream worked its way through her exhausted brain. Qiu Qianwei had been trussed into a chair at the foot of the bed, facing Simon. He was wide awake. Every so often his hands gripped the arms of his chair in a spasm of sheer frustration, straining against the ropes that bound him. He had remained thus throughout the night, never taking his eyes from Simon's face.

Now the early morning sun began to filter through the thin curtain, drowning out the candle's gleam and throwing his gaunt, clammy appearance into sharp relief. The strain of constant watchfulness showed everywhere—in his sunken cheeks, in the droplets of sweat on his forehead and the malicious stare of his feverish eyes.

Jinny sat bolt upright in a chair placed with its back against the only door. She held the heavy revolver in both hands, keeping it trained on Qiu. Of the four people in the room, she looked the least tired. As Simon turned away from the window she said, "I think you had better go out, or they'll start to get suspicious."

"I don't like leaving you alone with him." After last night he knew she couldn't bring herself to use the gun. "I may have to be gone quite a while."

"So? Many hours must pass before they decide what to do in Beijing. Qiu Qianwei is tied into his chair, he can't move. We'll still be here when you return." Jinny sensed her husband's unspoken fears and she flushed. "I'll not be weak again!"

She stood up, taking meticulous care to keep the gun pointing straight at the center of Qiu's body, and kicked her chair to one side with her foot. Simon laid a hand on her arm, but the gesture provoked no response from his wife. As soon as he'd closed the door behind him he heard the sound of Jinny's chair being replaced against it on the inside.

The living room was deserted, but Simon registered sounds coming from the kitchen. He tiptoed across to the front door and quietly eased it open. For a moment he stood on the threshold and watched Mingchao walk up and down in front of the house with his friends. They were like children. Every so often one of the young men would raise a hand to the sun before slapping it against his forehead with a laugh. Their faces wore expressions of total incredulity. China was not like this. Just because you were getting married, that didn't mean you deserved good luck on a scale of such magnitude. It was Sunday, a day off, Mingchao's wedding day, and the weather was beautiful. Mingchao caught sight of Simon and grinned at him.

"Good, hah?" He had waited all his adult life for this.

Simon smiled. "Very good. When are you setting off to fetch Zhaodi's belongings?"

"Soon, soon. Do you want to come, Brother-in-law Simon?"

The Englishman hesitated. He was reluctant to stray far from the house, in case Jinny needed help, but it was essential for him to be seen acting normally. "If I may."

"You may, please do."

Zhaodi's parents lived at the other end of the village, near where the track came down from the hills. Fortunately the distance was not great, because there were a lot of things to carry. Zhaodi's mother was a tough negotiator. Mingchao had been saving up for the past five years. He was obliged to buy his fiancée a treadle sewing machine, a bicycle and a watch: the "three wheels," a sort of bare minimum deposit without which nothing could be done. His gifts had been stored in the bride's house, on permanent exhibition, for some months; now they had to be transported back to the eastern side of the village where the couple were to live.

As soon as the party arrived at their destination, Simon walked straight up to the heaviest item, the sewing machine, without waiting to be asked. As the tallest man in the village, he knew that this was his duty. No one said anything but there were smiles all around.

"Hey, Brother-in-law Simon . . ." He turned to see Mingchao happily puffing away at a cigarette. "D'you want to smoke, hah?"

Two groups of men had met at the gate of the bride's parents' house. In accordance with tradition, it was necessary for Mingchao to bribe his way past Zhaodi's brothers with cigarettes, a ritual that they dispatched in no time at all.

"No, thank you."

"*Maotai, yao bu yao?*"

"I would like a drink, thank you." Simon accepted the cup and nodded to the bridegroom. "Longevity!" Zhaodi's elder brother scowled at the presumptuous Westerner, screwed up his mouth as if preparing to spit, then changed his mind and smiled at him instead. "There's nothing like this in the West," he asserted.

"That's true."

"Good." The brother seemed well satisfied at getting the better of the exchange. Then his face darkened. "That cadre is not with you?"

"No. He's still recovering from his injury. His wife's looking after him. I don't think we'll see him today."

"Then that is good, too. He's not invited to this wedding. Better he does not show his face, hah?"

"I agree. It would be unwise to disturb his rest."

Zhaodi's brother seemed pleased by this show of solidarity, for he nodded a great many times and smiled at Simon. Then—

"Mingchao," he said peremptorily. "It's time for us to go."

The sewing machine was strung up between two poles. Simon

led the way, head bent under the weight of the ungainly, old-fashioned treadle. Mingchao came next, clutching a bundle of brightly colored quilts on top of which ten tins of cakes perched precariously. There followed a wardrobe, some chairs and a table, a chest of drawers, more quilts, clothes, a bed and enough food to feast the village: steamed buns, savory rice, vegetables, sugar, fish, and flask after flask of the inevitable *maotai*. Kaihui leaned out of her kitchen window, saw the procession approaching and gaily clapped her hands together.

"Hurry, hurry," she cried. "Much to do." She had been up since before dawn, nursing the fire and apportioning culinary tasks between the neighbors.

Simon lowered his end of the sewing machine to the ground by the front door and went inside. Kaihui beckoned him into the living room. "Come over here," she hissed, as she placed her ear against the connecting door to the Qius' quarters. "What do you make of that?"

While Simon was still half a dozen paces away he could hear the sound of a woman softly keening, her tears falling as interminably as the rain that separates spring from summer. Qingqing must have woken up, then. Kaihui raised her head and looked at Simon with a strange expression in her eyes. "She asks over and over again, 'Where is my child, where is my child?' It's true that I haven't seen the child today. What do you know of this?"

Simon Young surveyed her thoughtfully for a moment, weighing his next words. At last he said: "Tingchen has gone, Kaihui. My own children have taken him away."

Kaihui gasped and shrank back from him. As she looked at Simon she noticed how his flared nostrils gave his face a cruel look and she felt a little sick. "Do you know what you've done?" she asked in a hushed voice.

"I do know. But we must get out; and this is the only way. Believe me—the only way."

The woman held her trembling hands up to her cheeks. "I suspected you were plotting. I knew Linhua was making a secret store of food. Does Linhua agree with it?"

"My wife . . . consents, yes."

"Of course she consents. She's your wife! But does she *agree* with it?"

When Simon offered no reply she went on, "And what of us? Of the villagers? There will be trouble now, terrible trouble, and you'll be to blame. Have you thought of that?"

"We'll have to see."

Kaihui had long ago sensed that this Englishman was made of steel. She pondered the situation for a while; then she asked, "Is little Tingchen safe?"

"Oh yes. Of course!"

She read the shock in his eyes and was partially reassured. "At least that's something. Where is he?"

"It is better that you don't know."

"Yes, better so. Then, if I'm asked—"

"You can tell them nothing. Exactly. Kaihui, you must help us now."

"I?" She looked up at him in fear. "How?"

"You must act as if you know nothing. Continue with the wedding preparations as if everything were normal."

"How can I do that? People will notice. They'll see the cadre is not around, they'll miss the child. None of us like the cadre or his wife, but people like Tingchen."

"We'll have to cope with that as best we can. What I need now is *time*, do you understand? Time to let things happen. We must prolong this day as much as we can."

"Why?"

"Because last night the cadre radioed Beijing. The village will have visitors today, I'm sure of it. They'll take us away when they leave. Then no more cadre; no more English."

"And no more sister." Kaihui looked at the ground. "I see. Well, you had better eat something." She sighed. "This will be a long day."

There was a commotion outside the front door, near where Mingchao and his friends had built a rough brick fireplace in which to cook the pig. It was the first time that the villagers of Chaiyang had ever attempted to roast an entire animal and no one was quite sure how best to proceed; various solutions were being proposed, with an altercation as the inevitable result.

Kaihui took a last look at the Englishman's face. "You want me to act normally?"

"Yes."

"Then I had better go and make peace between those blockheads." Her lips turned down in a rueful smile. "They'll expect me to interfere—as usual."

She bustled outside with a bundle of herbs and soon managed to quiet the protagonists. Simon watched her from the doorway. As she came back, wiping her hands on her apron, she tossed her head in the direction of the pig and said, "Hope they don't get it back without its tail, ah?"

"What?"

Kaihui grinned, her fears apparently forgotten for the moment. "You don't know that?"

"No."

"Right. Wait there, then; I'll fetch you some *doujiang*." She bustled away to the kitchen and emerged a moment later with two steaming wooden bowls of the soybean soup. "Sit, sit! Breakfast!"

"What about next door? Jinny's in there, guarding the cadre and his wife."

Kaihui pondered this latest complication. "Feed you and me first," she said at last. "One thing at a time. Sit!"

Simon did as he was told. Kaihui sat down opposite him and began to slurp gruel. In between mouthfuls she told him the old peasant legend. "If the husband sends the pig back without its tail . . . on the third day after the wedding . . . it means his wife was not a virgin. You did not know that?"

"No. I'm sure it will not happen in this case."

"Hah! So romantic! But I think you're right."

Outside they could hear snatches of song from the men tending the fire: "With pitch and prong the whole day long we both were making hay . . ." Although it was still early, the *maotai* already flowed freely. There would be upset stomachs and sore heads in Chaiyang on Monday morning. Kaihui noticed Simon's sardonic smile and said curtly, "I know you think we Sichuanese are bumpkins, but we have very good morals."

"I never doubted it."

"We've aways been poor, of course. A lot of women were sold in Sichuan; a good daughter could fetch as much as one thousand yuan or more."

"I'm sure the Party has taken steps to eradicate such abuses."

"Party, bah! More gruel?"

"No, thank you. What about next door—perhaps they'd like some?"

"Yes. I'll fetch it. Wait there."

When she came back with three more bowls on a tray Simon rose and went to knock on the connecting door. "Jinny—it's me."

He heard the scrape of her chair and the noise of the bolt being drawn back. When at last the door opened a fraction, he saw Jinny standing with her back to it, feeling for the jamb with her free hand while she continued to point the revolver at Qiu.

"Breakfast," Simon murmured. "Let us in."

As Jinny advanced a step Kaihui pushed against the door with the laden tray, knocking her off balance. In a trice, Qiu, still tied to his chair, somehow managed to stagger upright and launch himself forward, carrying the chair on his back. Disorganized impressions flashed through Simon's brain: one of the cadre's hands was free, he had managed to loosen the ropes around his legs . . . less than three feet separated Qiu from Jinny. His legs again became entangled in their bonds. He staggered, was on the point of falling . . . he threw his whole body and the chair as well into a horizontal tackle, butting the woman in the stomach with his head. Jinny gasped with pain, and dropped the gun.

Throughout this scene Qingqing had been lying on the bed. As soon as her husband moved, however, she leaped upright; and when Jinny dropped the revolver she dived for it.

Simon elbowed Kaihui out of his way with a brutal shove. The tray went flying. Qiu lay on top of Jinny, pinning her to the floor by the weight of his body and the chair. His head was mere inches away from Simon's foot. The Englishman delivered one savage kick to the center of Qiu's forehead, making the cadre scream.

Qingqing had succeeded in retrieving the gun. Without pausing to think, Simon hurled himself on top of Qiu and Jinny, scrabbling for the cadre's free hand and the arm of his chair. Qiu groaned. Simon jerked the chair upright.

"Now," he panted, "put down the gun, Qingqing."

Qingqing saw that the foreigner was using her husband as a shield and slowly lowered the revolver.

"The woman, you fool!" Qiu's voice rose in a screech. "Shoot the woman—shoot Linhua!"

Qingqing's scared eyes darted to where Jinny was lying on the floor. Clumsily she began to aim the gun downward. In her split second of hesitation, Simon picked up chair and occupant and swung both of them forward with all his strength. Qiu cannoned into Qingqing and they fell sprawling to the floor together. Simon bent down to recover the gun from Qingqing's limp hand and saw that Qiu Qianwei had fainted. A lurid purple and black bruise was beginning to show on his temple. So puny—he reminded Simon of a broken doll, a child's toy cast aside by its owner.

"Are you all right?" he asked Jinny as he helped her up.

"Yes. Bruised a bit, that's all."

"We had better clear up, then." Simon gestured wearily at the mess on the floor where the gruel had been spilled. "I'll get a cloth. Take the gun."

Simon turned his attention to Kaihui, who was painfully levering herself to her feet. "Are you hurt?"

"Not much." She made an attempt to wipe the gruel from her apron, then abandoned the effort as a waste of time. "I'm fast running out of gruel."

He smiled. "There will be enough, I'm sure."

When Simon returned with a cloth, Qiu had already regained consciousness. He was moaning softly. The Englishman untied him and helped him sit up. When he saw that Qiu was still too weak to walk, he lifted him onto the bed. The cadre's eyes fluttered open. "What happened?" he croaked.

"You behaved stupidly," Simon snapped. He wheeled around to address Qingqing, who had taken the chair at the foot of the bed, the one from which he had recently freed Qiu. "Please don't be so foolish again," he said in Mandarin. "You are not used to guns. The only person in danger of being shot is your husband. Remember that."

Qiu struggled to sit up. After a couple of abortive attempts, he succeeded. He swung his right arm to and fro tentatively, as if fearing it might be broken.

"You look terrible," said Simon. "Do you want to eat gruel?"

Qiu shook his head.

"Water?"

"No. Leave me alone."

"I'll leave you alone as long as you behave."

Qiu sneered. "The army will come. You'll be arrested. Shot." He directed one of his most venomous looks at Kaihui, who had just reentered the room. "This village will be decimated. *Decimated!*"

Kaihui wilted under his scorching gaze.

"Don't listen to him," Simon rapped. "He's raving."

But he could see that Kaihui was not convinced. He drew her aside and said quietly, so that no one could overhear, "When does the wedding take place?"

"The wedding . . . ? There . . . there is no ceremony. The papers were signed a few weeks ago, the Party secretary's certificate . . ." She swallowed hard, trying to ward off tears. "The feast begins at midday."

"So we have until then before anyone starts to get suspicious."

Kaihui nodded, not trusting herself to speak. Simon released her arm and turned back to face Qiu.

"There will be no more heroics; you don't have to prove your courage to me." He raised his voice. "We'll wait here. All of us, except Kaihui, will remain in this room. The window will stay closed. The curtain stays drawn."

Qingqing started to protest, but Simon rounded on her, his face angry. "Enough!" he said. "You'll do as you're told!"

Shortly after eleven o'clock, they heard a thunderous knocking on the front door.

The temperature inside the Qius' room had grown almost unbearably hot. Sweat was pouring down all their faces. Simon had been wrestling with sleep. Now he roused himself, rose quietly to his feet and went to lean his head against the connecting door. Kaihui was talking in the next room—trying to keep people from coming in, by the sound of it. Suddenly her voice rose to a crescendo and died away. The door swung open, giving Simon a nasty bump on the temple and at the same time revealing the hostile countenance of Weidong, the tavern keeper, at the head of a large group of villagers.

For a moment Weidong said nothing, while he slowly realized that things were not quite as they should be. Qiu and his wife sat next to each other on the bed. The foreigner's wife was in a chair opposite them, with a revolver in her hands. Weidong's bulging eyes slowly assimilated first the gun, then the bruise on Qiu's forehead and finally the knowledge that there had been an astonishing reversal of roles. "What's going on here?" he growled.

Qiu jutted out his chin. "This barbarian has stolen my child. Kidnapped him."

"What?" Outside, in the living room, the sea of heads bobbed with astonishment; Simon heard the news ripple through it and did not like the sound.

"Is it true?" Weidong had already crossed the threshold, and now he was followed by several more of the village men, together with Kaihui. The Qius' bedroom suddenly seemed very small. Simon backed away until he found himself hard up against the wall and could retreat no further. Weidong, seemingly undeterred by Jinny's revolver, advanced on him in a menacing fashion. "It is true that I have not seen Tingchen this morning. Did you steal this man's child?"

"Of course not. My children took Tingchen for a walk."

"It's not true, it's not true!" Qingqing's shriek made them all jump.

"It is true," Simon said quietly. "They'll be back shortly."

Weidong's eyes narrowed while he thought about that. Then he looked down at the gun in Jinny's hands and for the first time its significance seemed to dawn on him, for he backed away a couple of steps. Simon tried to calculate the odds. If the villagers were brave, they could overcome him and Jinny without difficulty, although they would inevitably lose one man, perhaps two. Sheer weight of numbers would win out in the end. But—were they brave? *Were they?*

Suddenly Weidong turned and addressed himself to the body of villagers. "Has anyone here seen baby Tingchen today?"

There was a chorus of nos. Weidong faced Simon again, "I think you are lying."

Silence. Simon's eyes flitted between Weidong, the villagers, Qiu. Within seconds, he knew, Weidong would have given his verdict in favor of the Qius. His muscles tensed. He was not going under without a fight. Somehow he must find a way of protecting Jinny . . .

A movement caught his attention. Kaihui had been staring hard at Jinny. Now Kaihui turned her head away, looked back and seemed to make up her mind.

"I saw Tingchen, an hour ago," she said.

Every eye in the room was instantly directed at her, and she quailed under this sudden onslaught of attention. For a moment nobody spoke. Then Weidong said slowly, "Is that so?"

"Yes. He was going for a walk with the foreign children. They said they were going to visit the shrine."

"She's lying!" Qiu exploded. "Don't believe her lies! The boy has gone, I tell you."

Weidong frowned. "Who are you accusing of lying?" he asked. His voice was ominously quiet.

"I—"

"She's from Chaiyang. We know her. We all know her." Weidong allowed his words time to sink in. "But we do not know you, cadre. You are government. You are Party, yes. But she"—he nodded in Kaihui's direction—"she is village."

Simon waited a second longer, then drew a deep breath and seized the initiative. "How can we help you, Weidong?"

The tavern keeper did not answer at once. He continued to stare between Qiu and Simon, as if something still caused him doubt. At last, however, he raised an accusing finger and pointed it at Qiu. "You," he said. "This box of magic tricks, this what-d'you-call-it. This film machine—it doesn't work."

"The film machine . . ." Simon tried to make his voice sound even. "The projector has broken?"

"That's what you call it? Pro-jec-tor? Yes. No life in it."

"Perhaps I can help," Simon said.

Weidong's attention instantly reverted to the Englishman's face. "You?"

"Perhaps. Is the generator working?"

"*I* don't know. How should I know?"

Qiu looked from face to face, not believing what he heard. "You fools!" he yelled. "How can you be talking about the projector when this man has stolen my child?"

Weidong slowly turned toward the cadre with a look of intense dislike. "He says . . . his children have taken your son for a walk."

"He's *lying!*"

"So you say. Kaihui doesn't agree." He turned back to Simon. "Production Brigade headquarters have sent a, a . . . projector and a film. *Maidens of Diamond Mountain.* For the wedding. In this village we have not seen such a thing before. There is something called a generator. But there are no instructions and nothing works. Can you really help?"

"If it is a simple matter of the generator or the projector, I think so."

"But—how can such a thing be? You are not an engineer."

Simon's confidence was growing. "When I was younger, I studied electronics in my spare time. It's a useful skill in this century, especially to a man whose businesses include much in the way of technology."

Weidong puffed out his cheeks. "Come," said Simon quickly. "Let us examine this projector of yours."

But it was not quite so simple. Weidong looked down at the gun in Jinny's hands. "You do not own that."

"No," she agreed.

"*He* owns it."

"Yes."

"You should give it back."

This time it was Simon who spoke, very quietly. "No."

"Take it!" Qiu cried. "Take the gun away."
Weidong rounded on him. "*You* take it!"
Qiu gasped. "I . . . I am sick."
"So am I. So are we all. Sick of you, sick of cadres. Pah!"
Weidong addressed himself to Simon. "We go to see the projector machine. Then we will discuss this man's child. Yes or no?"
"Yes. The cadre and his wife come too, though."
"If they must, they must. Come on, then!"
Jinny stood up and plucked her husband's arm. "Why must they come?" she said in English. "Leave them here—"
"So that they can use the radio? No. Besides, if they come, progress will be slow. Qiu is limping badly. Things are going too fast. *We have to slow them down.*"
Weidong looked back from the threshold of the house. "Come," he said. "It's getting late."

The projector and its generator had been dumped in a corner of the cooperative barn near a puddle of stagnant water. Such rural indifference to modern methods proved too much for Qiu Qianwei, even in his weakened state. "Peasants!" he snorted.
Simon took the gun from Jinny and made a show of checking that the safety catch was off before handing it back. "Watch them both." He deliberately raised his voice. "Only kill them if you must."
For a long time Simon merely stood and stared at the garish, orange-colored generator. Then he approached it and began a minute inspection of all its moving parts, at last unscrewing the filler cap. When he peered inside a smile creased his face. "No petrol. Weidong, do you have petrol?"
"We have." Weidong jerked a thumb toward the back of the barn where jerry cans were stacked in an untidy heap.
"Then let's put some in and see what happens."
The barn was filling up. Curious villagers and their children quickly learned that the wedding was not the only source of entertainment in Chaiyang that day; the high foreign devil had thumped the cadre and was tinkering with machinery. Simon soon found himself surrounded by a circle of eyes. At first the villagers were silent and watchful, but soon the bolder spirits, doubtless encouraged by *maotai*, were offering advice and criticism.
"Careful how you pour. . . . Use the filler, no, *not* like that. . . . Mind you don't spill. . . . Here, use the funnel. Where is it now? . . ."

Simon continued to pour the petrol slowly, careful not to spill the villagers' precious allocation. He replaced the cap, gave the cord a couple of twists around his hand and yanked hard. The generator coughed, shuddered and subsided. A twitter of excitement, reminiscent of birds in an aviary, rippled through the spectators. He tried again. The machine came briefly to life and died. Now the excitement was more vociferous. "Third time lucky," he muttered to himself; and it was so. The generator fired. The villagers cheered.

Simon stood back and wiped his brow. How much time had passed since they'd arrived at the barn? Ten minutes? Fifteen? He knew he had to consolidate his position. He could not go on tinkering with the machines forever; sooner or later he was going to have to get to grips with the disappearance of Tingchen. If nothing happened soon, if Beijing had weighed the matter and decided to leave Qiu to his fate . . .

He was sweating now. Take a chance. Look decisive. Act. Test. Provoke. "Fetch me a screwdriver, Qiu Qianwei," he said hoarsely.

Qiu scowled. The villagers had begun to be amused by this reversal of authority; Simon was aware of comments, none-too-discreetly uttered. "That's it, you tell him. . . . Damned cadres. . . . Why shouldn't he do some work for a change?"

Qiu turned on the watchers. "These people have stolen my child!" he barked. "Yet you stand there and gape! He orders me about, and you do nothing. Accounts will be settled here, oh yes!"

He lurched forward, throwing off Qingqing's supportive arm, and the circle of peasants yielded a pace or two. Qiu limped slowly along the line of faces, peering closely at each one as if to imprint it on his memory. Minutes ticked by. No one spoke—the whole barn was reduced to tense silence. Then, just when it seemed that Qiu was about to speak again, at the back of the crowd someone shouted: "*Shit!*"

And the barn erupted. "That's right, tell him. . . . All you've done is talk shit since you got here. . . . You just look out for yourself, cadre. . . . Yes, go tell them that in Beijing, get out, go on. . . . Go piss off back where you came from. . . ."

Fists were shaken under Qiu's nose. He retreated rapidly until he was standing next to his wife, who held up her hands as if to protect her head. Qiu Qianwei looked from face to face and saw no comfort anywhere. The circle was closing in on him now; soon he would be entirely surrounded.

"We've taken all we're going to take. . . . Yes, we don't have to stand for this. . . . Has anyone seen a chit for this fellow? . . . Where's the bit of paper says we have to put up with him, aren't the local swine enough? . . . Settle accounts, indeed—let's settle up with him, for a start!"

Suddenly a loud voice cut across the rising uproar. "*Stop!*"

The noise subsided. The villagers looked away from Qiu and saw that the tall Englishman was holding up both his arms. Simon waited until the barn was perfectly quiet before saying, in his normal voice, "A screwdriver. Please."

There was another moment of ominous silence while the villagers looked at one another. Then the twittering began again, only this time it seemed muted.

"For goodness' sake, find the poor bastard a screwdriver. . . . Fetch it quick, before he gets fed up. . . . Weidong's got one. . . . No, there's one right here in the barn. . . ."

Simon expelled a long breath. For a moment he did not trust himself to move. At last a screwdriver was produced and passed from hand to hand until it reached Qiu, who hesitated, then held it out to Simon with something approaching diffidence. Simon stood in the center of the circle, hands on hips, and did not condescend to take it immediately. When at last he did stretch out a hand, the barn fairly shimmered with excitement.

"What are you doing now?" Qiu's quavering voice resonated with suspicion, as if he feared Simon might be about to sabotage the village film show. At once the muttering began again. "Let him work, why don't you. . . . Fat lot you ever did. . . . At least he knows what he's doing. . . . Yes, why don't you just shut up and have a bit of patience?"

Simon laboriously connected the generator leads to the bulky old transformer, checking everything he did twice over. How long had he been in the barn now? Twenty minutes? More? His heart was thumping unpleasantly.

At last he could fiddle no longer. He stood up and turned to face his supporters. "This is necessary," he explained loudly, tapping the box, "because the generator produces more current than the projector can handle. It must be reduced from four hundred volts to two hundred and twenty; also, it must be transformed from direct to alternating current."

The barn, hugely satisfied with this majestic mumbo-jumbo, sighed with satisfaction. Through some miracle of coordination there was a lead fitted with a plug that matched the projector's terminals. As Simon tightened the last nut he drew a deep breath and prayed, conscious of the many hopeful eyes glued to his back. After such a tremendous buildup it had to work. It just had to.

He pressed the main switch and to his enormous relief the pilot lamp came on. He wiped the sweat from his hands with a rag, taking his time over it. Now for the real test . . . a flick of the master control and with a noisy clatter the spools began to turn.

"It works," he said superfluously; and once again the barn cheered him to the echo.

He made his way toward the door through a barrage of thumping hands and raised thumbs, accompanied by loud "*Hao*"s; but his heart still beat very fast.

"Well done, darling," Jinny said quietly, handing back the gun.

"The projector doesn't matter a damn in itself; it's the breakthrough with the villagers that counts. They're on our side—for now."

"I know. You were wonderful."

"We've bought a little more time, that's all." Simon sounded unhappy. "The villagers are with us at the moment, but once they start to worry about Tingchen not turning up they'll swing back to the Qius just as easily."

"Why should they? They hate the Qius."

"But they're injured parties, parents. If a kid goes missing anywhere, it's serious. Here, it's a major catastrophe."

As they emerged from the barn together he glanced around him. Nearly all the villagers had gathered in the square. Now they were friendly, but Simon knew the mood of a crowd could change in a second.

"Listen, ah . . . ." Weidong plucked his arm. "Shall we go and see if your children have returned with the little boy?"

Simon managed a smile. "Why not?" He looked around. "Qiu Qianwei and Qingqing will walk in front, please."

Jinny linked her arm in his and they began to walk back toward Kaihui's house. They did their best to go slowly, but still their progress seemed terrifyingly fast. "What do we do when we get there?" she murmured.

"God knows."

She glanced back. "They are all coming, Simon. Every one of them."

"Yes."

She reached out to touch the gun in his hand, but it gave her no reassurance. "What will they do when they discover that Tingchen has really gone?"

But he walked on in silence, having no answer. And by now they were nearly at the house.

27

Robert Zhao handed the fireproof safe-deposit box to his pilot and received in exchange a small leather case secured by a combination lock. He watched the helicopter until it had disappeared over the horizon in the direction of Kai Tak Airport. That was the last shipment of jewelry. The house had been stripped of its valuables now and whatever was left in the way of furniture or fittings would just have to stay there. This was not the first time Zhao had abandoned an asset. Life was more important than money.

He ran back up the steps to the terrace, taking the stairs three at a time. He was in a hurry this morning. The stock exchanges would be open first thing on Monday; there was still a lot of business to be done.

He carried the leather case into the main living room and spun the locks. The lid sprang open to reveal ten thousand United States dollars, neatly packaged in bundles of hundred-dollar bills.

He looked around him, searching for a temporary place of concealment. Nearly all the servants had gone by now, there was nobody left except one trusted houseboy, but Zhao was not the kind of man who took unnecessary chances. There was always the possibility, however remote, of an unexpected visitor.

Visitors . . . the thought made him shudder. He had been lucky to get this far. After today, they could whistle for him and their precious Founders Shares.

Zhao made up his mind. He went down into the sunken square that formed the room's focal point and folded back the carpet to reveal a metal plate with a membrane-covered keyboard by its side. When he tapped out half a dozen numbers on the membrane the plate slid open to reveal a deep cavity. Zhao reached down into it and pulled out a Colt .45. He weighed it cautiously, licking his lips. The penalty for importing such merchandise into the colony was death, but occasionally even outsize risks like that were worth taking. He laid the gun aside and rummaged about in the cavity until his hand made contact with the certificate relating to Simon Young's Founders Shares. He shook his head and smiled. What good would those shares be to the Russians; or even to the Chinese, come to that? Whereas in the hands of a seasoned businessman, an entrepreneur . . .

He could not resist unfolding the cream-colored certificate for another look. The document was, without any possibility of exaggeration, unique. Zhao had always had a soft spot for bearer shares—no messy registrations in some distant office, no scrutinizing of signatures, no hassle. The certificate itself *was* the asset—or as good as. All you had to do was pack it away in your briefcase and choose a politically stable destination with a nice climate. The certificate, in other words, was tantamount to cash. One hundred million pounds worth of money, comprised in a single sheet of paper ten inches long by fourteen inches wide.

Zhao dropped the certificate back in its hiding place together with the leather case and laid the Colt on top of both. As he did so, his fingers made contact with something else and he frowned. He could not recall having left anything other than the gun and the certificate in the safe. What could it be, now? A plain brown envelope . . .

He recognized it as soon as he drew it from the cache, and his frown softened into a hesitant smile. Of course: the personal life. Well, there hadn't been much of that lately. He opened the unsealed envelope. Three or four letters, his mother's wedding ring, a locket, a photograph . . .

The print was quite old now and its colors had faded somewhat with the passage of time. He remembered taking it. He remembered quite clearly.

Zhao sat down on the carpet and held the picture out in front of him. His birthday, seven years ago. The photo, taken on his yacht, showed a tall Westerner and a beautiful woman relaxing with their backs against the sternrail. Zhao concentrated on the woman. She was smiling into the sun with the kind of rueful expression that people wear when they don't want to be photographed and have been protesting right up to the very second before the shutter clicks.

The woman in the photo was Chinese. She wore white slacks and a navy blue blouse, a thin gold chain around her neck. She must have been in her late thirties then, but she looked much younger. Her face was bare of makeup. She could have been a model, her face had such good bones.

Zhao held the photograph up to the light and stroked the paper with a finger that trembled slightly. It came to rest on a tiny mark at the hairline, just above the woman's right eye.

A mole. A minute black mole.

Jinny Young.

Zhao continued to study the woman's face for several minutes longer. He remembered how Jinny had taunted him with the ghastliness of that day, in front of Qiu. Too much to drink. The agony of watching her laugh in the sunlight with her husband. The clumsy pass he had made. Memories . . .

At last Zhao stuffed the photograph into his pocket and threw the envelope into the floorsafe. He tapped some more numbers on the membrane, the plate slid back across the mouth of the cavity. Moments later the room once again looked just as it always did.

He walked through into his study and sat down at the desk. When he reached for the telephone his hand was not quite steady; Zhao slammed down the receiver with a curse and banged his fists on the desk. Only when he felt calm again did he reach for the typewritten list of investments that lay on the blotter in front of him.

Zhao dialed his stockbroker's home number and asked to speak to him. He ran swiftly down the list, marking up Saturday morning's bid price against each share, worked out some figures on his calculator, then gave terse instructions. "Call me first thing tomorrow morning, as soon as you've dealt," he concluded, before replacing the receiver on its rest.

Now it was only a matter of waiting. He drummed his fingers on the desktop. He might as well use the time to work out where to go first. Paris, perhaps? No, not Paris—his face clouded—Mrs. Zhao lived in Paris. New York? He stood up and walked across to the bookshelf, which housed, among other works of reference, an international airline guide. It was a long time since he'd been free to amuse himself in this way.

Before he had leafed through many pages, however, the phone rang. He answered it without thinking and instantly regretted it.

"Zhao. Zhao? Can you hear me, Zhao?"

"I . . . I hear you, Mr.—"

"*Yes!* 'Mister' will do all right."

"How . . . how are you?"

"I am very well. I think you should assume that this is a shared line, Mr. Zhao. Do you understand me? A *shared* line?"

The implications of what his caller was saying hit Zhao and his jaw dropped. "Yes, I understand." But his voice was not as firm as it might have been.

"Good. It is time we did some business together, wound this thing up. I want to see you."

"See me? Here?" Zhao forced a laugh. "But my dear . . . man, you can hardly show your nose here. Not in Hong Kong."

"I'm here already."

"You're *what?*"

"I'm here. I landed this morning. Hello? Hello?"

"I'm sorry! I didn't hear you. I thought you said you were here, in Hong Kong."

"So I am. What is wrong with you today?"

"I . . . I'm surprised, that's all. Where are you staying?"

He heard only a soft laugh at the other end of the line. Then: "Arrange for our *official* friend to be at your house tomorrow morning, at ten o'clock. With his chop. I'll be there to take delivery of the commodity."

"You want a magistrate? Here?"

"Of course."

"But, why? The . . . the commodity we are discussing, it can be taken away quite simply, no formalities are required, I don't—"

"I want a legal title. A witness. No messy loose ends. Oh, and Zhao . . ."

"Yes?"

"Don't try to leave the house between now and then, will you?"

"I have business to attend to—"

"On a Sunday?"

"This is Hong Kong, not—" Zhao, on the point of saying "Moscow," remembered the admonition about a shared line and hurriedly substituted "London."

"Let it wait."

"I can't, it's urgent."

"It is not that urgent. Stay where you are. And believe me when I say that I'll know if you don't."

The line went dead. For a long moment Zhao stared at the receiver in terror, as if he suspected it of harboring some deadly virus, while he fought to control himself. Why the hell was Krubykov here, in Hong Kong—just about the most dangerous place on earth for a Soviet agent? Was it a coincidence that he should turn up as Zhao was on the point of disappearing?

The Chinese was not superstitious; he did not believe in coincidence. But whatever the real explanation might be, he didn't propose to stay and find out. The house was under Russian surveillance, it seemed. Very well—but they could hardly watch the place after dark: there were no streetlights within miles and Zhao had long ago made highly confidential arrangements for leaving, should the need arise. He looked at his watch, calculating times, then reached for the phone and dialed. "Hello, Cathay Pacific? I want to reserve a seat on tonight's flight to Tokyo, please. First class."

He had been on the point of saying "one way" when he remembered what Krubykov had said about a "shared line" and he paused, aghast at the realization of how panic had nearly led him astray. "Return," he said smoothly. "Book me one seat on Wednesday's inward flight."

He could always cash in the return half of the ticket, he reflected, as he put down the phone. And even if he couldn't—as he'd reminded himself earlier—some things were more important than money.

28

The procession of villagers, headed by the Youngs and the Qius, came to a halt outside Kaihui's house. The walk had gained Simon another fifteen minutes, thanks to Qianwei's injured leg, which kept progress to a crawl. Simon realized there was no point in dallying further. He walked straight up to the front door and raised his hand to knock.

"Simon," breathed Jinny. "We can't go back inside. Tingchen isn't there. When the villagers see that—"

"What choice do we have?" He was about to say more, but Qiu had come to stand by his shoulder and Simon compressed his lips. He raised his fist and brought it down against the door. Kaihui opened it almost at once. Simon saw that she was holding something, a paper, but before he could speak Qiu had grabbed Kaihui's arm.

"What is this thing?" he said, unfolding the paper. "A map!"

"I . . . I found it, I was looking for—"

"You!" Qiu waved the map under Simon's nose. "This is yours!"

Before Simon could speak, he heard an unfamiliar noise and looked up quickly, shading his eyes against the light.

"Simon," said Jinny, "you have to think of something."

"Shh! Listen . . ."

No, he had not imagined it. Engines. Rotors.

Qiu Qianwei also looked up, then turned back to face his captors. "A helicopter," he said.

"I know," Simon replied tersely.

"You see. The army have come. You must give up now." He stuffed the map into his pocket. "Give me the gun."

"No."

Qiu wiped the perspiration from his forehead. He could hardly stand. "You'll be quite safe. I give you that promise. Give me back my gun."

"No!"

By now the sound of the engines had become almost deafening. The helicopter circled overhead while its pilot looked for a place to land. The villagers scattered with cries of alarm, locking themselves inside their homes until this terrifying invasion from the sky was over. The lanes of Chaiyang were empty, except for the Youngs and their prisoners.

"He's landing—there!" Simon began to run along the lane, leaving the others far behind him. As he reached the outskirts of the village the helicopter settled in a field where the water buffalo were penned for the holiday, forcing the terrified beasts into a corner. Two soldiers jumped down from the helicopter, shouldering their rifles, followed by a thin, elderly Chinese wearing spectacles. Simon, anxious not to pose a threat, eased his pace so that by the time he came up to the man he was walking quite slowly; but still the soldiers eyed his astonishing height with trepidation and, seeing the gun in his hand, raised their own firearms.

For a long moment the Chinese and the tall Englishman surveyed each other in silence. At last Simon seemed to reach a decision, for he tossed Qiu's revolver onto the ground, whence it was swiftly retrieved by one of the soldiers. The old man, seeing that Young was no longer armed, held out his hand. Simon hesitated an instant, and took it.

"My name is Sun Shanwang."

"My name is Simon Young."

They released hands and Simon stepped back a pace. "You are where, Comrade Sun?"

The old man hesitated, but only for a second. "I am the deputy controller of Central Intelligence. I have come to collect you and your family. It is time for you to leave this place."

The elderly Chinese smiled; and Simon liked him for it. "I imagine that there's a business negotiation ahead of us," he said gently.

"There is," Sun replied. "But it can wait until Beijing. Now you must prepare for the journey. Your wife and children are where?"

"My wife is coming, Comrade Sun. My children are not in this place."

"So Qiu told us. Where are they?"

"Where you will not find them quickly."

"I accept that." He shook his head in unwilling admiration. "Why did you do such a thing? The risk . . ."

"It was necessary to do something. And I am a risk-taker."

"But to involve a child in your plan, here, in the Middle Kingdom—"

"I had to be sure that you would listen. Also, I had to protect myself. If I had merely passed on Robert Zhao's information about the family settlement and your Soviet opponents wanting the shares, you would have thanked me and left me here."

Sun shook his head emphatically. "There was never any question of that. But I think you are a risk-taker indeed. Now, where are the children, please?"

Qiu came limping up, along with Qingqing and Jinny, in time to hear these last words. "Hah, Comrade Sun . . . here is a map! It was found at the house. Look!" He held out the map, jabbing with his forefinger at the line that Simon had drawn the night before. "They went southeast!"

Sun studied the paper for a moment, then raised his eyes to Simon's impassive face and sighed. "I could bring up a brigade, search all the countryside to the southeast of here. Yet something tells me I would be wasting my time."

"How can that be?" Qiu was almost apoplectic with rage. "It's my child's life at stake here!"

But Sun pointedly turned his back on Qiu and addressed himself to Simon. "We think the information you gave us about Zhao

Yi Qiang is almost certainly correct. A Soviet cruise liner, the *Crimean Star*, sailed past Hong Kong early this morning. She dropped a small boat, just before dawn. Our tracking radar lost it. We do not know who was on it, but I can think of only one thing important enough to lure a Russian into the colony at this time."

"The shares."

"Yes. So you will return to Beijing with me now, please."

"What guarantee of safety can you offer?"

"It is very simple. Zhao has the share certificate. The Founders Shares are bearer securities, so his position is a strong one. But it suffers from one weakness—his title depends on a forged mortgage, a forged memorandum of deposit. Unless you come forward to prove that, however, his title will remain unimpeached. Without you, your physical presence as a witness in a Hong Kong court of law, we are powerless to prevent him selling the shares on." He shrugged. "So you see, we have no choice but to take you back. Also, I give you my personal assurance that your hardships are at an end. How quickly can you be ready, Mr. Young?"

"Very quickly." He turned to face Qiu. "Your son and my children are in the caves to the southwest of the village, behind the shrine."

The haggard cadre stared at him in disbelief. "You're lying! They went southeast, toward Hong Kong." But Sun Shanwang had already beckoned the soldiers' officer and as the man came up he gave his orders: "Get a villager to show you the way to the shrine."

"I will go," said a quiet voice. It was Mingchao, who had joined the party unnoticed.

"Very well." Sun Shanwang addressed himself to the officer. "Two men will be enough. The rest of us will wait here."

A circle of villagers had gathered at a safe distance away from the awesome flying machine. The soldiers fanned out, pushing the curious and more daring peasants away. Jinny edged up to Simon and groped for his hand. "What do you think?" she murmured. "Do you trust this one from Beijing?" But Simon merely shrugged.

Time passed slowly. Sun Shanwang retreated inside the helicopter, leaving his soldiers to stand guard. Jinny wiped the perspiration from her forehead and lowered herself down on the grass. Simon continued to stand, looking over the heads of the assembled villagers in the direction taken by Mingchao and his escort. After what seemed like an age, he reached down to shake Jinny's shoulder. "They're coming."

Jinny scrambled to her feet. The peasants, seeing the tall Englishman's excitement, turned as one to face the village. Diana was the first to appear at the end of the alleyway, carrying Tingchen in her arms. As she came level with the last house she whispered something, pecked his cheek and lowered him to the ground. For a second he hesitated, still clinging to her skirt; then he caught sight of his parents and began to run.

Qingqing swooped to catch him up. She could not speak. The little boy seemed glad to see her, but otherwise none the worse for his night in the caves. At first Qiu Qianwei looked on impassively, without saying anything. Then he began to stroke Tingchen's cheek, tentatively at first but soon more boldly. The child looked up from his mother's breast, smiled and reached out to put his arms around Qianwei's neck. The cadre grimaced with a sudden spasm of pain, but managed to bear his son's weight and hold him tight. He turned away at once, so Simon could not see the look on his face, but his quivering shoulders told everything.

Diana, white with strain, flung herself into her father's arms. Mat sank down on the ground, exhausted. "It worked," he said softly. "It worked, it worked . . ."

"It's worked so far, Mat. We're not out yet. Come on—let's pack."

He disengaged Diana tenderly and helped his son to rise. As they began to walk back to the house, Jinny slipped her arm through Simon's. "Are you all right?" he asked in a low voice.

"Yes."

There was a silence.

"Sure?" he prompted her.

"Of course. Only . . ."

"Only what?"

"I . . . I never expected to come again to this place. Once here, I never dared hope I would ever be able to leave it. Escape was a dream." With her free hand she brushed away a tear. "Now it's here, I . . . Kaihui . . ."

Jinny's voice faded. Simon squeezed her arm, but could find no words to say.

They reached the house to find Kaihui on the step, waiting for them. She looked into Jinny's eyes and seemed to read there all she needed to know, for at once she wiped her hands on her apron and merely said: "Right. Help you to pack, Elder Sister."

Packing did not take them long, for the Youngs had few possessions in Chaiyang. Kaihui made up a parcel of food from the wedding feast, still uneaten, and pushed it into Jinny's hands. Until that point, Jinny had been in reasonable command of herself. Now she crumpled and began to sob.

Kaihui held her sister close and rhythmically began to rub her back. "There, there," she murmured, "don't cry. You see, I'm not crying? I know you'll be happy where you're going. I'll think of you there, happy." She held Jinny at arm's length, so that her sister could see she was smiling. "And you must think of us here, too. We'll be happy too."

"Come with us," said Jinny; but Kaihui smiled and shook her head. "It wouldn't be right, Elder Sister. Too old. I need my own things. I need my people." She saw how Jinny would not be able to cope with parting thus and she relented slightly. "One day I'll visit, maybe. Until then, be happy, be happy. See—I'm not crying, am I?"

But when Diana embraced her she did cry, after all, and when Mat kissed her cheek she hugged the boy close with a convulsive squeeze, hiding her face in his chest so he would not see the tears and despise her for a stupid old peasant woman. Yet it was Mat who surprised them all. He kissed his aunt again, and said in Mandarin: "We'll come back."

Simon, already at the door, turned in amazement. For the first time in his life he was hearing his own son speak like a man: in a voice that was firm, but also gentle. Mat smiled, and repeated: "We'll come back, Kaihui. We all will."

Then the family walked together to the helicopter. Diana was the last to board. As she began to mount the steps, Kaihui reached into a deep pocket of her jacket and thrust something at her niece, closing both hands around hers. "*Gei ni, gei ni,*" she whispered. "For you . . ."

Diana looked down. It was a bottle of Chishui. The girl turned without speaking and ran up the steps, but not before Kaihui had seen tears flowing down her face.

The steps were winched in, the rotors began to turn, and then they were up. Simon looked out the tiny window to catch a last glimpse of Kaihui, a little apart from Mingchao and Zhaodi, who stood hand in hand, waving.

His face set. He would remember Chaiyang.

The helicopter hovered, turned and began to rumble toward the northwest, flying into the gorge that sealed the valley at its far end. For a moment the sound of its engines was thrown back by the towering walls, making speech impossible. Then they were through and once more the lush, green plains of Sichuan opened out beneath them.

Simon twisted around to look over his shoulder. In the seat behind, Mat sat forward, his head in his hands. Diana was looking out of the window, an intense stare on her face, as if striving to capture every detail of this last view of the village, her village—and in that moment Simon knew that his children also would remember the heritage of Chaiyang.

"Kaihui, Mingchao—so many years." He sensed from the sound of his wife's voice that she was close to tears and he put an arm around her. Jinny looked up, half expecting to see the stern expression that had become second nature to him over the past weeks, but instead his face was smiling and kind.

"Is it really over?" she asked timidly.

"Yes. It's over."

He drew her down into his arms, cradling her close throughout the long flight to Chengdu while he struggled to prepare himself for what lay ahead.

It was late afternoon when they arrived in Beijing. All of them—Sun Shanwang, the Qius, and the Young family—were ushered into a limousine that was already waiting on the tarmac when the aircraft taxied to a halt. At last they reached the city and without stopping the car swung in through the heavily guarded entrance to Zhongnanhai compound, home of China's leaders. It swept along a broad, tree-lined avenue before suddenly turning left and descending a long slope. Simon stirred from his reverie.

"It's true, then," he said.

Sun Shanwang half-turned in the front seat and said, "What's true?"

"There's an underground passage connecting Zhongnanhai with the Great Hall of the People."

"It's true. See how you are favored, Comrade Young."

"Are you empowered to negotiate with me, Comrade Sun?"

"I am."

"That's good. Thank you."

The car pulled up in a spacious underground vault and soldiers came forward to open all four doors simultaneously. Simon was glad to stand up once more. He stretched and yawned extravagantly.

"Come this way, please."

Sun led the way up a flight of shallow steps culminating in a pair of heavy studded doors brilliantly lit by spotlights. A television camera mounted high up on a stalk swiveled with maddening slowness until its lens pointed directly at the group. After a pause the doors opened wide enough to admit them one by one.

A long, bleak corridor, no more than a rough concrete tunnel, stretched out in front of them. Light bulbs strung along a heavy black cable provided the only means of illumination. Sun marched briskly down this passage until he came to a pair of doors leading off into a stairwell. They descended three levels before turning into a corridor that exactly mirrored the one above; but here armed guards were stationed at fifty-meter intervals and Simon was conscious of a low hum coming from somewhere nearby. As they marched along the passage the sound grew louder, until suddenly they were confronted with another studded door made of steel. A second camera surveyed them for a moment; then the door slid back.

They had reached the communications center of all China.

It was a large, low-ceilinged room, carpeted throughout in bright red to match the color of the telephones banked along the far wall. Before each phone was set a black leather swivel chair, a table, reams of paper and pencils. Above them hung a wall chart bearing lists of numbers; even from the far end of the chamber Simon could see the boldly painted prefix 39 at the top of the list, and he knew that he had come at last to the hub of all power in the Middle Kingdom, for numbers that began with 39 were assigned to members of the Politburo.

Sun beckoned one of the soldiers who had accompanied them from the car and gave terse orders. "Escort these people"—he pointed to the women and children—"to the guest rooms. They will wait for us there. Clear the center."

The room emptied, leaving Sun alone with Simon and Qiu. The old man pulled three of the chairs away from the bank of telephones and arranged them equidistantly from one another, facing inward. "Please . . ."

Simon sat down and waited while Sun and Qiu also took their seats. The only sound in the chamber was that same relentless hum that might have come from a powerful generator. Sun cleared his throat and began to speak.

"You mentioned a negotiation, Comrade Young, and that is right. May I please begin by stating what we want and what we offer in return?"

Simon inclined his head.

"It is necessary to undo some of what has been done. We acknowledge that. The first thing I must do is apologize." He frowned at Qiu in such a way as to make it clear that this expression of regret did not embrace his subordinate. "We have strayed from the correct path. Although . . . well, it is not an excuse, but it may perhaps be said in mitigation of our offense: we have been impressed." The respect in his eyes was manifest. "We did not think any Westerner would be capable of surviving the trial of life in Chaiyang."

"Indeed. You must have thought us very weak."

"Physically weak, no. But there are other stresses associated with rural life. Psychological stresses."

"I see."

"Yet in spite of everything, you did more than survive. You rose above it. You perfected an escape plan. And you kept your family united behind you. That is true leadership, Comrade Young. Leadership, patience, humility"—he shook his head—"such a man may go wherever he pleases."

"You spoke of it as a trial. What was its purpose?"

"It was necessary to prevent you from having an opportunity of raising the money to pay off the Soviet Communal Bank."

"I follow that. But why keep us in Chaiyang? Prison Number One here in Beijing would have done just as well."

"We wanted to see if you were as good a Chinese as you like to think you are. It is true, you are. You are Chinese in stoicism, in thought, in way of life. Also, you have much sympathy with the Chinese people. We have many plans for your future, once 1997 has come."

Simon's eyes widened but he said nothing. This did not appear to surprise the old man, for he continued, "You have guessed, I think, what our plans were. The proposal which Qiu made to you, here in Beijing, represented only half of our intentions. We did mean to betray you and collect your Founders Shares for ourselves, although Qiu Qianwei did not know it at the time. This was a short-sighted policy which we now recognize to have been misguided. The shares must be returned to you forthwith."

"What?"

Sun saw the look of utter amazement on Simon's face and smiled. "We are pragmatists. Zhao has betrayed us. The only way we can be sure of preventing the Founders Shares from getting into Soviet hands is by producing you, your testimony. Which in turn of course means that the shares will have to be returned to you. There, am I honest enough for your English taste?"

Simon ignored the irony. "And how, exactly, do you propose to do this?"

"It is necessary for you to return to Hong Kong to reclaim what is rightfully yours. For that to happen, there must be a trial. You will have to give evidence to the judge, swearing that neither you nor Magistrate Hua ever signed the documents on which Soviet Communal Bank relies."

"You place great store by my testimony. Please explain."

"Is it not obvious?"

"Not really. Why do you not simply ask Magistrate Hua to give the necessary evidence?"

"Because he can tell only part of the story. And, above all, he cannot initiate the process. Magistrate Hua cannot invite the court to set aside the forgeries; only you can do that."

"Of course. Yes, I see now."

"There is need for great haste. Zhao is on the point of leaving Hong Kong for good. We have arranged for a call to be made from this place to your lawyer, Sanditon." Sun looked at his watch. "In twenty minutes."

"Then this is a forced negotiation."

"I'm sorry, but it must be so."

"Continue, please."

"We wish you to tell your lawyer that one of our representatives will call on him later tonight, with the original documentation relating to the Soviet Communal loan. That documentation is, of course, ineffective to create a security over the shares, because the memorandum of deposit was witnessed by Luk, instead of a magistrate. We wish you to instruct Sanditon to take steps immediately—I stress, *immediately*—to have the judgment in the bank's favor reversed."

"I see. Of course, no one but I can give such instructions. Certainly, Hua could not. What else?"

"We rely on your discretion, and the discretion of your family, with regard to the experiences of the past few months."

"And in return?"

Sun removed his spectacles and began to polish them with a piece of tissue. He looked old and vulnerable. "In return, we offer all that we have offered already, and more. You are a friend of China, Comrade Young, especially after Chaiyang. The gains, the benefits to you, are incalculable. You know this."

"I know it. I know also that you have betrayed me once. Why should I trust you again?"

"Do you have a choice?" Sun's face remained amicable but his voice had taken on a sharper edge.

"I think I do. Before we come to that, there are some questions I would like to put."

Sun looked at his watch again. Although well versed in the art of concealment, he could not wholly succeed in erasing the look of anxiety from his face. "Proceed, please."

Simon laid his hands on his thighs and deliberated for a few moments before he spoke, while Sun fidgeted in his chair.

"First, I would like to know what became of Mr. Ng and his sister, Maudie. Are they alive?"

"They are alive. We encouraged them to take a holiday away from Singapore, that is all."

"Are they your agents?"

"Not as you would understand the term. Qiu Qianwei correctly briefed you as to their status. On occasion they are useful to us, no more than that."

"Yet the boy who took Maudie's place, he was no longer useful to you?"

"Please do not waste time thinking of him." Sun Shanwang's face betrayed impatience. "He had committed many offenses of spiritual pollution."

Simon allowed the silence to develop a little, watching to see if Sun would realize the awfulness of what he had said. But there was no reaction, so he went on. "My next question is this. Why is there such need for haste?"

"I have already told you: because we ourselves have been betrayed."

"Explain, please."

"Our man in Hong Kong, Zhao, now has your shares. As I constantly remind you, they are bearer shares. You English have a saying, do you not—'Possession is nine points of law'? In the case of bearer shares, ten points. Zhao's duty was to transfer those shares to us. But he has made preparations to depart and we believe that he plans either to sell the Founders Shares to the highest bidder or keep them for himself."

"Ah!"

"You guessed this, I think?"

"I long ago realized that Zhao was involved in your scheme. It was one of the two things that gave me hope. Knowing him as I did, I felt sure that in time he would try to deceive you, for that is his way. If that time came, I knew I would once again achieve value in your eyes."

"I see." Sun knew a moment of genuine curiosity. "What was the other thing that gave you hope?"

"You kept me alive. That spoke for itself. But, tell me, Sun Shanwang—why did *you* suspect Zhao's treachery? What alerted you to your danger?"

Sun's face closed up. He did not think that the Englishman would be likely to appreciate the power of the *I Ching*. "We have . . . certain methods."

"And why must you prevent him from making away with my property?"

"Why? Because the prospect of those shares finding their way into hostile hands or being kept by Zhao is as unwelcome to us as it must be to you. Think what enemies could do to your beloved Hong Kong between now and 1997, with a seat on the Corporation's board and, as we now realize, the power to dissolve the bank. You don't know what we plan to do with your colony, not even *I* know that. But it doesn't require much imagination to see how great a destruction could be wrought. Is that what you want?"

"Perhaps. I don't know."

Qiu, who had been fidgeting restlessly, now sat up straight in his chair. Sun grimaced and repeated the phrase that Simon had used earlier. "Explain, please."

"Is it not simple?"

"I don't find it so."

"It's not possible to rewrite the past. There's too much to be undone in this case. In order to steal my shares you first swapped forged documents and then you deliberately blew up my desalination plant. True or not true?"

"True. We arranged the explosion because we knew we could not rely on you to refuse to repay when the time came. We had to make sure that you *could* not pay."

"You've murdered my servants, whom I liked and trusted. True or not true?"

"True. It was their fault: they tried to obstruct our men."

"You've brought ruin on my family, distrust into my marriage. Did my son obstruct your men? Did my daughter?"

This time Sun did not answer; he merely spread his hands in a gesture of assent.

"And you have driven an irremovable wedge between my father and myself, having first put him in danger of being murdered along with my daughter Diana. I ask you again: Is this true or not true?"

"Not the whole truth. The antagonism between your father and yourself was well known long before we commenced this operation. And I would remind you that it was not we who endangered your relatives—rather, it was we who rescued them."

"Even so, Sun Shanwang, the crimes you have committed against me are many and grave. Why should I help you now?"

There was a long silence. Qiu looked fixedly at the floor while Sun Shanwang stared into Simon's eyes, trying to assess what he read there. "You know the alternative?" he said at last; but his voice was hesitant.

"Chaiyang is the alternative. That, or a bullet. I know it."

"There will be no bullet; but Chaiyang, yes—you and your family could be compelled to live and work there all your lives."

"I have done it. I can go on doing it."

"You, maybe, although I beg your leave to doubt it." Sun hesitated. "No, perhaps you could. But what of your wife?"

"She is your servant. You will, of course, dispose of her as you wish, whatever I may say. As you disposed of the Luks, perhaps."

"Your attempt to deceive me is as valiant as it is unsuccessful. We know just how much you love your wife. You are not indifferent to her fate. But even if you were, what of your son and daughter?"

"My son is not interested in my achievement. He longs to do something different with his life. Chaiyang is not, perhaps, what he wanted, but at least it is *different*." Simon's voice rose. "And, in any case, you, as a Chinese, will acknowledge my right to rule my own son's destiny."

"Diana, then?"

"She grew to like the village. You saw her distress when the time came for us to leave. No, Comrade Sun—you cannot threaten me."

"You're bluffing."

Simon merely smiled.

"You do not think so? Well, let us see. I have been threatening you with Chaiyang. Now I will show you Chaiyang in another light—not as a threat, but as an inducement."

"I do not understand."

"Chaiyang is the essence of China. There lies the heart of the Middle Kingdom. But it needs modernization. It needs money—the kind of money that only Hong Kong's wealth can provide. Tell me, please—do you regard yourself as a pragmatist?"

Simon thought. "Yes."

"As I've already said, we too are pragmatists." Sun addressed himself to Qiu. "Tell him about the opium."

Red Dragon's eyes widened in surprise. "The opium? It is a state secret."

"*Tell him!*"

Qiu reluctantly swiveled his chair to face Simon. "We produce opium. Of course, you know that. What you perhaps you do not know is that in 1968, the Mah-jongg Brigade set a production target of thirty-five thousand tons a year, to be exported to the West. This target has been periodically revised . . . upward. It has become an important instrument of our foreign policy."

"And here?" the deputy controller prompted him. "What is the penalty for use and possession of opium in the Middle Kingdom?"

Qiu shrugged. "Death."

Sun turned back to Simon. "Yes, we are pragmatists. We will do whatever may be necessary. We will overcome our population problem—did you know that in the frontier areas to the north we are founding all-male communities, whose production figures outstrip those of the rest of China by in some cases as much as ten percent? Such communities are scarcely conducive to human happiness, but if the population falls and there is rice to eat, what of it?

"We will take back the things that are ours, Hong Kong and Taiwan. We will sap the strength of your youth through drugs, if we think it is to our advantage in the unending struggle. So yes—we have killed, we have betrayed, we have done all these things. As have you, in your fashion, over the years, Mr. Businessman-*tai-pan* Young."

"I? I have not killed."

Sun laughed. "Not with your own hands, perhaps. But does the name Ao mean anything to you?"

Simon said nothing. Qiu was struck by the extent to which the Englishman's face had changed during his stay in Chaiyang. His eyes, set deep in their sockets, had begun to smolder. Qiu was half afraid of this new Simon Young.

"Ao was a pirate," said Sun Shanwang. "They found him floating in Hong Kong harbor. Who put him there?"

Simon examined the backs of his hands, but still he said nothing. Qiu tried to look into the Englishman's eyes but now they were almost closed, leaving only two tiny white slits between the lids.

Sun repeated his question, very deliberately. "Who . . . put . . . him . . . there?" He shrugged. "You covered up well; we shall never know the whole of that secret, unless you choose to reveal it to us. But we are quite sure you were involved in Ao's death. Somehow."

"*Aiya*," Qiu murmured softly. "My God . . ."

Until this moment Sun Shanwang had scarcely raised his voice. Now, however, he unexpectedly threw back his head and cried, "Yes, we are pragmatists! All of us! We must take back the shares but this we cannot do without producing you, whole and alive. So, tell us the price!"

He rose, went across to the bank of telephones and picked up a receiver, holding it out to Simon. "But first . . . make your call!"

Simon stared at Sun Shanwang through his half-closed eyes for a moment longer before levering himself out of his chair and walking across to join the deputy controller of Intelligence. But instead of taking the receiver, he pushed Sun's hand away. "No."

"Why?"

"Terms first. Then the call."

"Go on."

"First and most important, my wife must be released from any further obligation to you."

"Of course. She has served her purpose. We have no further need of friendly eyes and ears within your home."

"Next. You will do all that you promised before: most privileged trading status, irrevocable *written* guarantees securing Ducannon Young's position."

"Yes."

"You will rebuild my desalination plant, stone by stone, brick by brick, at no cost to me; and then you will run it and maintain it for all time."

"Agreed."

"And finally . . . finally, Sun Shanwang . . . you will give me security for all these things."

"Security?"

"An irrevocable banker's draft, drawn on the Bank of China, for one hundred million pounds sterling, which I will keep during my lifetime; coupled with a deed covering the draft and expressed to be granted as security for the due performance of your obligations."

"No."

"Please think again."

Sun gnawed his lower lip. "I will have to report this," he said at last. "Even if it is agreed, which I doubt, it will cause delay."

There was a long pause. At last Simon said, "Then to show my good faith, I shall make the call to my lawyer in Hong Kong." Seeing the deputy controller's face light up, he raised a cautionary hand. "But that is all. Until I have the draft, the deed in my hands, my memory is closed. That is what I will tell the judge in Hong Kong: I have no memory of the matters in question." He lowered his hand and smiled bleakly. "Then the judgment will stand; the shares will vanish. For a time. Until they reappear in the possession of a purchaser, or until Robert Zhao is ready to deploy them against you. Tell me, Sun Shanwang, for I would value your opinion—if Zhao were to sell, who do you think the purchaser would be?"

For a very long time the two men stood face to face, not speaking, their eyes locked. At last Sun turned away with a dismissive shrug, saying, "I think this is yet more bluff. You have no intention of giving up all that Hong Kong has to offer in exchange for a life, an *existence*, in Chaiyang."

"Perhaps you're right," Simon said thoughtfully. "But at least in Chaiyang I'm assured of a welcome. Whereas there are difficulties about my returning to Hong Kong."

"What difficulties?"

Simon laughed. "Do you really think it will be possible for me just to start up again where I left off? There was a court case, remember, a scandal? A final break with my father . . . many, many things."

"And do you, for your part, really think that we have not

considered those things? Assistant Commissioner Reade is helping us already: it was a simple matter to brief him to put about the story we wanted told. You had a mental breakdown; the shock of the murder attempt, the bombs . . . these events unhinged your mind."

Simon let his astonishment show. "You talk of Peter Reade as though he were working for you. He isn't."

"Oh, is he not?" Sun laughed. "When I said earlier, 'We are all pragmatists,' I certainly meant to include the British government in my statement." His laughter faded. "Your own side have used you, I should think so."

"But that's utterly inconceivable—"

"Nonsense. Any government would have done the same. No, you are unlikely to find yourself prejudiced in Hong Kong. And there is something else you should remember."

"Which is?"

"You were instrumental in ruining a Russian bank. Plenty of people will be ready to forgive much to whoever did that."

"Oh? And the depositors with that bank—what of them? Did my government's grasp of political realities extend to ruining them as well?"

"Of course. Don't try to carry altruism too far. There are limits to the extent to which we are prepared to indulge your self-esteem. No, I say again, you have no intention of surrendering your comfortable life in Hong Kong."

"And I, too, say again: perhaps. How interesting it will be to find out." Simon looked at his watch and said, "The call, Sun Shan-wang. It's time."

29

Throughout the whole of Sunday, Sun Shanwang's army rolled quietly into Hong Kong; by nightfall it had vanished like a wave draining into the sands.

His men had begun to arrive shortly after first light.

Immigration Officer Tok was nearing the end of his shift at Kai Tak Airport. He had been on duty for almost nine hours, with only a short meal break, but since things were fairly quiet during the latter part of the night he'd had ample opportunity to flirt with Alice Chan, the other occupant of his double desk. Alice was engaged to be married to a customs officer who showed no sign of being in a hurry to arrange the ceremony; and Alice—an attractive, healthy young woman—saw no reason why she should not spend some of her free time with Ricky Tok. True, Ricky was married and his wife had recently given birth to a daughter, their first child, but what of it? reasoned Alice; it always paid to get on well with colleagues . . . especially the good-looking male ones, on the upper end of the salary scale.

So when the early morning plane from Xian disgorged its load of passengers the two officers looked at their watches, exchanged lugubrious glances and prepared to give their scant remaining attention to the last immigrants of a long night.

Ricky beckoned, and a well-dressed Chinese stepped across the yellow line. The officer examined his passport, issued in Beijing three years before, compared its photograph with the smiling face on the other side of the desk, and consulted the two-volume "bible" of prohibited persons.

"Purpose of visit, Mr. Wang?"

"Business trip. I am with a delegation from the Xian Chamber of Commerce, here at the invitation of the government. This person"—the immigrant pointed to where Alice Chan was processing another Chinese—"is also with the same delegation."

Ricky looked at the two passengers. Both wore dark gray suits, ties, and spectacles: a couple of studious business types. They were in their late twenties or early thirties, he judged, and that coincided with the date of birth entered in the passport he was holding.

"How long do you intend to remain in Hong Kong?"

"Two days."

"Sponsorship?"

"Here." The passenger produced a letter signed by the colony's commercial secretary. Ricky ran his eye down it. He had seen hundreds of such documents; this one was not in any way unusual. While he was scanning the last paragraph his hand was already reaching for the rubber stamp. Belatedly he remembered the official courtesy campaign. "Enjoy your stay."

"Thank you."

The visitor from the mainland picked up his passport and went through. Thirty more immigration officers sat at identical desks on either side of Ricky, filtering the never-ending influx of passengers from all parts of the world. His eyes strayed to the clock on the wall. Another ten minutes and he'd be free. Maybe Alice would like some breakfast, there was this new place he'd discovered in Mody Road . . . He raised his hand and another passenger stepped across the line.

Meanwhile, Mr. Wang and his nine colleagues passed through the customs hall into Hong Kong, unremarked and unremembered.

*   *   *

A few miles to the north, Constable Pang Kai Mun stood at the Hong Kong end of the covered bridge that links the People's Republic of China with the New Territories. This morning, his job was to guard the heavy sliding gate into the customs and immigration area. He watched as the first of the day's five passenger trains from Guangzhou to Kowloon halted in Lo Wu station and passengers began to stream past him. Always the same boring people, he was thinking—peasants with sacks, old women lumping heavy baskets, the odd handful of better-dressed Hong Kongese on their way home from visits to relatives in the People's Republic. Pang did not relish this duty. His talents, for which he had a high regard, were wasted on it.

Suddenly one of the passengers attracted his attention. While the man was still ten yards off, Pang knew that here was something different. He advanced purposefully to pluck the peasant out of the slow-moving throng.

"Name?"

Pang soon realized that the man was simple. He grinned at the officer, muttered some words in an incomprehensible dialect and started to move on. When Pang jerked him back the man's inane smile did not falter for an instant.

"*Name?*"

"Ah, ah, ah!" The peasant put down the canvas sack he was carrying over his shoulder and began to rummage around inside it. Pang used the opportunity to take a good look at him. He was about twenty-five, the policeman decided: tall for a Chinese and with a sturdy body in good shape, apart from the slight stoop that a lifetime of rural toil always inflicts. Spiky, close-cropped black hair, sunken cheeks, brown eyes, tanned skin—nothing unusual. Yet, in spite of his run-of-the-mill physical appearance, there was something odd about this man. Pang rubbed his jaw thoughtfully. Something, quite apart from the peasant himself . . . *smelled.*

The hayseed stood upright, or as nearly upright as his overworked frame could manage, and stuffed a bundle of papers into Pang's hand. The policeman rummaged through the documents and made a face. Residence permit. Grubby visitor's pass. Letter from Party District Committee authorizing a twenty-four-hour visit to Hong Kong for the purpose of selling fruit and vegetables. Pang mentally noted the man's name, which meant nothing to him, and handed back the papers. It took a little while for it to dawn on the peasant that he was meant to take them.

Pang slowly began to walk around the man, who at once swiveled with him. "*Stand still*, can't you?" Pang snapped. No, there was nothing, nothing at all suspicious. And yet. And yet . . .

"I haven't seen you before," he said. "Have I?"

"Ah, ah, ah . . ."

"Is this your first visit?"

"Ah?"

Pang peered down into the canvas sack. Lettuces, somewhat the worse for their journey. He reached in and felt about, muddying himself in the process. Nothing. Pang straightened up, rubbing his hands together to shake off the remnants of soil and grit still attached to them. He saw that the man's attention was fixed on the customs hall behind his back and wheeled around to catch sight of another group of about a dozen peasants, each with an identical sack, grinning at him.

"You're arresting Old Li, hah, hah!" They seemed to find the prospect amusing. "Two nights in jail, maybe three, hah!" "Yes, a longer visit than you bargained for, Old Li."

Out of the corner of his eye, Pang spotted the inspector approaching and he hastily jerked his head toward the waiting group of peasants. "On your way. *Move!*"

Inspector Spurr came up to Pang and followed the direction of his gaze. "Anything wrong?"

"I do not think so. But"—Pang shook his head as a sign of irritation—"all my experience tells me: not quite right."

Spurr shrugged. "Who the hell ever knows with those people?"

"But that's bad. We ought to know."

The inspector placed a friendly hand on his subordinate's shoulder. "Come on, Pang, we all realize that land immigration into Hong Kong's a joke. The real work gets done on the other side, in Shenzhen. No one comes across that bridge as a legal immigrant without the mainland's permission."

"Do we not have a say?"

"Oh yes, we have a *say*, all right. But no means of finding out about the ones they send us." The inspector pointed at the group of peasants, who by now had cleared customs and were lining up for the train again. "Why, for all I know, that lot could be the bloody Politburo!"

Pang frowned and shook his head. "They are too young," he observed.

*　　*　　*

The human waves continued to roll smoothly in from the mainland throughout the morning and most of the afternoon. The guns came right at the end, when dusk was already falling.

A police cutter inched its way through the crowded waterway, out into the main stream of harbor traffic, and headed slowly toward the open sea. Sergeant Cheong-Leen raised his binoculars to his eyes and scanned the horizon. Rain, nothing but rain and more rain. The weather forecast for the next twenty-four hours was the same. And of course, tomorrow was, it had to be, the sergeant's day off.

He sighed; then, as the regulation black leather belt bit into his ample stomach, breathed in sharply. Sergeant Cheong-Leen was too fat and he suffered from indigestion. Lesser men might have allowed these misfortunes to affect their disposition; but the sergeant was too nice a man to work off his aches and pains on inferiors.

"Rotten weather," he said pleasantly to Probationary Constable Lum, who stood next to him on the bridge. The young Chinese coughed nervously. "Yes, Sergeant."

"I hate these days, you know. 'Blanket cloud, choppy gray sea, heavy rain, visibility poor and decreasing.' How many times must I have written those words in the log." Cheong-Leen sighed once more. "Just the weather for illegals, too."

He raised his glasses again and studied the harbor. Suddenly he stopped in midsweep and lowered his elbows onto the ledge in front of him to steady his gaze. "Vessel approaching, two o'clock, one hundred yards, inner channel. Ready to go about for boarding."

"Aye!" said the helmsman.

As the cutter came alongside, Sergeant Cheong-Leen stepped quickly over the rail with an ease that came from long practice and jumped down into the boat. The craft was typical of Hong Kong's Aberdeen Harbor fleet—wooden construction, twenty feet long, high in the stern, covered with a green tarpaulin stretched across round hoops that ran the length of the hull and powered by a rackety inboard engine. The policeman looked around him. Usual mish-mash: a dozen or so passengers, chickens clucking, a piglet, baskets of spring onions, greens, gingerroots, crates of beer, crates of Coca-Cola, two large wooden chests. That shouldn't take long, then; which was as well, bearing in mind the rain and the heat.

"Good afternoon, ladies and gentlemen." He repeated the words in Mandarin, looking carefully to see if anyone registered, but

□ 415 □

nobody did. Oh well, thought the sergeant, never mind; although it was funny how often an illegal could be flushed out by the sound of a few words spoken in his own language.

The passengers were the usual motley crew: six women, eight children, two men. The NCO did his rounds quickly, convinced before he started that he was going to find everything in order. He knew the captain of this ship, had checked him out many times before. As he'd anticipated, all the passengers possessed regular identity cards. The policeman turned his attention to the cargo.

"What is in those chests, please?"

One of the two men looked at the sergeant, smiled and murmured a few words.

"What did you say?" Cheong-Leen bent down low. "I did not hear you."

"I said, Sergeant Cheong-Leen, that it is good to see you again. You will remember us, I think? And you will remember the circumstances of our previous meeting? The white powder?"

The sergeant straightened up very slowly, his good-humored smile a thing of the past. He scrutinized the face of the man who had spoken. Yes, the face was familiar . . . then the other man also smiled and, using only the third and fourth fingers of his left hand, reached up to scratch his right shoulder.

The probationary constable was watching all that took place from the bridge of the police cutter. He had seen Sergeant Cheong-Leen inspect the passengers' papers, then go forward, under the tarpaulin, out of range of vision. Now, only seconds later, he emerged at a fast clip. The young policeman looked on in astonishment as his superior scrambled over the side of the detained vessel and made his way forward to the bridge. Why did he not check out the cargo? What had gone wrong?

Lum knew his place. It was not for him to question a non-commissioned officer. But as Cheong-Leen regained the bridge and breathlessly gave the order to get under way, the younger man couldn't help noticing how the sergeant's hand shook as he wiped the sweat from a face that was suddenly almost green in color. Lum discreetly turned his head to port and busied himself in a scan of passing vessels. But when the boat they had detained was far behind them in the main channel, and Cheong-Leen still had not told him what entry to make in the log, he screwed up his courage to ask timidly: "What should I write, please, Sergeant?"

"Write," the sergeant snapped; and Lum swallowed, his mouth suddenly dry. Cheong-Leen had always seemed so genial in the past.

"Write," Lum repeated. "In the log . . . ?"

The sergeant subjected him to a long, hostile stare. Just when Lum had started to wonder if Cheong-Leen had heard his question, the NCO banged both fists on the chart table. "Nothing!" he shouted hoarsely.

Lum jumped backward a step. "But, but . . . Sergeant, the rulebook says—"

"Of course the rulebook says! Write . . . write that we stopped a vessel, the time of day, the location, the . . . the harbor number." Cheong-Leen rested his palms on the table and let his head drop forward so that Lum could no longer read his expression. "Nothing suspicious," he muttered to the tabletop. "Nothing suspicious at all."

There was a moon that night, but the gods were kind: they hid it behind a massive bank of clouds that reared up over the mainland in the shape of an angry dragon. The valley beneath Ak Tai To Yan was black. When they brought Simon Young to the foot of the hill he blundered against Qiu Qianwei and even then could not see him.

Qiu clasped his hand. "Welcome," he hissed. "You are a little early; it is only a quarter to one."

"The junk landed us ahead of schedule and the captain thought it best if we came at once."

"Better early than late," said another voice, a woman's voice: and Qiu snapped, "Who's that?"

"My wife. She insisted on coming."

"That was not part of the arrangement! It was not! Linhua and the children were to be returned to your house."

"I know. But my wife does not trust you, and, as I say, she insisted."

"Do you not have any control over your own wife?"

"Your question is offensive; it also betrays gross ignorance of Western ways. Besides, why should I deny her requests? She has endured too much on my behalf."

"I stay!" said Jinny; and Qiu snorted. "Yes, that's quite right—you will stay here, on this very spot!"

"I—"

"If you argue, Wang Linhua, I will have you and your husband bound and gagged and left here, alone. I mean it!"

There was a long silence, broken by Simon. "Very well. I'll ask her to stay here and wait. Jinny?"

"If you say so." Her voice was sulky. "If *you* say so."

"Please."

"Huh." Qiu was annoyed. "Now I will lose two of my men. Someone will have to look after you."

"No need."

"Yes! Your husband says you don't trust me. Well, I don't trust you, either!" He raised his voice a fraction. "Captain!"

Another man answered: "Sir?"

"Come here . . . take this woman, see that she remains here. Mr. Young, you will come with me, as we agreed."

Simon reached out to take Jinny's hand. "Go with them," he said quietly. "This shouldn't take long."

"You'll be careful?"

"I will."

She squeezed his hand and released it slowly, as if her fingers were reluctant to sever contact with his. Simon strained to hear her leave, but all was quiet. One moment she was standing by his side, the next she had gone.

Simon strove to pierce the darkness that hung in front of his face like an impenetrable blackout curtain. "I can't see," he breathed.

"Then all is as it should be. My face is darkened, my men wear black."

"Men?"

"Yes. I'm a colonel in the People's Liberation Army. I've brought a unit with me, although you can't see them."

"How many?"

"Two hundred."

"Two hundred!"

"You think it's not enough?" Qiu sounded doubtful. "Perhaps you're right, I should have brought more."

"That's not a rescue operation, Colonel Qiu. That's an invasion."

"Then we are a few years early." Qiu's voice betrayed a rare flash of humor. "Although you didn't seem to mind that when we conducted exercises in Ocean Park, one famous Tuesday."

"Exercises?"

"Oh yes. That operation was a very useful test of our state of preparedness. It's silly to talk of invasion, Mr. Young, for we're here already. In the streets, the restaurants, banks, offices, shops— the mainland *has* repossessed. Only the formalities need to be completed and, to a Chinese, a decade or so is nothing." He shrugged and changed the subject. "I'm surprised to see you here. I thought you would be in Macau, spending your hundred million pounds."

"That's trust money, Colonel. The interest is mine, but the principal will come back to you intact, one day. And I'm surprised to see *you* here: I thought you were still recovering from the wound you received in Chaiyang."

"I'm feeling better. Besides, wounded or not, I have no choice. This is the conclusion of a long project, *my* project. I must be here."

A human presence glided past Simon; the grass rustled and he felt the air move. He heard voices whispering, but he could not distinguish the words. When Qiu grasped his hand, he jumped.

"We are ready. Zhao's not alone."

"How do you know?"

"We have his houseboy here, in a sack. Mind your feet, please; if you tread on him he may cry out. He was very communicative before we put him in the sack. Zhao has a visitor."

"Who?"

"We don't know. The houseboy's powers of description are not good. But—a Westerner, not an Oriental."

"Borisenko?"

"Or Krubykov, as we know him. Yes, perhaps."

"But when Zhao misses the servant, all he needs to do is phone for help—"

"The wires have been cut."

"Radio, then. Surely his helicopter has a shortwave radio, there must be a transmitter at the house—"

"There is. Unfortunately for Mr. Zhao, it's out of order. My unit captain has its main circuitboard in his knapsack. In any case, you didn't have to come. It was at your insistence that we brought you here to share these risks. We can deny you nothing now, it seems. What do you want to do—go back home?"

There was a long pause. A breeze fanned the hollow, making the sweat on Simon's forehead feel unpleasantly cold. "I want my shares," he said at last.

"Then let's go and get them!"

At once two shadows attached themselves to Simon, each inserting an arm through the crooks of his elbows. They guided him forward, out of the hollow and onto a track that led steeply upward. After a while he became used to the awkwardness, learning to match his movements to those of the guides. He could hear gravel crunch softly beneath his feet, but the accompanying shadows made no sound. How on earth could they see. . . ? Simon could perceive nothing except the lights of the solitary house high above them, but he sensed that the hillside was alive with people. They did not hurry. Just when the house seemed to be almost vertically above Simon his two companions guided him off the path onto grass, where his feet made no noise, and gently pushed him down to the ground. The three of them waited there in silence for what might have been ten minutes or an hour. At last Simon heard, or thought he might have heard, a high-pitched whistle, instantly stilled and not repeated. His shadows immediately hauled him to his feet and they began to run. By the time the three men reached the upper terrace Simon was completely out of breath.

The guides hustled him across the patio and in through the glass sliding doors. For a moment, all he could do was gulp down air. When at last he recovered and could stand upright again, it was to see a room full of still, silent figures, like actors on a film set awaiting their director's cue.

Robert Zhao stood in the sunken, square center of the large room, arms folded, one calf angled elegantly across the other so as to leave the toe of his right foot resting on the black carpet. His face expressed mild irritation tinged with boredom. At each corner of the square stood a man clad in black, his skin smeared with burnt cork, training a MAC-10 semiautomatic pistol on Zhao. Qiu, also wearing lightweight black pajamas and plimsolls, stood midway between Simon and the former group. The man whom Simon knew as Borisenko was sitting on a sofa, his face blank.

"Simon!" drawled Zhao. "My very dear chap, how nice to see you again. Do come in, won't you?"

He was frightened. It showed, not in his well-mannered phraseology, but in his eyes. He was more than frightened. He was terrified.

"Good evening, Robert . . . Mr. Borisenko." By now Simon had recovered; he saw no reason to mar the meeting's calm atmosphere. The Russian made no response, but Zhao seemed nervously eager to talk.

"If you'll forgive me for saying so, you appear to be really rather under the weather. You look like a man who's had adventures. I hope I may hear about them sometime. Family well?"

"Quite well, thank you."

"Strange company you keep, these days. Would your friends mind if I smoked?"

"Ask him." Simon pointed at Qiu.

Zhao cocked his head in Red Dragon's direction, raised an eyebrow and said, "Is it all right if—?"

"You may not smoke, Zhao. We have come for Mr. Young's property."

"Please be specific."

"His Founders Shares in the Pacific & Cantonese Banking Corporation."

Borisenko spoke for the first time. "You amaze me," he said softly.

"Why?" barked Qiu. "What business have you to be amazed? What business have you to be here at all?"

"I had an appointment with Mr. Zhao—"

"Yes, at ten o'clock tomorrow morning. We know all about that; this man's phone has been monitored for months. What brings you here nine hours early?"

When Borisenko grunted but said nothing, Qiu went on: "Is it because you trust him as much as we have learned to do?"

"I trust no one, particularly when it comes to the affairs of Soviet Communal Bank. And it seems I am right not to trust." He pointed an accusing finger at Simon Young. "Why do you say that the Founders Shares are *his*? If you had said *your* property, *tongzhi*, I could have understood it. But *his* . . . that's quite another thing." He frowned at Simon. "Do you say they are your property?"

"Yes. I claim them."

"And what about the judgment of the High Court, which gives my bank full authority to dispose of them as it thinks fit? Or is Ducannon Young now in truth above the law"—Borisenko's voice changed to a snarl—"as it always imagined itself to be?"

"My lawyers are already working on that. The judgment will be set aside in a few days."

"I see." This time it was Zhao who spoke. His eyes glazed over and Simon knew that he was calculating. "On your evidence, I suppose?"

"Yes."

"And so what a marvelous coincidence it is, you coming back

at just the right moment . . ." He cast a hostile sideways look in the direction of Borisenko. "So many unexpected visitors, all at once on a Sunday evening; I'm almost beginning to feel that no one trusts me at all." His eyes reverted to Simon's face. "Let's hope nothing else happens to you in the meantime, eh? Rather an important witness, aren't you?"

Zhao addressed himself to Qiu. "There's been a misunderstanding. Naturally, the shares are at the disposal of the People's Republic." He winked at Borisenko, then shrugged resignedly. "My dear chap, they do have the weaponry, after all! And in any case"—he turned back to Qiu—"when have I ever denied it? Am I not your nominee?"

"You are. On behalf of the People's Republic, I call for the share certificate. I direct that you shall deliver it to this man, Simon Young."

"Of course." Zhao spread his hands and smiled one of his most winsome smiles. "I'm standing on it."

"You are what?"

"Standing on it. There is a safe embedded in this floor, under the carpet." Zhao directed a mockingly conspiratorial glance at Simon. "So much more secure than the Corporation's smelly old vaults." He turned back to Qiu. "If you'd call off your guards, I'll lift up this table and raise the carpet."

"The guards remain where they are."

Zhao shrugged. "As you wish." He bent down to the table beside him, but before he could touch it, Qiu said, "I encourage you to move very slowly, please."

"Certainly."

Zhao once more bent down to the table and, with carefully judged movements, lifted it onto the upper-floor level. Then he raised one corner of the carpet and peeled it back to reveal a metal plate. Simon, moved by curiosity, advanced a few steps. To one side of the plate he could see inscribed numbers from zero to nine. Zhao looked up, caught his eye and said, "Dreadfully clever, this. Japanese. Well, everything is these days, isn't it?"

He tapped on the membrane that covered the numbers and the plate at once slid aside to reveal the hole. Zhao smiled at Simon for the last time and casually reached down into it. With a single, smooth movement he drew out the Colt .45 and leveled it straight at the Englishman. "Everyone stand back!" he said. "I'm leaving now. Young—move away from the terrace doors. Qiu, tell your men to put their guns on safety and drop them. *Now!*"

For a split second everyone froze; then Qiu said: "Do it."

Four MAC-10s fell to the floor.

"That's right. Good. Now tell them to move back, away from the safe."

Qiu made an impatient gesture with his right hand. The four gunners retreated.

Zhao was sitting on the edge of the floor cavity, with his legs out of sight. He reached down into the hole with his free hand and pulled out a leather case, a folded sheet of cream-colored paper and a brown envelope, all of which he placed next to him. The same hand jabbed at the membrane again and Simon heard a rumbling sound under the floorboards. Zhao risked a quick look down and tossed the case and other items back into the recess.

Zhao spoke. "Young—walk over here, very slowly, with your hands on top of your head."

Simon obeyed. As he passed the sofa on which Borisenko was sitting, the Russian silently eased himself to his feet and backed toward the terrace doors. His shoes made no sound on the thick black carpet. All attention was concentrated on Zhao; no one noticed.

Simon Young approached to within a few feet of the lip of the hole in the floor and looked down. Now the recess was not a recess at all, but a shaft without visible bottom; he could just make out the first two rungs of a metal ladder let into the side of it.

"Stop!" said Zhao.

Simon obeyed. Qiu was standing to his left, half a pace in front of him. Zhao's eyes darted between the two men. "I don't like long good-byes," he said abruptly. "I've got your share certificate now, and I can do what I fucking well like with it. The only person in the world who could ever prevent that, Simon, is you. 'Rather an important witness,' I said—Christ, what an understatement! No one else can sue for the return of those shares. No one!"

Zhao paused. He seemed to be having trouble with his breathing, as if he had reached the boundaries of self-control. "Sorry, old man," he said quietly. He might have been commiserating with a heavy loss at backgammon. "Not at all what I wanted."

A number of things happened very fast. Zhao aimed the Colt at the center of Simon's chest. Borisenko turned and sped for the terrace doors. Zhao's eyes flickered away, saw Borisenko's departing back, widened in shock and instantly reverted to Simon. Qiu leaped sideways into the direct line of fire. When Zhao pulled the trigger, the click of the hammer falling on an empty chamber reverberated through the still room like a thunderclap from heaven. Zhao jumped.

They heard him land with a grunt. Almost instantly a heavy panel slid across to seal the tunnel and once more turn it into a cavity-safe. Qiu threw himself on the touch-sensitive membrane, searching in vain for a key; at a sign from him his men dived for their pistols and started to blow the floor panel to smithereens.

Qiu scrambled to his feet and grabbed one of the gunners by the arm. "Out!" he screamed. "Onto the hillside—alert the brigade, then get me that Russian!"

The man raced to obey. As he reached the door, Qiu shouted: "Wait! Take Young down with you."

"I'm coming too," said Simon.

"No!" Qiu beckoned the gunner back. "You're responsible for this man, look after him. And tell the unit captain to spread out in a cordon, round the hill. Zhao still has to get out of here. That tunnel must have an exit somewhere."

"*Hao.*" The gunner took Simon's arm and held it tightly. Simon struggled, but the man's grip was unbreakable. Qiu watched until the two of them had passed through the terrace doors before once more directing all his attention to the tunnel.

The metal panel had been destroyed. Now one of the remaining soldiers lowered himself into the cavity. As his legs swung over the edge, the sound of a shot echoed upward from the tunnel: the man screamed in agony and rolled aside, clutching his thigh. A second gunner fired a quick burst into the hole: when his fire was not returned, he launched himself down, out of sight.

Qiu nodded to the remaining soldier, who clambered onto the metal ladder and slid down it. The cadre leaned over the edge of the cavity. "All right down there?"

"Yes. It's a drop of about two meters, Colonel."

"Have you light?"

"Torchlight only. There's a tunnel. We can feel an air current."

"Proceed with care. I'll follow."

Qiu jumped into the void. As he landed he felt his ankle twist, but managed to rise. The cadre fumbled for his torch and flashed it around the chamber.

He was standing at one end of a narrow, low tunnel, about five feet square. Its floor and walls were nothing but compressed soil, reinforced in places by steel girders and breeze-blocks. The gunner had been right: warm air was flowing along the passage. Qiu began to follow his torchbeam.

Voices up ahead. His men must have made contact. Suddenly the muffled sound of a shot echoed through the darkness, instantly followed by several bursts of automatic fire. Qiu ran forward, blundering painfully into the walls as the passage snaked left and right.

He turned a corner to find himself confronted by a square of light some twenty meters dead ahead. A figure leaped across the illuminated gap and Qiu thought he recognized Zhao. Another burst of automatic fire followed.

Qiu advanced slowly toward the light. Almost immediately he stumbled across his two gunners, lying flat on the floor of the tunnel. "What's happening?" snapped Qiu.

"There's a sort of cave ahead, Colonel. We can see a car. The Chrysanthemum has taken cover behind it."

"Idiots! Zhao has a handgun, you have semiautomatics. Overpower him!"

As if in answer, another burst of fire thundered out from the floodlit cavern in front of them. Qiu flung himself to the ground, covering his head. Bullets clanged off the nearest iron girder, sending a shower of earth cascading down on the three men. Simultaneously they heard a car door slam and the sound of an engine starting up.

"He must have had another weapon here in the tunnel," Qiu muttered. He rose to a crouch and tapped one of his gunners on the shoulder. "Cover me!" The man straightaway began to loose off rapid volleys. Qiu stood fully upright and sprinted for the opening ahead.

He kept going into the light, with the second gunner following some way behind. But while Red Dragon was still yards short of his goal his legs became entangled in an obstruction and he fell, dropping the torch. He managed to struggle up, cursing, and run on. Ahead of him was a blue Mercedes 500 SEL, Zhao already in the driver's seat. As Qiu flung himself at the nearside door he gleaned a vague impression of a natural stone underground chamber, dripping with water; floodlights; petrol cans . . . then the car's engine revved and exhaust smoke filled the cave.

Something black was coming down across the mouth of the passageway, closing it off from the main chamber. A steel shutter. The soldier who had followed Qiu felt his feet ensnared by the same obstruction that had floored the colonel. He tripped, landing on top of his MAC-10, and yelped with pain. Now his body lay directly in the path of the shutter.

The first soldier stopped firing. He could just see his colleague writhing on the ground across the entrance, with his feet entangled in a wire—of course, a tripwire that operated to bring down the shutter, Colonel Qiu must have set it off . . .

The light at the end of the tunnel was virtually gone. Only a thin strip showed between the shutter and the floor. The hydraulically powered steel plate reached the trapped gunner's body. He shouted for help. Suddenly his voice rose to a tortured, high-pitched scream.

The first gunner covered his ears with his hands, but only for an instant; then he raised his semiautomatic and ran forward to pick up Qiu's torch, guided by its faint beam. The voice somewhere near his feet was emitting sounds he would not have thought possible—the kind of ululating squeal that goes with the slaughter of pigs, almost high enough to transcend the outermost range of human hearing.

In the light from Qiu's torch he saw that the second gunner's body was all but severed. He swallowed back vomit and fired a single, merciful shot.

As Qiu grabbed the handle of the door, Zhao's foot pumped down hard on the accelerator. The Mercedes shot forward down a slope, its headlights illuminating what looked like a blank wall straight ahead. Zhao slammed on the brakes and immediately accelerated again, hoping to throw the cadre off the car. As its back wheels spun wildly, throwing up showers of earth, Qiu managed to wrench open the door and throw himself half onto the front passenger seat.

Zhao smashed his Colt down on Qiu's hand. The colonel felt dizzy with pain for a second, but then his head cleared and he saw that Zhao was wrestling to keep control on the slimy mud surface of the cave's floor. As Qiu swung one leg into the car, Zhao, distracted, took his eyes off the road. The Mercedes swerved to the left, forcing him to grab the wheel with both hands; and the Colt dropped into his lap.

He had very little leeway in which to maneuver. He turned hard right, instantly straightened up again. The effect was to slam the passenger door. With a mighty effort Qiu hitched his other leg inside before the door could close on it.

He knelt hunched up on the front seat with his forehead almost in contact with the automatic-gear lever. The car ran through the "wall," in fact nothing more than a densely woven screen of foliage draped across the cave's mouth, and emerged onto a bumpy gravel track.

Zhao took a swift look through the windscreen to check his course, then focused all his concentration on Qiu Qianwei. Red Dragon was struggling to squeeze his legs off the seat. Zhao grabbed the cadre's hair and used it to jolt his head down on the gear shift. Qiu, grappling blindly with his right hand, made contact with the steering wheel and gave it a wrench. While Zhao fought to keep the car going straight, Qiu clutched the back of the driver's seat for support and tugged the wheel again. The car slithered to the very edge of the track, its far wheels sending up cascades of earth and stones. Qiu, aided by the lurch, went sliding down into the passenger seat.

Then his eyes flitted to the windscreen and widened in horror. "*Aiya!*" Zhao looked. About fifty yards away, down the slope, the track swarmed with people. Some of Qiu's troops were running up the hill toward the car, Young at their head. Zhao accelerated hard, pointing the Mercedes at the Englishman as though it were a gunsight.

Forty yards . . . thirty . . .

Qiu battled for control of the wheel, but Zhao was too strong for him. When the cadre struck at the side and back of the driver's head Zhao retaliated, poking his fingers at Qiu's eyes, pulling his hair.

Twenty yards to Simon Young, to the last obstacle in Zhao's way.

Suddenly he remembered the gun. He scrabbled about in his lap until at last his hand made contact with the Colt. He lifted it, taking rough aim at Red Dragon. But as his finger tightened on the trigger the car swerved again and Zhao glanced at the track. His mouth fell open, his eyes widened in stupefaction. For Simon Young had stumbled and fallen to one side, revealing behind him a lone figure seemingly dressed all in white, the color of death, its arms raised high.

Ten yards to the waving white figure . . .

"Jinny," shrieked Zhao. "*Jinny!*"

All his muscles suddenly went limp. Qiu grabbed hold of the wheel with both hands. He managed to swivel around until he could look out of the windscreen, but could scarcely bring himself to believe what he saw. Jinny Young was running into the path of the car, arms raised straight above her head, her pale face spectral in the headlights . . . then, with awful suddenness, through the windscreen he saw nothing but black night.

Zhao screamed.

Qiu Qianwei jerked the wheel to the left and saw that the ground rose gently into scrub. He succeeded in holding the wheel steady, without protest or struggle from Zhao. The Mercedes ran up the slope and came to a halt. As it began to slide backward, men from the Mah-jongg unit emerged out of the surrounding darkness and wrenched open the doors. Zhao fell sideways to the ground.

Qiu yanked hard on the handbrake, leaped from the passenger seat and ran back down the hill. A group of soldiers had already gathered around Jinny, who lay in the center of the track, motionless. Simon Young was kneeling beside her and as he reached for her wrist Qiu knew instinctively that there would be no pulse, no heartbeat.

But at the last minute Simon could not bring himself to touch his wife. He stood up awkwardly, incapable of shedding tears before these strangers, and ran a few steps, holding his hands up to his eyes. The cordon of troops opened to let him through.

After a while he regained sufficient control to return to the body in the road. It was necessary to make arrangements. A calm voice inside his head repeated the word over and over again. Arrangements, arrangements. When a person died, there were formalities to be attended to. Someone must tell the children. Of course: he must do it. Arrangements—such a comfortingly neutral word. Then it was necessary to call an ambulance. There would be papers to sign, more arrangements. His whole body was cold and numb with shock.

Simon sat down on the stones and took his wife's clammy hand, rubbing it gently with his own. Qiu left him there. He went back up the hill to find Robert Zhao kneeling between two soldiers. The Chrysanthemum looked at Red Dragon through eyes full of pain.

"Dead," said Qiu laconically.

He snapped his fingers and a brace of MAC-10s blew Robert Zhao to pieces.

A split second after the shots echoed out across the hillside, Jinny Young's eyes opened and she sat up. "What was that?" she said.

"*Wa . . . a . . . ah!*"

The troops, who had withdrawn to a respectful distance, could not contain their astonishment. Simon stared at his wife, suddenly back from the dead, and opened his mouth. No words came out. He went cold with shock; then relief and gratitude overwhelmed him. "*Jinny!*"

Jinny turned her head so that she could see him properly. "What was that?" she repeated.

"You're all right! You're alive!"

"Yes, I'm alive." She seemed puzzled by his ardor. "I tripped and then I fainted when the car ran over me."

Simon had lived in the Far East for most of his life; communication with the Chinese had become second nature to him. He was used to filling in the minor gaps that inevitably occurred when thoughts were transferred across the cultural divide. But because shock had numbed his responses, for a few seconds he failed to realize that his wife was speaking literally: she had fallen down parallel with the track, the car had passed over her body without any of its wheels actually touching it, and she had fainted. The car had run over her.

Then the truth dawned; and Simon laughed out loud for joy.

Another kind of dawn had come by the time Qiu's unit finished clearing up. It was a remarkable operation. There was nothing to show that Zhao had received visitors during the night. Indeed, there was nothing left of Zhao at all.

Qiu came out of the house to find Simon leaning on the terrace balustrade, staring out toward mainland China. The clouds had rolled away to disclose the first faint pale blue beginnings of a resplendent tropical morning. Qiu rested his back against the low wall and lit a cigarette. After he had smoked in silence for about a minute Simon stood upright. "Where are your men, Qiu Qianwei?"

"They've gone."

"I didn't see or hear them."

"Good."

"And Borisenko . . . or whatever he was called. Have you found him?"

"No."

"Are you going to?"

"Not this time, I fear. If we were going to track him down we would have done so by now. No, he's slipped through the net. But we shall find him. One day."

"And when you do?"

Qiu drew hard on his cigarette. "We shall kill him. Now, I must take you home. We have a car waiting, but it's necessary to walk a short way to get to it. Your wife is already there. Quickly, please—it's getting late."

They descended the steps to the helicopter pad. There was a muddy path leading from it, heading south, toward Kowloon. The two men followed it through the scrub for about a quarter of a mile before emerging onto a wider track roughly made up with stones, where they found a Toyota. Jinny was already in the backseat. Simon got in next to her, while Qiu sat in front with the driver.

Red Dragon felt inside his jacket and removed a sheet of stiff paper, folded into four. "Your share certificate."

"Thank you." Simon swallowed. "Thank you very much."

"*Nali, nali.*"

As the car moved off, Simon put the certificate in his pocket and leaned forward to tap Qiu's shoulder. "What are you going to do now?" he asked.

"Me? I shall go back to China, of course."

"For another assignment like this one?"

Qiu laughed. "There are no assignments like this one! I will go wherever I am sent, do as I am told." He made a rueful face. "Perhaps they will send me to some quiet provincial university where I can be a professor of economics." His shoulders sagged, but he put a brave face on it. "Probably not."

"You don't like being a colonel?"

"It's not a question of like. I think I've become too good at it for them to release me now."

"Will we meet again?"

Qiu shrugged. "Who knows?"

Simon gripped Qiu's shoulder, and the Chinese started. "I'm sorry I had to use your son," Simon said, after a pause.

"Yes." For a moment Qiu let his old malevolence show through the affable exterior. "So am I. Perhaps time will cover up the memories; who knows?"

Simon compressed his lips. "Time is on your side, Qiu Qianwei, not mine. You go; your duties are at an end. Mine are just beginning."

"Good. New starts are always good."

"Not this one, I think. It's hard to begin again, at my age."

"I don't agree, Mr. Young. We have a saying: 'Difficulties are like springs; if you are weak, they will be strong; if you are strong . . . they will be weak.' The five million Chinese citizens of Hong Kong are very strong. So are you. And you have help."

"I do?"

"Indeed." Qiu rested his arm on the back of the driver's seat and turned to smile at Jinny. "Good sister—I enjoyed that bit of the make-believe. A part of me envies you, Mr. Young. Yes, you have help."

Jinny frowned at him. "No thanks to you."

"All is now in the past, Wang Linhua."

"Don't use that name!"

"Sorry, sorry. New start, hah? New name, new desalination plant, everything begins again."

"People don't find it so easy to start afresh," said Simon. "I'm no different. My business reputation is destroyed."

Qiu tossed his head and laughed offensively. "I thought you understood us!"

"What?"

"Did Comrade Sun not explain it to you? We Chinese see only the facts of life. If I lived here I would see a desalination plant, rebuilt and functioning, but I would not see a Russian bank. Did you know Soviet Communal Bank closed its doors on Friday?"

Simon shook his head.

"It is a fact. It is one thing to have a High Court judgment, another to collect. The bank did not collect and now it never will. We have ruined it, you and I."

"Ruined it and how many others? What of the people who deposited their savings with Soviet Communal?"

"Most of them took their money out a long time ago. It helped us, in fact—there was a minor run just before it ceased to trade. As for the rest, well"—he smiled his usual, unemotional smile—"it serves them right for dealing with the Russians in the first place!"

"You make things seem very simple."

"And you insist on complicating them. You'll find that your reputation is scarcely dented, Mr. Young. The plant you built will soon be at work. The court case which you must now fight will justify your actions publicly. And we on the mainland stand behind you. No, I do not think you need worry about your reputation."

"My father—"

"Another pragmatist. Wait. Allow time to pass. Your father is like the bamboo he affects to despise: he will bend to the wind, rather than break."

"If you believe that, you don't know him."

"Oh, I think I do. But in any case, we should soon have an opportunity to find out."

"Meaning what?"

But Qiu merely shrugged.

The journey took less than an hour. At last they were turning off the road into the driveway of a home Simon had never thought to see again. As he got out, he saw that a car was parked beside the terrace and he looked at Qiu with a questioning glance.

"Wait," repeated the cadre.

Simon ushered Jinny inside. As the front door closed behind them, Diana and Mat rushed out of the living room to throw themselves on their parents, hugging and kissing them in rapturous welcome. Simon looked over Diana's shoulder and to his astonishment saw another person emerge, somewhat diffidently, into the hallway.

"Father . . ." Simon disengaged his daughter's arms and walked slowly up to Tom Young. "I wasn't expecting to see you."

Tom grunted. "Well. I thought perhaps the children might need . . ." He was silent for a moment. Then he said: "This isn't the time."

"No."

"But Peter Reade's been telling me some things. About the ruining of Soviet-backed banks. Operational necessities."

When Simon said nothing, Tom went on. "Look, Simon, I won't pretend I've absorbed it all yet. I've got a lot to think about. But . . . perhaps we could talk about it, one day soon."

Simon surveyed his father for a long moment. Then, still without speaking, he nodded. They held each other's gaze for several more seconds: long enough to register and convey the beginnings of respect. Then the older man withdrew, with a smile for Jinny and a wave to the children.

"See?" Qiu Qianwei had been watching the scene with evident satisfaction. "New everything, just like I described." When Simon did not speak, the cadre cocked his head. "Nothing to say?"

"Actually, I was thinking of that bastard Reade."

"Ah! A useful bastard, all the same." Qiu pointed to the terrace outside. "I will speak to you in private one last time, please."

The two men went out to the pool and stood facing the sea. Qiu rested his back against the ledge of the wall. "It is important that we discuss Assistant Commissioner Reade. You called him a bastard, and I understand why, but you would be surprised to know how assiduously he has been protecting your reputation here, in your absence. He spread all the right rumors: the children on a visit to friends in Europe, you suffering a nervous breakdown, recuperating abroad with Jinny . . . do not underestimate your own secret intelligence service, Simon Young. We are very pleased with Reade."

"I do not underestimate Peter Reade. Nor do I trust him."

Qiu shrugged. "That's your choice. Just remember, please, that he has an important part to play here, between now and 1997. You must learn to work with him, if you wish to work with us."

Qiu reached inside his jacket and pulled out a thick envelope, sealed with green wax. "It is late, I must go. But first I am to give you this."

The Englishman took the package from him and opened it. The envelope contained a thin brown booklet. At the top, the seven characters that stood for "People's Republic of China"; beneath that, the five stars of the Middle Kingdom and a representation of the Great Hall of the People set within a gold wreath; below that, finally, the ideographs for *hu zhao*, passport.

A Chinese passport, made out in the name of Simon Young.

He turned it over and over in his hands, not quite crediting the evidence of his own eyes. No one could put a value on such a document in the hands of an English ruler of an English *hong*. "Is this the price?" he said at last.

"Price?"

"Of a career. A desalination plant. Trusted servants."

Qiu shrugged again. "If you say so. I leave now."

But before he could depart Simon seized him by the elbow and held him fast. "Last night you would have saved my life at the expense of your own," he said quietly. "You deliberately walked into Zhao's line of fire."

"Yes."

"Why? After all I did to you, through little Tingchen. Why?"

Qiu looked at him, smiled and shook his head. "I really did think you understood us," he said. "But perhaps you do not know the East at all."

"Why?"

"Because without you, without your evidence, the judgment could not be set aside. Because we are many and you are one; yet for a brief moment the many have more need of the one than he has of them."

Simon stared at him. "Who are you?" he said at last.

Qiu looked down at the white hand on his black sleeve before raising his eyes to the Englishman's face. For a moment they held each other's gaze; then he said, equally quietly, "I am the dragon."

A tug, a flash of black cloth against gray stone, and he was gone, darting down the ramshackle wooden steps to the quay, where a speedboat awaited him. At the foot of the stairs he turned and waved for the last time before jumping aboard and taking his seat in the stern. The Englishman stared after the boat as it pulled away from the jetty, quickly gathering speed into the open bay, while he struggled to understand Qiu's enigmatic farewell.

Jinny came to stand beside him. When, after a moment's hesitation, she laid a hand on his arm, he looked down at it with a smile. Eventually he stretched out his own hand to cover hers. "What do you think?" he said.

But Jinny did not speak; and after a while Simon Young turned to rest his arms on the parapet. In the far distance, on the other side of the bay, he could see Kowloon: and he knew that beyond Kowloon, under its mauve catafalque of early-morning mist, lay all China: a land of fascination, wonderment and power. A land of remote things.

His eyes strayed to the passport which lay on the ledge beside him. The Middle Kingdom. Another country. His.